REEDHIMA MANDLIK

Heartbeat- A Novel

ISBN: 0-6154-3620-X
ISBN-13: 9780615436203

DEDICATION

For my wonderful friends, Camille Westfall and Alexis Garoufalis, and also for my parents, without whom this book would never have seen the light of day.

CONTENTS

ACKNOWLEDGMENTS

This book would still be sitting in the three journals I had written it in, thoroughly unreadable and a horror for the public eye to behold, if it weren't for these people. First and foremost, thank you Camille Westfall, for helping me create this dream three years ago, and transforming it into something beautiful. Thank you also for creating the brilliant cover art of this novel! Without you, this book would literally not exist. Thank you Alexis Garoufalis, for your cynical and wonderful remarks that transformed each chapter into something worth reading, and for believing in this book's potential, no matter how horrid the first version was. From Verses to Heartbeat, both of you stuck through it all, and for that I am forever grateful. Thank you to my wonderful parents, who put up with my anxiety and restlessness over the smallest changes in the manuscript. Thank you to my wonderful friends, for believing in me and helping make this dream a reality. Thank you especially to two friends of mine (you know who you are) who just happened to be in the right place at the right time, proving that inspiration can come from anywhere, and that timing is indeed everything. Also, I would like to thank the incredibly large spider that gave its life for our entertainment during a particularly long editing session. Without you, our edits would have been excruciatingly boring. And finally, thank you, lovely reader, for reading this. Smile! You're included, too.

"If you've ever heard a beating heart
a rhythm for the songs we're too afraid to sing
nobody here is perfectly fine
a delicate frame, a fragile design"

- Bigger Than Love, My Favorite Highway

Chapter 1
In Another Light

"Look at that beautiful sky!" Saphirra exclaimed. The sky was an endless cerulean blue, dotted here and there by wispy clouds that drifted slowly overhead. Lofty oak trees left streaks of shadows on the grass, their leaves rustling nosily in the wind. Flowers bloomed beautifully, visited by fat lazy bees every few minutes. For the last day of her freshman year of college, it was perfect.

"Can you believe it's almost over already? It seems like we just got here," Claire remarked, loosening her strawberry blonde hair from its tight ponytail. Saphirra nodded as she slowed her pace on the sidewalk, peering at the crowd around her.

"Everyone else is already leaving," Saphirra sighed, gazing out at the Rose University of Chicago. It was hard to imagine her grandfather had built the thick castle-like structures around her, and even harder to imagine Claire's relatives being involved. Their families were extremely close, thanks to some political compromise decades ago. Saphirra dumped her almost empty book bag onto the warm grass, glad she and Claire weren't in Europe with their parents. Of course, no one had asked her whether she wanted to stay here or not. Her father rarely asked anything of her anymore—they hadn't had a real conversation with each other in years, and Saphirra was more than happy to keep it that way. She refused to be anywhere near her father or his many estates around the country, so he left her at the university instead.

Her father had ordered for the university to be closed and for the staff to be dismissed while a new wing was constructed. That meant that Saphirra would have been utterly alone on the 1,000 acre campus by next week. She liked having the place to herself; if staff couldn't stay, the students couldn't either. Thankfully, Claire had been forced to stay with her too, to watch over the campus as maintenance crews came and left.

At least I won't be alone.

Claire dropped her book bag next to Saphirra's, the resulting loud thunk jarring Saphirra from her thoughts. Saphirra wasn't surprised to see it stocked with textbooks—Claire liked to reread them during the summer. Although she would never do so herself, Saphirra could faintly see her point. Mythology books had to be the most interesting textbooks on the planet, full of tales and myths for the students to analyze. Saphirra stared at the colorful books absentmindedly, relaxing on the cool grass. The sun warmed her back for the first time in weeks. Students were stretched out on blankets all over the grassy main quad, soaking in the few rays of sun they could get. It had been an unusually rainy year for Chicago, and the sun had rarely more than peeked its shy golden rays out from a cloud before it disappeared again. Claire sat down next to Saphirra rather anxiously, checking her watch for what seemed like the fifth time that hour.

"Saph, we've got ten minutes-"

Saphirra waved Claire's warning away, scooting over so she was in the shade. Even though their parents were close, the two girls had never met until they found out they were sharing a dorm room. Now Claire was her best friend—sweet, bookish, bubbly Claire, who looked uncharacteristically tired as she leaned against the cool bark of the thick oak tree for support.

"Fine. We're going to be late for Professor Tundlebrown's last class of the year, and I'll blame you," she teased.

"Speaking of professors, did you hear the rumors? Professor Lockson practically *begged* to stay here this summer. Apparently, my dad told him no exceptions. Lockson is furious."

"Yeah, but they're just rumors. That really doesn't sound like him to me."

Saphirra could feel the edge in Claire's voice, and shut up at once. As Claire dragged a thick book out of her book bag and opened it with a huff of impatience, Saphirra glanced across the central quad of the university. It looked like a fairy tale; the tall trees that surrounded the campus swayed in the light summer breeze, making the quad look like a spring meadow. Past the Frisbee-playing college students and the large fountain that marked the entrance to the Natural History buildings, two students were talking animatedly. She zeroed in on them, watching pensively.

"Claire, look over there." She nodded over towards two students, watching the tall one with flaming red hair. Their eyes met and she ducked her head, immediately annoyed at herself for not having the courage to hold his gaze.

"I know that guy from somewhere," she repeated for what felt like the hundredth time, raising her eyes to him again. He stood out in the sea of blonde and brunette hair, and was easy to spot. He'd gone back to talking to his tall dark haired friend, pausing to throw his books onto the grass beside him. Claire nodded slowly, talking as she would to a three year old.

"Yes, I know you remember. You've pointed out that guy so many times I could pick him out in any crowd! We've been over this a thousand times, Saphirra. You keep saying you know him, so chances are that he knows you too," Claire said sternly. She glanced at Saphirra's far-away expression over the edge of her book, biting her lip. "You're both anthropology majors, you can talk about your classes or something! He's really smart, you're really smart. Hell, everyone in this place has to be smart." When Saphirra didn't respond, Claire let out a huff of impatience. "This is really irritating. If I didn't know better, I would think you don't know how to talk to people."

"*Seniority,* Claire. It's just so awkward. Plus," she added, "I'll never get the chance to say what I meant at all."

They went through this conversation practically every week, and she still couldn't bring herself to tell Claire that she knew exactly where Alex was from, and how she knew him. She remembered it clear as day; he used to be her best friend back in Boston. After she moved, Saphirra had always wondered how he was doing, knowing it was silly to do so, bordering on just plain stupid. It had been a miracle that she'd even seen him again, let alone talk to him. She hadn't even noticed that they went to the same university until he'd walked straight up to her friend a few months ago.

"Quinn, did you turn the paper in for Tundlebrown yet? I wanted to see how you phrased the introduction," Alex had asked, walking up to Quinn in the east quad. It had been early spring, and the sun had just begun to paint the trees a golden yellow. The wind had blown into their little group, making it hard to hear. As Quinn turned away from Saphirra to see who was speaking, Saphirra did the same, and nearly dropped her books. It wasn't his face that registered to her; no, she'd recognized him for his eyes, bright blue and electric. Saphirra barely had time to process that Alex was directly in front of her before Quinn had started speaking.

"Yes, actually I turned it in." Quinn had said apologetically. "Sorry, Alex."

"It's okay."

He had begun to walk away when Saphirra decided to call after him.

"I read it, though. It doesn't seem that hard at all. All you'd have to do is check out *Babylon Untamed* from the library, it should help you analyze the metaphorical value of the colors surrounding the palace," Saphirra had blurted out. It was as if her mouth had a mind of its own. Alex gave her a hesitant nod accompanied by a look that seemed to say '*Oh. Is she talking to me?*' Before Saphirra could elaborate, he'd turned away as if she'd never said anything at all.

Somehow, the blow to her stomach from his expression was just as painful as seeing him again. Saphirra had managed to pick apart the grass around her, still absorbed in her reverie. It took her a moment to notice Claire hadn't said anything at all. As she looked up at the oddly still Claire she jumped, startled by her expression. Her friend's eyes were widening, staring in a direction a bit to the left of Saphirra's shoulder.

"Claire, I can't just walk up to him randomly. I'll sound so stupid. No, I already *sounded* stupid last time. I just want to let it go." She paused, waiting for some sort of reaction on Claire's end. Claire gave her a panicked stare. "Claire?" she continued, annoyed at her friend's lack of interest. Claire It wasn't until she felt a tap on her shoulder that she realized what Claire was staring at. A voice she hadn't heard address her in five years echoed behind her, making her jump.

"Hey, do I know you from somewhere?"

Alex watched West's mouth move, barely hearing the words. He kept glancing at a girl across the grassy quad, completely absorbed in a conversation with her blonde friend. From what he could see, she really wasn't that different from before. West had stopped talking, watching Alex's face expectantly, but he barely noticed. He watched Saphirra take a seat next to a tree on the warm grass, and it took him a moment to realize she was returning his gaze. His azure eyes locked on her emerald ones, and he quickly looked away towards West to distract himself. How did she still have that effect on him? After all this time, he felt like he'd been plunked right back into middle school, all because he was hiding from her glance like a little kid. He'd barely recognized her when he'd asked Quinn about her paper all those months ago. He hadn't even realized it was her voice until he'd been too far away to react, and had been kicking himself for it ever since. The one person who had given him purpose had moved away ages ago; the one time he had a chance to see her again, and he'd blown it. West followed his gaze, and let out a short laugh.

"This is stupid. Just talk to her," he said knowingly, brushing his hair from his eyes. West could have rolled into a mud filled ditch and everyone would *still have* loved him. He never seemed to notice, however, and Alex liked that about him.

His thoughts turned back to Saphirra as self-doubt clouded his mind. What if she didn't remember who he was? Chances were that she didn't even want to talk to him again. She had her own life, and a bit of the past probably wasn't welcome. If he didn't do something now, he might never be able to do anything again. It would nag him in the back of his mind forever if he didn't at least talk to her.

"I should say something," he said quietly, his hair flopping into his eyes. West watched him, a tiny smile playing across his lips. His dark brown hair was messed up by the wind, and his piercing grey eyes studied Alex quizzically.

"Wow, you *just* figured that out. It's been bugging you since spring. I'm surprised you haven't done anything yet," West said sarcastically.

"Not bugging me, really..." Alex trailed off, unsure of what exactly he wanted to do. Talk to her or ignore her and let the moment pass? West gave him an incredulous look.

"Really," West said dryly. "Well then, I guess you don't mind if *I* go say hi..." He began to walk off, but Alex stopped him by grabbing his shoulder.

"Fine. I'll do it."

West smirked at him as he squared his shoulders and took a deep breath in anticipation. "If she doesn't remember me then well... then she doesn't remember," Alex said grudgingly. He tried to shake himself out of it.

"Well, good luck," West said, trying and failing to keep his amusement out of his voice. He slapped his back and started walking off towards the Ancient Ruins research building, leaving Alex to stand awkwardly in the shade of a tree.

He wished he was calmer, but it was hard. He could make a complete fool of himself. His legs were moving towards Saphirra automatically, his arms swinging at his sides. He immediately stopped swinging them—he looked like a bizarre metronome. He swept his fiery bangs away from his eyes nervously, but they just flopped back down again. A few moments later, he was directly behind her.

"Claire?" Saphirra said to her blonde friend, who sat staring at Alex in frozen wonderment. Before he knew what he was doing, he had said it.

"Hey, do I know you from somewhere?"

That had to have been the stupidest sentence I have ever said, Alex chided himself. His face immediately flushed as Saphirra whirled around, her green eyes widening in surprise when she looked him over.

"Oh! Aren't you an anthropology major? You're friends with Quinn, right?" she asked curiously.

Alex's heart sank and he nodded. *She doesn't remember me.* He started to form an excuse in his head as the silence stretched. *Sorry,*

I must have thought you were someone else, don't mind me, I'm going to leave now, sorry for bothering you—

"No, I mean from anywhere else? Boston, maybe?" he blurted instead. After a moment something seemed to click, and her face lit up.

"Oh! You're *that* Alex! Alex Waterford, right? From Boston? That's so weird, how we're at the same university, and just noticed each other just now, right here..." She shook her head, apparently trying to rid herself of something. "I mean, how are you? What are you doing here? I can't believe it's really you!" she exclaimed a little too brightly. Alex shrugged.

"It's been alright," he started. *That's an understatement.* "I was actually wondering if—"

"Waterford!"

Alex was broken off by the enigmatic Professor Lockson. He was the mythology theory professor at the university, and he also happened to teach Alex's last class for the day. Professor Lockson's golden eyes flashed in the sunlight. His black hair, short in the back with shaggy bangs in the front, flopped over one eye. College girls craved to be near him, but Alex couldn't see why. Lockson leered at everyone who passed, and seemed like the type of person that hated sunny days and young children. He was young, too; he looked barely over the age of twenty–five. He passed by their tiny group, his peculiar tawny eyes glittering with malice.

"Mr. Waterford, you aren't planning on missing my last class, are you? I know we've had some...*issues* with your attendance in my class before...You wouldn't want to be dropped from the course just minutes before it's over, now would you?" he said icily, his eyes roaming, then locking on Saphirra. Alex bit his tongue to keep back the words that popped into his head—*Anyone would jump at that chance*—and nodded at his professor instead. Alex glanced at Saphirra apologetically.

"I wouldn't miss it," Alex mumbled to the professor. Lockson wasn't about to give up, though; he remained rooted to the spot, ignoring Alex as if he hadn't replied at all. He cleared his throat loudly.

"Now, your father," Lockson snorted at Saphirra, "is kicking me out along with all the other professors and staff this summer. Something about needing to add a new wing to the university, right? Tell your father thank you, Miss Rose. Just in case I cared to rob the very administration that gave me a living, I have now been hindered from doing so. Congratulations," he added accusingly. When Saphirra made no retort, he stalked off towards the Mythology building, muttering insults under his breath. She looked like she was about to say something, but thought against it.

"Pleasant, isn't he?"

Saphirra laughed at Alex's dry tone, and his mood lifted a little. He turned towards the buildings again, frowning slightly.

"Sorry, but I guess I have to go to my last class. How about we meet here later? Catch up on some things," Alex suggested hopefully. Her blonde friend cleared her throat loudly, and he jumped. He'd completely forgotten about her.

"Oh, and you should come, too," Alex suggested regretfully. She smiled ruefully at him.

"No thanks, I've got something to do later anyway."

Saphirra threw a look at Claire. Was it relief?

"See you later."

He waved goodbye, grabbing his books as he walked towards the Mythology building, unable to keep a small spring out of his step as he went.

❧

Saphirra plopped into her seat in her ancient ruins class, smiling widely.

"He actually remembered me," she sighed, pulling her books out onto the table in front of her. Class hadn't started yet, but Saphirra already wanted to bolt from the room. Claire rolled her eyes and smiled.

"Really? I thought *you* didn't remember him at all," Claire said accusingly. Saphirra adjusted her pile of books on the table, fidgeting under her gaze.

"I didn't want to sound stupid, that's all. What will I talk to him about now? What should I say?" she asked worriedly, pushing her books to the side, and then moving them back again. Claire shrugged.

"I don't know. It's your problem, not mine. And stop fidgeting," she said indifferently.

The girls were forced to stop conversing as their ancient ruins professor, an old man named Tundlebrown, walked into the room and began handing out their finals. Claire turned to him attentively as he wrote on the board, adjusting the same dull green suit he always wore. It wasn't long before Saphirra had finished her final. Soon she had zoned out completely, annoyed at the fact that Tundlebrown required his students to remain there until the hour was over. She thought back to when she had first met Alex instead, recalling the end of sixth grade. It still amazed her how he'd changed her whole life.

He'd shown her that there were people in the world that wouldn't criticize her when she opened her mouth. He'd shown her that there's nothing to be afraid of. For a seventh grader, that was quite an accomplishment. She wanted to thank him now more than anything. He was just so *kind,* nicer than any person she'd ever met. He had changed her, and she couldn't help thinking that she owed him some gratitude for his unwitting act of kindness.

The rest of the class inched by in a haze of boredom. Saphirra's eyes were trained on the clock on the wall, watching the second hand tick by. Finally, a coughing fit cut Mr. Tundlebrown off mid-sentence, and before he could get the words "Okay class, you're dismissed" out of his mouth, they had rushed out the door to escape.

Saphirra turned out of Tundlebrown's classroom and frantically raced to Professor Lockson's class, her last class of the year. If she was even one second late again, the professor would have her head. Her footsteps echoed in the deserted hallway, and delicious wafts of summer air breezed through every window, tempting her to ditch class and enjoy the day. She couldn't risk skipping the final, however, so she ignored the laughs and shouts of college students outside and raced into Professor Lockson's class just as he had begun to close the door.

"Nice of you to join us, Saphirra." Professor Lockson smiled coldly at her, his golden eyes flashing with anger. He never liked Saphirra, and she had no idea why. She hadn't done anything to make him mad, but he just *hated* her. She shivered under his cold gaze.

"Sorry," she said meekly, slipping into a desk in the back row. He always *had* to make her feel insignificant, like she was a small bug he could squish at any moment. Scowling pointedly at her, he walked up to the dark green board and began writing.

"Class, please return your final to my desk when you're done." he paused, waiting for the rustle of pages to stop, and then sat down, looking like he wished he could be anywhere but here. Saphirra opened the test booklet, for once agreeing with him.

As Saphirra handed in her final an hour later, Lockson looked around, expecting an alert class. Most were asleep, the others gazing absentmindedly out the window. Saphirra longed to be one of them. Only a few people, mainly Claire, were busily working.

Mythological theory can be so boring. *And Lockson makes it even worse.* Saphirra thought. She began to doze, her head resting on her arms.

She was walking towards Alex, who seemed incredibly drained. They weren't anywhere she recognized; she could see a city skyline in the distance, its twinkling lights cut off by the trees surrounding her. It was so dark; she reached out to him, to ask if he was alright. His violent shuddering calmed a bit at her touch. She looked up into his piercing blue eyes, studying the panic within him. She saw his head turn and she followed his gaze, searching. As he turned back to her, his body became rigid. She looked up into his eyes and started at the bright violet staring back at her.

"Alex, what-"

It suddenly occurred to her that he wouldn't answer her, that he couldn't; he was somehow incapable. She tried to say something more, but she couldn't move her lips. She was frozen to the ground, and she felt the breath leave her body as her surroundings dissolved into piercing darkness—

"Saphirra Rose!"

Saphirra jerked awake with a start, knocking her books to the floor.

"Yes?" she looked around frantically, and realized the classroom was empty.

"Sleeping in my class is unacceptable, even for the founder's granddaughter!"

Professor Lockson's cold voice shot at her through the deserted room, making her cringe. *Everyone else was sleeping, too!* Saphirra wanted to shout. Instead she nodded, barely listening to the rest of his lecture as she gathered her fallen books and shoved them into her bag at top speed. Her dream had scared her, but it was only a dream. Or was it a nightmare? Sighing, she turned to the window, panicking a little at the orange tinge to the sky. *It must be late.*

"I am late for a meeting with the Board thanks to you. You will meet me here at seven sharp. I need to talk to you about your lack of respect," Professor Lockson continued. She nodded absently and he took this as an acceptable response. He gave her a dirty look before he left, muttering about disrespect. Saphirra rolled her eyes, dismissing the strange feeling Professor Lockson always gave her. She quickly pulled out her cell phone and sent Claire a message telling her that she'd be late and that she had to talk to Lockson, and dashed out the door.

Alex leaned against the trunk of a tree, waiting for Saphirra. *She's just late,* he assured himself for the fifth time. He gazed out at the almost deserted quad, watching the sunset. Most students had already left the campus, anxious to get away from school and head for home, where they could reunite with all their old friends. He didn't mind staying for a little while longer.

Alex sighed, settling into the warm grass as the sun sank lower in the sky. He touched the necklace his mother had given him before she'd left them, remembering when she'd told him to keep it safe. He'd worn it ever since. It was just his dad and his sister back at home now, and he couldn't exactly depend on them again. He had received just enough money to pay for a dorm and living expenses, and for whatever his scholarship didn't cover. If he went home to the apartment over the summer, he'd only make it harder on his dad. He thought of his sister, who was at that awkward transition between middle school and high school, and his heart gave a small twinge.

Reedhima Mandlik

Something moved out of the corner of his eye, and he turned to see a figure racing towards him from the opposite end of the quad, her raven hair flying out behind her. A moment later she flopped down beside him, out of breath.

"Hey! Sorry for being late. Professor Lockson held me behind for a minute." As Saphirra swept her hair behind her, and Alex felt relief flood into him.

"How was your last class with Lockson?"

Saphirra groaned.

"Please, don't even *mention* Professor Lockson. I think he's out to get me," she grumbled. Alex laughed. Now *that* was the Saphirra he remembered.

"I heard you were staying here. Why?"

Saphirra shrugged. "Well, my dad can't have professors and students milling about the university while they renovate, and he thought it easiest if I stay here to watch over the place when no one else was around." Saphirra let out a frustrated sigh. "Long story short, we're stuck here all summer," she explained sourly. Alex shook his head incredulously.

"So your dad left you here by yourself instead of letting you go home? Can't he just-" he cut himself off. "Right...you don't like your dad..."

She shook her head and hugged her knees to her chest.

"I'm surprised you remembered that," she said quietly.

The silence stretched again, and Alex spoke.

"So, why did you move?"

Wrong question. She hugged her knees tighter.

"Well, since Mom died, we wanted to leave the place and memories behind, I guess. Start over, you know?" she mumbled. She suddenly became very interested in a bug crawling its way up a blade of grass. She smiled up at him, but he could still see traces of sadness in her eyes.

"It's a gorgeous sunset, isn't it?"

"Yeah. It is."

Silence stretched between them. Saphirra glanced at his neck and noticed a delicate silver ring looped around a thick leather cord.

"That's a beautiful ring," she said appreciatively. Alex nodded, toying with the ring absently.

"My mom gave it to me. It was her engagement ring," he replied, his voice taut. Saphirra nodded, understanding the heavy silence that had floated in between them. She rested her chin on her knees.

"I'm sorry," she said, gazing out at the sunset forlornly.

"It's alright."

The awkward silence stretched between them, until Saphirra finally checked the display on her cell phone. "It's getting late, and I was supposed to talk to Lockson around this time..."

"Well, I guess I'll see you later, then?"

Her eyes sparkled as she got to her feet, smiling warmly at Alex. "Of course."

He watched her leave, and then followed a little while later; he'd realized that he'd forgotten his textbook in Professor Lockson's classroom anyway. He crossed the quad towards the Mythology building, watching as Saphirra turned into one of the hallways that lead to his classroom. As he turned the corner into the hallway a few minutes later, he heard a slam, then a long, drawn out scream.

Chapter 2
Saved By a Broom

Saphirra left Alex sitting by the tree reluctantly. If she hadn't fallen asleep in class, Professor Lockson wouldn't have made her come in and she would have been able to spend more time catching up with Alex. *Figures. I was done with the test anyway, and everyone else had fallen asleep too!* Saphirra grumbled to herself. She wondered what the professor could have in store for her as she walked.

The crickets were chirping their symphony, filling the night air with an evening song. It was steadily growing darker around her. As she crossed the quad, she accidentally stepped on a Frisbee that lay long forgotten in the grass. As she walked, her mind wandered to Claire. *Where did she disappear to?* It wasn't like her to miss out on a perfectly sunny day like today, or the sunset that followed, for that matter. The summer was colder than usual in Chicago this year, and a day like this one was an opportunity that Claire would never miss. Yet, Saphirra hadn't seen her after class.

Maybe she's at the fountain, Saphirra thought. The fountain marked the entrance to the Natural History buildings, its stony visage resembling a book spouting water from its marble pages. Engraved on the rim were sayings like, "the pen is mightier than the sword", and "to gain knowledge is to lose belief". It also happened to be Claire's favorite place to draw. As she neared the fountain she noted Claire's familiar figure, outlined by the setting sun. For a moment she considered walking over there and ditching Professor Lockson. Something told her that was a bad idea, however, so she kept walking, lost in thought.

The faculty of the university had left almost as fast as the students did, anxious to leave and gain a month or two of peace before coming back to the hectic world of teaching. And yet, Professor Lockson remained. Her father had forbidden anyone from entering the university until the third week of July. This quickly made him the enemy of Professor Lockson who, for some unknown reason, liked spending his summers at the university. Some students here actually liked Lockson, but she couldn't think of him as anything but a cold-hearted teacher that overreacted about everything. He seemed to hate her for no good reason, and that made her furious. She couldn't help but feel that something was off about him.

What did he have against her, anyway?

She turned into the Mythology building and walked down the brick hallway towards his classroom, climbing up the small steps as slowly as she could. Even the hallway he worked in felt like a prison, keeping her from where she wanted to be the most. *The sooner I get this over with, the better,* she thought as she rounded the corner.

She turned into the dimly lit office and squinted, looking for the professor. He appeared from behind a large stack of books, smiling coldly.

"You can start by sorting these—" He pointed to a mountain of books, "by author, then by title." He smiled coldly down at her.

Saphirra stared at him. *You have got to be kidding me.*

"What? You said you wanted to talk to me, not put me to work," she said as politely as she could, gritting her teeth. "*Sir,*" she added at his reproachful look. *What's his problem?* Professor Lockson smirked.

"Well, this mundane task should keep you awake in my class, and any others that you deem so unimportant that you can sleep through. Get started, or I'll keep you here until midnight." He laughed to himself as she struggled with a tower of books. Saphirra glowered at him, muttering curses under her breath. *I should get him fired for this.* Grumbling to herself, she accidentally dropped them at the foot of a shelf, knocking over a vase with a resounding *crash*. Nervously, she turned around to gauge Professor Lockson's reaction. His face was smooth and unreadable as his tawny eyes surveyed the damage. After a moment's hesitation, his voice rang through the classroom.

"Now you've done it."

His voice was dangerously low, and somehow it sounded almost as if he'd been waiting for this moment all day. He slowly turned to look at her, and the fury in his golden eyes made her flinch. His sudden uncontrollable anger made his young face look twisted and scarred.

"Professor...?"

Her voice came out as a nervous squeak, and his tawny eyes flashed. Within seconds, the door of the classroom had slammed shut in a gust of air, and with more speed than she thought was humanly possible, Professor Lockson's face was inches from her own. The sudden mood swing had her backing away from him, frantically searching for an escape. Saphirra's heart began to race. She heard his ragged breathing and before she could comprehend what was happening, she had been slammed into the wall behind her. Saphirra let out a terrified scream, and the professor hesitated as the sound washed over him. Within moments, however, he snapped out of his trance and, in a whirl of black and gold, her air supply was cut off. One powerful arm pushed her waist against the wall as another gripped her neck, choking her. She tried to scream again, and he slammed her head against the wall, drawing blood and causing stars to burst in front of her eyes.

"W-what are you doing?" she gasped weakly. How was this possible? The strength he used against her was too much for his scrawny arms to possess.

"I think I should let you know this—you will not get out of this alive. Tonight, you will die. It's nothing personal; it just happened to be your fate." His voice was dangerously soft again as he clutched her neck tighter. She couldn't panic, she couldn't think; as his grip grew stronger her attempts to escape grew weaker, until finally her arms fell limp at her side. She couldn't breathe. Black spots swam across her vision, obscuring what little view she had of the room. After a moment's hesitation, he tossed her across the floor with the ease of a child throwing a doll. She sailed through the air and crashed into a pile of books. She screamed again as a burst of pain shot through her wrist.

"Ah, I forgot just how fragile you are!" Lockson roared with laughter as he ran towards her again. Within milliseconds, he was crouched down next to her. Saphirra squinted up at the professor she once thought was at least sane, her vision blurring at the edges. As her heart raced, she saw him give her the tiniest smile.

"What...are...you?" she gasped. She felt a trickle of blood drip down her neck, but she was too preoccupied with his eyes to care; they'd changed from golden amber to bright violet. He leaned in close and bared his teeth.

"Now, Saphirra, if you would have paid attention to class at all this year, you would have known what I am by now, wouldn't you?" he asked softly.

Saphirra couldn't muster up an answer. She was petrified. *Could he really be?*

"Now, I would have liked to do this a different way, but since you wandered into my grasp so willingly, I can just as easily get rid of you now. You, Saphirra, could ruin everything." He took a deep breath and reached out a hand to touch her bare shoulder, his eyes closing lazily. It almost looked as if he was meditating, his arms reaching for something invisible. She flinched, snapping his concentration; within that second, an unearthly snarl escaped his lips. From where he was holding her something pierced her skin, sending jolts of pain through her body.

With no air to scream, she glanced at her arm instead. Claws— big, black, dragon-like claws—protruded from his fingers, causing beads of blood to slide down her skin. He loosened his grip on her almost unconsciously. She gasped for fresh air, too dazed to move.

This can't actually be happening!

"I'm sorry! I'm sorry!" she was sobbing now, straining to get the words out of her mouth, the sound coming in short gasps. He, of course, ignored her.

I'm going to die.

She winced as his grip on her arms tightened.

"Ah, you think I would even give you a chance to survive? Not after this. Not after so many years." She saw sticky, clear liquid dripping from his teeth. She was going to die in the hands of a monster.

What a strange way to die.

The professor closed his eyes again, feeling something she couldn't feel, sensing something beyond her abilities. His mouth crinkled into a dangerous smile.

"You've got something different about you. It's...special to me. It could ruin all my plans, you see. I couldn't get rid of you before, but who's stopping me now?"

He gripped her with one cold hand and forcefully tipped her head up with the other, making her feel as if he was trying to snap her in two. She could feel his lips less than an inch from the hollow of her neck and she closed her eyes, bracing herself for pain—the pain that would end everything.

Suddenly, the door across from them burst open and someone barreled into the room, wielding a broom. He swung the handle wildly, crashing it down so close that it narrowly missed Saphirra. He swung a second time, this time hitting the professor squarely in the head. Lockson roared as the handle snapped over his skull, but he barely seemed disoriented. He pushed Saphirra aside, twisting to see where the blow had come from. As she fell on her arm, she bit her lip to keep from screaming. She gulped in the fresh air, choking on it. Professor Lockson stared at her savior, murder in his eyes.

"Get away from her," the person growled as threateningly as he could. Saphirra felt a burst of panic at the sound of Alex's voice and she whipped her head up to look for him. There he stood, wielding the broom like a sword, looking unsure of what to do next. Saphirra wanted to scream at him to get out of the way, to run while he still had a chance.

"*You*," Lockson snarled, diving at Alex. Lockson's claws barely raked his back, but it was enough to make him yell both in pain and shock at his attacker. Lockson swung again, this time leaving deep, long gashes that streaked his arms and his face. She watched in mute shock as Alex snapped out of his stupor and nodded to her, signaling that she should move. Saphirra began dragging herself towards the door as quietly as she could, to no avail. Professor Lockson was at her side in a flash.

"Oh no, I've waited too many months for this, I'm not going to wait for permission anymore! I'm going to kill you tonight, before this gets any worse!" he hissed, his sharp, perfect teeth glinting in the dim light.

"*No!*" Alex shouted, shoving Saphirra aside. She fell to the floor with a thud, wincing in pain. She looked up just in time to see Lockson sink his teeth into the hollow of Alex's neck, where Saphirra's would have been a moment ago. Alex could only shout in pain as Lockson spit out his blood, grimacing at the unwanted taste.

"No!" Saphirra groaned weakly. Alex clutched his neck, where blood was seeping through his fingers at an alarming rate.

"You've ruined everything, you idiotic boy!" Professor Lockson shrieked, his voice unnaturally high in panic, his fingers fumbling behind him as he backed away. His eyes were bright violet, glowing eerily against his black spiky hair. He surveyed Alex, one gash bleeding down his neck and dripping onto the tile, the other slowly soaking his shirt with blood, and Saphirra, lying on the floor almost blinded by pain and frozen in fear. In a last ditch effort he dove at her, and she felt his long claws make contact with her skin.

She felt Lockson try to bite her, and braced herself for the same pain Alex was going through. When nothing happened he seemed annoyed, grunting with the effort of holding her still. She saw him try to bite her again in the reflection of the darkened window, saw his jaws come within an inch of her shoulder then stop, as if barred by something. Frustrated, he cast her aside, and she hit the floor hard. Out of the corner of her eye she saw something flash; Alex's ring seemed to be glowing a bright white. She blinked, and the light was gone.

"I don't understand this! I'm done. The prophecy is a lie!" he shouted in fury. He backed out of Saphirra's vision and then he was gone, disappearing in a whirl of black and white. Saphirra lay on the cold linoleum floor, trembling in shock.

Alex groaned as he sank to the floor, clutching his shoulder. She struggled to her feet and staggered over to him, wincing with every step.

"Alex, can you talk? Answer me, please!" she said desperately, kneeling down next to him. He nodded towards his pocket, and with her good hand she reached into it and pulled out his cell phone.

"Call..." He groaned weakly. Saphirra tried to fight back the blundering fog that obscured her mind so she could think clearly. She punched 911 into the cell phone.

"Emergency response, what is the nature of your emergency?" The operator asked coolly. Saphirra hesitated.

"Some rabid dogs came in through the forest and attacked myself and a friend. They bit my friend and he's losing blood...Okay, were on the Rose Campus of Chicago Yes, it's a safe location–"Alex snorted incredulously—"Yes, we're in my professor's office, room 201...please hurry!" she invented wildly. She told the address of the university and the name of the building they were in to the woman, who told her to stay on the line. She covered the mouthpiece and slumped against the wall next to Alex.

"You really shouldn't have done that," she told him wearily. He glanced down at her.

"I'm glad I did. Did you know he was a...a..." He couldn't get the words out of his mouth; they were just too bizarre. Saphirra shook her head.

"I knew he hated me, but not this. You shouldn't have gotten hurt. You shouldn't have-"

Alex cut her off, and she had to bend lower to hear his next words.

"You'd be dead otherwise, and then where would I be?"

"Safe."

He looked like he wanted to say something contradicting, but he slumped down instead, slowly succumbing to unconsciousness. She felt herself being dragged into the same darkness, and could dimly feel people swarming around her moments later, shouting various medical terms. Within moments, sirens flashed outside the university, people rushed in with stretchers, and everything dissolved into the dark.

Chapter 3
Teeth, Claws, and All That Jazz

Claire ran out of the stuffed classroom, breathing in the warm summer air.

It's over! She thought excitedly, practically sprinting to the fountain in her rush to leave. Her last class had finally let out, and, in her haste, she hadn't been able to find Saphirra. She'd been bustled out by the army of college students that were even more anxious to get out than she was; she assumed Saphirra would try to find her later.

Claire neared her favorite fountain that marked the entrance to the Natural History building, ignoring the shouts from various students around her. The massive book spewing water from its thick stone pages was a favorite of many students, and it was rare to see it so sparsely populated. Jubilant, she sat down on the wide, bench-like rim. The stone was pleasantly warm, and she relaxed for a moment, basking in the glow of the sun. School was finally over, she had the entire summer to herself, and she was determined to enjoy every second of it. After a moment, she reached into her full book bag and took out a dark blue notebook. It was filled to the brim with her sketches. When she was bored, or saw something that interested her, she drew it into the notebook. Each pen stroke held all her secrets, each sketch her emotions. She carried it everywhere.

She flipped through the worn pages to a clean spot, and set it on her lap carefully, trying to decide what to draw. She rummaged through her bag until she found it. It was her mythology textbook, which was full of information on creatures of all sorts. She had to return it soon, so she wanted to sketch the creatures as long as she could before it was gone.

Reedhima Mandlik

It was ludicrous in itself that there was even a textbook for the subject. It had everything from Sirens to Pixies and Griffins to Elymphs. Why someone would even bother making it into a college subject, she didn't know, but she loved it anyway. Learning about mythical creatures let her mind flow and her imagination soar.

Thumbing through it carefully, Claire finally found something she wanted to draw- a lesson from the beginning of the semester, a Viceprus. This creature looked like person with sharper teeth, skin that seemed to glow, and burning violet eyes, all accompanied by a large set of black, feathery wings. She started sketching, working on the finer details of its perfect, oval shaped eyes. She could feel herself tuning out the shouts and laughter all around her, and her eyes narrowed as she erased the teeth she'd just drawn. If she could just get the points right...

"It looked fine before."

She looked up in surprise to see the person she'd seen talking to Alex just this morning interrupting her, jarring her concentration. He stood next to her, watching with mild interest. She blinked at him.

"You're Claire, right?"

She nodded and then ducked her head. This guy was cute—his grey eyes watched her intelligently. She tried to ignore him, but he didn't move. Finally, she gave in.

"Yes, I am," she clarified. He sat down next to her, and she shifted away automatically. *Yes, go ahead and sit down. I wasn't doing anything that needed concentration,* she thought, prickling with irritation.

"Hey, I'm West. Pleased to meetcha," he said. She nodded at this statement and resumed drawing, becoming more annoyed by the second when he didn't take a hint.

"Did you know Professor Lockson used to be a doctor? Then his patients started disappearing and now he's a teacher," West said conversationally, blatantly unaware of her snort of irritation. All she had wanted was a few hours alone to finally draw something, and now *this?*

"Yeah, I heard about that. I bet it's just a silly rumor though," she said indifferently, bending down to work on her drawing. She felt extremely self-conscious, as she always did when people watched her

24

draw. After a moment, she felt an uncomfortable prickling on her neck, and turned around. West was watching her.

Again.

"What?" she was thoroughly aggravated now.

"What are you drawing? Can I see?" West asked curiously, trying to peek over her shoulder. She covered her drawing hastily with her hands. This guy was so random that the thought of having an entire conversation with him scared her.

"I...I don't really like people seeing my drawings and..." He completely ignored her, reaching out instead to grab her notebook. Before she could stop him, it was in his hands. He simply stared back and forth from the textbook to her sketch, and she squirmed.

"What? Is it bad? It's bad, isn't it? I knew I should have darkened his eyes more, but..." she trailed off at the incredulous look on West's face.

"Are you kidding? It's like an exact copy of the picture! You're a pretty good artist," he said with awe. Claire twisted her hands shyly and switched to another subject, hoping he wouldn't see her blush.

"So, what are you still doing here? Most of the students here have already left," she asked curiously. Once she gave up her attempts to concentrate, he seemed a lot less exasperating. West's expression changed abruptly.

"Actually, I was going to stay in Alex's apartment with him, since my job is so close by." He shrugged, but wouldn't meet Claire's eyes. *He's hiding something.*

"Where do you work?"

"Five Staffs. It's a pretty boring job, but it works," he shrugged. "Anyway, what are you still doing here?"

"Saphirra and I are stuck here in the university over the summer, to make sure it doesn't blow up, you know," she joked. West smiled.

"Wow, I'm sure Alex will like that," he muttered. Claire tilted her head quizzically. *What is that supposed to mean?* She let it drop.

"Why aren't you staying with your family?" He asked. She couldn't avoid talking to him now, so she gave up drawing and turned to West. Something about him was off. He seemed gentle, and yet...

The look he'd given her drawing—the way it seemed to both frighten and anger him—worried Claire.

"My mom is working in Europe," Claire said quietly. "I can't exactly join her." She shrugged, hearing the uncertainty in her own voice. It wasn't bad, living alone all the time, but it did get lonely. She started to draw again, trying and failing to concentrate.

"Well then, we both have something in common. We both had crappy childhoods," West said, a hint of a smile stretching across his face. Claire tilted her head to one side, surprised.

"I never said-"

"I know. It was a joke," he explained. She frowned at him, puzzled. *I can't get a read on him.* It unnerved her how incapable she was of telling when he was serious or not.

"Oh. I- I'm sorry?" she began.

"Don't be, just forget it." He waved her apology away, taking her sketchpad away from her again and erasing something. She began to protest, but he'd handed it back to her before she could get the words out of her mouth. The lopsided teeth she'd been having trouble with were now perfectly proportioned. She glanced at him, mouth agape.

"How did you—"

"My mom taught an art class." He shrugged, grinning at Claire's dumbfounded expression. His voice was strained, however, and she narrowed her eyes suspiciously. *He's definitely lying about something.* The thought worried her.

"You know, maybe you could visit me at work one day! It's pretty boring and altogether uninteresting, so it would be nice seeing a friendly face once in a while," West suggested.

"I would like that," Claire nodded appreciatively, effectively killing the conversation for a few minutes. She made many more attempts to complete her drawing, each thwarted by West, who had apparently nowhere else to be. He was easy to talk to, however, so Claire forgave him. It wasn't until she noticed the cold night breeze that Claire realized how much time had really passed.

"West, what time is it?" she asked him, glancing around as if in a daze. Did time really fly by that fast?

"Uh…It should be about eight by now, shouldn't it?" he replied, checking the digital watch on his cell phone. A moment later he jumped up, as if the rim of the now silent fountain had shocked him. He checked his cell phone anxiously.

"Oh no, it's eight already?"

Claire got up too, watching him curiously.

"Are you expecting a call?" Claire peeked at his cell phone, but he snapped it shut.

"Yes, I am, actually. You know, I better head back, it's getting kind of late, anyway." He glanced at the ever darkening sky, now dotted by thousands of glowing stars, his expression suddenly serious. He started walking away from her but Claire skipped over to him, matching his long stride with some difficulty.

"Hey, want to come with me? I was going to walk with Saphirra to the dorms but I haven't seen her. I think she might be in Lockson's office—he asked to talk to her anyway." She smiled hopefully at West, whose worried expression softened at her voice.

"Sure, why not?" He still sounded distracted as he turned his phone to vibrate and shoved it back in his jean pocket. *Who could be calling him this late? Probably his girlfriend.* Claire thought dejectedly. They walked across the deserted quad in silence, each absorbed in their own thoughts.

"It's weird. She was doing better in Lockson's class than I was. He should have finished talking to her by now. Where is she?" she thought out loud. West shrugged.

"Maybe she forgot something."

"Yeah. Maybe."

Claire knew the second she turned the corner towards the building that something had gone horribly wrong. Police cars had pulled into the sidewalk and onto the grass and policemen were walking about, drawing yellow caution tape across the entrance to Professor Lockson's classroom. There were no voices issuing from the classroom, and its door was ajar. She quickened her pace, dashing towards one policeman writing on a clipboard.

"What *happened*?" Claire asked, aghast, as she surveyed the scene. The policeman ignored her, pausing to call someone on his cell phone. West stepped in front of her, looking the man square in the eye.

"My friend was in there. What happened?"

The policeman shook his head. "It's confidential, no one is allowed back there," he told them. West rolled his eyes and tugged at Claire's arm, pulling her towards the entrance.

"West, we can't go through here!" Claire hissed as West ducked underneath the caution tape. He pulled her through, and set off down the hallway, not pausing for her to catch up.

"It doesn't matter—" He cut himself off, stopping suddenly as he peered into the room. Worry gripped Claire's heart as she turned into the room herself, nearly knocking into West.

It looked like a tornado had ripped through the room—the desk was toppled over, papers were scattered everywhere, and the window at the very top of the room was ajar. There was blood on one end of the wall, and the remnants of a broken vase littered the floor. She scanned the room, looking for signs of Saphirra having been in the struggle.

"Saphirra? Professor Lockson?" she called shakily, walking into the room. She almost immediately tripped over something, and when she bent down to see the obstruction, she noticed it was a broom. There was blood on the handle.

What the hell happened here?

"Let's go. They can't be here. *We* shouldn't be here," West said stiffly.

"Why?"

He backed out of the room slowly. "We could get arrested for disturbing the place, for one thing. We should probably figure out where they went."

They retraced their steps, ducking back under the tape and running through the darkened quad towards the gates, unnoticed by the preoccupied policemen. As they ran, a light flickered on in the infirmary, and West paused. Before Claire could stop him, he'd changed course, dashing towards the infirmary.

"What are you *doing?*" she shouted for the second time that night, breaking into a sprint after him. West got there first; he opened the double oak doors with a bang and ran over to the receptionist's desk, Claire following him closely. She saw him slam his palms onto the desk, startling whoever was behind it.

"Ms. Stone, where did the ambulance take Saphirra and Professor Lockson? The policemen won't answer any of our questions. Where are they?" West asked the woman anxiously. She didn't even look up as Claire finally arrived, gasping for air. Claire looked around, realizing that the entire infirmary was empty except for Evelyn Stone, the young and slightly dense head nurse that took care of college students in the main ward. Ms. Stone tucked a strand of honey brown hair back into her messy bun and flipped the page of a magazine.

"They left. I'm the only one that's stuck here until tomorrow," she said monotonously as a response to Claire's glances around the empty ward.

"What happened?" West asked through gritted teeth. Ms. Stone glanced up reproachfully at his tone, her strange greenish yellow eyes glinting irritably.

"Two students, Saphirra Rose and Alex Waterford, were sent to the hospital an hour ago. They were bleeding pretty badly. Now leave me alone," Ms. Stone said in a bored voice, tapping a pen against her lips.

"Wait, Alex was in there too?"

Claire felt her stomach drop. *Why was Alex with Saph in the first place? What happened to them?* Claire and West stood open- mouthed, staring at Ms. Stone. When they didn't move, she added casually, "They said something attacked them. I think they said they were dogs."

West groaned in frustration and stalked away, muttering darkly about incompetent nurses, while Claire stood motionless, stunned. *What kind of dog destroys an entire room?*

"But Professor Lockson—" Claire started, but Evelyn held up a finger.

29

Reedhima Mandlik

"Is perfectly fine, and is resting in his home. He tried to defend the students, I believe."

When Claire didn't move at this response, West sighed, frustrated, and stomped back to Claire.

"Come on!" West said, tugging on her arm.

Saphirra awoke in a room filled with the repetitive beeping of computers. She sat up suddenly, wincing in pain from the effort. Her arm was bandaged in a slippery tarp-like sling, and a long bandage stretching down her shoulder prickled her skin as she moved.

What am I doing here?

It was pitch black in the ward, except for the glowing of the monitors. She heard a groan, and looked at the other bed a few feet away. A tuft of red hair poked out from under the stiff bed sheets. As if a switch had been turned on in her brain, the night's events flooded into her memory.

Monsters shouldn't exist- they were mythical creatures, like gremlins and unicorns. They shouldn't be able to harm other people, and they certainly shouldn't attack college kids, snarling something about the importance of "life force". Saphirra paused, biting her lip. *Come to think of it, hadn't Lockson tried to bite me, too?* Why couldn't he bite her, when he could bite Alex? She thought back to that moment, and Alex's glowing ring stuck out in her mind's eye. *Had it been glowing?* She wasn't sure anymore. The constant stream of questions made it impractical for Saphirra to even think of returning to sleep. This was all so surreal, so impossible. *And poor Alex, getting caught in the whole mess,* she thought, glancing over once again. Other beds lined the opposite wall and surrounded her own, most seemingly recently vacated. An old man slumbered noisily in the far corner of the ward, much too far away to hear their voices. As he gave a particularly loud snore, she decided to move. Swallowing her fear, she got out of her bed cautiously and began to walk towards Alex's bed. Fear radiated through her as she came closer. Why was she walking closer to him? She didn't know what he would be like after the bite or whether he was himself at all.

"Alex?" she whispered, staggering as her feet slipped on the unfamiliar floor. She felt strangely lightheaded as she passed the window, and paused to breathe in the night air. The full moon illuminated the city below it, making the buildings glint in the silvery orb's soft light. She reached his bed and sat down beside his curled frame, unsure of what to do next.

"Alex, are you awake?" Saphirra asked quietly.

"Mmf," he grunted, flipping over to his side. She tentatively moved to the edge of his bed, and he shifted slightly.

"Alex...I'm scared."

His eyes fluttered open, glowing strangely in the darkness as he looked at her. She turned her gaze to the ceiling, trying to ignore the small prick of terror his gaze gave her. *This couldn't have happened. It's just not possible!*

"What happened to Professor Lockson? To us?" she continued, shifting her gaze to the clock on the far wall. Its bright red electric lights burned in the darkness. 11:58 PM.

Alex sat up gingerly, and the bedsprings groaned.

"Whatever happened was weird, and definitely not normal, but no human could do this." he lifted the gauze from his shoulder and revealed a set of tiny puncture marks on his neck, nearly healed. Saphirra groaned. *So this wasn't all a bad dream.* What were they going to do? They had no idea what Lockson was, let alone if Alex had become one of them.

"But...he couldn't bite me, Alex. It was like his body refused to do it. My neck repelled him like a magnet. If he couldn't bite me... how come he could bite you?"

Alex looked nervous at this new information. He frowned, thinking hard.

"I have no idea. This whole thing is weird. He's never taught about something like this in my class. Didn't you take mythology with him this year? Maybe he taught about what he was?" he asked curiously. Saphirra shrugged.

"He might have, but the only way I could check for sure is if I had the book, and I'd have to borrow it from Claire..." A new problem had just occurred to her. She was supposed to go back to the dorms with Claire tonight. Surely she'd notice Saphirra was missing, and go check Lockson's room. *And if the police are still there...*From what she could tell of the paramedic's mutterings in the ambulance, they didn't buy the wild animal excuse, and Saphirra couldn't blame them. The classroom was much too torn up for that. If they didn't believe it, Claire wouldn't either. She'd want the whole story, but how was Saphirra supposed to explain *this*? Alex seemed to be thinking the same thing.

"We can't tell anyone about this. Not unless we want ourselves locked up. Even your friend Claire," Alex said. He winced in pain, and Saphirra reached over to help prop him up. His forehead had a bandage wrapped around it, barely masking a nasty looking bruise. Fatigue was etched in every line in his face, and yet his eyes were bright and alert. Anyone would notice that something had happened to them both, especially a friend like Claire. Maybe it was best not to attempt to explain. She nodded in consent.

"This *would* be hard to explain," she admitted. "Will you be okay?"

Alex felt his neck and smiled.

"Well, I still have a pulse, that's something. This bite hurts like hell, though. You know what, Saph? I think I'll be just..." Alex clenched his mouth shut as his whole body convulsed in a spasm of pain.

"What's wrong?" Saphirra asked, startled. Alex was writhing now, his fingers digging into his pillow. The clock beeped and Saphirra whipped around. 12:00 AM.

"No..." she whispered in horror as Alex began to sit up, his body convulsing. His hands gripped the pillow, and as he let go the pillow fell to the floor, feathers flying in every direction.

He has *claws*.

She stared at his rigid form, outlined fiercely in the moonlight. He got up slowly, staggeringly, and his eyes gleamed bright violet, boring into her in the darkness. He snarled, revealing a set of sharp teeth.

It was as if she'd been transported into a horror movie.

"Saph...Leave...Get away from me!" he shouted, gritting his teeth from the effort of keeping still. Saphirra backed away, but she couldn't take her eyes off the ravenous monster.

"What *happened* to you?" she tried to say, but her brain only managed to vocalize the first word. Alex didn't seem to know what to do. It was as if he was possessed, cringing in pain at the sight of his own body in the fallen mirror beside him.

"*Run!*" he roared before he launched himself at Saphirra. She dodged him and he hit the dresser, spilling bottles everywhere. Saphirra froze—this was all too much.

"Move!" he yelled, struggling to get up. For a moment, his eyes had flickered back to blue, and they were widening in fear. Then they flickered back to violet and he snarled viciously. Saphirra backed away, into the middle of the room, transfixed. *How is this happening? Why is this happening?* Information frantically flitted though her brain, but she couldn't make sense of any of it. Her knees were wobbling, and she collapsed, unable to stand any more. The room was spinning uncontrollably, making it hard to focus on anything. She braced herself as Alex lunged at her, knowing if she moved she'd simply hit something else. He landed directly behind her and pulled her to his chest. The spot where he touched her began to glow, and she stared at the sudden golden light, panic overwhelming her senses.

"Alex, what are you doing to me? Stop!" she cried, her body quaking under his touch. Alex ignored her, sweeping her black hair away from her neck. His warm breath washed over her as he whispered in a broken, horrified voice, "I am so, so sorry."

She wasn't sure whether she could move. Her whole body felt numb, still shocked at what was happening around her. She closed her eyes tightly and braced herself for pain for the second time that night, but it never came. The room was suddenly flooded with light. Claire was at the door.

"I try to find you to walk you home, and then I see *blood* in the room, and Ms. Stone says you were at the *hospital*! What the heck happened?" she asked shrilly, taking a step into the room.

It was then that she saw the two kneeling on the floor, Alex's teeth bared inches from the hollow of her throat.

"Oh...oh my god...he's not human...He's a Vic-" she started, but apparently her knees had chosen that exact moment to give in; seconds later, she'd collapsed to the floor in a faint. The light seemed to have stunned Alex; his grip on her loosened and he pulled away from Saphirra suddenly. His claws had dug into her shoulder, and as he scooted away they scraped at her arms. Confused, Saphirra turned around to face him. Why hadn't he bitten her already?

"Alex? Are...Are you back to normal?" she asked bravely. Her arms were bleeding slightly onto her shirt now, and she winced again as she clambered onto the edge of her hospital bed, never taking her eyes off of Alex for fear he'd start again. He seemed frozen in shock at what he had almost done. He shrank away from Saphirra, his expression filled with disgust, staring at the spot where Claire had fallen. Saphirra watched Alex uncertainly, and then took the opportunity to get unsteadily to her feet and cross the room, dropping down next to Claire. With her good arm, she shook Claire's shoulders gently.

"Claire! Claire, wake up!" she cried desperately. Claire's eyes fluttered open.

"Wha- what happened? Why am I on the floor? Why-"She got up unsteadily on her elbows, and as she looked into the room she caught sight of Alex. She let out a weak scream.

"Shh!" Saphirra hissed, clamping a hand to Claire's mouth.

"Mmmf!" her eyes widened as they glanced from Alex to Saphirra in mute shock. Saphirra looked down both sides of the deserted bleak white tiled hallway, then dragged Claire inside the room and locked the door.

"What are you doing?" Claire asked in alarm, her voice a high pitched squeak. "He's...he's got *claws*! How is that even possible?" she asked in a horrified whisper. Saphirra sat down next to her, hugging her knees.

"I-I don't know. He just got this way. Lockson did this to him."

At Claire's shocked expression, Saphirra explained to Claire what Lockson had done just hours ago.

"Then why would you locking us inside with him? He tried to hurt you! You could have been killed!" she argued, glaring at Alex.

Saphirra felt guilty as she watched Alex slowly get up and move over to a hospital bed, staring off into space.

"He-he wasn't himself, and I don't know *what* he is anymore..."

"But she does."

Alex's voice was low and gravelly as he addressed Saphirra. The old man in the corner of their ward grunted a little in his sleep and flipped over, completely oblivious. Claire looked nervously at Alex, who was staring at a spot on the wall as he spoke.

"She started to say it before she fainted. Saph, you heard her, didn't you?" he asked quietly, shifting a little towards the broken mirror. Claire flinched at his movement.

"What did I say?" she asked Saphirra beseechingly. Saphirra thought back.

"You cut yourself off...but I think you said Vampi-"

"No, no, that can't be right!" Claire said shakily, inching over to where Alex sat. She pointed at him, her finger shaking. "I don't know how reliable the textbook is, but it's got to be right about one thing—he is *not* a Vampire. He's not anything like that, from what I can tell." She paused. "I know I wouldn't have said that. Creatures like that are supposed to be carnivores. That is," she said scornfully, "*If* they even exist. Alex doesn't seem as dangerous. See?" she tilted Alex's chin up to the light and he glared at her. Claire ignored him. "He's got bright violet eyes. Look at them! They're nowhere near red, like a carnivore's should be. For another thing, look!" She tilted Alex's mouth towards hers, and stepped hard on his foot. As he shouted out in pain, she clamped his mouth open with her fingers. "Saph, his incisors aren't long and sharp. In fact, they're pretty dull compared to the rest of his teeth. Aggressive creatures usually have long incisors." Claire seemed oddly calm now; she walked around Alex, studying him intensely. "Finally, creatures like that go nuts for blood or flesh, don't they? Come here, Saph."

"Are you serious?" Saphirra asked incredulously. "How can you be so calm about this? You were ready to bolt out of here a moment ago!"

"That was before the fact that this is *real* sunk in. I can't avoid helping you now," Claire said, her voice shaking a little. "Just come here. Trust me," she insisted. Saphirra did so cautiously, nimbly avoiding the broken glass as she went. The thousands of tiny shards reflected the moonlight up at her, creating tiny stars on their darkened ceiling.

Claire continued after a moment of surveying Alex.

"He's not watching your arms. He's not trying to hurt you. That proves it!" she said triumphantly. She rocked back on her heels to look up at Saphirra, who was thoroughly puzzled.

"Of course I wouldn't," Alex said though gritted teeth. He kept watching Claire's face, looking for...what? An explanation? "So?"

"You aren't vicious. You just proved it yourself," Claire said smugly. "You may have lost it a moment ago, but you're fine now." Alex sighed and sank further into the shadows.

"Then...what is he?" Saphirra asked tentatively. Claire frowned.

"That's just it—I can't remember! I swear I've seen something like him before..."

Alex let out a frustrated groan. "Then what do I do? I can't just sit here and go mad in a hospital!"

When Claire could only give him a shrug in an answer, he threw up his hands.

"I give up."

Saphirra took a deep breath and looked over at Alex. He was glancing from his claws to Saphirra's bleeding arms in a kind of sad horror. She quietly went over to the smashed first aid table and re-wrapped her bad arm as best as she could. She wondered if anyone else had heard the racket they were making; judging from the silence outside, they hadn't. Marveling at the incompetence of the hospital personnel, she began to walk cautiously towards Alex.

"What...why are you coming towards me? Stop! Do you know what you're doing?" he asked, panicked. "I might try to hurt you again! Get away from me before I do something else!" Saphirra ignored him and sat down next to him, pulling her knees to her chest. She was shaking, but she knew he needed someone to show him he wasn't to be avoided. He needed to know it wasn't his fault.

"I'm okay," she assured him. Alex looked at her incredulously, his expression pained. He glanced down at the bandages on her arm, and looked away just as quickly.

"Are you kidding me?" he said in a strained voice. Saphirra shook her head in frustration.

"You won't attack me again." She said this with such certainty that Alex snorted with laughter.

"I just tried to kill you, Saph. I'm sorry, but you should probably stay on the other side of the room."

She glared at him, unfazed by his words.

"Well, you seem to be in your senses now, don't you?"

"Yeah, but I don't know why. And if something snaps again, you'll be hit first."

"I can handle that," she said defiantly. They sat together like that for a while. Claire watched Alex warily as she crossed the room to sit on the edge of a bed. She put her hand over his, startled to feel how heated his skin had become.

Badump.

Alex seemed to have felt it too- he had started suddenly, glancing at Saphirra. His violet eyes were slowly changing back to blue.

Badump...Badump thump thump thump....

"Is that...your heartbeat?" Saphirra said slowly. Alex nodded at her, alarmed. "Is your pulse supposed to be this obvious?" she asked, afraid to move her hand away. Blood seemed to be pounding through his fingers about ten times faster than it had been before. Warmth swept through her as she realized it- *something was reversing the effect.*

"I think...I think I'm becoming normal again," he said in a broken voice, looking around in what she guessed was relief. His eyes had almost faded back to their original piercing blue, and his pulse seemed to have slowed down. As Saphirra made to let go, Claire jumped to her feet.

"Don't let go of him!"

Saphirra looked at her, startled.

"What? Why not? He's turned back, he's human again!"

Claire shook her head exasperatedly. "No, look at your hands!"

Saphirra looked down and nearly jolted apart from him in shock; where their skin touched, a faint golden glow emitted, so dim it was barely visible even in the darkness. Clouds covered the sky outside, obscuring the tiny stars. Alex looked up at her, eyes wide.

"What's going on?" Saphirra asked, startled. She resisted the urge to tear her hand away and turned to Alex instead, looking up at him imploringly. "What does this mean—" Saphirra started, but Alex cut her off.

"It *means* that I'll be able to hurt you the second you let go, whether I want to or not. You probably shouldn't let go for a while, if you want your body to be intact," he snapped. He twisted so he was more comfortably propped against an empty bed frame.

"Just stay here, please?" he added after a few minutes of awkward silence. Saphirra smiled back up at him, shifting until she leaned against the wall. Her touch seemed to keep Alex at bay, and she sighed in relief. She didn't think she could survive another attack.

"That's fine, I won't move. And if you wouldn't have saved me, I would be dead by now. So thanks." Saphirra paused, surveying the damage around her. "Claire, we can't let anyone see this! Please turn on the lights and help me clean up, so no one sees this mess." Saphirra's voice went an octave higher than usual in panic. Claire nodded and flicked the light switch. Aside from the random scuffles and clanks of fallen pill bottles hitting the wastebasket, silence blanketed the room. Alex's voice broke the stillness.

"Should I tell West about this? We do live in the same dorm, after all. What will happen if we get attacked again? What will happen *tomorrow*?"

"It's like you said, Alex. Let's not tell anyone, keep them away from danger for as long as possible, you know. We'll help you for as long as it takes, and we'll be able to find out more about what you are tomorrow."

"I swear I know what you are," Claire added musingly. "We'll find out, I promise."

"Let's meet at the roof of our dorm tomorrow, then," Alex decided, staring at the clock in boredom. "That way West won't hear if I make a noise."

They nodded in agreement, as Saphirra followed Alex's eyes to the digital clock.

1:00 AM.

"Only a few more hours to go before daybreak..." Claire sighed.

West lay in his bed, staring up at the ceiling, unable to sleep. After they had run to the hospital, they discovered the hospital policy only allowed once visitor at a time. They had decided Claire should check on them tonight. Visiting hours had been over a while ago, but Claire assured him she'd be back soon. He stood there waiting in the hospital reception area for a good half hour before calling Claire's cell phone. When she didn't answer he decided Claire must have already left and he had missed her somehow. As he'd taken a cab back to the dorms, the dreaded phone call came.

"West."

"Yeah, boss? Is there another assignment?" West had asked wearily.

"No, I just want to keep you on your toes. There's been one of *them* spotted near your campus," the voice said.

"Well, what do you want me to do about it?"

"Let's see what this one does. Maybe he's powerful, but I think we need to keep him alive for a little while longer just to make sure. I'll keep you posted." His boss hung up abruptly. He *always* hung up abruptly.

This job really isn't worth the money, West thought as he stared up at the clock through bleary eyes.

3:00 AM.

Being a Viceprus hunter is not worth the effort.

Chapter 4
Viceprus

Saphirra had slept in the same position all night, her head barely resting against Alex's now warm shoulder, her hand still lightly touching his. Claire had collapsed on a hospital bed nearby, and was snoring slightly, her strawberry blonde hair fanning out all around her. Alex was still leaning against a bed frame, but he hadn't been able to sleep; he could see too many things in the darkness. He was afraid to let go, afraid to fall asleep for fear of turning back into that monster when he awoke.

He'd known he wasn't a vicious kind of mythical creature the second he'd changed. He'd just felt different somehow. His back had felt like it had split in two, and his hands now burned from where the claws had receded. That pain was too much to bear if he had to go through it every night from now on.

Am I stuck this way?

The thought made him flinch. Saphirra and Claire's sleeping frames were no longer outlined with a soft golden glow, but simply by the rays of sun streaming through the window. Turning into this psychotic monster that saw light emitting from human beings as if they were light bulbs...Every *night*...he couldn't bear the thought.

How could he even have attacked Saphirra in the first place? Alex felt terrible. Her arms were covered in bandages, and yet she was sleeping peacefully next to him. He had felt disgusted with himself when he had wanted...*what, exactly?* He couldn't put a definition on it. All he knew was that the thing he had been after was connected to the light that surrounded Saphirra and Claire. It was horrible. If Claire hadn't come when she did, Saphirra would...she could have been *dead* in his hands. Alex shuddered at the thought. If the light hadn't shocked his mind back to a sane state, he would have killed her right there, and probably Claire for good measure, too. And to think, it had all started with Professor Lockson. What did he want with Saphirra, anyway?

What would have happened if I hadn't come in when I did? Alex wondered, rubbing his neck. It continued to pulse with a dull throb, and he gave up on lessening it as he surveyed the damage around him. The mirror fragments had been picked up, and the tables had been returned back to their original state, thanks to Claire.

Alex thought he heard footsteps coming down the hallway, and frowned. He could definitely hear something; the pounding of heels on tile were soft, measured...a woman's footstep. He heard the noise pass them faintly, and frowned. But how was that possible? Through the noise of the busy hospital, he'd managed to hear this?

Humans shouldn't be able to hear things that well...should they?

But I'm not human anymore, am I? He reminded himself sadly. Saphirra shifted, distracting him. She looked up at his face, her emerald eyes squinting sleepily in the strong daylight.

"Morning," she mumbled, yawning widely.

"Morning," he replied as cheerily as he could, watching her tuck a strand of raven hair behind her ear. The footsteps seemed to be getting louder. Whoever was walking was on something that made an echoing clang at each step—a stairwell, probably. Then he heard a woman's voice.

"Okay, I'll go check on the patients in the emergency ward now, doctor...No, one of them has a slight sprain; I better check to see if that's healed." The person seemed to be a nurse. Her footsteps quickened, and Alex knew they were headed towards this room. He thought hard, glancing around the cluttered room apprehensively.

"Someone's coming. Follow my lead, okay?" Alex grinned at Saphirra's confused expression, then hoisted himself onto one of the abundant beds and closed his eyes. Saphirra did the same, her head hanging slightly off the edge of her bed. The footsteps paused at the door, and the nurse walked in, talking rapidly.

"Well, good morning, Mr. Waterford, Miss Rose, and..." The nurse stopped in her tracks, her hazel eyes surveying the damage, and then Claire's sleeping frame.

"Who are you?" she demanded shrilly. Claire jerked awake, rubbing her eyes sleepily.

"What *happened* here?" The nurse asked, aghast, surveying the broken mirror and random fallen objects. Alex pretended to stir feebly.

"I think that man over there was walking around in the middle of the night," he mumbled with fake sleepiness. The nurse looked suspiciously towards the old man, who was still tucked safely in his bed on the far corner of the room. "He was blundering about, but this girl here helped him back to bed. We didn't know the damage was this bad, though." Alex said, gesturing to Claire. The nurse *tsk-tsked* at the fallen mirror, but miraculously she nodded and sighed with relief.

"Oh yes, that has been happening lately. I keep telling them to move him to a mental patient ward, but apparently his heart isn't doing too well," she muttered darkly, bending down to pick up the spilled food. "I'll get a doctor in here immediately to tend to your wounds. Maybe we should move you two to a new room...get someone to tidy up in here..." she nodded to herself and bustled out the door, mumbling apologies for the wizened old man. The minute she left, Saphirra sat up.

"You blamed it on that poor man!" she said reproachfully. Alex grinned sheepishly.

"Well, it worked, didn't it?"

Saphirra nodded at him then did a double take. A smile slowly spread across her face.

"You're finally normal!" she sighed happily as she got to her feet, wobbling a little as she began to walk. A relieved sigh from Claire reminded Alex that she was still here. She was now sitting curled up at the edge of the starched white sheets. Saphirra sat down next to her, wrapping an arm around her shoulder.

"I swear I know what you are," Claire told Alex stubbornly for the tenth time. Alex smiled shakily at her.

"Trust me, we believe you. Do you know how you can find out? The sooner the better."

Claire nodded at him .Then her gaze fell on Saphirra's bandages. She started away from her.

"What happened to your arms? They're worse than before!"

Saphirra looked down at them, flexing the one in a sling. Removing it, she moved her arm around slowly in a circle, stretching the muscles.

"I think it's healed," she assured Claire. She then began to unwrap the bandage on her other arm, surveying the damage almost amusedly. It was covered in small scratches and cuts where the fallen mirror had hit her skin, and bruises from where Alex had grabbed her. Four long cuts marked where Alex's claws had been.

"It's not so bad," she murmured to herself. Alex stared at her, now worried for her sanity. *That looks painful, even to* me, *and she says it's nothing?* Saphirra gave Alex a fleeting look that seemed to hold both assurance and sympathy. Worried, he opened his mouth to say something, but he heard heavier footsteps a few floors below. They were climbing into what Alex assumed was an elevator, because the buzz of voices was rapidly growing clearer.

"Old man Roulkin went off on them? Well that's strange. I'll be there as soon as I can." It was a strong male voice this time. Alex's heart started racing.

"The doctor's coming," Alex said sharply, sitting bolt upright. Saphirra looked puzzled at his change of tone.

"Alright..." She said warily. He glanced up at the corners of the ward, searching for the telltale red light. Finally he found it. Alex strode across to the other side of the ward carefully, out of view of the blinking red light as he made his way to the corner. He began to lift the man named Roulkin off of his bed.

"What are you doing?" Claire whispered in alarm. Alex ignored her and put a finger to his lips. He then moved the still sleeping Roulkin to the front of the surveillance camera in the ward, blocking its view. He made it look like Roulkin's hands reached behind the camera and not his own as he dismantled the piece.

"Alex!" Saphirra hissed at him. He ignored her too as the camera fell open in his hands. He grabbed the disk inside and snapped it in two, tucking it safely in his pocket. After carefully replacing its base, he moved Roulkin back to his bed and crossed back to the girls.

"What did you *do*?" Claire asked, aghast. Alex shook the pieces of the memory chip at them.

"It was too dark last night for that camera to have spotted us from so far away; plus, we were on the floor most of the time. But to-day morning was a whole different story. If Roulkin is actually mentally sane, he'll protest being blamed for damaging anything, now won't he? And if they decide to review the camera...They could see us."

"So you just move a drugged patient in front of the camera?" Saphirra asked dryly. "How is that supposed to help?"

"Then it would look like *he* took the camera's memory and not me."

Saphirra and Claire looked at each other.

"Please tell me you haven't done this before," Saphirra asked. She sounded like she was only half-joking. Alex offered her a smirk.

"What do you think?" he asked sarcastically. Saphirra didn't speak, so he continued. "Please show the doctor your arms, okay? Make up anything you want about what happened last night, as long as it sounds plausible. I'm going to be fine, but I'm not so sure about you. I can't be here, or they'll know something's wrong with me. Especially if I change again. I'm going back to the college." And without looking back, he abruptly walked out of the room, passing the nurses' station as he went. The busy college student behind the desk didn't bother to give him a second glance as he headed towards the elevator, his footsteps muffled by the noise of the busy hospital. His insides churned when he thought about what he had almost done. *How could I have gotten into this? Does Saphirra not notice danger when it's straight in her face?* Alex thought angrily, stomping into the elevator. He glanced at its mirrored walls as it started its slow decent, and was shocked by his own reflection. His hair was sticking up on one side, making him look like he was wearing an absurd toupee. His navy blue shirt had dark streaks on it where Saphirra's blood had rubbed onto it.

Saphirra. He shivered as he remembered just a few hours ago. He had heard someone coming, but had no idea it was Claire. He could feel the presence of power far beyond human strength, and his human consciousness seemed to slip, giving in to the new monstrous side of him, the side that wanted to kill. He had known, calculated even, that he could strike and kill Saphirra in the matter of seconds he had before that person opened the door. He'd even tried, and if Claire hadn't shown up at that very second, he would have succeeded.

Would he become a murderer if he kept this up? Would that be what he'd be reduced to? If Saphirra had paused for even a fraction of a second more, he would be holding her lifeless body in his arms. Alex shook his head at himself as he entered the hospital lobby, disgusted. How could he even have thought of hurting someone like that? Why was he such a...a monster? His chest had burned, almost as if he had been choked, as if someone had set fire to his lungs. The feeling had been unbearable. Just seeing Claire look at him like that, with horror and fear, gave him a reality check. The light had jarred his mind back into place, and gave him back the consciousness that he needed. It had taken all his self-restraint to not kill them, but he'd managed. What if it was like that next time? What if...what if he killed someone? What if he turned on West or Claire this time? Lost in thought, he nearly knocked into a bleary-eyed nurse, pushing a cart blindly through a door. His bizarre appearance went unnoticed as hospital personnel rushed by him, not even bothering to spare him a glance. He walked out of the hospital in a daze, not bothering to check himself out. Claire and Saphirra would cover for him. He hailed a cab and told the sleep-deprived driver the address of the university automatically, still lost in thought.

Saphirra was too nice to him. When Claire had screamed, he wondered why Saphirra hadn't, too. All she'd done was look at him, and her eyes were filled with *pity*. Not hate, not fear, but pity. He wanted to talk to her again, to apologize, but he was afraid. What if she runs away, like a delayed reaction? What if she understood how dangerous it was to be around him, and told him she never wanted to see him again? He didn't think he could stand it.

"The further I am from her, the happier she'll be..." Alex murmured to himself. *And the less danger she'll have to face, I suppose,* he added sadly. The driver's voice startled him out of his thoughts.

"Fight with your girlfriend, mate?" he asked sleepily, scratching his five o'clock shadow. Alex shook his head sadly.

"Not even close."

Saphirra shielded her face from the blazing sun, her green eyes searching the deserted front gates anxiously. Normally, the entrance would be filled with students talking or playing Frisbee. Now, however, it was completely empty. A few birds pecked at the ground and squirrels darted here and there, but no sign of Alex was to be found. West had agreed to staying at the university until Alex came back, admitting that Alex had the keys to the apartment anyway. West had then disappeared back into the dorm room he shared with Alex, and hadn't made a reappearance since.

"Where *is* Alex?" Saphirra asked, frustrated. Claire shrugged, her eyes searching too.

"I honestly don't know. Even West hasn't seen him, and they're inseparable." She shrugged, smiling regretfully. "Sorry."

Saphirra couldn't help but be annoyed. They'd searched for Alex all over campus after they'd returned from the hospital, with no luck. Everyone was breaking their necks out of concern for him, and he was still missing.

"He couldn't have just disappeared off the face of the earth! His stuff is still in his room, West said so. It's been a week, so *where* could he be?" she said angrily, stalking away from Claire. She had so many questions for him about that night. What did she do wrong? Should she have not fallen asleep where she was? Should she have stayed awake with him? She'd felt the pain of his claws piercing her, but she was afraid of telling Claire, afraid her prejudices towards Alex would only get worse. Saphirra had thought that Alex didn't know that she'd feigned disinterest in her wounds that day, but his sharp eyes had told her otherwise. Listening to his steady breathing next to her had made her feel calm; it had eased the panic away like a child listening to a lullaby.

Saphirra let her mind drift to that night. She'd liked the fact that she was able to help him somehow, even for a moment. *It must have been terrible for Alex,* she reasoned. Saphirra couldn't fathom what had brought that tortured, pained expression onto his face that morning, but it was as if it was imprinted on her eyelids. Had he left because of her, or himself? Had he been suffering for over a week and a half every night, alone and lost?

She had thought Claire's jaw could drop no lower when she told her about Professor Lockson—she was pretty surprised about that— but it had dropped straight to the floor when she'd heard about what happened before she came into the hospital room they were in. She'd told Claire about how Alex had grown claws and how his eyes had switched sharply from an intense blue to bright violet, trying to cushion the impact of her words the best she could. She couldn't help hoping Claire wouldn't think it was Alex's fault, as he seemed to think himself.

"Weren't you scared?" Claire had asked, astonished. Saphirra's protective answer was *no,* but her real answer was *yes.* She was terrified at the sudden strength Alex had seemed to possess, and the murder in his then-glowing violet eyes had frightened her as well. She couldn't help but wonder if she would have been able to stop him if Claire hadn't shown up. Claire seemed to think it was Alex's fault he was now a monster, and that annoyed Saphirra the most.

Why didn't anyone see how it was *her* fault Alex was like this? That it was her fault that he'd gotten bitten last week? She'd somehow caused her professor to go insane, and now Alex was missing. How long could his self-control last? Eventually, the pain would get to be too much and he could do something drastic. *And if he's been going through that weird change every night, who's to say he isn't already hurt... or worse?* Saphirra thought worriedly, following Claire as they made their way towards the main entrance to the university.

Claire had finally remembered where she'd seen the creature's telltale violet eyes before; she'd begun to sketch them in her notebook. When she'd gone back to look for it, however, the drawing had been torn out. They searched the mythology book Claire frequently used as well, only to find a whole chapter had received the same fate. The only thing they could get out of that book was the creature's name from the table of contents: *Viceprus.* Someone didn't want them to know what the creature was, or what it did. Claire and Saphirra could barely remember the properties of the creature, let alone what it needs. What could she do, go to the library and check out a *Vicepruses for Dummies* book?

"Hey, get away from there!" Claire's yell broke through Saphirra's thoughts, and she hurried to catch up with the running Claire, shooing away a group of teenagers spray painting something on the Rose university entrance sign. The baggy sweatshirt-clad boys snickered as they ran away, tripping in their oversized shoes as they went.

"Idiots," Claire muttered, shaking her head.

"Great, now we have to clean *that* up too." Saphirra ran to grab a rag and some cleaning supplies from the nearest dorm, returning to find Claire turning her head this way and that, trying to make sense of the tumbleweed of black spray painted over the university sign. From where she was standing, it looked horribly like claws.

Saphirra lay in her dorm room that night, staring out of the small window at the starry night sky. What if Alex didn't show up? She told herself this worrying was only natural; he had been her best friend, after all. She turned the night's events over in her mind for what felt like the thousandth time. Why was Professor Lockson after? Her death or something more? If he had wanted blood, he could have attacked Alex thoroughly and drank *his* blood. But he had spat it out, hadn't he? He hadn't torn Alex limb from limb either, he'd just ran away. It just further proved Claire's point that the creature, the Viceprus, probably wasn't too vicious. Why couldn't Lockson bite her? All she knew was that she and Claire would have to do more research. The university library had an abundance of mythology books, so they'd look there first. It was obvious someone didn't want them to know what a Viceprus was—the torn edges were a clear message—but that only made Saphirra want to search more.

Saphirra gave up on sleep; it was no use trying with all these questions swirling around in her brain. Instead, she hopped out of her bed and slipped out the door quietly, so as not to wake Claire up. She walked down the stairs and into the quad, marveling at the emptiness of the place. Without students, it just looked lonely. The long grasses brushed her bare feet as she walked to her spot on the lawn. She now had a new reason for the tall oak tree to be her favorite spot; it now marked the renewal of an amazing friendship. A light summer breeze tickled her face, and as she turned to face the wind, she saw it—a tuft of copper hair sticking out from the trunk of the tree. She sped up, heart pounding, not daring to believe it. Too late, he saw her coming and hastily tried to walk away, gliding over the grass as if his feet weren't even touching the ground.

"Oh, no you don't! You aren't disappearing this time!" she hissed at him. He started to run, and Saphirra knew it was useless to run after him. She simply sat on the ground, ignoring him as he ran circles around her. She watched with mild interest, and after a moment, she could tell he was slowing.

"There's no point in leaving now. I've seen you, and once West finds out, he's going to kill you for not telling him where you were," Saphirra said flatly. He was acting like a little kid; once they know no one is playing their game, they lose interest. Alex stopped running the now worn track around her, and the wind immediately ceased as he walked over to her.

"What are you *doing* here?" Alex asked her through gritted teeth. The happiness that she had felt from seeing him vanished in a second.

"I happen to *live* here," Saphirra snapped back as she straightened up, her eyes flashing dangerously. "What did you expect? You disappear for a week, scaring me half to death, and just when we were about to send a search party out for you, I find that you were out here all along! We were worried about you, we missed you, and *I* was worried about you, damn it!"

Tears pricked the corners of her eyes, and she swiped at them angrily.

"Why are you crying?" Alex asked, startled. He flopped down next to her, unsure of what to do next. Saphirra irately wiped her tears away, only to have them replaced with new ones. His irritable expression was replaced by a look of concern as he tried to touch Saphirra's face. She slapped his hand away.

"Because I'm *angry!* How could you just...just leave, especially now? We thought something had happened to you, I..." She couldn't finish the sentence. Her furious stance collapsed, and she hugged her knees, shaking. She felt like a little kid, and she didn't like it at all. Her vision of the dark grounds was blurred, and she didn't move away as Alex laid a comforting hand on her shoulder. She listened to the steady beats of her heart, trying to calm herself down, and he waited patiently as the trembling gradually subsided.

"Feeling better?" Alex asked quietly. Saphirra blushed.

"I'm still mad at you," she said stubbornly. Alex tousled his hair, chuckling to himself.

"I forgot how much you cry. Remember that one time, back in middle school? You were so sad, all because the school bus had run over a bird." His eyes twinkled, and Saphirra felt herself blush two shades deeper, bypassing crimson and going for a deep maroon.

"Well, it was a dead bird! I was *twelve.* And I wasn't crying!" she protested, amazed he'd remember something so insignificant. Her anger had vanished; she didn't think it had even existed in the first place.

She decided to change the subject.

"You can sleep, can't you?"

Alex's face fell.

"Yeah, I can," he said cautiously. He seemed to be waiting for something, watching Saphirra carefully.

"Why do you even want to leave? What's so important that you can't stay?" Saphirra finally burst. "And why are you looking at me like that?" she added. She could feel her face getting hot again at the intensity of his gaze.

"I figured that I'd done enough damage. I wasn't here the whole time, either. I'd actually come back to grab some stuff from my dorm and then leave again," Alex said after a while. Saphirra frowned. Alex sighed exasperatedly at her expression. "The whole point is so I don't hurt anyone again. The further away I am, the less damage I cause," he explained. Saphirra hated how casually he said it. He looked into Saphirra's eyes, almost pleading with her. *That* was what he was worried about?

Reedhima Mandlik

"Alex, you never asked for any of this! How could you have known this was what was going to happen? And," she added as an afterthought, "I wouldn't have left, if I were you. You had us worried sick. We looked all over for you! West wanted to call the *police*. Do you know how hard it was to come up with a good excuse for him not to when we wanted to do so ourselves?" she chided, keeping her eyes trained on his face. She waited for a reaction, but he kept his expression carefully blank.

"I'm sorry."

"You should be."

They sat in stony silence for a moment, both staring at the sky.

"Saph, I never changed to what I was that night again."

Saphirra turned to him, eyes wide. "What? How is that poss-"

"I don't know!" Alex threw his hands in the air. "I just don't know. I don't know what I am, or what I can do, let alone if that night was a one-time thing or if I change sporadically...I don't know if I'm stuck with this forever or not..."

"But we *do* know what you are! At least, we know the name of what you are," Saphirra said excitedly. "You're a *Viceprus.*"

Alex looked at her as if she'd just expressed an intense desire to become an Eskimo.

"A what?"

"That's the thing. We don't know what a Viceprus is. And we were too busy looking for you," she paused pointedly, "to do any actual research." She told him about the torn pages and the ripped out drawing in Claire's sketchbook.

"So someone doesn't want us to find out what it is," Alex mused. "Well, whatever a Viceprus is, it must be pretty strong. Saph, I think it's becoming a huge part of me. I can run really fast now, but only at certain times. Plus, I have better reflexes than before. It feels weird."

Saphirra stared at him, incredulous. He was such a *guy*. Didn't he realize the danger he was in?

"What, no super strength?"

"Nope, that happens when I become an actual freak," he teased back. Saphirra smiled. *He's taking this better than I thought.* Suddenly, Alex stopped laughing.

"Are we supposed to be out here?"

His face turned serious as he scanned the air around him.

"No...I don't think so, at least. Well, you're not even supposed to be here. But West decided on staying here because of how close his job is, so you can too, I mean, if you want to," she babbled, caught off guard at the sudden mood swing. His eyes narrowed at a rooftop at the far end of the quad.

"We're being watched. Don't make a sound," he whispered at her, and in one fluid movement, Saphirra somehow found herself in the grass, her face pressed protectively against the ground. Saphirra could feel her face getting hot again as Alex lay down beside her. His breath tickled her neck. He glanced about, as if he was looking for something.

"Alex? What-"Saphirra began to whisper, but Alex put a hand over her mouth. A moment later, he pushed himself upright.

"What the *hell* was that all about?" she whispered, disgruntled. She hated being taken by surprise, he knew that. What was he *doing?*

"Would you rather be dead?" he asked, irritated. The closeness between them was making it very awkward.

"What are you talking about?" she asked suspiciously.

She glared at him as she got up, wiping mud off her knees.

"And you attacked me because...?"

Alex pointed at the tree where they had just been. Saphirra peered closer, her eyes slowly adjusting to the darkness. Right where her head had been moments before was a single, pointed tranquilizing dart, buried deep into the bark.

Chapter 5
Five Staffs

West yawned widely as he walked out of the bathroom, freshly showered and clothed. He stretched his arms over his head as he stared around the messy dorm room that he shared with Alex. He wasn't surprised to see a tuft of red hair poking out of his friend's covers that morning, and he wasn't sure if he had enough energy to care, anyway. It had been another long work night, and he hadn't come back to the dorm till four in the morning. He liked his job; he was good at it and it paid well, plus he was able to kill Vicepruses; the same kind that his mom had warned him about all those years ago. Still, it got incredibly tiring. He didn't bother to ask Alex why bits of grass clung to his t-shirt as he got up and disappeared into the bathroom; he was just glad that his best friend was back.

"Where were you this past week? We were worried, and you wouldn't pick up your cell phone," he asked curiously as Alex shoved piles of clothes aside, looking for a clean t-shirt. Drying his wet hair with a towel, West watched his fruitless progress.

"Oh you know, around," he said nonchalantly, succeeding in finding a green one. *How specific.* West let it drop, walking over to his messy bed instead.

"So did you ever come here to shower, or is this the first time in a week you have?" West teased, resulting in a pillow getting chucked at him from across the room. "Of course I took a shower," he grumbled, slipping the shirt on and walking out the door bleary-eyed, tripping over a book as he went. "Meet me in the food court when you're done," he called over his shoulder.

"Sure," West answered, his reply muffled by his towel. As the door slammed, West wondered about where his roommate had been. *Wherever Alex was last week, it seemed to have made him more guarded,* West thought, tousling his hair once more. West couldn't put his finger on it, but Alex had somehow changed. He seemed high strung and more suspicious of the world. West had no idea how to help him; not only did Alex seem more cautious, but it looked like he'd hid in a gym for the last week. He seemed...stronger, somehow. Different. He was more agile and had much better reflexes than before. Wherever he'd been, it seemed to have done something to him. West shook off his nagging doubts. *I must be imagining things now,* he thought, grabbing his wallet from the top of a cabinet and slinging his wet towel over his shoulder.

Have Saphirra and Claire seen him yet? He wondered, pulling on a navy blue polo. He could guess their reactions—Saphirra furious, Claire relieved. Or would it be switched? Regardless, the two would definitely have a few things to say to Alex. West groaned at the thought of having to sit through Saphirra's impending lecture.

As he was about to leave, he surveyed the room. It looked like a tornado had hit it. *No, a tornado would have made it cleaner than this,* West decided. *What's one more?* He shrugged, throwing the towel on top of a mountain of clothes carelessly as he strode out of their dorm.

Minutes later, West walked casually into the food court. Narrowly avoiding knocking into the group of chairs planted sporadically in the aisles, he headed towards Claire, who was staring at the empty food stands as if they were an interesting television program. Now that school was over, the empty cooking center looked like a ghost town, boring and forlorn. His footsteps echoed off the worn tile walls as he walked closer to Claire, his stomach growling.

Claire waved towards him energetically. Her wavy blonde hair fell to her shoulders, hiding her face as she turned back to the table in front of her. She was sketching something on the drawing pad that always seemed attached to her; her hand danced across the page, the strokes turning her surroundings into charcoal. He involuntarily smiled as his eyes locked with her hazel ones. Whenever he was around her he couldn't help smiling; it was a kind of reflex. She flipped the page, and he noticed her fingers run along the edge of a torn one; she frowned and flipped past it, eyes clouded. He balled his hands into fists.

"Hey, Claire," he said, already feeling more awake. Claire positively radiated energy; it was impossible not to absorb some. He realized he was still smiling like an idiot and relaxed his face as he sat down next to her. Claire's eyes shone.

"Hey! The others aren't here yet but-" Claire stopped abruptly. Her face swam for a second, and then he promptly rested his head on the table, hiding his face so she couldn't see his weary smile. *Falling asleep at a lunch table. That's a new one.* He snorted as he felt himself drifting into a groggy stupor. His job had made him so tired he could barely think straight. Seconds later, Claire's warm fingers were brushing his messy short brown hair off his face.

"I'm tired," he attempted to explain, his voice muffled by his arms. He heard Claire laugh beside him.

"You're really random, you know that?" she joked, her eyes now back on her drawing. She furrowed her brow in concentration. "What's got you so tired?"

He straightened up, his sudden tiredness vanishing as fast as it had come.

Oh, just you know, killing a few Vicepruses with a dagger the length of your forearm. Oh, and after that I went back to the dorm and slept for about three seconds. How was your night?

"I was up late last night. Work, you know."

He was so tired that he felt dazed, as if he was living in an extremely vivid dream. If he drove, he'd probably crash into something.

"Really? I thought Five Staffs closed at ten," she said, suspicion clouding her hazel eyes as she took them off her drawing. West gulped. *How do I explain?* He tried to come up with something to say.

"I have another job, but that's not what I wanted to talk to you about." He broke off, wondering what to say next. Claire watched him expectantly, tilting her head to one side.

"What are you drawing?" he asked instead, turning her sketch pad towards him. His jaw dropped in awe as he took in the perfect drawing of the Rose university gates and the impeccable lettering entwined around the thick golden bars. The trees swayed in a breeze frozen forever on the page, the grasses dancing to a tune no one could hear. She smiled down at it fondly.

"Do you like it? It took me a while."

West nodded, his eyes traveling the treetops, where the roof of one of the buildings was barely visible. There were two small people on the roof, half finished, but detailed all the same. The girl had long flowing hair, her body embraced by the man beside her. Neither looked willing to let the other go.

"Who are they?" he asked, pointing to the two people. They were barely the size of his finger. She blushed, pulling the pad back to her.

"No one. I mean, someone, but--nothing, just random people," she stuttered, snapping the pad shut. West stopped her from tucking it away, holding it open instead to drink in its pages. He'd gone through them all before, but he couldn't help but stare at them in awe as he flipped through the book for a second time. A frozen deer in the wilderness, a pitcher of glass at a window, a circular room with no exit, a girl sitting peacefully in a meadow, a solitary sock tucked hastily into a dresser...Each drawing was so real, so perfect, that it was as if she'd taken a snapshot of each moment. West got to the ripped out page, and he ran his fingers along the edge. All too late, he realized he'd lingered on the page too long; Claire's intelligent eyes were watching him with a newfound suspicion. He felt a twinge of guilt, but he pushed it aside and forced himself to flip the page. West knew he had to distract her, and fast.

"I have the day off tomorrow, so would you like to come to Five Staffs with me?" he asked hurriedly, staring at a spot on one of Claire's drawings. She seemed caught off guard at his question. West reached over, amused, and handed back her sketchbook. It was almost scary how easily he could distract her. "You don't have to go...I just thought, you know..." West continued, shrugging. Somehow he felt a twinge of sadness, as if she'd already said no. Claire paused for a moment, and then finally opened her mouth.

"Yeah I'd—"

"Hey, what are you guys talking about?" Alex called as he entered the room, cutting Claire off. Saphirra trailed behind him, holding fast food bags in her arms. Both West and Claire slumped back down in their seats; he hadn't realized he was even leaning that close to her. Alex dumped the food onto the table and pulled up two chairs, the screeching metallic sound jarring West's sleep-deprived brain.

"Oh, we were just planning going to go to Five Staffs tomorrow," West said casually. *Of all the times he had to come back...*

"That sounds like fun! I love that place. Mind if we join you?" Alex grinned at him, completely missing the point. West silently cursed, and then smiled tightly.

"Sure, you guys can come, too." He heard the strange dejectedness in his voice as they plopped down next to him. Saphirra exchanged an apologetic look with West. He would rather go only with Claire, but what could he do? *Maybe it's easier this way,* West reasoned. *She'll never know what a Viceprus is as long as I'm around.* Claire, meanwhile, was staring at Alex openmouthed.

"Where *were* you?" she asked incredulously. Saphirra piped up, unnaturally giddy for a Monday morning.

"He went to the emergency room because his uncle had a heart attack," she informed Claire, barely managing to add a sorrowful note at the last second. West could tell it was a complete lie, but he didn't pry. Claire exchanged a knowing look with Saphirra, as if she knew everything already. *Girls.* West shook his head. How they understood everything in a split second baffled him. He clapped Alex on the back.

"I'm sorry. Is he alright?" West asked, faking concern. He knew perfectly well that none of Alex's relatives lived within the country, but it seemed like more fun to make him squirm.

"He passed away on Tuesday," Alex said, looking completely unconcerned at the fate of his supposed uncle. West shook his head.

"That's tough. Have you had the funeral? Do you want me to come with you if you haven't, for moral support?" he asked, reaching into the bag of food and taking out its greasy contents.

Alex shook his head, stammering, "We already had it, it was a quiet ceremony, you know." He shrugged, diving into his burger with more enthusiasm than necessary. Claire and Saphirra exchanged another look as West continued, trying to keep a straight face.

"Oh, that was fast, wasn't it? You had enough time to do all that? And leaving everything here, too...Must have been sudden, huh?" he bit his lip to keep from laughing. Alex shifted uncomfortably in his seat.

"Mmhmm..." He mumbled incomprehensively as he took another large bite. West shifted his chair and whispered into his ear,

"You *will* tell me the real story later."

Alex looked startled, but merely nodded. Claire glanced between them and said loudly,

"So, West. What's your other job that's keeping you up so late?" It was his turn to choke on his food. Swallowing hard, he stared at Claire, wondering. *How do I tell her I kill mythical monsters on a daily basis? Wait, why am I even considering telling any of them, let alone Claire?* He shook his head at himself, disappointed in his irrational thought. The sleepless nights were finally getting to him, it seemed.

"It's a secret," he replied mysteriously, shoving a handful of fries into his mouth to avoid answering anything else. Claire smiled uncertainly, but seemed to understand she shouldn't ask any more questions. As Saphirra took over the chatter, West sighed with relief. It surprised him how easily Claire held back her suspicion. *She probably could care less, anyway,* West reasoned. *Maybe I won't even have to tell her.* But somewhere deep down, he knew she'd find out eventually.

Claire walked towards the Grand Five Staff's front gate, finally spotting West. He towered over all the moms and their screaming kids, and was currently waving her over like a traffic control cop. She waited patiently until there was a gap in the ever thickening crowd and then made her way over to him. As Claire sped up she made it to the entrance faster than expected.

"Hey!" she said brightly as he straightened up. West seemed amused at her reaction, but his grey eyes were clouded. Claire looked away, unsettled.

"Hey."

She smiled at the natural greeting, which somehow sounded better when he said it. She threw a questioning glance around her, looking for Alex and Saphirra. All she could see were the towering roller coasters and food vendors everywhere. West answered her un-asked question, yelling over the din of the crowd. "Alex and Saphirra are already here. I told them to go ahead."

"I thought you said meet here around three. I didn't realize I was late," she told him, barely audible over the boisterous crowd be-hind them.

"It's alright. I don't mind. I guess we can go through the Kiddy Staffs entrance now. There's no point in going all the way to the front, anyway," he assured her as he scanned the crowd again. Claire tried to ignore the twinge of suspicion she felt as she allowed herself to be pulled into the park by a very distracted West. Noisy families pushed past her, making her collide with him. She had been counting on Alex and Saphirra making it a little less awkward, and falling over West every five seconds wasn't exactly helping their situation either.

The part of the park they had entered into was meant for kids rather than the general public, and Claire couldn't help a pang of dis-may at the thought of just how long of a walk it was to get to the main attractions. Bright, colorful posters papered the wall beside them, advertising for a new ride based off of a giant teddy bear. Children ran about, their parents trying to stifle cranky wails for cotton candy and popcorn as they went. As they milled about the park searching for an exit out of Kiddy Staffs, Claire no longer felt self-conscious. She glanced around, trying to distract herself. There was no way she could have a decent conversation like this.

They walked in silence for a while until West spoke.

"Hey, are you alright? You seem kind of quiet."

"I-I'm fine. Just thinking, that's all," she scoured her mind for something witty to say, anything to keep herself from saying some-thing stupid. Then she spotted a vivid sign, the words unreadable be-cause of the glaring sun.

"Why don't we go on that ride, since we're still in Kiddy Staffs? What's it called?" she squinted towards the sign, but it was West who answered.

"Spinning Water Squirting Bumper Car Rubber Duckies of Doom. Sure, it seems like fun!" he said sarcastically. Claire grinned up at him.

"What, now you're too cool to go on a kid ride? What's the problem? It's just a giant plastic duck!" she teased as they began to walk away from it. West seemed to change his mind; he gripped her wrist and turned her around, pulling her towards the ride.

"Fine, let's go on it," he said determinedly. Claire gave him an appraising look.

"Are you serious? I was joking!" she protested as they neared the ride. West gave her a mischievous smile.

"Completely. If I have to suffer, so do you," he said playfully, and she consented to being towed into the almost empty line. She stared at the ride, which looked like a carousel filled with giant rubber ducks of various colors, their rubber bottoms attached to the floor below. Metal poles connected them to the ceiling, and metallic paths had been carved into the floor, presumably so the ducks could move anywhere. At any rate, it looked incredibly stupid. She instantly regretted mentioning the sign as they pulled through the line, reaching the attendant much too quickly.

"Aren't you two a little too old to be on this ride?" The attendant asked them as they showed him their neon green wristbands which served as passes. West looked up at him incredulously.

"Sir, I've been waiting for years to go on this ride! It's the highlight of my day," West told him seriously. He gave them a weird look before shrugging and lifting the red velvet rope leading to the steps of the ride. Claire felt herself blushing again as she tried to suppress a laugh.

"Step right up, and sit tight!" The man called after them. They chose a particularly fat yellow duck, sitting onto its metal bench designed for people about fifteen years younger than themselves. It was a tight fit, but they managed. After a moment, the attendant pulled a lever in the control panel jutting out of the ground next to him. Safety bars snapped down over their heads, and before they knew what was happening, they were spinning.

West was laughing again, reaching for a tiny wheel she had never noticed before, attached to a control panel in front of them filled with blinking buttons.

"Hey, this ride isn't too bad! Let's steer, maybe knock into some people?" West offered. But steering was physically impossible. Claire couldn't tell what was left from right, and the world wouldn't quit *spinning*. A balding man's face, a little girl screaming gleefully, twins waving their hands around as their mother frantically tried to keep them inside the duck , completely unaware that it was spinning; each image flashed before her eyes, blurring into one jumbled mess. She tried to focus on the various knobs in front of her instead.

"Should I push this?" Claire asked, pointing to a big flashing blue button. West shrugged so she pressed it, unleashing a jet of water on a neighboring duck. They retaliated instantly, drenching them.

"What was *that*?" West spluttered. Claire shrugged, wiping water off her face.

"I think that's the water squirting part."

Finally the spinning stopped, and the whirl of colors formed shapes.

"This must be the bumper car part," West informed her as a duck bashed into them. They attempted to hit other passengers, but the controls were too small; they ended up dodging others instead, until suddenly all the ducks shut down. West jerked at the wheel, which stubbornly refused to work. West wasn't controlling their duck anymore; it moved on its own, forming a neat line behind the others. The steering wheel moved by itself, facing their duck towards a gaping tunnel that she hadn't noticed before.

"Please keep all limbs inside the duck at all times. Hold onto the bar and *have a nice drop*!" The attendant's voice boomed over the loudspeaker. The tunnel seemed to get wider and wider, until it swallowed them whole.

"Welcome to your doom," a voice whispered out of the darkness, eerily close to Claire's ear. She whipped around searching for the voice, but all she saw was darkness.

"West, did you hear that?" she asked.

"Hear what? Oh don't tell me you're scared of a kiddy ride now," he joked. Claire was about to reply that that wasn't what she meant at all when the word *doom* echoed all around them once more. Claire turned around again; she was sure she'd heard it from behind her this time. It was then that she saw it—a pair of violet eyes snaked with gold, glowing eerily out of the darkness. Before she could react, Claire heard a metallic squeak as the metal pole connecting the duck to the ceiling fell away.

Suddenly, they were falling.

Chapter 6
Assault

"Are you sure West and Claire will be able to find us? Maybe we shouldn't have left that early..." Saphirra trailed off, worried. When they'd been pushed into the park by the constant swarms of people, West had seemed completely at ease. Still, she couldn't help wondering if they should have waited longer for Claire to show up.

"They'll be fine." Alex shrugged, and Saphirra calmed a bit. He was right. What could possibly go wrong in an amusement park?

"So, where to? We've got the whole afternoon."

Saphirra squinted in the strong sunlight, searching for a fast ride. She glanced around, watching a little boy buy a lollipop twice the size of his head from a street vendor. He stood under a deathtrap of twisted metal and squeaking hinges.

"How about that one?" she asked, peering at an interesting sign pointing at it. The sun beat down on her neck mercilessly, and she moved into the shade of a tree for a better look. She had loved roller coasters even when she was a little girl; she loved the adrenaline rush she got from them. This one loomed eerily above them, its dizzying height countering the terrified screams issuing from it.

Perfect.

"Let's go on it! That is," Saphirra corrected herself, "if you want to." Alex laughed at the eagerness in her voice.

"Sure. Why not?"

Soon enough, they were waiting in line. Saphirra couldn't get over the beauty of the park. Trees lined every pathway, and flower beds surrounded each noisy attraction, as if to mask the mechanical whirr of its motors below. Whoever had designed the park had obviously tried their best to hide the whirring mechanics of the attractions within their carefully constructed garden; for her, it was working.

As they neared the entrance to the ride, her thoughts shifted to Alex. Lately, he seemed distant, not at all the Alex she remembered. He refused to talk about the possibility of him undergoing another attack, or even an attempt to research what a Viceprus was. Above all, his ego had blasted through the roof. He seemed to get worse with every passing day, making snide comments now and then and completely avoiding Saphirra's attempts at conversation. He was becoming a jerk, and that annoyed her.

A lot.

She looked up at him, deep in thought. That stupid smirk was still on his face, as if he had better things to do than wait with her—as if he was *humoring* her by being here. And yet, his appearance hadn't changed; his reddish hair still flopped into his eyes with every miniscule step he took towards the ride, and his eyes still pierced her every time they met. He looked the same, but it just didn't seem like him. As they stepped onto the ride, she wondered if she would ever get the old Alex back.

Five curves and three stomach-dropping falls later, they had come to the end of the ride. Saphirra was impressed—she was actually excited for the end, something she hadn't been for years. She screamed just for the fun of it as their coaster car went on a vertical drop of more than sixty feet. She could hear her heart pounding in her ears, and she was gripping the safety bar so hard that her knuckles were white. Finally, she saw a spark of light at the end of the dark tunnel, and as it leveled out beneath them, they were plunged into the afternoon sunlight. Saphirra blinked to get the stars out of her eyes.

"Wow! That was fun. Kind of scary, but fun," she said shakily, climbing out of the car. She tottered slightly while getting off the platform, still dizzy from the ride. Alex smirked at her again, climbing out after her.

"Are you kidding? That wasn't even remotely *close* to the rides I've been on. What a waste of time," he scoffed. She glared at him. *Wow. Now he's insulting the rides too?*

"Whatever you say Alex," she said monotonously. *What has gotten into him?* Alex walked away from her blindly, leaving her to follow in his wake. She groaned as she tried to steady herself. The world was shaking too much to move any more without her stomach emptying its contents. She sank down into a nearby bench, holding her head in her hands. It took Alex a little while to notice she wasn't following, and, quicker than it was humanly possible, he was back by her side.

"Hey, are you alright?" he asked softly, bending to sit next to her. Saphirra's cheeks burned. How could he be so indifferent one second, then completely sweet another? Was this happening because of the Viceprus bite, or was this his true nature? She closed her eyes and talked as steadily as she could.

"Y-yeah, I'm fine. Just dizzy, that's all." She heard her hollow voice; it was her lying voice. When she felt Alex stiffen beside her, she knew he'd recognized it.

"No, I want to know what's really going on. What's wrong?" the tone of his voice made her look up at him, and she saw his eyes held nothing but concern. *Why is he acting like this?*

"I just don't *understand*! What's up with the weird mood swings?" she asked, anger flaring up suddenly inside her. Alex stared back at her, a peculiar expression on his face. He sighed, looking around the park as if the words would pop out for him from a nearby bush.

"I don't know. I don't know what's going on with me. It's like one second I'll feel like blowing everyone off, and another I'll feel horrible about it. I'm sorry, Saph." She could see that he was sincere, and her anger melted away faster than it had appeared. At her continued silence, he shifted uneasily. "Listen, I don't know when I'm going to...I don't know, *attack* someone, I guess. I'm on edge the whole time. I can barely sleep. So I'm sorry if I get angry, it's not just at you." Saphirra nodded, his words hitting her hard. *He hasn't slept? How much is this really affecting him?*

"It's okay, I understand," she told him. "Do you think it's out of your system? Like a one-time deal?"

Alex shook his head, refusing to meet her eye. "I don't know. I don't feel normal, at least."

Saphirra frowned at him. "What do you mean?"

"I don't want to talk about it."

Saphirra's anger flared at his cold tone. *I was just trying to help,* she thought, but she pushed her resentment aside and stood up instead.

"Let's go get some food," she said, eager to change the subject. Together they walked towards a lone churro stand in the middle of the amusement park street. The sweet cinnamon smell made Saphirra's mouth water, and as they walked closer, a new sight caught her eye—a flash of black hair, a spark of golden eyes. She stopped dead in her tracks, staring in horror at the spot they'd disappeared into. *Was that—?* She whipped around wildly, noticing for the first time how deserted their pathway was. Even the street vendor had left, even though Saphirra could have sworn he'd been there just moments before. Alex looked worried for her sanity.

"Saphirra? What's going on?" he asked slowly. Saphirra ignored him and began to walk towards the shrubbery instead, searching. As she stepped onto the neatly mown grass, someone pushed her down. A whistling sound pierced through the stillness, stopping short with a dull *thunk.* Saphirra tried to move, but Alex had already released her. They both looked up at the tree together; a long, thin dart was stuck fast in the bark, right where their heads had been moments before.

"Alex, *run!*" Saphirra screamed as more and more darts whistled past them. They scrambled to their feet and scattered. Within moments, Alex was far ahead of her, his feet a blur as he ran with superhuman speed. He turned the corner, not even bothering to check if she'd been hit. Her heart raced as she ran, turning the corner so much later than Alex did. After a moment, Saphirra couldn't hear anything behind her, so she turned around. The flash of black and gold appeared again, this time with a face; Professor Lockson scowled down at her from the branches of a tree, his eyes glinting maliciously as he looked her over. Within seconds, he'd vanished.

"Alex! Alex, they aren't chasing us anymore!" Saphirra called, snapping herself out of her fear. But when she looked over her shoulder, Alex was still running, leaving her in his wake.

⚬✺⚬

Claire screamed. They were freefalling on a rubber *duck*. If anything, it was an extremely weird experience. She grabbed West's arm as they slipped down an incredibly steep slide, eyes watering as air rushed around her. Claire had to wonder at the practicality of putting this section in a kiddy ride—nothing seemed to be moving except for the walls, rushing past them at alarming speeds. She only had time to look behind her and see an equally alarmed set of kids fall through the hole after them before the duck shuddered violently as it hit water, splashing them briefly as it settled. West let out a shaky laugh.

"That didn't seem like a kid's slide to me," he joked halfheartedly as the safety bars around them lifted. Claire shook her head, still searching for those eyes. *It was my imagination,* she told herself firmly. As the ride came to a stop, West had to help her out of the duck. When they walked slowly towards the door, the attendant smiled haughtily.

"I hope you've enjoyed the Spinning Water Squirting Bumper Car Rubber Duckies of Doom. Please come again soon!" he said snidely, thoroughly annoying Claire. She was visited by a violent urge to kick him.

"Well, they can't get sued for false advertising, that's for sure," West commented. She nodded, afraid of opening her mouth. The park was spinning a little too fast for her liking, especially since she couldn't concentrate on anything but that voice. *Welcome to your doom.* Was that part of the ride, or was it...something else? Claire shivered. The voice hadn't been harsh. In fact, it had sounded downright pleasant, almost musical–which is why Claire had been so unsettled.

"What were you saying back there?" West asked her suddenly, causing her to nearly trip.

"I thought I heard a voice. Something about doom," she told West. He seemed unfazed.

"It was probably part of the ride," he assured Claire. She studied him, looking for some sort of clue. If he had heard it, maybe he'd seen the eyes, too. But if he hadn't and it was indeed part of the overall attraction, then she had nothing to worry about. He made no indication that he was lying, however, so she relaxed.

Still, she couldn't help but compare the way the eyes had glowed to the way Alex's had back in the hospital. What scared her most was that the way they pierced the darkness was almost exactly the same, except for the streaks of gold that laced through the eyes she saw. Deep in thought, Claire barely noticed when West stopped walking, and consequently almost knocked into Saphirra. She was standing in the middle of the regular amusement park pathway, just waiting to become a human speed bump.

"Saph, what are you *doing* here?"

Saphirra didn't even look back when she answered. "That...that *jerk!*" she told Claire angrily, still glaring into the distance. Claire followed her gaze for a moment, and then gave up. All she could see was shrubbery.

"Right," she said disbelievingly. "Well, we have to move, unless you enjoy getting run over," she added as a couple carting a stroller along knocked into them. She steered Saphirra out of the busy walkway and onto a bench. Saphirra resumed glaring into space, apparently thinking hard, and didn't even blink when West waved his hand in her face.

"Wow, she's really out of it. What happened, Saphirra? Where's Alex?" West asked. She snapped out of it at the mention of Alex, turning to Claire and giving her a look of desperation.

"Everything's fine, West. Alex just went to the gift shop or something; he said he'd be back soon. Claire I have to show you something." her voice was hollow; she was lying. "Just come with me for a minute, there's this really nice shop I want you to see. I have to leave after that, but you should probably stay. You don't mind if I steal her for a bit, do you West?"

West opened his mouth to say something, but Claire elbowed him in the ribs. He closed his mouth at once, but she could tell he wasn't fooled. Saphirra looked determined to do something, and bounced off with too much energy towards the park gates. West looked at Claire, his eyes questioning.

"A gift shop. What could possibly be so damn important about a gift shop? And where does she have to go, anyway? Weren't we supposed to wait here for Alex?" he asked, dumbfounded. Claire shrugged.

"Saphirra will always be Saphirra."

And before West could swallow her noncommittal answer, she ran to catch up to her friend.

After milling about the park for a good two hours, Claire decided there wasn't much left to do. It was gradually getting dark, and from the unresponsive glare Saphirra had given her, Alex was somewhere off on his own. Saphirra had shown her the darts embedded in the trees and bushes as they pulled them out, explaining what had happened yesterday with the dart as well as seeing Professor Lockson again today as they went. Claire had in turn told Saphirra about the eyes she'd seen, but she couldn't make sense of them, either. Saphirra had decided that she couldn't wait for Alex any longer; she would research what a Viceprus was, whether he wanted her to or not. As Saphirra stalked off towards the university, Claire was left to find West again. Neither had any idea of what to do, and Saphirra had left Claire with a deadening, hopeless feeling that seemed to wash everything else away. As she'd talked to West, however, she was pleased to discover that their conversations flowed easily, and Claire felt herself relax. Finally, the crowded pathways started to thin out as it neared sunset, and Claire knew she should check up on Saphirra.

"Hey, West? I have to go back to the college soon. I have some stuff to look up," she told him regretfully.

"Yeah, that's fine. I'll meet you there later, okay? I might as well go look for Alex. He probably forgot his cell phone again..." He muttered, glancing around the park for what Claire guessed was Alex's vivid red hair. She left him to search for his missing friend, climbing into a yellow cab as quickly as she could. She sighed, watching shops trickle past her window. At the rate the traffic was going at, a snail could have gotten to the university faster. She just hoped she could get there in time, before West did.

❧❦

Alex ran as fast as his legs would carry him, passing entwined couples and gleeful children hollering for ice cream. He heard Saphirra shout after him, telling him the onslaught of darts had stopped, but he ignored her. *Why wait? I can run faster, I'm stronger. I don't need her, I don't need anyone!* he thought to himself, picking up his pace. His feet pounded the pavement, and he felt another burst of energy course through him. It had been happening often lately; he'd get random flashes of strength and velocity, and his body temperature would skyrocket. For a second, he would be able to see these *lights* around him, all in various shades of gold, each emitting from a different person. Before he could do anything about it, however, it was gone in a flash. He would flush with heat, almost as if he had a fever, and suddenly he wouldn't be able to move.

After a moment, Saphirra had stopped calling after him. As he turned the corner, he looked back and saw her standing in the middle of the pathway, watching him with disdain. That was when he felt his first twinge of regret. As he slowed down a bit, he took in his surroundings—no one was around. The pathway was deserted again.

Then it hit him.

He *was* acting different, and he'd left Saphirra by all those darts containing who-knows-what. The look on her face suddenly made sense, and he stumbled again as the flash of energy receded. He suddenly felt more tired than he had ever felt in his life, and he felt his footsteps falter underneath him as they tried to adjust to his slowing speed. *Why? Why do I keep messing everything up?* Alex thought angrily. He collapsed onto a wooden bench, putting his head in his hands. His skin burned and his vision became blurry.

What have I done?

Alex felt horrible. *She must hate me,* he thought sadly. He couldn't blame her. He'd run away so fast, he never bothered to protect her, let alone wonder why he needed to get so far away from her in the first place. Now that he thought about it, he'd seen something around her; it was a kind of glow that seemed to emanate from her skin like it had that night in the hospital. It had pulled him to her, its intensity throwing off all reasoning he'd had, and he knew he had to get away. The truth is, he'd *wanted* her, in a way. He'd wanted to have whatever that sphere of light meant. It was a craving his body couldn't explain, something beyond human desire—something *ancient*. He hoped he never found out what it was. *What's wrong with me?* Alex thought, disgusted. Why was he still affected by the bite? He couldn't describe the feeling he got when he looked at the strange aura around Saphirra; all he knew was that it felt pure. It was like he could tell how people were by the aura their body radiated. A man passed him and Alex's head whipped up as he watched him pass. He was pale and badly scarred on one arm, but his *aura*...it looked greenish and strange, almost polluted. Alex was unsettled. The burning in his chest wasn't as powerful as that night, but the craving still gnawed at his insides. *I'm a monster. I shouldn't put everyone in danger like this...I should leave the park before I hurt someone. Heck, I should just leave the city.*

But Saphirra would hate you if you left; a tiny nagging voice reminded him. No one knew where Professor Lockson was now, and he could show up any time. The darts were probably his fault, too. But that didn't mean he should put everyone in danger by staying, especially his best friend. Did West know he was living in the same room as a monster? Was West even aware of the danger of Alex being a half-Viceprus who didn't even know what was wrong with him?

He sat there on the warm bench for what felt like forever, mulling over where he could go, what he should do. He didn't think he could even muster the energy to get up; the run had drained him of all his energy. It was getting dark faster than usual thanks to a large purple storm cloud that covered an otherwise beautiful sunset.

Another day gone. How long could he stay like this?

Maybe I should tell Saphirra about the flashes, he wondered for the hundredth time. *Maybe I should actually research something. It's not like I can avoid it.* Then he heard someone calling his name.

"Alex! Where the *hell* have you been?"

It was West, running towards him with exasperation on his face. Alex didn't bother moving, and he looked down again as West approached him.

"*Well?*" he demanded. Alex met his gaze reluctantly.

"Well what?"

Reedhima Mandlik

I was looking for you for the last two hours! What happened between you and Saphirra? She was like in a trance when we found her, and then she just walked off."

"I was...thinking some things through," he said nonchalantly. "I thought Saph went off to find you."

West's eyes flashed with anger.

"She had no idea where you were! And now I find you, sitting on a bench, *'thinking things through'*," he mimicked, "and I could have been anywhere else! Why the hell don't you carry your cell phone?" West asked exasperatedly.

"I usually don't need it–"

"Well you needed it this time, didn't you?" West snapped angrily. The two stared at each other in stony silence, until Alex spoke.

"Is Saphirra okay?" he asked. West rolled his eyes and hauled Alex off the bench.

"Come with me."

Chapter 7
The Prophecy

"Why do computers hate me?" Saphirra grumbled to herself, hitting the keyboard in frustration. The computer monitor made no response, staying stubbornly as blank as ever. She'd gone to the nearest internet café, only to realize that all the computers were down. Out of frustration she'd marched back to the university to check those, but of course they were down too, because of construction. What would she have to do, borrow a smart phone and type into the tiny screen? She gave up on trying making the computer cooperate and sighed, slumping back into her chair in defeat. Why didn't anything want to work around here?

Still grumbling, Saphirra stalked away from the computers, now searching the extensive isles of the library. The bookshelves reminded her of Professor Lockson's neatly filed ones. She shuddered as the memory of the neatly lined walls in his office popped into her mind. *That's one night I definitely don't want to relive.* She scoured the shelves, looking up anything to do with mythical creatures. Pixies, Centaurs, even Sirens could help at this point. She began randomly pulling books off the shelves, sneezing as they fell with a dusty thud to the thick carpeted floor below. Saphirra skeptically pulled out a book titled *Mythical realities of fiction*, frowning as she flipped through its thick pages. She turned to the about the author section apprehensively. After reading about how the author had five cats and thought fish could speak, Saphirra flung it aside, annoyed.

As she bustled about the dimly lit room, she couldn't help wondering about Alex. She was completely nonplussed by him; why didn't he bother to stop when she'd called him? *What is going on with him, anyway?* Saphirra wondered, bending down to pick up the enormous pile of volumes at her feet. She heaved them onto an empty table, scattering them along the glossy wood surface. *Still, it's not like he de-*

cided to be this way, Saphirra conceded. It really wasn't fair to blame him, especially if he wasn't getting any sleep. *That's probably the least of his problems,* she thought. Saphirra felt guilty. It was partly her fault he was like this, no matter how much he denied it. She sighed as she flipped open a book, forcing herself to skim its musty pages.

She couldn't resent him for not stopping for her as much as she would have liked to, though. If he knew about her past, he would ditch her. He'd run away as fast as his legs could carry him, and she'd accepted it long ago. Keeping that secret was hard enough, and even then...it seemed like the world knew. She didn't know how long she could keep that particular secret from Alex; she never was good at lying to him. *Now it might be easier, though.* She reasoned with herself. *It's been a few years. Five, at the most. Alex isn't acting like himself; maybe he'll never notice.*

Saphirra gave up on the book in front of her and threw it to the floor, cringing at the loud thunk that seemed to echo around the deserted room. Saphirra thoughts turned to the only other Viceprus she knew existed—Professor Lockson. Were all Vicepruses surly pig-headed jerks by nature, or just him? She compared the two.

Yep, they probably are. She reasoned, remembering Lockson's smirking face as he'd flung her across the room, and Alex's matching expression today morning. She shuddered again and opened the nearest book, accidentally inhaling a large cloud of dust. Coughing, she flipped through it, only to pause at some pages that had been torn out. Her finger traced the jagged edge where a whole page should have been, and she looked back to the table of contents, puzzled. *Viceprus Indicium.* Saphirra stared at the words, dumbfounded. The letters on the page weren't just in some strange calligraphy, impossible to read even to the well-trained eye—it was Latin. Normally students didn't care enough to rip out pages from dusty old volumes, let alone if it was in a different language. She flipped through more pages, searching for another jagged edge. The whole book was in Latin! She turned, shoving books aside until she found another book, with the same result. Pages were ripped out, and when she went to what she assumed was the table of contents, it only supplied one sentence—*Vi-*

ceprus Indicium. Finally, she found a book that had something written next to the words, scribbled in by a student long ago—*Oraculum.*

What could it mean? Saphirra wondered. Every time she found the same words in any book, whether it was English or Latin, she got the same result. A ripped out page.

Where the heck am I supposed to get a Latin translator? Saphirra thought irritably, flinging the third load of books off the table. They were scattered everywhere near her tiny workspace, and she had no desire to pick them up again. Whoever had ripped out those pages was successful—she now had no way of finding anything on the creature. Just as she was about to give up, a thick leather-bound volume caught her eye. She reached for it and flipped through it, noting that it was considerably less dusty than the rest. She knew she wouldn't find anything; it most likely held the jagged edges of yet another ripped page with words she couldn't understand. Saphirra turned to the table of contents, her eyes hunting for the words she now hated. Finally, she found them. *Viceprus Indicium—Oraculum.* She flipped to the page, and there it was. No rips, no tears, just a beautiful paragraph, clearly visible:

Unus imperium mens,
Alius pectus pectoris.
Suum corporis ferus,
Suum pectus pectoris sanus.
Utriusque capessunt vita,
Atqui vereor nex.
Ut cruorem colorat divum
Quod luna videor two vicis ,
Fortuna vadum exsisto ostendo sum.
Unus mos reperio pacis ,
Ceterus traditio.
Suum key ut superstes
Est occultus intus gemma.

Saphirra looked at the words, dumbfounded that she'd actually managed to find something.

"Looks like they forgot to tear this one out," She told herself smugly, hugging the book to her chest. As she began to copy the words down to put through a translator later, she saw a flash of light and looked towards the double oak doors, startled. Claire left the doors open behind her, letting in the fluorescent light of the hallway. It bleached the carpet around her a pale white.

"What are you doing in here? No one uses this part of the library anymore," She asked, walking into the room. Her hazel eyes widened in surprise as she surveyed the piles of books around her. Saphirra looked up at her, then at the windows that displayed the grey, rain-laden sky. She hadn't even realized it had become dark outside; this section of the library was so dim itself that daylight barely made a difference in the gloom.

"That's exactly why I decided to come here in the first place. I was hoping I'd find something on Vicepruses, but I had no luck. Someone had ripped them all out, just like your sketchbook, and the textbook."

Claire gave her a worried look.

"Who keeps doing this to us?"

"Professor Lockson, most likely," Saphirra replied bitterly. "I bet he did this even before he attacked me, just in case someone saw what happened and wanted to find out what he was."

Claire bit her lip, conveying exactly what Saphirra feared; what if Professor Lockson was still around the campus? He could even be somewhere in the library, watching their fruitless progress. The thought sent chills down her spine.

"Then what's that?" Claire asked curiously, pointing to the half-written page in Saphirra's hands.

"This had been ripped out of every single Latin book, and I finally found one that was intact," Saphirra responded. Claire walked over to her, narrowly avoiding tripping over a mountain of books. She sat down next to Saphirra and bent down, rereading the passage a few times before looking at Saphirra with awe.

"How did you find this?"

Saphirra shrugged.

"I'd been looking up stuff on Vicepruses all day through books, since the computers are down. I couldn't find anything until I came across this. Everything else was gone."

"Then where did you get these Latin ones from?" Claire asked interestedly, scooting over to the pile to rummage through it. "*Viceprus Indicium—Oraculum*'...Saph, this is a prophecy about Vicepruses...It's got Viceprus information." She looked up just as thunder rolled through the sky outside, frowning disapprovingly at the lack of light. The giant glass windows that made up the east wall of the library shook in their panes as storm clouds rolled by, covering up the once cloudless sunset. Lightning ripped through the sky, and rain started to fall, splattering the windows. "Great. West's out there looking for Alex. They'll be soaked," she muttered.

"They were in the very back. But how do you know what it means?" Saphirra asked inquiringly.

"I knew the Latin because I tried to learn it. It didn't really work out, but I can understand some of it." Saphirra shook her head in awe. Claire was such a *braniac*. Her friend bent down to the book again and read the passage out loud, trying to translate as much as she could. "'*One controls the mind, another the heart.*' then there's a few lines I don't understand..." She screwed her eyes up and read on, slower still. "'*When blood hangs in the sky, and the moon appears twice*'...something. I can't understand what it says. The last part I understand, though: '*Their key to survival is hidden within the jewel.*'" She looked up at Saphirra. "I can't read more than that without frying my brain, but I know I could get it if I tried hard enough." She shrugged. "Why don't we just put it through a Latin translator?"

"The computers are down everywhere around the university. The guy at the internet café said it had to do with our network or something."

Claire gave her a frantic look.

"But this is important! It says something happens '*when blood hangs in the sky.*' And it's talking about survival. Saph, what if it's about us? Why else would someone try to keep us from finding out about it?"

Lightning ripped through the sky, and the already dim lights flickered ominously. As Saphirra stared out into the gloom, she realized something.

"Wait. Did you say *West* out there? With Alex?" Saphirra asked Claire, jumping to her feet.

"Yeah, West said he'd find him. Why?" Confused, she watched Saphirra as she waded through the pile of books to get to the doors.

"Professor Lockson tried to hit us with those darts again, and Alex hasn't been himself all morning. Something's really ominous about this whole thing. What if something happens to them? What if Professor Lockson finds them again?"

Claire picked up another book and flipped through its pages, not really reading them.

"I doubt he'd attack again. Don't worry about them. They can handle it," she told Saphirra reassuringly. Saphirra paused by the door and began to pace. She couldn't help but worry. Professor Lockson showing up in the middle of the amusement park had scared her out of her mind. What made it worse was that he'd simply stared at her instead of attacking. If anything, she now felt more paranoid than before. If he was so intent on killing her that night, why did he let her go? They were facing him, a prophecy that no one could understand, and a new Viceprus who had no idea when he'd act up again. How couldn't she worry? She doubted any of the books in the library had any relevant information besides the book that held the prophecy—so many pages were ripped out of the books she'd looked into, she doubted there was any information left to discover. What if they never found out what a Viceprus could do, and Alex attacked someone again?

"That's the problem, Claire! I don't know anything that would help him! What if he attacks West?" she stopped pacing, leaning on a bookshelf and watching the dreary weather outside. She was anxious. How couldn't she be? Claire was watching her as if she thought Saphirra would explode or something.

"Why are you looking at me like that?" Saphirra demanded, getting up to start putting the useless books away. Claire helped her, and they worked in silence for a minute. Then Claire spoke.

"Well, you seemed...weird, when we found you. You looked so distracted when West mentioned Alex. It worried me." She shrugged, and then continued when Saphirra didn't say anything. "When he'd said Alex's name, you acted like you had snapped out of a trance. What's wrong?"

Sometimes Claire is a little too observant. Saphirra had no idea how to respond. She didn't know what was wrong herself. It wasn't the first time in her life that she'd felt loneliness, but it still hurt. She'd realized at that moment that she couldn't just sit there and sulk—it was her fault he was like this, so she might as well take some responsibility for it. After shifting though some other books, Saphirra tried to explain.

"I don't know...He kind of left me there. And I got to thinking...He's acting strange, you know? Not like himself. I don't know how to help him, but I've got to try, haven't I? Especially if he isn't willing to do it himself."

"Well he should be helping us instead of running around an amusement park," Claire retorted, her nose buried in the shiny red volume once again. Saphirra knew it would be pointless to try to get him to do so, and she shoved her worry for Alex aside. Right now, the Latin was more important.

"According to you, this prophecy was in a lot of books, right? That must mean it's important, or that a lot of people know about it. I just wish I understood more Latin!" Claire fretted, tying her long blonde hair into a bun.

"It sounds like you need me then, doesn't it?" A voice, strangely familiar, shocked Saphirra. She whipped around, looking towards the door. West was standing there, his chocolate brown hair soaking wet.

There was someone behind him, half hidden by the giant oak door. A red haired, blue eyed, sheepish someone.

❦

Saphirra simply stared at him. Her expression was blank, and he couldn't fathom why. He'd imagined her angry, maybe even to the point that she'd stubbornly ignore him, but he didn't expect her to do *nothing*.

"Saphirra? Claire?" he asked tentatively, walking further into the library. Both West and Claire were giving him reproachful looks, and he didn't even bother to retaliate. Saphirra stared at him for a second, twirling a lock of her raven hair around her finger unconsciously. Then she blinked and smiled.

"Look, I've...*we've* found some information for you! Isn't that great?" she said brightly. West looked from Saphirra to Alex then back to Claire, confused.

"Why are you all in here?" West asked, puzzled. Claire piped up, her petite frame hidden by the mountain of books in front of her.

"Alex needed some information on...on a summer course, for Professor Lockson. I promised I would help," she invented wildly. *Actually, that sounds pretty plausible,* Alex thought appreciatively.

"That's...great! Thank you," he managed, watching Saphirra carefully. Why wasn't she mad? She was acting like nothing had happened at all today.

"So what did you need Latin for? I'm fluent in Latin," West said interestedly, trying to take a peek at the passage Claire was skimming. She snapped the book shut and positively beamed at him.

"No, I don't think we need it that bad. It was for Alex's research, it's not that important." She widened her eyes at Alex, who nodded. "Would you mind leaving us alone for a minute please? We need to discuss something." She smiled kindly, and West gave her a confused look. Alex waited for West to question them some more, but instead he shrugged and walked away without comment. *The effect Claire has on West is unbelievable*, Alex observed. Normally West would want to know everything.

"Meet me at the food court later, okay?" West called as his footsteps receded down the hallway. Alex walked into the room, closing the oak doors softly behind him.

"So, you're back. How nice," Claire said coldly, turning her back to him. Saphirra glared at her for a moment, and then smiled apologetically at Alex. The smile didn't reach her eyes, which seemed distant.

"It's a prophecy. Claire said it could have something to do with us and Vicepruses, and she managed to decipher about three sentences," Saphirra summarized.

"What were they?"

"*'One controls the mind, another the heart'* and *'when blood hangs in the sky and the moon appears twice',* and *'Their key to survival is hidden within the jewel.'*" Claire told him stoically. "That's it. That's all we got."

"But you just said it yourself. There are fragments we don't even understand, and a few hours ago we didn't even know there *was* a prophecy! How do we know it's about us?" he asked. It all seemed so suspicious that such an important thing was related to them. They were only college kids, after all.

"It was listed under 'Viceprus Information', for one. And I thought it had to do with us because someone had ripped the page out of all the books here." Claire explained. At his alarmed expression, she told him about the missing pages, and Claire's ripped out drawing.

"Well this sucks!" Alex grumbled, kicking a book out of his way. He immediately inhaled a cloud of dust, and sneezed.

"Well, it would have been easier if you had *helped* in the first place instead of skulking around," Claire accused. Alex felt like shouting, but he knew that wouldn't do any good.

"Sorry," he said instead. Claire gave him a disapproving look before answering his unspoken question.

"You started transforming during that night when Lockson bit you," she said quietly. "The prophecy mentioned survival. I think someone might die."

The temperature in the room seemed to drop. Saphirra stared at Alex wide-eyed.

"Alex, do you remember what Lockson was saying before he disappeared?" she asked suddenly. Alex scoffed.

"I was a little busy trying to keep our heads from being ripped off."

Claire gave him a disapproving look, and Saphirra acted like she hadn't heard him at all. "He mentioned something about the prophecy not being a lie. Whatever happened that night, he hadn't expected it. And if he was looking at the same prophecy that we have...it *must* be about us."

Claire spoke up suddenly.

"Then that means the 'jewel' it's talking about is you. Your name, Saph. Saphirra, *sapphires*. He must have gone after you because it's about you."

"Just because my name has a jewel in it doesn't mean I'm suddenly the subject of some long-forgotten prophecy," she argued.

"What other explanation is there for him attacking you? I know it doesn't make the most sense, but it's all we've got."

Saphirra sank down into the nearest chair, her expression unfathomable.

"So what if it *is* about us? We should go get West to translate. He's fluent in Latin, maybe he can clear it up—"

"No! We can't tell him. If he finds out, he wouldn't believe us. And even if he did, then he might hurt you. We've been over this, we can't do it!" Saphirra interrupted him, sighing. Alex slumped against a bookshelf in defeat. They stood in silence for a minute, Claire eying Alex, who was watching Saphirra apprehensively. The rain slapped the windows monotonously, and the silence stretched. Finally, Claire slammed her book shut.

"I'm going to go look for Latin translators. There's bound to be some here, I bet you just didn't look hard enough, Saphirra. You two—leave. It's getting hard to concentrate," Claire ordered swiftly. Within a moment, both he and Saphirra had been shoved out the door.

"Why would it be hard to concentrate with us there? She was doing just fine a moment ago," Saphirra muttered darkly as the oak doors slammed in her face. Alex mulled over his choices in his mind. Option one—he could tell Saphirra about the bursts of power he now felt. He could explain to her how it was dangerous for him to be around other people, and try to convince her that it was okay for him to leave. Or, option two—he could try to figure out a way to handle it by himself and not tell Saphirra anything. *But what if that feeling...*

that pull *comes back, and I can't control it?* It had scared him how much her aura drew him to her that night. He glanced at Saphirra, who was watching the ground as she walked. Her arms were wrapped protectively around herself. He made his decision.

"Saphirra, could you come here for a second?" she looked confused, but followed him into a deserted study room anyway. *How naive.* Here she was, next to a half-monster, and she just trusted him blindly. He leaned against the wall, wondering how to start.

"Saphirra, why are you helping me?" he asked her curiously. She lowered her eyes, her fingers unconsciously digging into the desk behind her.

"Well, I don't...have to. If you don't want me to, I won't. You're my friend, and I just assumed you needed the help, so..." She trailed off. Alex shook his head.

"No, I mean, why are you still helping *me*? I just left you there, and I was acting like a jerk the entire day today. I mean, *I* would be mad, at least. Why aren't you?"

She sighed, as if it was completely obvious.

"I just assumed...it must be hard, dealing with all of this. Well, you said it yourself," She became defensive at the incredulous look on his face, "it's not really fair. And besides, I'm nowhere close to normal. I'm hanging out with a half-Viceprus." She smiled a bit, but he could tell something was bothering her.

"You really are an amazing person," he said in awe. Something about his words made her shake her head furiously.

"No, that's the problem! I'm not!" she cried, looking up at him. Her blazing green eyes held nothing but torture. "You couldn't possibly think that way if you knew–"She cut herself off, falling silent once more. Alex crossed the tiny space between them, sitting down next to her on a desk chair.

"Knew what?" he couldn't help himself. What could Saphirra, of all people, have done? He glanced at her arms, noticing something off about her skin. She saw his eyes on her and pulled her sleeves down over her arms, hugging her knees to her chest.

"It's nothing. At this point, I'm not sure I can lie to you or not, but please don't make me try." He couldn't tell if she was referring to her arms or her past, but he let it drop.

"Saph, I'm getting these weird bursts of energy, and they keep getting more frequent. I don't know what's right anymore! The thing is...I keep seeing this weird *glow* around people. I saw you today, and I just bolted. I-I couldn't handle it."

"What couldn't you handle?" Saphirra asked quietly. "Was it the same kind of glow I saw in the hospital?"

Alex nodded. It was so dark in the room that he could barely see her expression as she reached out to him and took his hand. As warmth flooded through him, the spot where they touched began to glow.

"Wow," she said softly. She tightened her grip and their hands shone brighter.

"I'm sorry. I didn't want to attack you," he finished half-heartedly, trying his hardest to ignore the renewed warmth traveling up his spine. She nodded up at him, but she couldn't quite keep the pain out of her voice.

"It's alright, Alex. Maybe there's a way to reverse your condition," she said hopefully. As if to prove Alex's point, a flash of pain hit him, and he shivered as his body temperature rose suddenly. She jerked away from his hand at the sudden heat.

"Is this what you were talking about?"

Her breath stirred the air, and he suddenly he could see her aura again—strangely pure, sweet...He sucked in a breath through his mouth, and it didn't help. It just made the burning worse. Saphirra touched his skin reassuringly, and the gentle pressure startled him. His heart faltered at her touch, but it seemed to be bringing him back to normal.

"You would give any doctor a heart attack if they watched your body temperature. You'd be a medical phenomenon!" she joked, and he was relieved the burning in his chest had died down. Their eyes locked, and suddenly Alex noticed how close he was to her. He opened his mouth to say something, but closed it just as quickly. He reached out to cover her hand with his own, and a wave of dizziness hit him, causing their heads to bump softly. She looked up at him, her face much closer he had thought.

Suddenly something outside their classroom fell with an almighty crash. Startled, both Saphirra and Alex leapt apart like they'd been electrocuted.

"What was that?" Alex asked in a panic.

*If someone had heard what we were saying...*Saphirra seemed to be thinking along the same lines. She dashed outside and looked down the deserted hallway, Alex in close pursuit.

"Who's there?" she called loudly. Of course, no one answered. She walked back to Alex, who shrugged.

"Maybe it was a cat or something," he suggested hopefully. As Saphirra bit her lip and stared at the doorway, Alex wondered what West had heard.

❧

West walked through the hallway towards the back corner of the library, bored out of his mind. His friends were taking too long to come down, and he was *hungry.* His stomach growled audibly, as if to prove his point. His boss was supposed to call tonight, and if West missed this call again his boss had warned he'd have his head.

Clutching the tiny cell phone in his left hand, West milled about the hallways anxiously. He desperately wanted to keep his slaying job, but he worried if that was even possible anymore. It usually took all night just to track one Viceprus down; by the time he'd killed it, he was always too tired to do anything else. Killing them wasn't easy—they were so much quicker and so much stronger than he was. Plus he only had a dagger to protect himself. His was infused with sundust, something it had taken him years to find. It was usually effective against even the stealthiest Vicepruses, but the hardest to kill were the purebloods—the only ones whose eyes changed from burning violet to a light gold. By the time he was done, his barely had enough energy to talk to Alex and Saphirra, much less Claire. The only reason he did it was for the money; it was five times his paycheck at Five Staffs per hour. He wouldn't have ever entered into the business if he hadn't been offered the contract that now bound him to the job by force, as well as what his mother had said to him five years ago.

*"You'd be crazy not to take that job, West. It's a chance to prove who we are...*what *we are. It's a chance to get rid of those Vicepruses we hate so much. They don't deserve to exist in the same world we live in."* His mother had *been folding a pile of laundry into tiny neat piles on her bed at the time. West remembered watching her fold methodically, swinging his legs back and forth. He remembered being unable to meet her eyes.*

"But I'm only fifteen."

"Your father would have been proud, sweetie. I would be proud. Do you remember the stories I used to tell you? They were all true. Every single bit of it. These are creatures that don't deserve—"

"Who are we *to tell them they don't deserve to live, Mom? They could say the same to us humans, couldn't they? They could have killed us at any second, wiping out our entire race. If they're so terrible, why would they leave us be?"*

His mother turned to him with an accusing look, almost as if he had slapped her. West regretted his words at once.

"They keep us alive for food, West. They need our energy to survive. And it's in your blood to kill them. I'm not letting you walk away from an opportunity like this!"

West tried convincing himself by toeing the carpet with his shoe. He knew he was losing a hopeless battle; the phrase 'Vicepruses are bad, bad creatures' had been ingrained in his brain since he was born. He'd never really thought twice about it until then. How was he supposed to kill an enemy he didn't have anything against? He asked his mother the same question.

"Oh West..." She'd sighed, finishing the laundry and reaching up to tousle his hair lovingly. "If only you knew just how special your father was. He didn't just disappear, you know." She stopped talking suddenly, as if she'd already said too much.

"Well what makes me any better than anyone else? Won't they just kill me, too?" West had tried, getting to his feet. His mother shook her head.

"You are the one thing a Viceprus hates the most. You aren't normal. Our family isn't normal. I hope one day I can tell you why. That time won't come for a while, though."

She'd laughed nervously to herself. West had studied her for a moment; her tired, brown eyes, her frazzled brown hair, her fingers callused from working too hard. He didn't have a choice.
"Okay, I'll do it."

He'd never been able to go back since.

I never should have signed that stupid contract, West thought regretfully. So what if being a Viceprus hunter was in his blood? It just wasn't worth it anymore. He was tired of the sleepless nights, wondering about what his mother meant by *'not normal'*. If he wasn't human, then what was he? Had his entire past been a lie?

His footsteps echoed in the brick lined hallway as he walked. The storm brewing outside threw a faint greenish glow into it, making the hallway look like a horror movie set. West was barely paying attention to where he was walking anymore, and would have walked into a wall if voices hadn't startled him out of his daze. They issued from a darkened study room. West crouched next to the door, listening hard. Was that Alex's voice? Was he talking to Saphirra? He heard the word *Viceprus,* and West nearly fell over in his crouched position in shock. *Vicepruses.* Did they know about his job? He listened harder, and suddenly everything became clear.

Alex is a Viceprus. And Saphirra knows.

Suddenly why Saphirra had run to the library made a whole lot more sense. It explained so much, like the random times Alex would cringe in pain, and how he'd suddenly become so fast and strong...

Saphirra muttered something, and then there was silence in the room, and West peeked inside. Alex was cringing again, and Saphirra was touching his arm for support. *She was touching a Viceprus.* His best friend was a Viceprus. This was bad. Very bad.

"You would give any doctor a heart attack if they watched your body temperature. You'd be a medical phenomenon!" Saphirra told him. Their hands were glowing eerily, throwing her face into relief; their faces got closer to one another, almost like in a movie. Alex reached out to touch her. *She's going to kiss a Viceprus. Does she not know how dangerous that is?* He thought furiously. Then his foot hit the doorframe, and he dropped his cell phone in pain.

CRASH.

Great. Now you've done it, he chided himself, scrambling to get away from the door. He sprinted out of the hallway, phone in hand, listening to Saphirra's voice echo though the hall.

"Who's there?"

He tripped over his own feet as he ran down to the food court, not caring if anyone was following him.

He's a Viceprus. My best friend is an evil, corrupt Viceprus, West thought, stunned, as he paused to catch his breath in the food court. None of it made sense! He passed a window, and noticed the rain had stopped, leaving behind the remains of the sunset. The sky was an eerie blood red, an ominous sign. Had he bitten anyone yet? Had he sucked the energy out of anyone? Taken over them? He'd been living in the same room with a...a *monster.* The same kind that he killed on a weekly basis. He stared at his reflection in the glass, and his shocked, pale face stared back. If Alex was a Viceprus, then what was he?

West's cell phone rang, cutting his musing short. The blaring noise ricocheted off the walls.

"Hello?" he asked sourly. He didn't have time for his boss's antics. Not now.

"You know who it is by now, West. You don't need to ask. No assignments this week—just a warning. Remember the Viceprus I warned you against? He's strong. We're going to try to locate him first, but keep yourself alert," He warned.

"Sure, boss."

The line went dead before he could even finish his sentence. West's heart sank, because he now knew exactly who his boss was looking for.

Chapter 8
Full Moon Arisen

Evelyn stared out of the rain splattered window, waiting. Tapping her foot restlessly, she swept her honey brown hair into a bun and let it fall gently onto her shoulders again. Normally the rooftops of the university were quaint, seldom-used places with little gardens on the sides of the rails. Tonight, however, they appeared soggy and forlorn. He'd said he wanted to talk to her, to tell her something he'd been meaning to for a while. He said he would meet her on the rooftop.

So where is he? She wondered idly. She watched a baby bird attempt to fly through the gale. *Birds are such stupid creatures,* she thought viciously. *The animals, the humans—they are all just meant to be tools for my kind.* When she had finished her transformation, Ry had suggested she take the place of the nurse. Of course, she got the pleasure of taking care of the previous one. Evelyn smiled at the memory, remembering the feeling of the nurse's energy flowing into her, surrounding her like a warm blanket. At that very moment the rain came to a sudden stop, and the clouds drifted apart to expose what little sunshine was left in the day. She walked onto the drenched rooftop, avoiding the puddles cautiously. As if on cue, Ry climbed onto the roof, his golden eyes blazing. She wasn't expecting the murderous look on his face, and flinched backwards as he walked towards her menacingly.

"Evelyn Jocelyn Stone, *what did you do?*" he asked her, his voice dangerously low. She hesitated—either way, she knew she was in trouble. She couldn't lie to Ry even if she wanted to.

"I didn't rip out all the information on your list."

Evelyn didn't know what she was expecting, but she certainly wasn't expecting this. Even the most dangerous beast would quake at the look he was giving her now.

"You let her find the prophecy! Why?" he asked her furiously, running a hand through his short black hair. "I told you to rip it out of all the books. It was such a simple task! All you had to do was disable the modem for a bit so they can't look it up online, which would have discouraged them, and they might not have found it at all. We went through all that trouble, and they *still* found the damn thing thanks to you," he growled. She shivered.

"I tried so hard, Ry. It was one book in the back of the library. Who knew they'd find it?" she replied innocently. Evelyn had thought her effort would earn some approval for once. Only now could she see to expect anything was a huge mistake.

"She is still alive, and she can still fulfill what she was born to do. If she didn't have the prophecy, she probably would have stopped searching by now. Once they translate it, there's nothing we can do. Do you see something wrong with that at all, or are you too thick to comprehend that?" he yelled at her. She felt like she'd been slapped, and cringed away from him as quickly as she could.

"I'm sorry!" she cried, but he wasn't done ranting. He glared at her, his face dangerously close to hers.

"Do you know why I didn't kill her that night? It wasn't because I was feeling generous, but because I *couldn't*. I physically couldn't drain the energy from that child."

"W-What? What do you mean you c-couldn't-"

"You heard me."

Ry didn't seem any happier about this piece of information than she was. Evelyn reached out to touch him, but he turned away from her.

"Do you know what would have happened if you had succeeded in killing her today? I wouldn't have a chance to fix this problem. Killing her would have ruined everything; I know that now." He seemed to be talking more to himself than anything, so Evelyn kept her mouth shut. "The council is trying to eliminate us as it is, and we don't need them to be suspicious. If we want our plan to be foolproof, we have to lay off hurting Saphirra for now. That prophecy...If it means what I think it means, I'll lose everything. I'm not willing to let that happen."

"What about that Waterford boy that was running around with her? You bit him, and he's one of us now. What are we supposed to do with him?" asked Evelyn, leaning against the rough stone edges of the rooftop.

"You're missing the point. Honestly, words are completely wasted on you," Ry hissed, stalking away from her. *Looks like I hit a sore spot,* she thought bitterly, glaring at him.

"I wouldn't walk away if you want to hear what happened *before* you showed up, Lockson."

Ry's back stiffened, and Evelyn gave him a wicked smile.

"What information could *you* possibly have?"

"After I shot the first few darts, Saphirra had tried to help the boy, but he didn't try to save her. He just kept running."

"So?" Ry asked irritably. Evelyn grinned, thoroughly enjoying her seldom gained upper hand.

"That's just it. He doesn't care about her. I saw it in his eyes. If the Viceprus part of him takes over, he won't protect her," she told Ry smugly. His tawny eyes lit up.

"How interesting."

She didn't even bother to ask what he was thinking; she had grown used to the cryptic way he spoke. She waited until he had cooled down enough to speak.

"You wouldn't have thought of the tranquilizing darts if It wasn't for me. You've got to admit that I did something right. Look at how far you've gotten now, Ry. If it wasn't for me you wouldn't have known if she had left Chicago, let alone that she was staying in the dorms. We can still make it work! She's made it too easy for us." She was quieted by a look from his molten golden eyes.

"It wasn't my fault." He sounded defensive, as if she was accusing him. "I was about to bite that girl, and *he* got in the way."

"Calm down. Maybe we can use him," Evelyn suggested. She studied him wonderingly. Why was he so bothered by this development? She knew they'd be able to control the Waterford boy if given the chance. Couldn't he see that panicking was useless?

"What are we going to do? We're running out of time, and if both of them aren't dead by that day..." Ry had never sounded so worried before. Evelyn attempted to lay a comforting hand on his shoulder, but he shrugged it away. As Ry started pacing, his footsteps quick and lithe on the flat rooftop, he seemed to make a decision. He turned to her, and she noticed his coy attitude was back.

"Did you think of a plan?" she asked. Ry smirked at her.

"Don't you know me? I always have a plan." She waited for him to elaborate, and after a moment of confused silence he obliged. "Waterford is completely averse to draining energy. We don't even know if he knows how to. If he goes long enough without energy from someone else, he'll drain his own and, in turn, die. Hopefully we won't have to do anything. Meanwhile, we can try to figure out what's wrong with that Saphirra girl, and why I can't bite her."

Evelyn stared at him. It was so simple; of course it had to work. Ry's plans always did. What startled her more is how quickly he'd managed to return to his unconcerned demeanor.

There was just one flaw.

"But we don't know what will happen at the full moon. If he loses control then and takes over–"Ry cut her off with a swift glance.

"He's too *nice*. He wouldn't hurt a human if it stood there with a neon sign over its head that read *attack me*. That isn't our biggest problem. What frustrates me the most is that I could have killed her ever since I started working here, ever since I knew who she was, and what she would become. But I didn't. And when I finally decide to throw caution to the wind, it turns out I can't bite her at all. Do you *know* how frustrating that is?"

Evelyn remembered all too well what the Council had warned them when Ry mentioned the prophecy: kill the girl and be killed yourself. The Council never was one for mincing words. Then again, Ry lived for the challenge, especially if his way of life depended on it.

"Evelyn, do you remember when I disappeared for a while?" Ry asked suddenly. She nodded, and he continued, his voice grow-ing soft. "I went to the Council in London again. They wouldn't let me hurt her in any way. According to them, she's only a human. Of course, they had no idea why she was so important to me." He con-tinued pacing, and she could practically see the gears whirring in his brain. Evelyn reached out a hand to stop him. She moved closer to him, almost unconsciously. The wind around them had settled, leaving a comfortable silence between them. Ry smiled. He knew exactly what she was trying to do.

"You did very well, Ms. Stone," he murmured, crossing the little distance between them. She knew she was nothing but a well-placed distraction to him, but she didn't care. She loved him, and she'd made that very clear. Yet, he'd never said it back. Not once. She decided to try again.

"I love you," she told him quietly.

"As you should." He smiled at her. Ry hadn't said it back, but it was enough. As he drew her closer, she knew she shouldn't let it go, that she should make him say the words back to her. But then he smiled at her, and she forgot everything. He bent down, his lips brushing her ear, and whispered,

"They'll be dead soon. And if they aren't, you will be."

Saphirra sat on her bed, looking out the window at the night sky. The stars twinkled cheerily at her, somehow visible through the thick evening fog. Tonight would mark yet another week that they'd failed to find information, and a month since the day they'd been in the hospital. The computers were *still* down, this time destroyed by some virus West had accidentally opened. Claire had managed to work through parts of the prophecy before West had crashed the computers, but large gaping holes were still missing. They still had no idea what most of it meant, let alone what would happen. Claire had resolved to go into the city tomorrow to research, and Saphirra had half a mind to accompany her.

She glanced around their dorm room, waiting for Claire to show up. It was tiny, but it worked. Their beds fit side by side, leaving barely any room to walk. Saphirra gazed back up at the sky, wondering about tonight. It was her turn to stay with Alex. How would he react? He seemed to be getting weaker somehow, and she'd noticed that his pain seemed to be getting worse. They'd quickly realized that Alex lost control when he slept thanks to West, who'd reported Alex's pillow having been massacred the next morning. They'd decided the safest bet would be to move him to a different dorm while telling

West that he'd moved back to his apartment in the city. *Poor West,* Saphirra thought. He knew that the group was keeping information from him, and he asked them about it daily. It took all of Saphirra's self-control to avoid telling Alex's best friend the truth.

Alex wasn't acting like an arrogant prick anymore, probably for her benefit as well as West's. He'd admitted one night that he couldn't sleep anymore, which worried Saphirra. He'd then tried to convince her and Claire that he could wait out the nights alone, but both had refused. Claire had figured out the one piece of information that had been alarming Saphirra for days; the glow that resulted when Alex touched anyone was from a transfer of energy between them. Claire had explained that the auras Alex claimed to see were the energies of the people around him, and that, as a Viceprus, he needed the energy from others to survive. When they began to glow on contact, Alex was unconsciously taking the energy from whomever he was touching. It was apparent in his eyes how easily this urge for energy tore at him, how much it hurt him to stay awake.

Why was it all happening so quickly? They needed more time to find a cure. For now both Saphirra and Claire were taking turns watching over him, to both make sure he didn't harm himself and also to give him their energy if he needed it. More often than not Alex refused to be anywhere near them, but once in a while, when he was at his weakest, he held out a tentative hand. By the end of the night Saphirra was always exhausted, and Claire the same, but it was the only recourse they had. Saphirra couldn't help wonder if they could turn him back. After all, if one could be turned into a Viceprus, then couldn't they be turned back into a human just as easily? The theory sounded plausible, but then again, they *were* mythical creatures. She knew something in the prophecy held the answer, but at this rate, they'd never figure it out. The answer was waving itself in her face, but every time she tried to reach out and grab it, it slipped from her grasp. The only answer they could come up with left them drained and listless.

Saphirra got up to open the window. The warm July breeze refreshed her, and she leaned against the tiny mahogany dresser, bored out of her mind. This was the one thing she hated—waiting, always waiting. She wanted to go up to the flat rooftops, to watch the Chicago skyline, to not have to worry about anything. But they still had false pretenses to upkeep, and Claire still had to watch for West. He was smart, and he'd eventually know something was up. *He probably already does.* Saphirra reasoned. How long would it take for West to figure out Alex had barely moved halfway across the campus?

Her mind drifted back to that night, two weeks ago. What had they been about to do? If they hadn't been interrupted, would anything have changed? *'I saw you and I just bolted...I couldn't handle it.'* What was it that Alex couldn't handle? The sight of auras around him, or her? She'd spent the last two weeks mulling over what would have been, and what was now completely illogical. She cared about him, maybe more than she should. He had protected her so long ago, and that wasn't something she could easily ignore. His presence brought up memories that would bring a smile to her lips even when she was so exhausted that she wanted to collapse.

But that still doesn't mean anything, Saphirra reminded herself. She frowned, tracing small circles into her felt pillow with her finger. What if everything had been different? What if she'd never met Alex by the tree, and had gotten killed by Professor Lockson? She'd thought about it too many times to count. No one would miss her, not really; her dad wouldn't bother himself to care. Her friends would be fazed, but only for a while; they'd learn to go on with their lives eventually. And Claire. What about her?

Pushing away the depressing line of thought, she pulled the red book from the dresser, opening it casually. They⬚d opened it to the same page so many times that it fell open easily, the binding cracking a bit in protest. She stared at the paragraph in Latin, hoping some of the words would just jump out at her and form a coherent sentence. They didn⬚t. Sighing, she tore a piece of paper out of a binder and began copying down the prophecy. What was that phrase Claire had partially deciphered? She couldn't remember.

Saphirra gazed at the words she'd scribbled on the page, trying to focus. It was impossible. She sank into the nest of pillows surrounding her, slowly losing herself in the comforting arms of sleep, phrases chasing each other around in her brain.

Colorful shards littered the pure white carpet beneath her. Saphirra grimaced at the ivory walls, hating them. Everything was white. Everything. Something smashed above her, and more broken glass littered the carpet, this time a dark green. The voices around her blurred into an incomprehensible cloud, and yet they continued to rise, growing shriller by the second. A second onslaught of glass fell around her, and Saphirra felt it pierce her skin, her arms. She looked down at herself, at her bare knees and her sleeveless arms. The world around her seemed to mute as she saw the carpet, this time colored by something else. Deep red stained the area in which she sat, chaining her there. As the world around her tilted, then dissolved, she couldn't help the calmness that stole over her; at least she wasn't surrounded by white anymore.

The door opened suddenly, the light starting Saphirra awake. Cold sweat dotted her neck, and she took a few steady breaths. Claire rushed in, grabbing earrings from the top of her blue bed. Her hair was up in a messy bun, and she straightened her navy blue blouse nervously.

"Hey, Saph. Do I look alright?" she twirled around once, her white skirt flying around her. Saphirra squeezed her tears back into her eyes, trying to focus on Claire.

"Perfect," Saphirra smiled at her as quickly as she could, and then turned back to the prophecy, which lay in disarray at her feet. With Claire in the room, it was getting harder and harder to keep her tears from spilling over and her voice from wavering.

"I'm going down to the quad soon. West told me to meet him there-" she stopped talking when she saw Saphirra's face.

"What happened?"

Saphirra busied herself by burying her face in the book that lay open at her feet and copying down the last sentence of Latin she'd fallen asleep writing.

"Just a bad dream," she said absentmindedly. *More like a bad memory.*

"Will you and Alex be alright? I know you told me to keep West from being suspicious, but—"

"Go ahead, and have fun. Don't worry, okay? Everything will be fine," she said as reassuringly as she could. Claire didn't seem convinced, but she nodded and left without comment. Saphirra put up a fake smile until Claire closed the door, and finally let the tears spill over.

Saphirra shook her head, trying to shake the thought out of her mind. She would *not* be haunted by memories, and she wouldn't shed another tear for the people she thought loved her. She'd promised herself that five years ago. Drying her eyes on the back of her sleeve, she looked out of the window again, trying to calm herself a little before going to find Alex. The deserted grounds looked peaceful. As she watched, a blur flashed through the darkness.

Saphirra jumped to the window, watching. Someone was running across the grounds, their feet moving so fast that the person appeared to float over the grounds. She tried to see who it was but she blinked, and the person was gone in a flash. She stood by the window for a moment, hoping he or she would show up again. Then someone slipped their hands over her eyes, and she screamed.

"Calm down, it's only me." A familiar voice laughed from behind Saphirra, and she sighed in relief.

"Oh thank god it's you; I thought you were Lockson or something," her smile of relief quickly turned into a frown as she watched him with accusing eyes.

"Wait. What are you doing in my room?"

Alex's face was flushed.

"Saph, I've discovered something. Something amazing. Will you come with me?" Without waiting for an answer, he grabbed Saphirra's hand and pulled her down two flights of stairs, tugging her out of the dorm and into the center of the quad.

"Is anyone watching?" he asked, scanning the area. Saphirra gave the grounds a weary glance.

"No, no one's here but us. West and Claire left together."

Alex smiled, then walked behind her and gently held her waist. She flinched, and he laughed at her reaction.

"Relax, I'm not going to try anything." She felt him bend toward her. "Don't move," he breathed in her ear, sending shivers down her spine.

And then her feet left the ground.

The grass seemed to fall out from underneath her, and the trees and buildings were getting smaller and smaller in the distance. The wind rushed past her face with more intensity than it should...they were *flying*.

"How...How is this *possible?*" She asked incredulously. "Did you drink Red Bull or something?" Alex laughed at her feeble attempt at a joke, tightening his grip on her as he flew higher.

"Red bull gives you wings, but not *these* kinds of wings."

He laughed again as she tried to turn around to see how he was doing it. "I told you, don't move! I'm not used to this yet! Just hang back and enjoy the ride."

But how is this happening? Saphirra wanted to ask, but she couldn't get the words out of her mouth. They dipped and dived rhythmically in the sky, and Saphirra watched the Chicago skyline grow smaller and further away until it seemed like she was looking at a dollhouse set. The city lights twinkled up at her, and she felt the air growing thinner and thinner around her. She'd never realized how Alex's body seemed to radiate heat around her, how she seemed to have trouble keeping her eyes open–

"How are you doing this? It isn't possible." she shouted at him through the wind. Alex sighed, and for the first time, she felt his claws around her waist, too.

"Will you wait for a second? It *is* possible, let me show you-"He cut himself off, and their ascent stopped abruptly.

Suddenly, they were falling.

Saphirra screamed, and Alex groaned in dismay as the heat left him as fast as it had come. Saphirra looked down, watching the buildings fly up at her at an alarming speed—they were going to crash, she was sure of it. At the last second, something snapped behind her, and Alex breathed a sigh of relief. Within moments she was uncomfortably warm again, and they stopped spiraling downward with a jerk.

"What just happened?" Saphirra asked breathlessly. Alex made no answer as he pulled her down to the quad again, trying to navigate.

"I don't know why that happened. I'm sorry! I had another lapse or flash or whatever, it shouldn't have happened. It didn't happen before..." Alex's voice sounded thoughtful as he let her down onto the ground. She staggered away from him, the quad spinning around her. She leaned against the big oak tree, waiting for the dizziness to stop.

Was that what he wanted to show her? How to have a near death experience? She rolled her eyes as he caught her shoulder. She couldn't deal with this.

Not now.

"Saph! Look at me, please," he pleaded, and she turned around. Her legs were still shaking.

"Look, I just—" Her jaw dropped when she finally realized what she was looking at.

Alex stood before her, two black, feathery *wings* protruding from his back. It gave him the bizarre appearance of a giant bat.

"Oh," she said in a small voice. Alex grinned at the expression on her face.

"Now you believe me?"

She could only nod as she walked over to him, her fingers stretched out to touch one wing. The feathers were soft to the touch and it was flexible, like the cartilage of an ear.

"How did you *do* that?" she asked him, appalled. Alex grinned widely, beating them once.

"Whoa," she said quietly, walking over to him. She tenderly ran her fingers over one wing, marveling at how big they were. It was such an out of body experience...so weird, so dreamlike, and yet so real. The wing felt so breakable, as if balsa wood made up the bones. Alex folded his wings back in, and she saw how they lay flat on his body.

"You've grown wings? When did this happen? I just thought...I thought that you'd drugged me or something," she said, not daring to believe her eyes. Maybe he *had* drugged her. This was just too unreal.

"Well, believe it, because it's true," he grinned widely at her, and unfurled his wings for effect, making her jump.

"You have no idea how strange that looks."

He only shrugged in response, turning instead to look up at the full moon. It cut through the fog and illuminated the grass below them, bleaching everything frosty silver.

"It s,"almost midnight," he informed her, gesturing towards the sky for emphasis.

"It is," she replied cautiously. She knew that tone. He was going to ask something of her.

"Would you mind if we went on the rooftops tonight? It's not too cold, and the fog is starting to clear up," he pleaded. She could only imagine his irritation at having to be stuck in the same room all night, especially in his new state. Saphirra felt a twinge of pity.

"Sure," she consented. Alex stiffened at her sympathetic tone, and she knew she'd hit a nerve. He hated the fact that they needed to look after him all night. He'd always hated causing others trouble, especially his friends. Somehow, he always missed the fact that neither of them really minded much. Before she could say anything, he pulled her to him then launched himself back into the sky, setting her down on the rooftop moments later. She gave him a disgruntled look and crossed to the far edge of the rooftop, leaning against the rough brick railing to steady herself. She already didn't like this new version of Alex.

The air was colder up on the roof than though her window below, and she shivered. Alex sat down next to her, leaning his head back to stare at the sky.

"Saph?"

She looked down at him, and he beckoned for her to sit. She slid down obediently, pausing to wrap her arms around her knees.

"Saph, I-I need to tell you something." His voice was strained, and when she looked up at him he seemed anxious. She twisted to face him.

"What is it?" she asked curiously. She pushed away the memory of the classroom that always seemed to want to resurface at times like this.

"Remember when I disappeared for a while? Remember how I said I had been near the university the whole time?"

She nodded, wondering what he could be getting at. "I had gone back to my apartment in Chicago. I was going to stay there for the rest of the summer. I never wanted to come back here." He swallowed nervously, and continued. "It got really bad. I'd be tired all the time, to the point that I didn't want to leave the couch, even for food. One night I just passed out on the floor...And I woke up near the oak tree in the quad. I don't know how I got there...*what I did* to get there. I think I might have attacked someone."

Saphirra didn't know what she was expecting, but certainly not this. She scrambled away from him, watching him through narrowed eyes. Alex sighed; he seemed to have expected this reaction.

"What exactly do you mean by attacked?" Saphirra asked, her voice louder than usual. Alex looked resigned.

"I mean I think I lost control and did something like what Lockson tried to do to you. I don't know if I did for sure, because I can't remember anything. All I know is that I could barely lift my head one minute, and the next I could run circles around you."

Saphirra was speechless. Did he hurt someone? *Kill* someone? It occurred to her how dangerous her friend had become. Alex wasn't finished speaking.

"I don't think you should be here tonight. Something doesn't feel right. I feel...Different somehow. You should go." He grimaced as a shudder swept through him. Saphirra shook her head.

"I'm staying. You aren't going to attack anyone else again," she told him firmly. He glared daggers at her, his eyes piercing through the night.

"You'll get hurt too. Go away."

"No."

They stared at each other stubbornly. Finally, Alex sighed and slumped down further in defeat. "Fine. Do what you want."

She settled down for the night, resting her head against the wall as his breathing grew more ragged. Saphirra reached out a hand, and he took it.

As the faint golden glow shone from between their clasped hands, Alex began to shudder, this time more violently. Saphirra made her grip on him tighter. His skin was icy cold beneath her fingers, as if the heat had evaporated into the air. He seemed to be in more pain than usual—he was craning his neck away from her desperately, almost to avoid seeing her. His grip was now vice-like on hers.

An unearthly snarl escaped Alex. His lips curled menacingly, and Saphirra had a clear view of his teeth; they glistened with invisible venom, venom reserved for his prey. She glanced at him worriedly as his body convulsed in pain. This had never happened before. He'd never been like this during the nights she'd stayed with him. She wanted to stop him, and she felt helpless when she realized she had no idea how. His blue eyes flickered to violet for a moment, and she let his hand go, alarmed. His eyes hadn't changed color like that since that day. She tried to move away from him but he just moved closer, his hands now brandishing claws. Alex stared at her with those strange violet, thirsty eyes.

"Alex, what are you–"

"Saphirra," he interrupted roughly, backing her into a corner. "Saphirra, give me your hand."

Saphirra's heart slammed against her ribcage as pure panic set in. Alex was acting almost exactly like he had a month ago. *Worse,* she decided as Alex loomed closer. She was scared, and immediately felt ashamed for admitting it to herself–Alex was her friend, after all. She'd consented to this, despite his warnings.

Saphirra desperately wished she'd listened to him.

"Alex, stop. You aren't yourself," she tried, but Alex just moved closer. She could feel his shirt pressing against her skin, and her breath caught. The closeness was extremely uncomfortable.

"Saph, *please,*" he breathed. She shook her head as his face drew nearer to hers. He wasn't looking at her anymore—he was looking through her.

"Alex, *stop,*" she snapped, but he seemed incapable of hearing her. His lips brushed hers, and for a moment she hoped it would be enough. Alex's eyes flashed back to blue, and for a brief moment she saw the apology in his eyes before they were swallowed again by the eerie violet. His hands held her forcefully against the brick behind her as he kissed her, and Saphirra knew no amount of struggling would have him release her. She fought against him but it was no use; she was exhausted already, as if she had been fighting him for hours and not minutes. She'd wondered how it would feel to kiss him, but never like this; not when he'd been taken over by a monster. She didn't want to find out this way. She wanted him to stop.

"Alex, stop. *Please,*" she said, her voice quivering in near tears. Alex ignored her and pressed his mouth to hers again, his lips moving urgently against her own. She tried to push him away but he simply moved to her neck, leaving her gasping for air. He stopped at the base of her throat, hovering over the spot Lockson had tried to bite.

I'm scared.

Her skin tingled where he touched her neck, and he clutched her closer, as if she could possibly run away. Her limbs felt sluggish and heavy, and Alex was now supporting all her weight. Her panic was frozen too—she couldn't feel anything but repressed calm, like anxiety that can't surface. It was smothering her.

Help me.

Dull panic was starting to edge though the haze in her brain, and she was starting to feel lightheaded. She tried to move her lips, but it was practically impossible. The numbness was getting more and more powerful with every passing second, and she moved her mouth over and over, finally able to form one word.

"Alex," she croaked nervously. He didn't hear her, and she was beginning to see spots in front of her eyes. She could hear a ringing in her ears as she fought to stay awake, and with a herculean effort, she lifted one arm from Alex's waist, and felt his grip on her waist grow stronger, almost iron like.

Let me go. Stop it!

Her cheek scraped against the rough edge of the ledge behind her, but she could barely feel the pain. Alex inhaled sharply and she twisted, trying to move away one last time. His fingers loosened, and she managed to pull herself out of his grasp a little.

It wasn't enough.

Alex bit into her skin, sending searing pain through her, blinding her. He shoved her away from him and she fell against stone, eyes watering from the pain. She couldn't make her mouth move. She couldn't speak. All she could do was lie there, watching Alex cower below the moonlit sky.

Claire walked with West on a cobblestone path, the neon signs of stores staring her in the face. She was still exhausted from yesterday night, because of the hours she'd spent with Alex's hand in hers, watching the golden glow of energy pass between them. Somehow her energy seemed dimmer than that of Saphirra's. Claire had gotten used to the awkward silences in the room, which she usually filled with the rustling of pages from books in the library. She'd found a legend on the internet that she wanted to look up, but of course West had managed to shut down their system before she could really read it. West had needed to go into town, and she'd agreed to go with him. She regretted it now, since their awkward silences were filled with tension, not impatience. "That sure is a beautiful moon," West commented, stopping in his tracks. Claire nodded as she stared at the lucent orb in the sky.

"Yeah, it is," she agreed nonchalantly. They passed an Internet café, and she wondered if West would mind her ducking inside for a bit.

"A beautiful moon, and underneath it, a beautiful girl," West said mischievously, turning to Claire. His steady gaze made her knees weak.

"Very funny," she said halfheartedly, turning to walk into a side street. West was nice most of the time, but his jokes had an irritating edge to them.

"I'm dead serious. I'm really lucky to have a girl like you. Thanks, Claire," he continued, grinning teasingly. Claire rolled her eyes, disturbed at how her heart had started beating faster.

"Why yes you are," she told him smugly. West laughed softly, brushing his fingers across her cheek. His touch sent a tingling shock through her, and it took her a moment to move away from him and start towards the university. *Why is West always so damn confusing?* Claire thought irritably. West skipped ahead of her, swinging his bag of groceries.

"Aw, come on! Cheer up," he said teasingly. Claire gave him a disapproving glance.

"Can't you talk normally?" she snapped. As West's face fell she felt a twinge of guilt. They passed the university entrance, heading towards the quiet, grassy quad, making light conversation as they went. Something was distracting West again—he kept fidgeting with his cell phone.

"Are you expecting a call?" Claire asked him. West dropped his cell phone back into his pocket.

"No, nothing important, anyway," he said quietly. That unsettled her, and she stared at him uncertainly. *It's past one in the morning, so Alex should be quiet by now.* Claire reasoned, glancing up at the dorms. She couldn't see a light in the windows, which meant they'd either fallen asleep or expected West to be there. Claire steered him to the fountain away from the dorms just in case and sat down on the rim. He followed suit, staring at the library building in front of them.

"Claire, what were you really researching that day?" he asked suddenly. Claire looked at him, startled. She knew he'd have a reason for dragging her out here.

"I...I told you, we were helping Saphirra and Alex–"

"No, I mean what you were *actually* researching. Come on Claire, I'm not dumb," he interrupted her, his grey eyes watching her face carefully. Ice gripped her heart as she struggled to make an excuse.

"I...Well, if you must know, I was trying to re-learn Latin. I couldn't remember it, and I was really impressed when you said you were fluent in it, so I thought maybe..." She shrugged, trying to make her voice carry across the quad so Saphirra and Alex would know they were there. She knew that it would be easier for West to swallow her lie than argue, and that was exactly what he did.

"Oh," he said quietly, watching the digital watch on his cell phone. She sighed. The excuses were getting harder and harder to keep track of; one of these days, she'd get tangled.

The two were startled by a door bursting open from the other end of the quad, away from the dorms. Voices echoed as the two figures neared them, one practically running after the other.

"Get away from me."

"Saph, I'm sorry, I didn't mean—"

"Get *away* from me!" Saphirra shouted at him, her expression livid. Claire's eyes widened as she took in Saphirra's cut cheek and the strange way she gripped her shoulder with one hand. Alex's hair was disheveled, his clothes bunching up in odd ways against his skin. Saphirra looked more exhausted than she'd ever been in her life, while Alex was positively radiating with energy.

Uh oh.

Both stopped in their tracks at the sight of West, who was watching them in bewilderment.

"What's going on? Are you okay?" he directed this question at Saphirra, who barely spared him a glance.

"Yeah. Fine," she replied curtly before stalking off towards the dorms. Alex looked up at them, and for the first time Claire noticed his eyes.

They were bright violet.

She felt West stiffen beside her and knew he'd noticed it, too. Before either of them could examine Alex closer, though, he'd bolted after Saphirra. West watched them go, eyes wide.

"What just happened?" he asked, running a hand through his hair exasperatedly.

"I'm going to check to see if Saph is okay. You want to help?" she asked halfheartedly. *If West convinces himself that Alex's eyes weren't violet at all, I won't have to explain,* she thought hopefully. As long as Alex's eyes were blue by the time they reached him–

"No, I think I'll just go back to the dorms," he said abruptly. His sudden change of tone startled her, but she didn't question it. As he made his way back through the quad, she didn't bother to stop him.

Chapter 9
The Tale of the Old Healer

Saphirra spent the next week researching in the inner city libraries. She was sporadically helped by Claire, and even those visits grew less frequent as time passed. Sometimes West would help, under the impression they were learning Latin. The only one she constantly avoided was Alex, who in turn tried to help her relentlessly, for lack of anything better to do. He followed her to every library, each time hoping to talk to her. He only increased Saphirra's irritation, however, because his useless presence only made it harder for her to concentrate.

Plus, he'd cut her time short. Everywhere she went she'd see him craning his neck to look behind a bookcase, searching for her. She didn't want to hear it; she knew exactly what he was going to say, and it didn't matter. She just didn't want to be anywhere near him. When he'd spot her and make his way towards her, she'd take that as her cue to leave. Saphirra left early in the morning and arrived back at the university late at night so she could avoid night duty for Alex. Poor Claire had no idea why Saphirra was avoiding Alex so much, since Saphirra hadn't bothered to inform her of what had happened that night. Alex had most likely told Claire what he knew, but Saphirra doubted it would suffice. Alex probably didn't even know the extent of what he had done himself, and Saphirra didn't want Claire to know. It would only make the situation worse, Saphirra had figured, especially with Claire's mounting irritation with Alex.

Saphirra could sense Claire's annoyance with her every time they met. She looked incredibly exhausted, and Saphirra felt the smallest twinge of guilt every time she saw Claire's face. She couldn't help but wonder how much energy Alex had sucked from her friend. The thought made her unreasonable anger swell.

Saphirra was now in a library, surprised she'd stayed so long. Alex hadn't spotted her yet so she'd been able to look for information longer than she usually would. Saphirra saw a flash of red hair out of the corner of her eye and slammed her book down irritably. He hadn't spotted her yet, but Saphirra knew it'd be only a matter of minutes before he did. Sighing, she stood to replace the book on the bookshelf, trying to push away the memory Alex's presence always brought to mind. Instead, she dwelled on the first time she'd had night duty with Alex. The memory popped into her mind so vividly that she couldn't be bothered to push it away.

"This isn't working."

Saphirra had glanced up at Alex, puzzled. They sat in an abandoned dorm room, Alex flicking through the books Saphirra had brought with her lazily. Claire was out with West in the quad, trying to coax him out to the city. She smiled a little at the way Claire had to occupy West; it felt like she was playing with a puppy. Alex had sighed and gone back to going through the pile of books that surrounded them.

"You don't have to be here, you know. I'll be fine," he told her for the umpteenth time. Saphirra rolled her eyes and turned back to the window, her breath frosting the glass as she spoke.

"Do you not want me here?"

"No, you know I didn't mean it like that–"

"Then what's the problem? I don't mind much," she told him with an air of finality. Alex didn't bother arguing, and instead returned to idly flicking through the pages of some book on folklore, attempting to read by the thin moonlight streaming through the window.

She turned back to the scene below, her eyes following Claire as she called out to West, arms beckoning. She saw a flicker of a frown on West's face, who was sprawled on the grass. A split second later, it was gone. He had seemed more resigned than usual lately, but Saphirra had passed it off as tiredness. West smiled up at Claire, and Saphirra could tell by the way Claire's shoulder's drooped a little that she knew something was off too.

The silence in the room was unnerving; it pressed down on them, making it incredibly hard to concentrate on anything. Saphirra glanced at her fingers subconsciously, wincing as the thin scars that crossed her arms were thrown into relief. She felt Alex's eyes on her, and quickly shifted so that they weren't visible. She turned her gaze back to Alex, smiling. Alex wasn't looking at her face, though; his eyes were trained on the arms she now hid behind her back.

"What happened to your arm?" he asked curiously, craning his neck to get a better look.

"What do you mean?" she replied innocently. Alex looked puzzled.

"I thought I just saw–"

"There's nothing wrong with my arm," she told him curtly. Alex looked taken aback at her change of tone, and she immediately felt guilty.

"Okay. Sorry," he replied, turning back to the book. Saphirra wanted to tell him what had happened. She had wanted to tell him everything, probably since the day they'd met again. She just couldn't find the words to explain, and she dreaded to see his reaction.

Then again, Saphirra argued with herself, *Alex's behavior isn't easy to predict.* Everything about him was so different than anyone else. The way he picked up one of the books, so carefully and gently, amused her. His eyes, which changed from blue to a blue green and back again, were watching her rather than the book. She felt herself blush.

"What, you don't like reading?" she asked jokingly. Alex shook his head and irritably flung his book aside.

"I hate reading," he grumbled. "Can't we watch TV or something? Please?" he pleaded. Saphirra smiled.

"We can't until West leaves the quad, or he'll see the light from it," she explained patiently. "Besides, don't you want to research your own kind?"

She laughed, and realized Alex wasn't joining in. He had a strange look on his face.

"I didn't realize I was a complete Viceprus now. I was under the impression I was still human. I guess I was wrong."

That sobered her right up.

"I'm sorry, I didn't mean–"

"I know."

Alex still looked sad, his lips pressed in a thin line, so she shut up for a while. The silence stretched, until she couldn't bear it anymore.

"Can you imagine this in an alternate reality, Alex? You know, like where this entire thing isn't as normal to us anymore. Have you noticed? We're getting too used to the supernatural." She sighed, stretching her arms out behind her. "If someone told you this was going to happen a few months ago, would you believe them?"

Alex had to think about that one for a while, studying the sky as if it was the most interesting thing in the world. He glanced back at her, and softness had replaced sorrow in his eyes.

"No, I guess not."

Something about the way he'd said those words hit her, even now. He'd said them as if he was admitting defeat, like he'd lost the battle between wishful thinking and reality by answering out loud. It worried her that he could give up so quickly, as if he'd already accepted the worst. Still, Saphirra couldn't help wondering if there really *was* no cure, if their searches were useless. Yet, Claire had mentioned finding something that morning that would help. Saphirra hadn't been able to see what it was, however, because Alex had been walking towards them.

He was walking towards her now.

Saphirra panicked. She hastily sprang out of her chair and headed for the nearest exit, weaving through bookcases in an attempt to deter him. As she burst through the doors and made her way onto the darkening street, she sighed. Avoiding him was getting harder than she would have liked.

"Saphirra!"

Alex had emerged from the library as well, and was heading towards her much too quickly for her liking. She tried to walk away as fast as she could, but his long stride easily matched hers.

"Saph, you can't keep avoiding me!" Alex said loudly.

"Just watch me," she hissed at him.

Alex narrowed his eyes. "I have a right to be *heard*. Just listen to me for ten minutes. After that, you don't have to even look at me."

People were beginning to stare at the scene they were making. Saphirra unwillingly pulled him into a nearby coffee shop, cheeks burning.

"Fine. Ten minutes," she told him sternly, sitting down in one of the booths. Alex slid in across from her. He looked anxious.

"I didn't expect to get this far," he admitted. "Listen, Saph, whatever I did that night, I'm sorry. I've told you a thousand times that I'm sorry. What more do you want me to say?"

Saphirra bit her lip, reading the exhaustion in his words. "Do you even know what you did that night?"

"No, but I *did* tell you to leave, I clearly remember saying that–"

"Did you actually expect me to leave you there by yourself?" Saphirra cried, her voice strained. "Alex, I'm your friend. You looked like you were in enough pain as it was. If I had left, who knows what would have happened? I couldn't just leave you there!"

Alex buried his head in his hands. "Okay. Tell me. What did I do?" he asked warily, his voice muffled by his arms. Saphirra tugged at her sleeves self-consciously, pulling them over her scars. *He doesn't remember.* The thought sent a wave of relief through her, tinged with something else...was it regret?

"Well..." she said tentatively, her voice low. "First, you cornered me. You kissed me..."

"How do I not remember that?" Alex interrupted. Saphirra ignored him. "Then you bit me." Alex's head snapped up. "I couldn't move for a while. I blacked out. When I came to you were still holding my hand. You didn't attack me after that, but only because I managed to get up. You drained me of my energy."

Alex looked stunned. "I-I bit you?" he asked hoarsely. "Then... Are you like me? Are you a—" he gestured to himself, and Saphirra shook her head.

"I don't need energy like you do. I don't see auras around people. I don't know what you did by biting me, but I think I'm still normal." She shrugged, turning away from him so he could see the faint bite mark on her shoulder.

"I'm sorry," Alex said in a hushed whisper, reaching out to take her hand. Saphirra allowed it. "You know I would never do that on purpose." Saphirra nodded, watching the barely visible glow emitting from their entwined hands. She glanced around them, making sure no one had seen.

"I feel normal. But when Lockson bit you, you started to change right away. I don't understand," Saphirra said quietly. Alex frowned.

"Maybe I'm not like him, since I'm still half-human." He whispered the last word, and Saphirra shrugged.

"Maybe we shouldn't talk here," she suggested, nodding her head towards the people around them. Alex agreed, and they walked out to the bus stop together, deciding to head back to the university. Saphirra felt happier than she had in days now that her anger had vanished as fast as it had flared. She was surprised just how easily they'd slipped back into their friendship. It was as natural as breathing.

She had wondered what Alex's bite would do to her for the past week, and had been checking to see if she had the same tendencies as he did. Surprisingly, she had felt no change within her. This only puzzled her more; shouldn't she be a half-Viceprus like Alex was? What was so different about Professor Lockson and Alex that his bite wouldn't affect her?

As the bus screeched to a halt near the university, they got down, only to be nearly run over by a frantic Claire.

"Where have you *been?*" she asked them. Before they could explain, Claire plunged on. "I found something that could help. Want to see?"

Without waiting for an answer, she dragged the two of them into the quad behind her.

⁕

Claire ran back to the oak tree in the center of the quad as quickly as she could, Alex and Saphirra frantically trying to keep up. Miraculously, she'd found just the source they needed that morning, in a book on ancient folktales. She'd gone through some lengths to get it. She had snuck into Professor Lockson's deserted classroom and gone through his drawers until she had noticed something that looked a little out of place. Amidst Professor Lockson's anthropology and mythical theory books was nestled a thin, brightly decorated volume. Its golden cover had nearly been swallowed by the sea of dull brown and grey around it. Curious, Claire had pulled it out, examining the nearly perfect condition of the book. The volumes around it had looked over-used, to the point that some were falling out of their bindings, and yet this one remained pristine. She had shrugged and taken it anyway, running out the door as fast as she could. Racing back to her dorm room, she'd tucked it into her bag for safekeeping, and hadn't looked at it until this afternoon.

She had been reading it outside, leaning against the giant oak tree in the quad, when she'd found the story. As Claire neared the large oak tree, she was relieved to see the book exactly where she had left it, its bright cover catching the waning sunlight. It was a beautiful day in Chicago, and the twilight filtered through the leaves, scattering a soft glow around her. Saphirra stared at it, uncertain. Claire bent down to pick it up, and rifled through the pages to try and find her place. The pages were still crisp and fresh, and didn't want to turn—obviously, Lockson hadn't read a single sentence.

"What is it?" Alex asked curiously, peering over her shoulder. Claire noticed faintly how Saphirra and Alex were still in the same area together, and smiled. She knew they'd work it out eventually. Turning back to the book, she flipped through it until she found what she was looking for.

"Listen to this," she said quietly, moving out of the shadows for a better view. "I found this in the back of the book. I think it would help explain a lot." She showed them the page, squinting to make sense of the dense lettering:

There once was a farmer who lived in a small cottage by the sea on the edge of an island village. The village they lived in was a kindly sort, one whose citizens always helped each other out in times of need. The farmer had twins, one daughter and one son, whose job was to fetch water from their well each morning. One day the daughter made her way to the well, pausing as she drew water to admire her reflection, as always was her custom. As she gazed lovingly her reflection, a voice interrupted her.

"Excuse me, but may I please have some water?"

The daughter turned to see the village healer sitting in the shade of an olive tree, watching her. Her countenance was ancient and grey, and her knobby hands rested wearily on her lap. The woman gave her a crinkled smile, gesturing to the bucket. "I wouldn't need much, but I am very thirsty."

The daughter considered the old healer, and then the amount of work it had taken to pull the bucket up from the well, and how it had already distressed her pretty hands. She stared down at the full bucket, then at the water in the well.

"I do not have enough water to give you," she told the healer. "Maybe another time."

With that, she began to walk back down the hill. As she passed by a merchant's stall, a wizened old man emerged, grinning toothlessly. She shrunk a little at his revolting appearance.

"Excuse me, but might I please have some water? It's terribly hot today, and I am very thirsty."

The daughter considered the tired merchant, and then the amount of work it would take her to refill the bucket from the well, give some to the old woman who was no doubt still there, fill it again, then walk all the way down. She thought of the impact that amount of work would have on her pretty feet, and stared down at the full bucket, then back at the man.

"I do not have enough water," she told the merchant. "Maybe some other time."

With that, she continued down the path. As she neared the seashore, a handsome young man walked up to her, his eyes as blue as the sea.

"Excuse me, but may I please have some water? I have been working all day, and I am very thirsty."

The daughter, stunned by the young man's appearance, didn't consider the amount of work it would involve to fetch another bucket of water, give some to the old healer who was no doubt still by the well, get more water, walk back down the hill, give some to the wizened old man who was probably still selling his wares by the road, walk back up to the hill, fetch another pail of water, and walk all the way down again. Nor did she consider the detrimental effects it would have on her skin for her to be out in the sun for so long. She instead gave it to the young man, saying charmingly, "Why of course."

When she handed the bucket to the man he transformed before her eyes first into the wizened old merchant, then just as quickly into the town healer. The old woman handed back the bucket, her eyes flashing angrily.

"You are vain. You would not give a drop of water to a poor old woman or a tired old man, but would readily hand this entire bucket to a person as young and healthy as yourself. For your vanity, your looks will now be a curse. Every full moon, your soul will be consumed by your conceited ways, until you have learned your lesson."

With that, the old healer walked back towards the well, leaving the daughter to run crying to her brother. She told her brother of the curse set upon her, and begged for him to help her. Now, her brother was a very lazy fellow, but at the sight of his sister's distraught tears he headed to the well, lamenting over his lost hours of sleep.

Sure enough, when he reached the well, the old woman was there, sitting underneath the branches of an olive tree. The woman sighed at the sight of him, retreating back into the shade. The brother called out to her. "Excuse me, healer, but could you please remove the curse you have placed upon my sister?"

She gave him a crinkled smile, gesturing to the olive branches above her.

"If you help me pick some olives from atop this tree, I shall reverse the curse. I have been walking all day, you see, and I am very hungry."

The brother considered the old healer, then the amount of work it would take to climb up the olive tree, pick the olives for the old woman, and climb back down again. He shook his head sullenly, stating,

"They are much too high for me to get them."

The old woman sat up, her eyes flashing angrily. "You are as selfish as your sister, and twice as lazy. You would not work to even save your sister from her cruel fate? Fine, then you deserve a curse befitting of your lazy nature. At every full moon you will crave the energy you need, until it swallows you whole. Until you learn your lesson, this curse will not be lifted."

With that, the healer walked away, leaving the brother to run to his sister. The two fought, blaming each other for their misfortunes. As they argued, the daughter began to change. She became one of the most beautiful maidens on the island, and her voice became as musical as the peal of bells. Her brother also began to change, for he knew he wanted to leave the island and explore. The brother grew wings on his back to effortlessly fly and long claws to grab fruit as he pleased. The son soon left the island, unable to bear his sister any-more, and the daughter remained in the cottage by the sea, both forever con-demned to their curse.

Claire finished reading, and looked up at Saphirra and Alex's faces expectantly.

"That's it?" Alex asked incredulously, trying to turn to the next page. "That's all you wanted us to see? What, you want to preach to us about selfishness now?"

Claire shook her head. "It's uncanny. When we were in Mythology, we were taught that all myths and legends held a small bit of truth. Well...what if this is it?"

Saphirra nodded beside her. "What if the son was the first Viceprus? What if when he flew away he had *wings?*"

Alex frowned thoughtfully. "Then what creature did the daughter become?"

Claire threw up her hands. "I wish I knew. All we know is that if this really is how the two were created, then we know *why.*"

Saphirra cleared her throat. "Even if this *is* the story of the first Viceprus, it doesn't explain much. Except..." she leaned closer, scanning through the story. "Here's something. It says the healer's curse takes place every full moon! And at the end of the folktale, it said the curse hadn't been lifted, which means..."

Alex looked at her, wide-eyed. "Maybe losing control is the curse? Maybe I have to stay away from people during the full moon?"

"The brother and sister split up, and it didn't seem to go too well for them," Saphirra pointed out. "I think the last thing you should do is stay away from people." Claire couldn't help but agree.

"But the next moon is in a week or two," Alex said cautiously. "What if I do something stupid again?" he glanced at Saphirra, whose expression had gone carefully blank.

"We'll just have to figure out what to do by then, now won't we?" Claire said quietly, putting the book down onto the grass. She was about to pull the prophecy out from her bag to show the two what she'd deciphered when a flash of red caught her eye. She turned to see West walking casually through the gate and into the forest in his bright red Five Staffs uniform, too far away to have seen them.

What is he doing here? Claire wondered. *I thought he was still on duty at Five Staffs.* She fingered the strap of her bag, torn. A moment later, she'd made her decision.

"Saph, you and Alex take this and try to decipher it. I have to... go."

Within seconds she'd handed her bag to a bewildered Saphirra and had taken off towards the forest that surrounded their university, running as fast as she could to catch up to West. She slowed down as she reached the first trees, her breaths shallow. As she wound her way through the thick trunks, she heard his voice.

"boss?"

She peered behind the trunk of a tree to see West talking into his tiny metallic blue cell phone.

Again.

He was *always* on the phone when he was with her. She'd watched his eyebrows furrow. Who was on the other side of their conversations? She couldn't help wondering who was worrying him so much, what was making him so nervous every time he picked up. The minute he hung up, he'd always have to leave, leaving a confused Claire in his wake. What could make him do that? The conversations were always so one sided that she could never tell what they were about— all she heard was West agreeing, saying he'd be there as soon as he could, and then hang up. She couldn't decipher a single thing from any of these conversations, no matter how hard she tried. She suspected West made it that way, so she would never know. It drove her crazy, and she couldn't help but wonder what he wasn't telling her.

Now was her chance to find out.

She carefully picked her away along the forest floor until she got a better view of him and listened hard.

"boss, you know I can't today. You aren't the only one I work for, I have a *real* job!" West protested. Claire noticed he was still in his Five Staffs uniform. He listened to the speaker on the other end and sighed, sounding resigned.

"Are you sure this one is a Viceprus? The four you sent me after last week weren't—" He listened again, and frowned.

"This isn't what you said I would have to do. I kill them, not take them hostage."

Claire gasped, and realized her mistake all too late; West whipped around, his eyes narrowed.

"Got it. Bye." He snapped his phone shut and glared at his surroundings.

"Whoever you are, you can come out now," he said loudly. Claire darted between two trees to his left, and he luckily didn't sense the movement. He stood there for a moment, his shoulders tensed for a fight, and Claire held perfectly still. He seemed to pass off the noise as a woodland creature and began to walk back to the dorms, glancing back to check behind him every few minutes. Claire followed him hesitantly, wishing she could scream. *West kills Vicepruses. Hell, West knows what a Viceprus is!* That in effect was shocking enough. As she darted into the dorms behind him, it occurred to her that he wasn't the person she thought she knew.

Alex's best friend was a Viceprus hunter.

And he was about to hunt one now.

Chapter 10
The Hunter's Secret

West stared at the floor of the dorm room, listening hard. He could have sworn he'd heard footsteps on the stairs...Shrugging, he pulled his red rug out from underneath a particularly messy pile of junk, and unraveled it to reveal a short, thin blade emblazoned with what West knew to be sundust. Sunshards were ancient stones supposedly found at the bottom of the ocean, where they'd first came into existence from the beginning of the earth. They were extremely rare, and supposedly very valuable; West couldn't fathom how his boss had so many. He pulled the dagger out of its sheath, examining its fine tip. The surface glimmered in the faint dusk glow that streamed through his window.

"We've got another one to kill tonight," he whispered to the dagger. It lay unresponsive in his hands. *Talking to inanimate objects. Not good.* West laughed at himself, straightening up slowly, cautiously. He heard the tap of footsteps on the metal stairs leading to their dorm room, and froze. Alex was coming. Who else could it be? He jumped onto his bed, forcing the blade under his mattress. He feigned boredom, watching impatiently for Alex to come in through the half open door. If he didn't hurry, he wouldn't get paid for the night's work. He heard the footsteps pause outside, then recede down the same hallway. West was puzzled but didn't question his luck as he unearthed his dagger and slipped it into his back pocket as he headed downstairs.

Ever since he'd found out what Alex really was, his job had become a chore. He'd pictured each Viceprus after that night as Alex, making the killing process a whole lot harder. He couldn't kill his best friend, even though he was a lowlife for sucking the energy out of his friends. He'd seen what Alex was doing to Saphirra, and the only thing he'd resented more was her willingness to help him. Didn't she understand that soon her energy wouldn't be enough, that he would want more? West was curious as to how she had handled the full moon, and had smirked at Saphirra's reaction. She'd been avoiding Alex all week, which only meant one thing; he'd lost control. West shook his head at Alex's stupidity. *He should know by now how to deal with it,* West reasoned. After all, Alex had to have been a Viceprus for quite a while to have been able to hide it so well. West was under the impression that all Vicepruses were evil, that none had a single redeeming quality; did Alex? He wondered if Claire knew what Alex truly was. Saphirra would obviously keep something so dangerous from Claire, wouldn't she? If Claire knew that Alex was a Viceprus, would she protect him? Should *he* protect the very creature he kills on a daily basis, the creature that he despises so?

The question bothered him. For the last five years, he'd killed Vicepruses. They were creatures that used their victims mercilessly, and they shouldn't be trusted. And yet...was Alex a good Viceprus? He couldn't understand what would make them good. Where did the line between good and bad blur? What would define Alex as either one? Was he simply the grey area in between?

His phone rang once again, and he snapped it open irritably.

"West," his boss said calmly in his young voice. It always caused West to wonder—who was he speaking to, really? It seemed so familiar; yet, he couldn't place where he'd heard it before.

"Yeah, boss?" he sounded wary again; it was automatic now.

"Your assignment moved." His boss sounded cold, indifferent. "She's north of Anderson St, in one of the office buildings Capture her and wound her so she can't move, and remember to *leave* her there. I'll pick her up later. Don't forget, she's a tricky one. I need my hunter, so don't die," The voice continued.

"But where exactly–"The phone line went dead. West snapped the phone shut in frustration. *He always cuts me off!* West thought, balling his hands into fists. The memory of his boss's words caused him to freeze as he walked on the cobblestone path towards the university gates–

"Remember the Viceprus I warned you against? He's strong."

Ice pierced West's heart. What if his boss was searching for Alex? West didn't want to have to deal with Alex, especially like this. He passed the entrance and walked out onto the street, turning the sheath of his dagger over in his hands. *How many hearts has this tip pierced?* He didn't know. Finally, he came to a stop at the foot of a building. It was the only office building north of Anderson Street, which meant West was in the right spot.

It's in there somewhere. He stared up at the tall building, knowing what was at stake tonight. It was then that he saw it through a window, glaring down at him with purple eyes. When the claws had ripped the shades closed, West knew his time was short. He climbed the stairs towards the apartment as fast as he could, hoping the Viceprus hadn't escaped. He was off his game lately; normally he would never let one of them catch sight of him. The wooden stairs creaked as he reached the landing, and he heard a door slam shut.

He headed to the only apartment with a crack of light streaming through the bottom of the door. He wasn't about to give it a chance to escape.

West burst through the door, dagger at the ready. He ran into the first room of the unnaturally tidy office.

Nothing.

West sighed, searching underneath the long desk warily. It was these tense moments he hated the most, the ones where he could be attacked by surprise any second. Then a flash of light caught his eye and he whipped around, not a moment too soon. The Viceprus was... *feeding.* Her hands held her victim's face to hers as the energy poured out from around them, making the air vibrate with a kind of electrified charge. It looked like she was doing no more than kissing him. He had to be no more than twenty, at the most. He was limp in the Viceprus's arms, and West could tell he was already dead. She absorbed his energy greedily, reveling in the soft light around her. She was completely oblivious to West.

Or so it seemed.

Before he could react she had lunged at him, her mouth still glowing eerily with leftover energy, and he dodged in the nick of time.

"Oh look, the food was delivered to *me* this time. And in fewer than thirty minutes, too!" her voice mocked him, and her silver blonde hair whipped at his face as she dived at him, her prey lying forgotten on the floor. Her voice was bubbly, pouring out of her mouth like a babbling brook. *I hate her already.* West thought, tensing up.

"Shut up," he growled, swinging his leg at the beautiful creature. The Viceprus was too fast and dodged, reappearing within seconds behind West.

"He was a pretty little thing, and it was easy enough to get him away from his friends. *'Hey, why don't you come with me? You're pretty cute, and I can show you a great time,'*" She mimicked, laughing evilly. "It was so easy. Humans really are stupid." West kicked out behind him, but the Viceprus vanished. He saw claws trying to break the door open, for her to escape. He thrust the dagger at her arm and she clutched at it, trying to snap it in half.

"That's one of the many things you can't break," West laughed as her hands started glowing and she shrieked, falling away from him. So she finally realized she was in danger. *Good.* He didn't like stupid Vicepruses; they were too easy to kill. And apparently he needed this one alive. Just as he prepared for a counter attack, she stopped and stared at him.

"You're not human."

Her voice sounded odd; thoughtful, almost spiteful. She cocked her head to one side, scrutinizing him. Her statement caught West off guard.

"What?" he asked before he could help himself. She grinned and spoke, almost to herself.

"Interesting. The Council would love to hear this. What is your name? I can spare your life if you tell me who you are. Or who your employer is," she added as an afterthought. West gritted his teeth. This was a new trick. How stupid did she think he was?

"That's not going to happen," West said through gritted teeth. The Viceprus sighed.

"Pity," she muttered.

Then her claws were inches from his neck, and he thrust the dagger blindly, but not before hearing a tiny gasp. He twisted around in midair, and saw Claire with her hand over her mouth.

"So, you brought your girlfriend along? Perfect."

Dread filled West's heart as the Viceprus changed course, diving for Claire. With speed and precision, West launched himself over the Viceprus, blocking its path with the tip of his dagger. An unearthly snarl escaped her lips as she dived again, ravenous. West threw it over his head, and a dull thunk told him he'd hit his target. He turned to pull the dagger out of her leg, ignoring her scream of agony. Bright golden dots started spreading over her skin, pooling over her wrists and ankles, chaining her. The spots grew into holes, shining with unbound energy. Writhing, she sank to the floor, her beautiful body now punctured with bursts of sunlight. West stared at her with indifference, flicking open his phone to call his boss.

"It's done," West told him. His boss laughed coldly.

"Good." The line went dead again without warning.

"What have you done?" The Viceprus shrieked at him. "You *dare* wound a member of the High Council–"

"Yes, I *dare*," West snapped at her. "You won't be dead until my boss reaches you." It was only with huge effort that he didn't stab her right there. He was blinded by fury, and anger at Claire for following him only added to his temper. He turned around to see Claire shivering by the doorframe, her eyes wide with fear.

"Why did you follow me?" he asked coldly, brushing past her as he walked out the door and down the stairs. Claire followed after him silently, speaking only when they had gotten out of the building.

"You mentioned killing someone. I had to know my friend wasn't some cold hearted killer," she said, staring up at the building. The light was still on in the room.

"She was still alive when we left, if you hadn't noticed. Weren't you listening?" West snapped at her. "Or did you hear what I had said to my boss, too? How long have you been following me?"

Claire gulped. "Since you got that call in the woods." West gave her a scathing look and stomped off, leaving her scrambling behind him.

"You...You're a Viceprus killer?" she called after him, her voice full of dread.

"Viceprus hunter, actually," West amended, not bothering to turn around to address her. Claire stared at him wide eyed, her face as white as a sheet.

"Oh...Well, that...that explains it," she'd said faintly, her eyes darting to the bloodied dagger in his hand and back to West's face in a kind of mute horror. He waited a full thirty seconds for it to sink in.

"You *kill* them..."

"Yes," he told her curtly. "Now you know. Never speak to me again and forget everything. Goodnight."

He turned away from her, expecting her to be discouraged. After all, she should at least be too confused to ask any true questions now. And that time was all he needed.

"West, I'm sorry!" she cried, startling him. "But you can't expect me to forget what I saw." West whipped around, eyes blazing.

"You *will* forget, Claire."

"Or what?" she lifted her chin up defiantly, eyes challenging him. He stepped back from her, running a hand through his hair. *I can't deal with this too. First Alex, and now this...*

"Fine," he snapped. "Just don't tell Alex or Saphirra, whatever you do. I don't want them thinking I'm evil or crazy or something. You won't tell anyone if you know what's good for you."

He turned away from her hurriedly, walking into the night and wishing that he hadn't seen the hurt in her eyes. Claire kept walking behind him, this time keeping her distance. Their footsteps echoed as they walked, each wondering about the other. Finally, Claire spoke.

"What if that Viceprus had killed you? She seemed fast enough," she said nervously. West scoffed.

"That's why I'm a Viceprus hunter. I never get hurt." Her voice had spilled relief though his body, and he relaxed despite the reality that Claire now knew. The fact that Vicepruses existed didn't seem to bother Claire. Rather, it didn't bother her as *much* as the fact that he killed them on a daily basis. They passed bright streetlamps and darkened windows of shops in silence, making their way slowly back to campus. The streets were quieter than usual with only the occasional bleary driver trickling past, not even bothering to look at the pair twice. He didn't want to have to relocate, to move to somewhere new. He was tired of all the pretenses, of all the stress he now carried. *Maybe it's a good thing she knows,* West thought, rubbing his eyes tired-ly. *Maybe I need a friend. A true friend.* He hadn't had one of those in years. Before he could even consider it, however, he'd decided against it. The thought of trusting Claire with his life was ludicrous.

Even so, the silence between them was unnerving.

"Do we make a left here?"

"Yeah."

Thoughts raced through West's mind. It must have horrified her to see him stab someone like that, making them scream in an-guish and pain. West paused for a moment. Did he actually feel pity for Claire? *She'd* followed *him.* He cringed at the thought. *I should have been more careful,* he thought angrily, kicking at the sidewalk. He saw Claire out of the corner of his eye watching his dagger, and he quickly hid it from view. He had to make a decision, and soon.

Either I could explain, or I could leave her in the dark, West reasoned. Neither option sounded appealing, because either way he knew she'd ask questions he wouldn't be able to answer. They made it back to campus quicker than usual. West walked Claire to the girl's dorms si-lently, and suddenly realized that this was it. Claire was mulling over something, searching for the words. She toed the grass nervously, and finally, she spoke.

"West...what I saw tonight...It won't change anything, I prom-ise. No one will know. I just hope that one day, I can tell you every-thing," she said sincerely, smiling up at him. It was the first time after seeing that Viceprus that she'd smiled, and West was caught off guard by his quickened pulse. Why did he suddenly want to comfort her, to apologize for something wrong that *she'd* done? He shook the feeling away, unnerved. She paused, her face still ashen in the moonlight.

"West, I have to know...What are you? Are you human, too?"

"I...I don't know."

She was waiting for an elaboration, and he knew it. How could he explain what he himself couldn't understand? He had never ques-tioned the fact that he was human until his mother had said he was *different*. That, plus what that Viceprus had said to him...he just didn't know. Before he could reply, however, he was startled by a strange sound. It was melodious, and something in his brain clicked into place. He turned away from Claire.

"Where are you going?"

Her surprised voice stopped him in his tracks. He shook his head for a moment, almost as if he'd woken up from a daze, but the voice sang again, and he forgot all about her.

It's beautiful. His brain registered. He walked towards the sound, completely ignoring Claire. He wanted to turn around to her, to pull her with him, but he couldn't control his actions anymore. He automatically turned the corner of the mythology building, and there she was. The person he was supposed to be waiting for.

Alex flew across the grounds, battling with himself. Part of him wanted to go back to the usual dorm room, where Saphirra would now be, but he didn't think he could stand another night of research. Besides, he needed to test his limits, to see if he could be on his own for a night or two. He perched on top of the library roof and stretched his wings, flapping them once or twice in the cool night air. He always got a kind of euphoria from flying, but it hurt when they materialized out of nowhere onto his back every single time a flash took over his senses. The need for energy constantly threatened to overpower him, ironically causing him to stay away from the people that could help him the most. Just being close to Saphirra was dangerous enough, but now that he knew about the full moon, he knew it'd only get worse.

Alex took off into the air again, flying easily in the night breeze. Cars honked below him and lampposts flickered in the distance, obscured by the branches of the leafy oak trees that surrounded the university.

The heart of the college was a peaceful place which always gave him the illusion they were in their own private world. Alex watched the breeze rustle through the trees appreciatively, wondering whether he could still be himself after tonight. Alex knew he'd lose control again at some point, and he refused to be helpless again.

Apparently, he'd kissed Saphirra. The fact that he'd even moved was strange enough to him, but to have done something like that, and not remember it...Alex was nonplussed. He needed some time away to think straight, he knew that...but how to do it?

Alex wandered the skies, searching for a flash of those tawny eyes that he knew so well. He knew looking for him was pointless—Lockson was smart enough not to come back here again—but he still couldn't help hoping to see him, especially when he was like this. He wanted answers.

He wanted *out*.

Swooping down, he landed silently on the soft overgrown grasses of the quad. A movement caught his eye and he walked curiously towards the infirmary, where someone was bustling about.

Who could possibly be here at this time of night? Teachers aren't supposed to be here, Alex thought suspiciously. All the professors of the university had left already, and no one was supposed to be there but Claire and Saphirra. Since Claire and West were out somewhere... who could possibly be in the health office? Alex walked through the side entrance and into the infirmary cautiously, his footsteps muffled by the plush carpet. A sharp clang came from the nurse's office on the left. He peeked in curiously, and to his surprise, he saw Evelyn Stone, the head nurse. She didn't even seem remotely tired, and was methodically stacking boxes and muttering to herself. Alex felt his wings evaporate on his back, and felt the rush of warmth that had surrounded him dissipate into the air. Staggering slightly at the loss of heat, he hit the metal desk with a sharp clang.

"Oh, hello Mr. Waterford. You scared me," Ms. Stone said in a bored voice, not looking startled in the least. "What are you doing here?"

Alex swore under his breath, massaging his foot before responding.

"I...needed something. Saphirra let me in." He eyed her suspiciously, watching as she piled prescription boxes into a corner. "Sorry, but aren't you supposed to have left the campus? Mr. Rose told the staff to leave a month ago..." Alex trailed off, watching Ms. Stone curiously. She'd straightened up suddenly, glaring at him.

"Yes, I *completely* forgot. Well, you can put this away, can't you?" she asked him monotonously, handing him a tiny pill bottle.

"What? But I don't know where these go–" Alex started, but Ms. Stone cut him off, fluffing her already balloon-like hairdo distractedly.

"I don't care, Mr. Waterford. They're for some student who needed energy supplements and didn't bother to take them. Great, I'm late," she said sullenly, checking her watch. "Put them on the shelf for me, would you?" she swore loudly and shoved past Alex out the door, slamming it in his face as she went. He stared at the shiny doorknob for a second, stunned.

What just happened? He wondered, studying the tiny pill bottle. Its label read *Navitas*. He stared at it, unsure of where to put it. *I've never heard of these energy supplements before...*Alex thought, turning it over in his hands. He glanced out the window warily, waiting until Ms. Stone had disappeared into the gathering darkness, before slipping the bottle into his pocket and heading out the door.

Chapter 11
Clandestine

Claire watched West walk away from her, completely baffled. She heard an indistinct buzzing noise, which was steadily growing louder. She saw West turn the corner of the mythology building and followed him at a distance, frowning. She felt disappointment welling up in her chest, but something about the situation told her not to call out to him. She hid behind the trunk of a tree and peered around it. Nothing.

Where is he? She thought irritably. The darkness around her made it nearly impossible to see. She felt her way through the forest, her fingers finally grasping the rough bark of a tree. She cautiously pulled herself onto the top branches of the sturdy oak, nestling herself between the rough leaves. There was West across from her, but another person was with him. This woman shimmered slightly around the edges, her silvery hair flowing like a sheet in the wind. They were talking, and as the wind died down, Claire heard what they were saying.

"...My name is Clandestine Margaux," a woman said, her voice musical and sweet.

"Clandestine..." West breathed, not sounding anything like himself. The woman, Clandestine, turned to face him. Her eyes were a deep violet, Claire noticed. *Is she a Viceprus?* She was undeniably pretty. It took Claire a moment to notice the grating sound she had heard was pouring from Clandestine's mouth. West seemed mesmerized; he gazed at Clandestine as if she was a goddess.

"Yes. You remember what you are now, don't you?" Clandestine asked softly, her voice like the peal of bells. Claire felt a stab of jealousy but pushed it aside. *Is this part of his job?* West had seemed caught off guard by the appearance of Clandestine, though. *What is going on?*

"I...My dad..." West seemed awestruck. "You know where my dad is. You were with us that day, weren't you? Where is he?"

Clandestine smiled.

"Your dad died a while ago, West. Nineteen years ago. Do you know why?"

West seemed hesitant, sounding almost like a lost child when he talked. "No."

"Your father was a Siren, West," she said. West only nodded, as if the information was perfectly normal to him. *Then again, he* is *a Viceprus hunter,* Claire thought. *The fact that mythical creatures existed must not surprise him much.* Clandestine waited, expecting a reaction. When she only got a blank stare as a response, she continued, seemingly satisfied. "He was on a raid for the Council, looking for human souls which were pure. They needed to prove they existed, because..." She trailed off, gazing into the distance. West continued to stare blankly at her, oblivious to the fact that she had been talking at all. Clandestine cleared her throat and continued.

"Anyway, your father had six months to seduce a human and take her soul. He chose your mother. From what I could tell, she loved him because of his Siren charm. At first, he would have to sing to her every time he met her so she would fall under his trance. Of course, after a while, your mother only needed to hear his voice. Your father did the one thing Council members are forbidden to do. He fell in love."

West nodded, almost hypnotically. *Sirens?* Claire wanted to scream. *First Vicepruses, now this?*

"Your father was supposed to capture her, kill her, and steal her soul. Instead, he chose to *protect* her." Clandestine sighed disapprovingly, as if it had been West's fault and not his father's. West continued staring off into space. "He starved himself for six months to hold on to her, to stall the Council. We aren't like those contemptible Vicepruses, who need energy all the time; souls are more of a luxury. Sirens are a pure race—they should never, under any circumstances, mix with humans. However, your father...he broke the code."

West nodded again.

"To protect your mother, he made her pregnant with you. The Council would not dare kill one of their own, so they bided their time, waiting. When you were born, your father fought them off, ordering your mother to go into hiding. Your mother moved here, to Chicago, with you. Your father died in battle."

West paused for a moment, and Claire stifled a gasp. *But...what does that make him?* She wondered. Their conversation popped into her mind.

'What are you? Are you human, too?'
'I...I don't know.'

Had he really not known? She recalled being confused by the hurt look on his face that he'd tried to conceal, and suddenly she understood. He hadn't known, had he? She'd said words that cut him deeper than a knife. West seemed to have broken out of his trance; he blinked furiously, working his jaw. Finally, he spoke.

"Then...Am I–?"

"You are a half-Siren, the minority of our kind."

"*Our* kind?"

Clandestine sighed impatiently. "Yes, West, *our* kind. You are speaking to a member of the High Council of the Siren division as well as a member of the Triumvirate. You have a choice. You can't shut away those powers forever, but you can be manipulated by them. You aren't as strong willed as true Sirens, because the human blood in you reacts to our power. Normal Sirens wouldn't be entranced by others' songs, as you have with mine. You would need the strength to overcome this power, and only strength outside your own can help you now."

West frowned and gripped his dagger, almost threateningly. This did not go unnoticed by Clandestine; her eyes fell on his dagger, and she let out a short laugh. "It wouldn't be wise to use that dagger against me, West. It would do nothing but wound me. *I* don't explode from an overdose of energy. *I* am not a Viceprus."

"How did you know—"

"I was the reason you have this job, West. Five years ago, I found your mother. If I hadn't kept quiet, you and your mother would be dead." Clandestine examined her flawless fingers with a smug smile.

"If you had decided against taking the Hunting job, I would have turned in you and your mother to the Council. Unless you want your mother dead, *you cannot leave your job.*"

West jerked back. Clandestine's eyes flashed to a deep gold as she spoke in a harsh whisper. West seemed frozen to the ground, mesmerized by her stare. Clandestine moved away with a satisfied smile, her long fingers brushing the branch beside her.

"It's your choice," Clandestine told him. "Either you obey me... or you and your mother die." she paused for a moment, looking up at the moonlit sky. Claire glanced around too, and saw something like an overgrown bat disappear among the line of trees on the far side of the university. Clandestine's voice shocked her as she jolted back to reality.

"Once you have heard the Siren call, you cannot go back. You've been awakened. *You have no choice.*" Her voice changed in tone to a harsh commanding whisper, and Claire saw Clandestine's eyes flash gold once again. West couldn't seem to be able to come up with an adequate response; he'd gone back to giving her a blank stare, his eyes glazed over. Clandestine smiled. "We will meet again, West Anastos." With a long look at West, Clandestine disappeared into the thick trees that surrounded the university. West stared after her as if in a trance, and he crumpled to the ground. Claire gasped again. *What did she do to him?* Claire felt like screaming at the woman, but knew she still might be lurking, so she kept to her spot. West stirred a few moments later, using the trunk of the tree to pull himself off the ground. He shook his head, holding it as if he had a headache. Claire watched him, confusion clouding her mind. *What just happened?* She thought again. West turned around to face her, and she saw his shoulders stiffen.

"Claire, you can come out now."
She nearly fell out of her tree.

Alex turned into his dorm, climbing the echoing metal stairs to the room he had shared with West. The rooms in their dorm were huge compared to other dorms around campus, complete with a mini kitchen and bathroom. Alex opened the door cautiously, stepping over a pile of clothes in the entryway. *The room got worse since I came back,* Alex observed, glancing around the messy dorm room. He shrugged, climbing over a fallen dresser drawer to his sink, and shaking a tiny red pill out onto his palm. Alex hesitated, wondering if this would actually help him. If the energy supplements at the drugstore hadn't helped him a month ago, why would these? He stared at the pill for one long moment, then drowned it in one gulp. Alex stared around the room, bored again.

Being an insomniac sucks. Alex sulked, walking over to the window.

It was then that his world exploded.

Everything around him burst into vibrant hues, drenching his dorm room in bright light. He staggered as his vision came back into focus and the lights faded, blinking rapidly. Warmth like he'd never felt before enveloped him, and suddenly he felt oddly calm and peaceful. He felt the best that he had in years, as if he had been suffering until this moment. It was the type of warmth that he knew he could crawl into and feel safe; it was protection.

Just as fast as it had come, it was gone, and he crumpled onto his bed in pain. He groaned and clutched his pillow in agony as his claws ripped it apart. He felt frozen one moment, and then overheated the next. With a shock of pain, his wings rematerialized onto his back. He twisted around, looking for something to hold on to, to crush the pain he was in, but there was nothing. Finally, the stabs of pain melted away, and he was able to get up staggeringly. Sighing, he scooped the destroyed pillow up, sneezing as feathers flew in his face, and dumped it in the trash bin. If it kept West from suspecting anything, he was willing to get a new pillow. Within seconds he felt a burst of renewed energy and strength, his muscles aching to stretch out in the night. Alex laughed to himself as he flew off to explore the city, and he couldn't help but wonder if he'd done the right thing. It wasn't until he reached the edge of the college that he saw it.

A flash of bright violet.

He started, whirling around in anticipation.

"By the order of the High Council, I order you to stop."

Reedhima Mandlik

Alex landed on the roof below him, wary. The person who had called out to him beckoned and he walked over cautiously, staying as close to the edge of the rooftop as possible. He looked like an ordinary middle-aged man, grayed with age and stress like all the rest. The man had large wings that resembled his own. Alex stared at him, unsure of what to do next. The man spoke.

"You're only a kid," he said, sounding faintly surprised. Alex raised an eyebrow, but didn't say anything. The man ran a hand through his thinning hair, sighing exasperatedly.

"Why are you here? You could be killed. I thought you were Ryan."

Alex blinked. "You thought I was who?"

The man shook his head. "Nothing." He started walking off but hesitated, turning back to Alex.

"It's really dangerous being here. And you don't look too sure of yourself, either. Are you a new Viceprus?" he asked curiously. Alex was taken aback by his blunt question.

"Y-yes, I mean...I think so. Are you?" Alex asked uncertainly. *This is just too bizarre.* He didn't know there were *more* of them. At least, not enough Vicepruses that he'd just happen to run into one randomly. The man let out a short laugh.

"Oh no, I've been a Viceprus for quite some time now." He searched the sky behind Alex, as if expecting someone else to accompany him. "Listen, you shouldn't stay around here. You should choose somewhere else. If you stay on your own like this, you'll be killed or kill someone, whichever comes first." He glanced around anxiously, as if he could pull the answer he was looking for out of the thick night air. "Listen, I'm late for a Council meeting, but if you want some help, come visit us. The Council can kill you, but we'll watch out for you. You should visit us to keep out of trouble, and stay hidden. People like you aren't supposed to exist, but I can help."

Alex could barely comprehend what he was saying. "What Council?" he asked, bewildered. The man sighed impatiently.

"I'll explain later. Come find us in Ontario. We'll be waiting for you. I'll give you a week or two to make up your mind, but I won't hold much patience after that. Many Vicepruses like you don't bother asking for help. However, I must caution you that it would be unwise to ignore this opportunity." He unfurled his wings suddenly, making Alex jump. He scrambled for words.

"Wait! What's your name? Who is 'us'? Where in Ontario?" Alex asked desperately. The man turned back to him, smiling pityingly.

"My name is Validus. I'll pass by here on the way back, so expect to find instructions on this roof within a few days' time." He hoisted himself up onto the ledge of the roof, then paused again. "What do I call you, kid?" he asked finally.

"Alex."

"Well then, I expect to see you soon, Alex. There is more than one Viceprus in the world, and we can help you. You can't do this alone." And with that, he took off into the sky.

Alex stared after him, dumbfounded. He wanted answers, but was he really going to trust this random stranger? He stood still for a moment, debating his options. All he knew was that Validus was right—if he was going to try to do this by himself, he could seriously hurt someone again. Saphirra's horrified expression popped into his mind, and he shuddered. Maybe he *should* trust Validus.

But Validus doesn't know about the pills, Alex thought, patting his pocket. The familiar rattle of the pill bottle made him smile. *As long as I have these, I'll be fine,* he reassured himself. After all, he now felt better than ever, right?

Alex sat down on the roof, stretching out to watch the night sky. It was peaceful here; the calmness helped him forget. As he lay out watching the stars, he told himself this was the reason he wasn't moving, and not because he couldn't. His energy hadn't run out as fast as it had come.

That's what he told himself, anyway.

Claire climbed back down the tree gingerly, nursing her arm. West was waiting for her, a slightly dazed look on his face. She stepped closer, trying to make out his expression in the shadows. His eyes seemed haunted.

"What were you thinking, Claire? Why were you watching me?" he asked accusingly. She fired up almost immediately.

"You walked off as if you were possessed or something! What was I supposed to think?" she snapped. West ran a hand through his hair, looking unsure of what to do with her. Claire didn't want to think about any of this. *First Alex, now him?*

"You were supposed to *leave me alone,* Claire. You weren't supposed to know about any of this in the first place." He sank to the ground, holding his head in his hands. Claire bent down beside him, putting a comforting hand on his shoulder. He was shaking.

"Hey, it's okay," she said softly. "You didn't know that this would happen..."

West looked up at her, his stormy grey eyes piercing her. He looked tortured, like a wounded animal.

"Claire, she *knew.* My mom knew this would happen to me." He grabbed fistfuls of grass, ripping the roots apart. "All those stories about Sirens she'd tell me at night, the folktale of the farmer and the twins, everything! *All of it meant something.* I was just too stupid to understand it." Claire stared at him, alarmed.

"The folktale? You mean the one about the old healer?" she asked, sidetracked. He nodded tersely.

"How do you know about that?" She asked curiously. West stared at the ground for one long moment, then back up at her. His expression had gone blank.

"Just forget it, Claire. Go away."

His abrupt change in tone startled her. She stood up.

"Fine, West. Good luck dealing with this yourself."

Shaking with anger, she started stalking off towards the dorms, when she heard a sound that stopped her in her tracks.

Music?

A beautiful song rose up around her, trapping her. She turned around, entranced. It was coming from West's mouth, but he didn't appear to be singing. The sound was like the breeze around her, integrating itself into the air, the rustle of the leaves, the whisper of the grass. He looked like he knew exactly what he was doing, and as his song grew in pitch, she walked over to him and entwined her fingers in his without meaning to. It was as if her brain couldn't control her body anymore; the sound overpowered all her senses. The sound made it hard to think straight or even concentrate.

Forget.

The command was not her own, and she fought against it, trying desperately to hold the memories of tonight in her mind. Even when he closed his mouth it was as if the song was still going on in her mind, completely brainwashing her. She tried to fight it, but it was no use; she couldn't do anything at all.

Forget everything.

"I won't!" she said loudly. She saw a burst of panic behind his eyes, but she was so furious that she didn't care. Unexpectedly, West's arms encompassed her, pulling her to his chest. Her cheeks burned as his lips kissed her hair gently.

Then the sound stopped. Feeling rushed back into her limbs and she pushed away from him, walking away as fast as she could.

"Claire!"

West's voice echoed throughout the campus, and she glared at him.

"What the hell did you just do to me?" she asked furiously. West opened his mouth, then closed it again, apparently at a loss for words. Claire had had enough. She stomped to him, her face dangerously close to his.

"Then answer this, West. What would have happened if I hadn't stopped you? If you'd kept singing?" she shouted at him. He looked like she'd slapped him, and she had a feeling that she wanted to. Instead, she turned away, walking into the night.

Chapter 12
Estranged

Ry walked through the gates leading to an old brick building, pausing for a moment to allow his eyes to adjust to the dim lighting. Its tepid walls seemed to crumble in the darkness, making his entrance almost ominous. At his appearance in the dull courtyard, a man stepped out of the shadows, his beady eyes searching the new arrival. Ry stopped walking, raising a hand through the gloominess to greet his companion.

"Aenor. You were sent to greet me?" Ry asked curiously, lowering his hand. Aenor did the same, taking a step towards the Viceprus cautiously.

"The Council is being careful, Ryan. I was sent here under the orders of the High Council. One of our own was taken a few nights ago."

"Who was it?" Ry asked. He feigned interest as well as he could as the two stepped into the building together. The corridor they chose was well-lit, and Ry could now see the faint scars from the First War that crisscrossed Aenor's face. Aenor wore them proudly, as Ry knew well; any Viceprus who had lasted as long as Aenor had would proudly wear his battle scars. They spoke of status, strength, and vitality; they also explained why he would have been chosen to be on the High Council. Aenor cleared his throat, answering exactly as Ry would have expected.

"It was Adela," he said uncomfortably. Ry suppressed a small smile, keeping his features carefully blank.

"But she was on the High Council!" Ry said quickly. "She was too smart to have been killed."

Aenor swallowed and began walking faster, his eyes trained on the end of the corridor. "She wasn't killed. A Hunter wounded her and took her hostage."

Ry understood Aenor's aversion to talking about Adela; after all, the two had been close. *Very* close. Ry frowned.

"But we haven't seen a Hunter in centuries," Ry tried. "Maybe she's just—"

"What, Ryan? *Disappeared?* Adela wasn't that stupid," Aenor said harshly. "The question is how did the Hunter know where she was? She was only visiting Chicago to meet Validus. She shouldn't have even been there. She shouldn't—" He cut himself off, taking a deep breath to steady himself. "Validus said he never saw you, anyway. Was he looking for you?" Aenor asked suddenly, turning to him. It was Ry's turn to avoid his gaze.

"I see no reason why he would," Ry told him. "I wasn't informed that he'd visited Chicago." He tried to keep his voice steady, hoping Aenor wouldn't detect the note of apprehension in his voice. It was a relief when they reached the large wooden doors that marked the entrance to the Council room. Aenor stopped in front of the door, nodding at a guard to unlatch the lock.

"What are you visiting the Council for this time, Ryan? Going to make another plea to stifle a human girl because her name reminds you of a jewel?" Aenor snorted, his mouth crinkling into a smile. "Did that *prophecy* of yours come true, or are you still waiting for another twenty years until a student named Ruby comes along?" he chuckled to himself, but stopped abruptly at the look on Ry's face. He quickly rearranged his expression to a placid, good-natured smile.

"Ah, Aenor, your jokes amuse me," Ry told him. "In fact, I came to London today to request a position on the High Council again. I'm sure Adela won't be returning to her post." And with a pleasant smile, Ry walked into the Council room, leaving a gaping Aenor in his wake.

Saphirra sat in the quad, eyes wandering lazily over a page from the folktale book Claire had found. She'd had more sleep in the past few days than she could ever remember; with Alex disappearing at night and returning by morning, Saphirra and Claire weren't constantly exhausted. Alex had explained that he didn't want another episode like the last full moon, and Saphirra couldn't help agreeing with him; still, it worried her when he spent that much time without their energy.

What if he attacked someone again? The question constantly flitted through her brain, but she never got the chance to ask Alex about it. Whenever she brought up the subject, he'd shrug it away, saying "I know what I'm doing. And see? I'm fine." Although it was true that Alex did seem more energized than usual, his noncommittal answer always made her cringe. The two of them had kept their distance in the past few days, at the risk of ruining their renewed friendship. Neither wanted to set the other off, but Saphirra couldn't help questioning his methods. She'd expected him to be dilapidated and sluggish in the morning, not cheery and excited. Saphirra didn't want to think he'd gone off sucking the energy out of random people, and yet she could think of no other explanation for it.

Even Claire had noticed how strange Alex was acting. This was unusual for her, especially since she's been acting so preoccupied as of late. Every time Saphirra brought up the subject, Claire would shrug and agree with whatever she'd said, as if she wanted to get off the subject as soon as possible. Her friends' strange behavior was irritating her to no end. *Why does everything have to be so confusing?* Saphirra thought exasperatedly. The only one who was acting remotely normal was West, but she couldn't tell him any of this. Poor West put up with their cryptic answers and winding explanations without as much as a suspicious glance. Saphirra wondered whether he didn't bother asking because he didn't care, or because he himself had something to hide. Before she could think too deeply into it, however, Alex's voice broke into her thoughts.

"Hey, there you are!"

She sat up, squinting through the sunlight as Alex walked towards her. As he drew nearer she laid back down on the grass, stretching her arms behind her head.

"Hey," she said peacefully. Alex sat down next to her, looking up at the cloudless sky. She turned to him expectantly.

"Why aren't you exhausted?" she asked finally. Alex raised an eyebrow at her.

"What do you mean?" he answered, avoiding her gaze.

"It's been almost a week. The last time you disappeared for a week you passed out from lack of energy. How are you perfectly fine now?"

Alex toyed with the grass absently as he spoke. "I'm using energy supplements."

"But you tried that before, and it didn't work," she said, puzzled. She remembered their trips to health stores quite vividly, as well as his disappointed expression when they had no effect. Alex ran a hand through his hair, searching for the right words.

"These work really well. They were supposed to be for some student here, but he didn't take them, so I did." He shrugged nonchalantly. Saphirra sat up and snorted incredulously. *Is he really that stupid?*

"You're taking pills designed for someone else, and you seriously think it won't hurt you?"

Alex prodded the ground, fidgeting with a fallen leaf. "Well, Ms. Stone told me to put it away..."

"Oh, even better!" Saphirra said sarcastically, standing up now. "Let's just *steal* medication from the university! Alex, it could have killed you for all we know. Ms. Stone isn't the most aware person on earth, what if she had no idea what it was—"

"Well it worked, okay?" Alex shouted at her. She was stunned into silence as he got up too, his eyes flashing dangerously. "It's been working for a few days now, Saph. I figured these were better than sucking the energy out of you and Claire!" he spat, thrusting the bottle into her face. She barely had time to see the label—*Navitas*—before he'd shoved it back into his pocket again. She took a step backwards, alarmed at the change in his mood.

"I was under the impression that *we* were helping *you*, not the other way around. It was our choice to let you use our energy, Alex. It's not like you took it forcefully and you're softening the blow with these." She pointed at the bottle, her finger shaking slightly. He stared at her for one long moment, his body tensed as if for a fight.

"I'm leaving," he told her abruptly. Saphirra blinked.

"What?"

"I'm leaving," he repeated. "Another Viceprus saw me and told me to come find him. He's part of some Council or something. He sounded like he knew what he was doing." He shrugged. "I figured I'd listen to what he has to say."

Her stomach contracted. He saw the look on her face and continued, his voice softening. "Saph...I've figured this out. I can't control myself very well, and what if I kill you at the next full moon? That Viceprus I met said I couldn't survive if I didn't have help." He explained to her how he'd met Validus, relaying to her their conversation. Her expression didn't change. She could think of a million reasons why it was a stupid idea, but she swallowed them. Another Viceprus had found them, and they might not get another chance to find a cure.

"Go," she sighed, taking Alex by surprise. "If it'll keep you from attacking people, go. Where is this Viceprus? Where are you supposed to meet him?" she asked.

"Ontario."

Saphirra gave him a questioning glance.

"Alex, that's just stupid, I–" She broke off as the words sank in, and her heart sped up.

"You're kidding. You're leaving to go to *Canada?*" she scoffed. Alex grinned a little.

"I have to fix this somehow, and I need your help to do it. I'm going to go over there and try to find help. I'll only be gone six days or so," he told her.

"Six days?"

"Travel will take longer when I can only travel by night, you know," he reminded her. "It'll probably take less time than that once I've found my way." She glanced at the ground.

"Alex, we don't know anything about these people. What if they're like Professor Lockson? He tried to kill us!"

"I trust him," Alex said simply. Saphirra stared at him, dumbfounded. Was he really going to accept it?

"Be careful, Alex. It could be a trick."

"You honestly think I haven't considered that?" Alex said exasperatedly. "I think we can trust him." At her incredulous expression, he tapped his forehead. "Instinct."

"How can I know that you'll be okay?"

Alex swallowed hard.

"If I don't call, or if I don't come back, something happened," he said, not looking at her. He unconsciously wove his hand into hers as he spoke, sending a jolt of electricity up her arm at his touch. Something kept her from moving away from him, and she looked up at his face, reading the panic in his eyes. She could feel herself shaking beside him.

"It's only a few days. When you come back, we'll finally know what's going on," she assured him. Without warning he pulled her to his side for a long moment, hugging her tightly. She could hear his heart slamming against his ribcage, and knew he could hear hers too.

"Every heartbeat tells a story. Yours is one I will never forget," he whispered in her ear. Before she could react to this he'd moved away from her, turning towards the university gates. With a final glance, Alex unfurled his wings and took off into the sky, disappearing over a rooftop. She sat back down onto the grass, unsure of what had just happened. Her hands curled into fists as she stared after him. *Why?* Why had he been so angry one moment, then so sad the next? She couldn't process it.

Hadn't she prepared herself for it? She'd sensed this would happen; Alex had been too quiet, too thoughtful for the last week. *What if he didn't come back?* But didn't they always come back? Wasn't that the major cliché in all the movies and books? Worry clawed at her heart. She hated the feeling of being helpless in a world where so much could go wrong in such little time.

She didn't know how long she'd sat there, just thinking. It felt like hours had passed. A bird's trilling chirp broke through her daze, reminding her that there were others that would wonder where she was. As she sat up, she felt her fingers bump against something in the grass. She picked it up, squinting though the strong sunlight to see what it was.

Alex's pill bottle.

She stared at the offending cylinder in her hands, dread washing over her. If he didn't have the pills, he didn't have energy. And that meant...

He might bite someone.

Claire sat by the fountain, sketching out a tree in front of her. The summer breeze danced lightly across her skin, wafting the warm smells from a bakery nearby towards her. She smiled contentedly as she sketched out the finer points of the tree bark. Sketching always let her mind wander; it calmed her. Not having to help Alex every other night made everything so much easier on her. She didn't know how she could have lasted if she had to endure another sleepless night, especially with the secrets she now bore. She tried to shake the thoughts away, but it was no use; she always panicked when she thought of West and Alex.

Why did West have to be a Viceprus hunter? Claire thought savagely, nearly poking a hole through her paper. It occurred to her that West might have known about Professor Lockson in the first place. *It would explain why he flipped out when Saphirra and Alex went missing,* Claire reasoned. Was it possible that West had only decided on the Rose university of Chicago because of Lockson? *Is West only here to hunt them?* Claire didn't know what to think anymore. First he was a Viceprus hunter, and now a Siren? She couldn't comprehend it. It was no wonder West wouldn't answer any of her questions; he was bound to be confused himself. She thought back to that night, her eyes trained on her half-finished drawing. Could she have made a mistake in following West? He was now not only a Viceprus hunter, but a Siren as well. The mention of the creature tugged at her mind, but she couldn't quite place the familiarity she felt with it beyond the obvious tales of destruction associated with them. She wanted to look at the folktale again, but Saphirra had it.

The folktale. Claire knew it was no coincidence that Lockson had kept it hidden in his office; it had to have some importance. Claire got up, shoveling her sketchpad back into her bag. She had to find Saphirra and get the book back. Together with the translated prophecy, they could figure something out. She walked into the student lounge, searching for Alex's telltale flame of hair, or Saphirra's long raven tresses. She finally found Saphirra fast asleep on a couch, a book strewn across her stomach.

"Saphirra. Saphirra! Wake up!" she shook Saphirra until she stirred, and when her eyes opened, she glared daggers at Claire.

"I'm going to have bruises now. Why didn't you just throw a book at me? It wouldn't have hurt as much," she grumbled. Something was wrong; her voice had an edge to it, something that had never appeared in her tone for as long as Claire knew her.

"Ah, Sleeping Beauty's awake!" West said loudly as he walked into the room, startling them both. He clapped in Saphirra's face, and Saphirra's glare of death turned onto him.

"I wouldn't be talking, boxers-with-hearts boy. You might as well have written Claire all over them," she growled, gesturing to his pants, where his waistband was clearly visible. That shut him up and caused Claire's cheeks to flare a bright red. Saphirra struggled to get up, and collapsed back down, sighing.

"What's got you so tired? I mean, you look like you've seen a ghost." A look from Saphirra's blazing green eyes made Claire fall silent. She watched as Saphirra got up slowly, staggering into the wall as she went.

"Where are you going, Miss Cynical?" West called, causing a book to be aimed at his head. He ducked, his shoulders shaking with laughter. Saphirra's green eyes sparkled maliciously, and she walked out of the room without a second glance. Claire glared at West.

"Wow, you're so mature."

"I have to be," he said smugly. He glanced down at the couch Saphirra had laid on, frowning at the book she'd left behind. Claire whisked it into her bag and sat down, glaring stoically at him.

"Where's Alex?" she asked. She completely forgot she was supposed to be mad at West, and cringed at her almost friendly tone. She'd just noticed Alex hadn't showed up with West. Alex and West were like a combined package—they just kind of showed up together. She was so used to the sight of them together she hadn't even noticed.

It explained why Saphirra was acting like she was. Suddenly Claire understood. West's calculating eyes met hers, and she looked away.

"I don't know. He told me he was going on vacation for a week or two," he said in a bored voice, leaning against the wall. She heard something crash to the floor in the hall, and got up to investigate.

"West, you'll have to excuse me for a moment. Or for a while." She gritted her teeth and walked away, leaving West to stare after her in bewilderment.

She found Saphirra trying to clean up broken glass, shaking slightly as she did so. Claire carefully sidestepped the broken vase and its scattered contents, and hugged Saphirra tightly.

"Sorry, I didn't mean to, I accidentally knocked into it..." She said shakily, shrugging towards the shattered blue glass. Claire nodded and helped Saphirra clean up for a while, wondering where on earth Alex was.

"Saph, what happened?" she asked, guessing the answer.

"Alex left to go talk to a Viceprus in Ontario," she told Claire. At her confused response, Saphirra explained about the conversation she'd had with Alex in the quad. She fell silent as West tottered past silently, watching Saphirra apprehensively as if she was an active volcano. Claire watched him go up the stairs and was surprised to feel a twinge of remorse at her abrupt departure.

"Do you think West knows about Alex?"

Saphirra took a while to answer. "I hope not, otherwise everything Alex left for would be pointless. He's been taking energy pills, Claire. *Navitas*. Ever heard of them?" she asked, handing Claire the bottle. Claire opened it, surprised to see less than a quarter of the bottle was full.

"How long has he been taking these?" she asked curiously, shaking a bright red pill onto her palm. *Navitas. Why does that sound familiar?* She wondered. Saphirra shrugged.

"He said he found those last week."

Claire frowned. "That's impossible. If this was a full bottle when he got it and he took one or two or day then he'd barely be halfway through this already." She stopped cold as the reality of it sunk in.

"Do you think he could have been...I don't know...*Addicted* to the pills?" Claire asked carefully. Saphirra refused to meet her eye.

"That's what I'm afraid of."

She broke off, cleaning up the glass with more enthusiasm than necessary. Claire helped her, uncertain of what to do. It was so obvious to her that Saphirra cared about him. It was logical, in a certain way. They'd been best friends for a long time after all, and they probably knew a lot about each other. Either way Saphirra was calmer now, running her hands through her disheveled hair unconsciously. She debated telling Saphirra about West, but something told her this wasn't the best time.

"You know, a famous writer once said 'the worst kind of torture is being stuck with your own thoughts, and the worst kind of pain is the pain of a broken heart. Neither can be fully cured, and neither can be fully avoided.'" She let out a shaky laugh. "I think I understand the first part now. I...I just don't know! What if he bites someone because he forgot these pills?" Saphirra took a shaky breath, and pressed her palm against her head. "I think I need a shower to clear my head. I'm going to go wash up," she said quietly. "You can just leave the vase for me later. Thanks, Claire."

Claire mumbled something along the lines of "No, I'll get it..." and watched Saphirra pick her way up the stairs cautiously, biting her lip. At that moment, West walked down the stairs, freshly clothed, his chestnut hair half dry.

"So, is she okay, or should I put some more vases in her path to knock over?" West joked, walking up to Claire. She turned away from him.

"She's just upset because he forgot to take something with him. It's no big deal, really," she said stiffly.

"Wow. She seems pretty shook up." West looked back at the broken vase that Claire was cleaning up, and bent down to help her.

"West?" she asked cautiously. He didn't look up at her, but she knew he was listening. "How exactly do Vicepruses...*die?*"

He frowned at the broken porcelain, apparently thinking hard. "Why do you want to know?" he said finally, brushing bits of the broken vase into a pile. Claire swallowed.

"Just curious."

He squeezed his eyes shut, speaking through gritted teeth. "If I answer you, will you let this drop?"

Claire found herself nodding, and West sighed, his eyes turbulent. "You give them an overdose of energy. My dagger has so many Sunshards that once it touches their heart they basically explode, or vaporize. The extra energy is too much for them." He stopped suddenly, as if he'd already explained too much. Claire bent down to the vase, pulling it towards her.

"Thanks," she muttered. He didn't respond and instead began to pile the shards up and into a cloth methodically. The silence between them was too uncomfortable. She spoke.

"I can do it myself–"

Their fingers touched, and Claire felt a jolt of electricity. Alarmed, she jerked her hand back and stood up.

"You know what? I don't care. Just leave me alone."

She walked away as quickly as she could, the bottle of pills clutched in her hand. It had finally occurred to her what *Navitas* meant; it was Latin for energy. The nurse had tricked Alex into taking the pills.

Alex took more pills than he should have.

It's an addiction.

Chapter 13
From Golden Eyes

Ry paced the length of his elaborate study, furious. His attempt to get into the High Council had been thwarted by Validus, who maintained the hope that Adela would return to her post. Ry opened a drawer and removed the bottom, taking a sleek gun out from underneath. Slamming the drawer shut he turned to the corner of his office, where a bedraggled woman was now chained to the floor, her clothes torn and her face bloodied. She turned her violet eyes upon him reproachfully.

"I should have known it would be you," she hissed at him. "You were always the desperate one. What, did you think capturing me would earn you points with Aenor? That's no way to get onto the High Council," she jeered, but for all her bravado was worth, she was weak. Her long silver hair was limp and lifeless, her features gaunt. Ry smiled and crouched down next to her, putting the cold metal of his gun to her temple. She stopped fidgeting and held her breath, her eyes boring venomously into him.

"For your information, I *would* have been on the High Council by now if it weren't for your friend Validus," he growled. "I see no reason in allowing you to return." He gazed at the barrel of his gun, almost lovingly. She watched his every movement, flinching when he moved closer to her. "What will they say when a member of the most powerful order is dead? Especially if we're *so* hard to kill." He tapped the gun against her skull and she shivered almost imperceptibly. Ry sat back, enjoying his power. She looked up at him.

"You want information."

It wasn't a question. Ry smiled wickedly and put the gun beside him, watching as she visibly relaxed.

"Of course."

She swallowed. "The Siren council refuses to send anyone to Siren Rock again. Not after what happened with Faron. They still haven't found the Emblem, either, which means we might find it first."

Ry nodded to himself as this last piece of news sunk in.

"Faron Anastos? The famed Siren that went soft?" he snorted. "That's not what I wanted to hear." He put the gun back up to her head, and she let out a gasp. "What do I care about the Sirens? I don't seek to keep the peace like the Triumvirate. I seek to destroy it." He cocked the gun, resting his finger lazily on the trigger. Adela flinched.

"Wait!" she cried. Ry was pleased to see she was shaking. "Wait, please...I know something else. Something about your prophecy."

Ry tried to contain his surprise. "I thought the prophecy was a joke," he said coldly. Adela shook her head feverishly.

"No, we knew. It's true. It'll happen. But Ryan, it's not what you think. It's not—"

"What would you know of what I have thought?" Ry roared, stunning her to silence. "This prophecy is about *me* and my *death* thanks to an ordinary human girl! What," he said through clenched teeth, "would you know about that?"

Adela shrank further into the corner. "We knew. We've been working it out, Ryan. But from what Validus has said, it's not solely about Vicepruses. Validus thought—"

"Oh, he *thought*!" Ry mimicked, standing up suddenly. "I don't want to hear this. This isn't what I wanted to hear. Goodbye, Adela."

Before she could respond, he'd shot her. She stared at the wound in horror as energy began to pour from the bullet, enveloping her in its unearthly light. She screamed as the patches of light on her skin that had chained her to the floor grew into holes, shining eerily. When she opened her mouth to scream again, the only thing that came out was pure sunlight. Writhing, she sank further into the corner, her beautiful body now punctured with bursts of light. It encompassed her whole and then rushed out in all directions, spreading everywhere. As fast as it had come, the light vanished along with the Viceprus, leaving only a scorched mark on his carpet. Ry stared at it with indifference, turning to put the gun back where he had found it. He couldn't listen to another word. Not when Adela had said the exact thing he'd feared.

He'd always questioned the prophecy and its origins, especially if it was destined for him. It had been made *for* him, after all. The Oracle had made it in his presence, had said specifically it had to do with him.

So why was this constant doubt plaguing his mind?

It was the same unvarying tug he felt at the thought of trusting anyone, especially Evelyn. A person could only deal with being in the dark for so long, and Evelyn seemed to be at her breaking point. *Evelyn.* She acted like a teenager, but her mind was brilliant. If only she could get past the material world, if she actually used her *brain* every once in a while, she would be smart—maybe as smart as him.

Ry shook his head, dismissing the thought. No one could ever surpass his mind *or* his abilities while he still had time to perfect them. He wouldn't allow it. After all, if Evelyn ever came close to matching his intellect, she would meet the same fate as Adela. Ry thought about that for a moment, puzzled by the strange wave of unwillingness that swept over him at the thought of Evelyn becoming nothing more than a distant memory. She was far too important to lose, an ally that could help him at the eclipse, if circumstance allowed it. Yet, the prophecy dictated his fate, which as far as he could tell did not involve her...Ry shook his head determinedly, pausing to watch the unchanging Chicago skyline out of one of his large windows. The twinkles of reflected sunlight winked at him, as if to say he couldn't change destiny. *There is always a way,* Ry thought. Somewhere, somehow, he must avoid that particular part of the prophecy... and he must do it without making Evelyn too greedy for power. He scratched his chin thoughtfully, walking to the center of the room. He had rearranged his office for what seemed like the thousandth time, but no matter how many times he changed the furniture, the room still bored him. He'd spent far too many hours in this room trying to find the missing link that could put his plan into place.

Ry traced the edge of his glossy oak desk, feeling the familiar grooves with his fingertip. Waiting was excruciatingly dull; he'd memorized his olive green office completely, and every vase, desk chair, and wall dent in his office now bored him. There was nothing left to explore. The only small comfort he had was the change of scenery outside his wall of glass windows. The midday sun scattered rays of sunlight across the tan carpet, drenching the room in light. He watched the sunlight dance across the carpet for a minute, and then sat down in his black leather office chair, putting the tips of his fingers on the armrests. This life was so monotonous, it was almost impossible to be excited about anything.

It did, however, leave plenty of time to contemplate his future.

Ry leaned back so that he was staring at the flawless ceiling, twirling a pen around with his long, graceful fingers. His race was full of secluded creatures, and keeping company was rare. Small gatherings dotted the planet, but only for Council purposes. The High Council knew he could surpass them in strength if he was given the chance, and would probably easily rid themselves of his tiresome presence if they felt it necessary. Ry thought back to Adela's words, regretting cutting her off. She had said the prophecy might not have to do with his kind.

Then why was it so important to the High Council to decipher and analyze it? Ry thought, frustrated. More importantly, why did they keep their analyzations a secret from him? None of the members had mentioned any of their speculation to him. Rather, they had mocked him for it.

Prophecies always came true. He knew that better than anybody. He'd *been* there to hear it. And yet, it was in every Latin book about his kind for a reason. Ry clenched his fists unthinkingly, crushing the pen in his hands. Ink flew everywhere, staining his fingers and the carpet around him. *The Council won't get rid of me that easily,* he thought savagely. Did they take him for a fool?

"Oh, is it time to redecorate the office already?" Evelyn's voice startled him as she walked into the room, closing the door gently behind her. Her hair was piled up onto her head in a messy bun, and her strange greenish eyes glinted in the setting sun. "Interesting," she said quietly, her gaze falling on his hands. "It makes you look like you got a bruise," she clarified. "You look as if someone had put in your place for once." She laughed.

"I've hardly walked away from any fight," he said, unable to keep a trace of amusement from his voice. She unearthed emotions in him that he hated to see still resided in himself. He'd thought he'd shut those away forever.

"Yes, but you will."

Evelyn never ceased to surprise him.

"What makes you so sure?" he said, turning away from her. Her arms were wrapped lovingly around his neck within a second.

"Because you are *Ryan Lockson*. Your plans never fail," she whispered in his ear, a hint of a smile in her voice. He laughed hollowly.

"Impending doom has never seemed so easy to avoid."

"That's because for you it *is*. Don't just assume you're going to fail. You've got me. What could possibly go wrong?"

He laughed with her on that. With Evelyn, what *wouldn't* go wrong?

"I have some good news. Your Hunter was finally caught in the act. Torturing Adela, no less."

Ry jerked away from her.

"How do you know?"

"Adela mentioned it when I came to retrieve her. Honestly, Ry, you should do your own work for once," she said in a bored voice. She casually glanced at the corner where Adela had been, and let out a short laugh. "You killed her already? Pity, she was interesting to talk to. You shouldn't let your temper get the best of you."

Ry didn't bother listening to the rest of her prattle. *How did my Hunter get found out?* It was an inconceivable theory, like Sirens taking over the Triumvirate, or his death. It just couldn't happen.

"How is that *good?*" he asked angrily. Evelyn held up a delicate finger.

"His friend Claire followed him. It's not much of a loss. I can interrogate her and kill her. She's bound to have some information for us."

"Like what? I know all I need to know about my Hunter," he said irritably. Evelyn rolled her eyes.

"Have you noticed the similarities between West and Faron?" she asked slowly. "Of course I have. We've both heard the stories of his escape. But Faron died years ago," he said dismissively. Evelyn raised an eyebrow.

"*Nineteen* years ago."

"It's obvious he's Faron's son, if that's what you're getting at. Their skills are unmatchable."

Evelyn shook her head irritably. "Don't you see? If they share the same skills, what else could they have in common?"

Ry thought about that for a moment. *Impossible.* Still, he had to make sure.

"Just go, Evelyn. Do something right this time," he heard the malice in his voice, and saw Evelyn shrink away from him a little. It felt nice to have power over her, and he turned back to the window, listening to her soft footsteps as she left the room. She would always be, no matter how hard she tried, only a tool to him. His mind turned back to more pressing matters. More time. That was all he needed...

Suddenly, he saw a telltale soft glow and a flash of blonde caught his eye. Stunned, he turned around to see what had produced it. The pleasant light grew irritatingly bright as it neared, and his brain barely had time to register exactly what kind of creature was behind him. He felt a tap on his shoulder, and reflexively grabbed the nimble fingers that held him in place.

"Looking for me?"

Her voice was like the peal of bells, her aura dark and venomous. He turned around to see who it was, and found himself staring into violet eyes crossed with gold. A rush of memories hit him, and he blinked them aside, too overwhelmed to make much sense of them. All he knew is that he'd stared at those eyes more than once.

"It's you—you, who made me what I am. You gave me these powers," he said, hardly daring to believe it. The blonde smiled at him. *A Siren was smiling at him.* He tried to jerk away, but was held steadfast in her grip. Sirens were just as strong as Vicepruses; they'd learned that in the First War. He wanted to fling her from the room.

"I hardly gave them to you. You had them all along, thanks to your father. My name is Clandestine Margaux. Pleased to see you again Ryan." her words had an old fashioned ring to them, and he shook her outstretched hand, a bit dazed. He wasn't used to being snuck up on.

"What are you doing here?" Ry tried to keep calm, his brain whirring.

"I've been looking for you," she said, eyeing his ink splattered hands.

"I've met you before," he realized suddenly, turning his golden eyes to meet her violet ones. A snake of gold flitted in her irises, giving her the appearance of the legendary queen demonic Siren, the alpha creature that caused devastation with one calling of their beautiful voices.

Clandestine's eyes flashed brilliantly gold, and the ribbon of gold in her eyes seemed to snake around her pupils, creating a blinding beam that dazzled him. He could feel his memories slipping, and he panicked. Ry lashed out at Clandestine, but was too slow. He fell onto the chair, and a harsh voice rang though his room.

"*Don't move.* Your mind is incredibly sharp—it's getting harder and harder to erase." she said the last words more to herself than to him, and he tried to struggle against invisible bonds that bound his feet to the floor. He couldn't move, and he hated the positively helpless feeling that was spreading though his body. He'd heard about Sirens with powers—hers must control minds.

"Good. Now, you will tell Evelyn to tell you all she knows, and everything the blonde idiotic college girl knows as well."

"Already done," he hadn't meant to say the words, but they'd come out in a mechanical sounding voice that wasn't his own.

"*Now, you will forget this whole conversation, and repeat anything you hear to me. You will forget who I am, and that we ever met,*" her voice was no longer delicate, but low and soft. Her fingers pinched his cheeks in an aggravating way, and the willowy blonde laughed evilly.

"You don't like this, do you?"

He felt helpless, powerless—like a human. He hated it. He watched her angrily, unable to speak. The room began to spin, and he crumpled to the ground.

"Such a good little tool."

Her laughter rang in his ears as he fell into unconsciousness.

Clandestine stared at the limp Viceprus in front of her. *Such a powerful mind, but such a sad excuse for a creature,* Clandestine thought as her hair returned to its original color. It always darkened in a Viceprus's presence. All Sirens' hair color did, and the same went for Vicepruses. She walked away from the limp body carelessly. He wasn't dreaming—no, *his* kind couldn't dream, no matter how hard they tried. She should know. She'd had enough time to watch others try to be normal and fail miserably—over five hundred years of time.

She could use anybody to do anything she wanted, and all with a glance. She didn't know what caused her powers; it just ran in the family. Akakios, her twin brother, held a power of his own; visions of the past haunted him, changing course with every person he touched. She had always resented her brother, for more reasons than one. It was clear that they couldn't live together anymore, and after a while Akakios had chosen to leave. Since then, she and her brother had agreed to meet, but never interfere in the other's private matters. They could kill each other instead of becoming allies, and she needed her brother alive.

Her plan had been to dominate, to rule. But she didn't have the ability that pureblood Vicepruses did. She couldn't convert humans into Sirens, but she could awaken the Siren blood that coursed through a select few. Her eyes would first flash violet, stunning the person in question, then gold, making them obey her every command. Ryan's powerful mind helped him to think, but it also helped him remember. His mind battled her control, a thought that was alarming to an effect. No one had battled her grip on their mind before, and *this* one she needed to keep in the dark. Especially since she needed him now more than ever.

It was strange, this feud between Sirens and Vicepruses. After the First War they had realized there was no escape from themselves, or the world around them. Maybe that was why they chose to fight. The Vicepruses saw Siren auras as dark objects, almost as if they were shielded. The Sirens saw Vicepruses as icy blue auras amidst the bobbing colorful human souls. Most Sirens didn't have a soul. Those that did...They were the most dangerous of all. Only the Triumvirate knew the true reason behind the feud, and they retold the story once a year to the new members of the Council. Any experienced Council member knew, however, that they managed to tweak it every year. Only she knew the original story.

She'd thought about it ever since she'd found Ryan and learned of the true nature of the prophecy. It was quite ironic, actually, since both races needed to be together, not apart, for it to be fulfilled. Prophecies were meant to be carried out, after all; it was a concept that Ryan couldn't seem to grasp. She sat down lazily in a worn out armchair and glanced out at the darkening sky.

Five hundred years ago, she would have been called an anarchist, maybe even a terrorist of sorts.

She was still one now.

Chapter 14
Bittersweet Life

West sat in his ticket counter at the Five Staffs entrance gate, bored out of his mind. It was a slow day, and it was only made worse by the unbearable heat. It was a sweltering in Chicago, only made worse when he was cooped up in a tiny room with only two windows and a broken fan for relief. West wiped his brow and chugged yet another bottle of water, exhausted. Matt, his co-worker, nudged him.

"You okay, West?"

He merely nodded and resumed gazing back out the window. He wasn't okay. He'd become the same thing he'd vowed he never would—a monster. He thought of the furious look Claire had given him, and shuddered. He'd never seen her so angry in his life; if only he could explain to her! If only he could explain how the powers over-rode all his common sense, how they...*he* could suddenly see her soul. A patch of glimmering white light in her eyes, and then...he didn't know what he'd done. He remembered an awful, luring sound coming from his mouth, and Claire turning to him, her eyes furious but her expression wistful. It was horrible. He didn't know why he'd done it, and he didn't want to think it was his sudden Siren abilities controlling him. It made him sound like he had split–personality disorder. He turned to his messy blonde haired, blue eyed, overly-eager coworker, and decided Matt had too much coffee today. Matt's voice broke through his thoughts.

"Slow day, eh?" he said, practically bouncing. West sighed in response, trying to avoid the flash in his eyes, where his soul undoubtedly lay. West saw it anyway; it glimmered, bright red and fierce, and West realized that he didn't want it like he'd wanted Claire's, like he'd wanted every girl's soul that waltzed past him today, unaware. Just as West opened his mouth to ask whether Matt wanted to take a few thousand laps around the park so his coffee high could wear down, someone banged on his counter, making him jump.

"We'd like two passes, West."

Saphirra's face peered at him through the ridiculously small window, a mischievous look in her eye.

"Two?" West asked tiredly, leaning across the counter. He could see Saphirra's soul, and he didn't like how half of him wanted it. *All monsters must have this kind of obsession,* West realized. *How can they possibly live with it?*

Saphirra shifted aside, and it was then that he saw who was behind her. Claire scowled at him.

"Hi," she said stiffly, avoiding his gaze. Saphirra at the two of them.

"You two are just being *so* mature. You should look at yourselves." Saphirra said chidingly. When neither responded, she glanced at them once more and blurted, "Oh. I left my purse back at the college. You know, I think I'll go get it. Bye," she turned hurriedly, and before West or Claire could say anything, she'd disappeared into the crowd. West stared at Claire in defeat, and she stared back. They hadn't spoken to each other in a week. Sighing, West threw his empty water bottle onto the littered ground and waved at Matt.

"I'm going to take my break now," he said nonchalantly. Matt watched him wordlessly as West shut the door in his face. He walked up to Claire, who was waiting for him, watching him studiously. She was beyond ignoring him now. West stood there for a moment, feeling incredibly awkward.

"Well, this was stupid. I'm going," he huffed, but Claire caught his arm as he whirled around.

"Please...just....will you walk with me? I won't waste your time, I promise."

Claire studied him again. She seemed to have been doing that an awful lot lately. He shrugged out of her grasp.

"I thought you said you wouldn't mention this again," he said through gritted teeth. The light behind her eyes shone with an intense ferocity he couldn't ignore, so he turned away from her.

"We don't have to, if you don't want to."

After a moment of silence, he consented. West turned with her out of the park and into the Chicago streets, and they walked in silence for a while. He was reminded of the night Claire had followed him; even then, he'd been trying to put what he was feeling into words. It was much harder than he'd thought.

"Claire...What I almost did...what I *did*...It was wrong, and I'm sorry, but you have to understand that it wasn't *me* doing all those things," he began, shielding his eyes from the incredibly bright sunlight to look at her. They walked into the shade of a building, and he stopped.

"You don't have to apologize. You didn't do anything," Claire said, her voice clipped. West put both his hands on her shoulders, and she winced. Her reaction sent a shot of remorse through him, something he shouldn't have felt in the first place. *She followed me,* West thought firmly. *She's right.* Somehow he couldn't agree with that anymore. He also couldn't keep himself from talking.

"I think Clandestine took control. It was like I couldn't stop myself. My body worked on instinct, like if I was hunting, and...I... I..." He could hear the plea in his voice, and watched Claire's hazel eyes switch from annoyance to exhaustion to understanding. She cocked her head to one side.

"You told me to forget everything, West. You nearly *made* me forget. You were right, okay? You're dangerous, and I should just leave you be."

West gave her a noncommittal nod and turned away, searching for something, *anything*, that would keep him from talking to her. He couldn't help wanting to tell her, but he knew he couldn't. The fact that she'd found out had done enough harm. Still, he felt like he needed to explain; if not for her, then for himself. He needed to know he couldn't be controlled by anyone, much less his subconscious.

"It was like I was trying to say something, but it twisted my words." He felt pathetic for admitting it, but he knew it was true. Claire's eyes widened in shock.

"Does it hurt you?" she whispered, all pretenses of anger gone. West shook his head, the urge to explain now gone. *You've said too much,* he told himself sternly. He couldn't let himself tell her.

Not this way.

Claire's hand brushed his, and electricity pulsed through him, so much more intensified than before. He jerked away from her and set off back towards Five Staffs, his cheeks burning. He wasn't going to let instincts take over anymore. He turned to see if Claire was coming or if she'd set off somewhere else, and saw her still in the shadow of the building, leaning against the brick wall resignedly. It took him a moment to notice Claire was crying.

Saphirra sat in the library with the prophecy in her lap, trying to stay out of the way. Claire had never returned to the university, which Saphirra took to mean that she was with West. It was irritating enough when two friends weren't speaking to each other, but when they were the only two people she could be around for the remainder of the summer, she couldn't stand it. Neither Claire nor West had bothered to tell her *why* they were ignoring each other, but Saphirra didn't mind; after all, she had secrets of her own. Feeling unable to process anything, she'd sank back into the safe confines of her chair, hugging her knees. Saphirra stared out at the midday traffic in the distance, wondering what Alex was doing, if he'd found Validus yet, and if he'd found a cure. The skyline was hypnotic, and as she gazed forlornly at the heat waves rippling the surfaces of buildings, her phone rang. She had to look twice at the caller ID before answering.

"Hey Quinn," she said, unable to keep the listlessness out of her voice. She'd been hoping it was someone else, *her* someone else.

"Hey, Saphirra. What's up? I just called to drop in. How's the looking after the campus thing going?"

"Pretty good," she lied. "How are you? How's Demitri?" she asked, surprised to hear a note of interest in her voice. Quinn sighed.

"Demitri broke up with me at the beginning of this summer. I have no idea why, I thought he was so into me! I mean, I look amazing, don't I?" she asked, a self-justifying note in her voice. Saphirra was unsure of how to respond, and was spared having to as she babbled on, "And speaking of *romantic relationships,* did you meet anyone new? A knight in shining armor, perhaps?" she asked slyly, her excitement practically pouring out of her receiver. She sighed. Quinn could sound incredibly dense at some times, and very perceptive at others.

"I'm sorry to hear about Demitri," she said sincerely. "And no, not a knight," She continued. *A Viceprus, maybe*, she amended silently.

"Well that's not good."

Her forlorn tone made Saphirra laugh. The silence on her end of the line seemed to cause Quinn to grow concerned.

"What's wrong? If anything is, I'll march right over into our college you are so diligently holed up in and bust down the door." The image of a thin and muscle-less Quinn trying to break down the door, her reddish-blonde hair tied back and her forehead shining with the effort, made Saphirra giggle.

"Nah, nothing's wrong, really," she lied, a guilty feeling in the pit of her stomach. *Just a psychotic professor attempting to kill me, that's all.* "Quinn, I'll have to call you later, okay?" It was hard to talk to the ever–cheery Quinn without being able to tell her anything. Her worry was starting to shine through, and sooner or later she'd notice it. Her friends were unusually perceptive that way.

"Okay. Say hi to Claire for me."

She promised she would and snapped the phone shut. What would happen to her school friends? She'd never even thought of that problem before. How would Alex be able to face them? They'd realize he was different sooner or later. And if he didn't survive the summer...

Don't think like that, Saphirra told herself firmly, pulling the book towards her. She had to try figuring out the prophecy, no matter how fruitless her attempts would be. After what felt like days Saphirra had reread the same word fifteen times before she gave up, throwing the book back onto the floor with a flourish. Nothing was making sense. She thought back to the folktale, thinking of the brother who'd turned into the first Viceprus. He'd had a sister, who'd received a similar, yet separate, fate. *What creature was she?* Beautiful, yet terrifying...Saphirra tried, and failed, to understand why it sounded so familiar to her. The one thing that had struck her as odd about the folktale was the tree the Healer had sat underneath—an olive tree. She had taken it as a metaphor to peace at the time, but what if it meant something else? What if it indicated where the two had come from, somewhere in the Mediterranean? She glanced out at the window, startled to see dusk approaching fast. A bird flew past, its dark wings reflecting the waning sunlight. *Alex, where are you?* She thought sadly. If he was safe, then it would be alright. She just wished she'd get a sign from him telling her he's okay. He'd called a few days ago, saying he'd be staying for a few more days than he'd originally said he would. Her cheeks were wet, and she was startled to see that they were tears, falling hot and fast onto her lap. The full moon would be soon. Actually...She thought back to the last moon, counting the weeks.

The full moon is this week, she realized. She wondered if Validus would be able to help him this moon. Hopefully, he'd be cured by the time he got back. She stared out at the window, losing every ounce of bravery she'd had. She never felt so alone before in her life.

Evelyn walked out of the office she loved so much, jubilant. She'd done well this time, and hadn't messed anything up—yet. She just had to keep it up until the eclipse, and everything would be perfect. Ry wouldn't tell her what was in the prophecy, but from what she'd ripped out of the books in the library, she thought she had an inkling. How did they fit together? She wanted to know, to understand everything Ry was working for. She wanted to help him, to save him from his treacherous mind. He hadn't ever expressed as much self-doubt before and it worried Evelyn. The fact that Ry, normally so self-confident and aware, could doubt a plan he'd been working on for years was alarming to her. She'd always thought of him as invulnerable, untouchable. *He needs a dose of reality sometimes. It would be good for him.* Evelyn thought, walking into her room on the third floor.

Ry had been avoiding her lately, which was understandable. He had little over a month left before the prophecy would be truly fulfilled, after all. *The anxiety must be catching up to him,* Evelyn reasoned. After all, what else could explain the tender look he'd given her? She wasn't foolish enough to believe he felt about her the same way she did, but today had her questioning his motives. Evelyn took down her bun pin by pin, setting them down methodically on the table as she worked. What did Ry want with her? She could never tell anymore if he loved her like she loved him. She knew that would be a warning sign eventually, but she didn't care. It would eventually work out. It always did.

Suddenly, a flash of silver caught the corner of her eye, and she whipped around. A woman stood at her door, blocking her only means of escape. Her silvery-blonde hair fell down to her shoulders, and her violet eyes glowed menacingly. *A Viceprus..?* Evelyn wondered. She tried to run, but the woman was too fast. She had Evelyn in a stranglehold within a second, flinging her against the wall. She sprang back to her feet as quickly as she could, twisting to see her attacker. The woman's eyes flashed bright gold, and Evelyn felt herself freeze on the spot, the sudden loss of movement toppling her to the ground. Her attacker was holding her against her will with some kind of demonic power.

"Evelyn, why do you always run? It's so...*boring.*" The woman laughed, sitting down lightly on the bed that Evelyn never slept in. "I have a job for you. *Sit.*" she spoke the last word in a commanding whisper, and Evelyn found herself sitting down on the floor automatically. Her expression must have showed her confusion and horror, because the woman laughed coldly.

"You Vicepruses are our enemies, and yet we're so very alike..." She seemed to be convincing herself of something, and that was when Evelyn first saw it. A dim glow emitted from her skin, surly and dark—a Siren stood before her, Evelyn knew it.

Before Evelyn could react, her captor's mouth opened, and a buzzing sound emitted from it like a babbling brook. It poured into Evelyn's ears, and she winced as pain like she'd never felt before pierced her head. She wanted to scream, but she was bound by the spell her captor had cast. The pain triggered a memory; she could see the small room she'd lain in, shuddering and weeping, as Ry poured life into her. She was a mistake. Her continued existence was a mistake. She should be dead. She wished she *were* dead.

"That's always fun." The woman spoke to herself softly, pacing around Evelyn as if she was a piñata and she wanted to find the perfect break spot. Evelyn stared at her frozen fingers, still outstretched in a reflex mode of panic. She couldn't feel them. She couldn't feel anything.

Evelyn gasped, trying to talk through the receding pain.

"Who...are...you?" she whispered in a strangled voice. The woman smiled jubilantly.

"Why, don't you remember me? My name is Clandestine."

Chapter 15
Secrets and Lies

Claire walked into the common room, yawning slightly. She'd just biked all the way to the closest internet café in Chicago to try and use their computer, and had finally found one. As she searched the internet, the same folktale from Professor Lockson's book had continued to crop up. She eventually gave up on searching for anything Viceprus related and instead searched for Latin translators, finally finding an adequate one that had translated the last few sentences she needed to piece the whole thing together. She copied and pasted the result of the prophecy and pressed print. Claire jumped as thunder raked through the sky, and read the translation as quickly as she could before she'd be forced to bike home in the rain:

One controls the mind,
Another the heart.
Their bodies fierce,
Their hearts sound.
Both take life,
And yet fear death.
When blood hangs in the sky
And the moon appears twice,
Fates shall be revealed.
One will find peace,
The other betrayal.
Their key to survival
Is hidden within the jewel.

Claire folded the paper into her jacket, her hands shaking. *Their key to survival...*Whatever it meant, it didn't sound good. She hopped on her bike just as the first fat raindrops started to fall from the sky, and she pedaled as fast as she could to the university. Saphirra *had* to see this.

An hour later she'd arrived in the warm common room, thoroughly soaked and shivering, the translated prophecy half wet. She'd run up to her room as fast as she could, before West could open his mouth to ask her why she looked like she'd walked through a waterfall. When she got into their tiny dorm room, Saphirra wasn't there. Sighing, she laid the paper down on the bed to dry and walked into the bathroom to take a hot shower.

They'd made so many pretenses to West that Claire couldn't keep them straight anymore. She suspected West knew more about Alex than he was letting on, but as long as he didn't ask about it, she was willing to pretend. West was acting strange; one moment he would be perfectly friendly to her, the next he would be closed off and quiet. Claire had stopped trying to make sense of his moody behavior a while ago, but she couldn't keep it from bothering her. She wanted him to be open with her, something she knew she could be if he let her. He seemed to be teetering on the edge of telling her something, and it took all her self-control to keep from pushing him. She felt guilty as is for following him, and as she towel dried her hair, she vowed she'd help as much as she could. She walked back into their dorm to find Saphirra sitting on the bed, reading the prophecy. Saphirra looked up at her as lightning raked across the sky. Raindrops pelted their windows as Saphirra closed the door.

"'*The key to their survival is hidden within the jewel?* Why am I the key? Is there something hidden in me or something? I can't save anyone!" she cried in dismay. Claire shrugged, returning the towel to its rack and combing through her hair slowly.

"Apparently you can," she said quietly, turning to sit next to Saphirra. "I'm more concerned about what it means by '*When blood hangs in the sky and the moon appears twice*'," Claire admitted. "We knew it had to do with you the second Lockson attacked you, didn't we?

The prophecy outlines when it is going to happen, and that's what worries me the most."

Saphirra held up a finger, pushing a lock of raven hair behind her ear before continuing.

"I think I figured that part out, or at least a bit of it. When a moon appears twice...it must mean twice in one month. Otherwise it wouldn't be unusual. If that's the case, it could be talking about the blue moon."

Claire felt dizzy. She'd never thought about that before.

"Saph, you *do* know when the next blue moon is, don't you?" she asked hesitantly. Saphirra raised an eyebrow.

"When?"

"Next month."

Saphirra gave her a panicked stare. "B-but blue moons aren't *that* unusual. I've seen some in the last few years. That can't be it."

Claire couldn't process it. None of it made any sense. If Lockson knew about the prophecy, then why did he wait so long before attacking Saphirra? Why couldn't he bite her? The translation of the prophecy only made everything more confusing.

"Well, maybe it's something unique. This must be something else." Claire nudged the book on folktales with her foot. "What is the other creature in this book? It could help with the rest of the prophecy."

Saphirra shrugged, looking hesitant. "Should I look it up? Maybe our computers are fixed, I think some of my dad's workers fixed them." She bit her lip, gesturing to the purpling sky outside. "I really don't want to go outside at this point, either."

Claire nodded. "Sure, why not. I'll catch up with you later."

As Saphirra walked out the door, Claire picked up the book on folktales and waited until Saphirra had reappeared in the quad outside, sprinting towards the History buildings amidst the light rain. She slid off the bed and ran downstairs into the common room.

She found West sprawled on a couch, the cheery daisy yellow walls looking oddly depressing when contrasted with the gale outside. West jumped up to greet her, talking fast before she could even open her mouth.

"Listen, I figured I should give you something," he said hesitantly. "That Viceprus saw you, and if she got away more could know about you. It wouldn't be wise for you to walk around without anything to protect yourself."

Claire watched him wearily. "What are you planning on giving me? Another dagger?" she asked icily. West shifted uncomfortably.

"Listen, the last thing I'd want is your death on my head." He looked away from her and resumed speaking to the daisy yellow wall instead. "Could you just keep it? Just in case?"

She gave him a weary nod, which he took as his cue to leave, and bounced up the stairs to his dorm room with more energy than he should have. Claire pulled out her sketchbook from her purse and began drawing her latest fixation while she waited, trying her hardest not to think about whatever West had in store for her. Something about the terse way he'd spoken aggravated her. Hadn't *he* been the one who'd initiated conversation with her? She hid the folktale book behind her back, deciding she'd show it to him later. If he suspected where she got it from, or what Alex was, it would cause chaos.

She'd drawn the outline of the fountain, and was working on one of the stone pages when her massive yawn broke her spell. She'd had a total of fifteen hours of sleep for the last five days, mainly because she was so used to losing sleep over the past month that the free hours she now had were useless to her. She was debating sleeping on the plush carpet when West trudged back into the room. He was holding something behind his back, smiling cautiously, as if testing the effect on her.

"What is it?" she said suspiciously. West held out a tiny blue box that looked as if something had been hastily crammed into it. She opened it and gasped.

"West...It's *beautiful*," she said, holding up the sparkling flower pin. Each intricate petal was inlaid with some kind of golden stone, which glittered beautifully even in the dim lighting of the room. She turned the light flower over, tracing the snaking golden ribbon of metal on the back.

"You *made* this?" she asked in awe. West laughed.

"Yep. It took a while, but I managed it. It's all made from the sheath of my dagger."

She stared at him in wonderment. "But don't you need it for–"she began, but West cut her off.

"No, I don't need it anymore. I have something better," he said nonchalantly. She held the glittering pin tenderly, unsure of how to take it.

"So the stones are–"

"Sunstones. Just in case," he said softly. She looked into his face, startled to see a mixture of resentment and vulnerability staring back at her. She tried to imagine losing him, and felt a pang in her heart even as she thought about it.

"What's wrong? I thought you liked it." His face fell as she tried to twist her grimace of pain into a smile.

"I love it," she told him. "I just don't understand why you'd take the trouble to make something like this."

West looked caught off guard. He frowned, apparently thinking hard. "You know.... I don't really know either. I just didn't want you hurt because of me," he said finally. "Don't go reading into it more than you should. I didn't mean anything by it."

Claire's cheeks burned. *What a jerk,* she thought sourly. "Just leave me alone, West."

He looked relieved as he walked away, whether because he didn't have to be in her presence or because she accepted his gift, she didn't know. She sank down onto a couch, holding the pin carefully in her palm.

What am I supposed to do with it? She thought, nonplussed. Unless the stone kept Vicepruses away like a repellent, she wasn't sure how she could use it as a weapon. Shrugging, she tucked it into her pocket and sank lower into her chair, closing her eyes tiredly. She heard muffled footsteps at the door and noticed they paused for a moment. She cracked an eyelid open, surprised to see West standing there, watching her. The look of tenderness in his eyes was the complete opposite of his curt attitude just minutes before, and it puzzled her. West sat down silently in the couch across from her, holding his head in his hands.

Reedhima Mandlik

"Claire...What am I going to do with you?" he whispered, his voice strained. She wasn't sure whether he thought she was asleep or not, but didn't say anything, just in case. Within minutes, he was fast asleep, his chest rising and falling gently with each breath. She wanted to wake him up, to ask him what he thought he was shielding himself from by acting this way, but instead settled back on the couch. She could barely keep her eyelids open. She promised herself she'd find Saphirra as soon as she woke up, and quickly lost herself in the comforting arms of sleep once more.

West saw Claire and Saphirra walk down the stone steps into the warm summer night, and fingered the package he held nervously. He saw them pause, and ran to catch up to Claire.

"Claire! Wait!" he pleaded. He saw her tell Saphirra something, nodding a little. Saphirra swept away to the entrance, wearing a shimmering blue dress. Claire wore a similar black one; her blonde hair was piled up on her head in elaborate curls, and West felt a pang in his heart.

"Claire!"

She paused, her back determinedly turned to him, tensed as if for a fight. He saw her fists curl, and silently kicked himself for everything he'd done. He didn't mean to do this to her. He didn't want it to turn out this way.

And yet, it had.

"Claire, I—I'm so sorry. Please—" his voice broke, and she turned around. Fury lit up her face.

"I gave you a second chance, and this is what you do to me. I have scars, West."

There was no fury in her voice; just disappointment. West winced as she turned to one side, and the scars he'd given her were thrown into relief in the moonlight, undeniably harsh. He didn't remember how they'd gotten there—all he remembered was that he had made each white stroke on her pale skin. Each tiny white line running the length of her shoulder cut West deeply in his heart.

"Please...please..." he pleaded with her, fighting to ignore the sphere of light in her eyes. It had dimmed because of him, and he briefly wondered how his father had managed staring into the eyes of the one he loved like this.

176

"West, I have to go. I don't have time for this."

She turned to walk away, and West slipped a corsage on her wrist.

"What—?"

"If I can't be near you, at least let my heart be," he pleaded. She gazed at him with a peculiar expression on his face, and he had to quell the sudden upsurge of music that threatened to pour out of his mouth. He hated himself for doing this to her, for taking the brightness out of her eyes. She watched him for a long moment, and then she turned wordlessly away, walking towards Saphirra. West watched her leave, noticing something glinting in the moonlight in the spot where she had stood just seconds before. He bent down to pick it up. The flower he'd given her lay in the palm of his hand, but the ribbon was nowhere to be found. She was gone, and she'd left his heart on the ground, to be trampled underneath her feet.

Suddenly, the scene changed. It was a stormy night...or was it day? Either way, it was dark, and he was running to Saphirra. He touched her head and pulled away almost instantly, his fingers sticky with blood. He listened for her heartbeat, and could hear nothing but a muffled noise.

"No!"

He turned to the screaming voice, and it was Claire's. He whipped around just in time to see the nurse grab her, jump on her...Claire was thrashing, then she stopped moving. Ms. Stone whipped around, carrying Claire like a rag doll, and disappeared. West looked down, panic racing though him, and saw the same flower Claire had trampled just minutes before, crushed and bloody in his palm...

"Claire!" West shouted, bolting upright. Claire had been in front of him a moment ago, hadn't she? He glanced around the common room frantically, his dream scaring him more than ever. Was she hurt? He heard screaming from outside, and he wrenched the double-bay doors apart and burst into the quad, blinking raindrops from his eyes. He saw his nightmare unfold in front of his eyes; Claire fell to the ground in front of him as something leaped at her, its ferocity horrifying. Her scream shattered the eerie silence that had blanketed the university, and thunder ripped through the sky. He saw someone tackle her. He barely had time to register it all before he saw Saphirra tackle the woman to the ground. Within moments Saphirra had been launched into the air. He heard a sickening crunch, and then Claire was gone.

Saphirra sat in the library, trying and failing to concentrate on the prophecy. Silence was never good; it let her mind wander. When would her defenses break? She'd tried not to worry about Alex but Claire still watched her carefully, as if she was a bomb about to explode at any second. Saphirra sighed, hugging her knees. She had walked into the common room, only to see West and Claire, sleeping. The moment was too sweet to ruin, so she had walked back to the library instead. It was lightly drizzling, but she didn't care. She liked walking through the rain; it made her feel calm somehow, as if each drop held a promise that everything would be alright. She sat watching the trees dance in the storm outside, thinking.

The full moon was a few days away, which meant it had been five days. Five long days. Their lives were now ruled by the full moon. It was ridiculous, but she liked knowing there was a certain time things were going to become more chaotic than usual. It gave her time to prepare. A motion on the grounds caught her eye and she turned to see Claire heading towards the library, covering her head as best as she could with a book as she ran. As lightning streaked across the sky, another figure became evident through the haze of rain. Claire seemed to notice the person too, because she seemed to be running faster than before, continuously glancing behind her shoulder. The person ran after her, and faster than humanly possible had launched at her. Saphirra ran outside just as someone who looked like Ms. Stone tackled Claire to the ground, both thrashing wildly. She heard a thud and then a moan as Claire stopped moving completely, her blonde hair spilling into the muddy ground. Saphirra screamed and shoved her in an attempt to break her grip on Claire, but she was pushed aside like a doll. Saphirra felt something crack, and then sickening pain shot through her, numbing her shock.

Why? She thought sluggishly, squinting through the rain that threatened to choke her. Ms. Stone's voice floated through the haze of rain to her ears.

"You know too much." Claire's scream pierced Saphirra's ear, and she struggled to get up, but her limbs were too sluggish. *Claire!* She tried to scream, and Ms. Stone was at her side in a flash.

"Shut up, you stupid girl! I want to kill you...but I like, can't." she seemed genuinely disappointed, and Saphirra gritted her teeth. Her head throbbed as if it had been split open, and she felt something hot and wet trickle down her neck, mixing with the rain that suddenly got heavier. She looked up into Ms. Stone's looming face, expecting a malicious smile. Glowing violet eyes stared back at her, narrowed viciously against the wind.

"Say goodbye to your friend," she sneered, and before she knew what was happening, the nurse's fist made contact with the side of her head, and she drowned in pain, falling reluctantly into darkness.

Chapter 16
The Murder of an Angel

West had been searching for Claire for four days, and he was seriously worried. Claire was gone without a trace. That night, when he'd called her cell phone in the vain, ridiculous hope that she'd pick up, with no luck. When he'd rushed to the spot where Claire had vanished, slipping a little in the wet grass, he had seen Saphirra. A bruise had begun to blossom on her cheek. He'd carried her to the university infirmary, hoisting her onto a bed and dressing her wounds as best as he could. Her head hadn't suffered a serious injury, but a wound on her neck had opened up, which had resulted in her blood loss. He'd bandaged her up as best as he could, using the same makeshift methods he'd used when a hunting job went awry. Saphirra stirred sleepily occasionally, mumbling in her stupor. Finally, she'd opened her eyes.

"Are you okay?" he'd asked. She blinked at him, and then sat up suddenly, cringing in pain.

"C-Claire got kidnapped by a–"Her eyes had widened as she realized who she was talking to, and she hurriedly rephrased her answer. "I mean, she was kidnapped. It was a woman, I think. I tried to stop her but..." she had shrugged and winced again, massaging her forehead. She had touched the bandages on her head gingerly, and then gazed at the gauze on her arms. "What happened to me?" she asked, glancing around at the large infirmary windows with new-found alarm. West helped Saphirra sit up, biting his lip.

"You got hurt because the person who took Claire slammed you to the ground. I wish I had gotten there sooner," West lamented, kicking the bed stand.

"It's not your fault," she had muttered drowsily, examining her bandaged fingers. West had shrugged as a bandage slipped loosely from her neck.

"Sorry. I'm no doctor but that was the best I could do," he'd replied as he helped her out of the infirmary bed.

"How'd you learn to fix me up like this?"

Her suspicious tone caught West off guard. "When you travel a lot you end up picking up some things," he had replied dismissively.

Together, they'd searched the whole college. Whenever he asked Saphirra about the intruder, Saphirra insisted everything was too blurry to make out. And yet, the figure had looked so familiar... He'd eventually realized that he wouldn't get anything out of her, and so he'd spent every day and night frantically searching for Claire. All he knew for sure was that the attacker had been a woman.

A woman with yellow-green eyes, which had flashed to a brilliant violet.

They'd shone through the pounding rain, and it had felt like they had been staring directly at him. With a vicious glint in her eye the woman had left, carrying Claire with her. West had to make a choice; chase after them, or help the soon to be unconscious Saphirra.

He couldn't help wondering if he had made the wrong choice.

Ever since Claire had found out about his hunting job, he'd been getting worse. He supposed that was why his responses were so clipped whenever she was around, and why he felt a small prick of satisfaction at the fury he could coax out of her. Still, somewhere deep in his heart, West knew he wanted to trust her. He wanted to sit down and tell Claire everything about his past, about his life. He'd never felt so strongly attached to someone before, especially someone who'd stumbled upon his secret by mere chance.

He'd resolved to keep one rule ever since he undertook the hunting job five years ago; don't trust anyone he wouldn't want hurt. *Maybe Claire is the exception,* he'd thought. Only now could he see how it was a mistake involving her. If only he'd taught her how to use the pin...but now it was too late. She was gone.

And it was all his fault.

By the midnight of the first day, they'd had to admit it. Her kidnapper hadn't simply dumped her on one of the side streets in Chicago; she was actually *gone.* He would never forgive himself if they didn't find her. His world had cracked straight down the middle. Who cared what was wrong or right anymore, if Claire was gone for good?

Claire. Despair clawed at his heart as he envisioned Claire being tortured, being tied up, and being held at gunpoint...he cringed. He didn't mean for her to get caught up in all this. He was torn between wishing he'd never met her in the first place and wishing he'd told her everything, so she would at least know what to expect. If the only Viceprus she had ever known was Alex, then she was woefully unprepared.

West didn't expect to see her again. The thought resounded with a dull ache in his heart. He'd caused her disappearance, and most likely her death. He should have been more careful. He should have watched for followers. He should have—

"West? West, are you okay?" Saphirra's voice broke through his thoughts. He looked at her, slightly disoriented. He couldn't even think straight anymore.

"No, actually," he admitted, leaning against a wall for support. *She won't come back. There's just no way.* Claire shouldn't have been this important to him. Losing her shouldn't have felt like this.

So why did he feel like he was drowning?

Saphirra sat in the shade of her favorite oak tree, waiting. Tonight was not only the full moon, but also marked the second day that Claire was still missing. She clutched her cell phone anxiously, waiting for his call, waiting to hear his voice. She missed him, and was glad half the worrying would all be over when Alex got back. With Alex, they could try to find Claire outside of the confines of the university. He might even know what had happened to her. All it would take was one smile from him, and she'd know things were going to be okay. She knew that no matter what situation a person was in, if they could smile—really, truly smile—then things would get better. If you were at a point that you couldn't smile anymore, you would need something or someone to help you back up. Otherwise, all would be lost. If you couldn't feel that wave of relief, no matter how momentary the feeling was, you were lost. Lost within yourself, lost in the world. It would be hard to bring you back. She couldn't even smile now, conflicted over what to believe. In truth, she was lost too.

West had asked to call the police after the storm had cleared, but when Saphirra had advised him against it, he hadn't panicked. In fact, West had been completely subdued about Claire's situation. Saphirra had figured at the time that maybe it was how he dealt with situations like this; shoving it down and burying it deep so that the pain was only evident in his own eyes. She had done that once. The scars on her arms tingled, and she crossed them across her chest, taking a deep, steadying breath. The loss of Claire left an empty hole in her heart, and it throbbed. Claire wasn't stupid; if she could handle Alex, then she could handle Ms. Stone.

She wished she were more convinced.

The quad was bathed in golden sunlight, drenching everything in a soft mid-afternoon glow. It was a perfectly normal day, warmer than usual because of the cloudless sky. A movement caught her eye, and she got up expectantly. Someone was walking towards her, their stride long and purposeful. Saphirra waited until the person got close enough so she could see their face before approaching them. As the figure walked closer, its features grew more distinct; honey brown hair, sharp, greenish-yellow eyes, and an evil smile. *Ms. Stone.* Saphirra's hands balled into fists. Ms. Stone walked up to her casually.

"Expecting a call?" she asked mockingly, stretching out a hand as if they were old friends. Saphirra glared daggers at her.

"Why are you here? What did you do to Claire?" Saphirra felt like punching her, but she knew that was asking for a broken arm. Instead, she crossed her arms over her chest sullenly as anger boiled up inside her. Ms. Stone laughed.

"I haven't done anything to her—yet. It's easier for me if I keep her sedated. She's still knocked out as I speak." She cackled as Saphirra made to punch her, grabbing Saphirra's arm and quickly and effortlessly shoving her onto the ground.

"I wouldn't attack me, if I were you. I might lose...*control.*" she scoffed at the shocked look on Saphirra's face.

"Why didn't you kidnap me instead? It would have been easier that way, wouldn't it?" she snarled at Ms. Stone. The nurse grimaced.

"I couldn't kill you even if I wanted to."

Saphirra scowled at her. "Then what do you want with me?" she asked warily. Ms. Stone laughed, her face lighting up almost immediately.

"Well, I hate to be the bearer of bad news. You see, I was...*bored,* yesterday, and decided to take a walk. Imagine my surprise when I see Alex heading right towards me! I invited him to take a walk and chat for a while, you know," she said, poison in her voice. Saphirra gritted her teeth, staring up at Ms. Stone with hatred. "But he didn't seem to want to, so I insisted. I guess I'd come on a little too...oh, how should I say this? *Strong.*"

Fear twisted in Saphirra's heart and choked her words as she struggled to talk.

"W-what do you mean?" she asked, dreading the answer. Ms. Stone rolled her eyes.

"Isn't it obvious? I killed him."

Saphirra stared at her wordlessly. *She has to be kidding. She's messing with my head.*

"It was so *easy,* I was surprised. The kid's not much of a fighter," she continued, sounding bored.

"I–I don't believe you," Saphirra stammered. *Impossible.*

"Oh, *don't* you? Well, I have proof. Here," she said, tossing something onto the grass. There, glittering in the afternoon sun, lay Alex's mother's ring, still entwined around a thick leather cord.

A deep red stained the edge.

"No..." She whispered. Her hands shook as she fumbled with it, trying and failing to pick up the delicate silver ring. She sneered down at Saphirra as mad fury filled Saphirra's heart. She wouldn't... she *couldn't*...The nurse dropped something onto the grass beside Saphirra, and with shaking fingers, she lifted it, staring at it in horror.

Alex's cell phone.

Ms. Stone stared down at her frozen frame, satisfied.

"Goodbye," she trilled, turning away from her. Saphirra wanted to run at her, to hit her, to kill her. Savage fury ripped through her lungs, and she screamed at Ms. Stone's retreating back. No, it wasn't possible, it couldn't be possible....

Alex was gone.

"NO! I am *not* going to let...you can't...I won't let you–" She spluttered, getting unsteadily to her feet. Pain as she'd never felt before pulsed through her, and somewhere in the college, a phone rang. Her cell phone, which lay in a bed of grass a few yards away, vibrated. She didn't bother to check who was calling. She couldn't possibly care anymore.

"Oh, but haven't you already?" Ms. Stone sneered, and before Saphirra could hit her with all her might, she vanished, leaving a broken Saphirra in her wake.

∾❦∾

Claire opened her eyes groggily. Where was she? What had happened? All she remembered was someone knocking her to the ground. She stared around a room unfamiliar to her. It seemed to be an olive green oval office, lavishly decorated, with elegant chairs pressed against every wall except one, which was an immediate copy of the library. She was in the center of the room, tied to one of the chairs. She tried to move and quickly discovered that she had been bound to it by thick ropes. She tried to move her lips, to scream for help, but her entire face was numb. She couldn't scream, she couldn't move—she was trapped. Was this a dream too? Her head throbbed a painful answer back. It had all happened, and it was all *real*. She struggled, and for the first time, she heard a soft laugh next to her ear.

"Struggle all you want, but you won't lose these bonds." The voice chuckled again. Claire felt herself start to hyperventilate as wave after wave of understanding hit her. This was no dream. Ms. Stone *had* attacked her, and taken her prisoner as well. Ms. Stone, the head nurse, had knocked her to the ground, her yellow-green eyes now a bright purple.

She's a Viceprus, too, Claire thought dimly. Were all the professors at Rose University Vicepruses? Claire stared out of the windows behind Ms. Stone into an inky black sky. Was it night, or early morning? *Where am I?* She couldn't remember seeing this office before on her routine checkups around campus; she must be far, far away from there.

"It's been a while, hasn't it, Claire?" Ms. Stone's voice dripped with sarcasm as she stepped towards her. Her voice seemed distant, as if Claire was listening to an old record player. *What is she going to do to me?*

"It's going to be a wonderful full moon tonight. It truly *is* a shame that you'd die before such an important day," the nurse said slyly, her shrewd violet eyes waiting for a reaction. Claire kept her expression smooth. Her mind, however, was whirring. She felt blood rush into her face, causing black spots to swim in her vision. The numbness had begun to wear off, and she worked her jaw, surprised that she could only move a small bit. She knew she should feel alarmed right now, but couldn't seem to conjure up the effort. *Ms. Stone definitely knows her drugs,* she thought savagely. Finally, she spoke.

"Why would it be important?" her voice came out slurred and raspy, and her tongue felt too thick for her mouth. Still, Claire knew full well what Ms. Stone wanted. So this was what it was all about. Alex. Maybe even West. The best she could do was play dumb while her mind started to work properly. She twitched her fingers, relief spreading though her as they responded. Blood rushed to the numb parts of her body, and she felt the uncomfortable prickle as she tried to move her legs, without much response.

"No, you damned fool! I know you know about West Anastos," she spat at Claire. She put a hand to her forehead in exasperation, then took a deep breath and looked back into Claire's eyes. As bright, glowing violet met hazel, something clicked into place. Ms. Stone reached out to touch Claire's arm. As her fingertips connected with Claire's skin, she sighed peacefully. The same soft glow that Claire had seen when she was with Alex poured out of her now, enveloping Ms. Stone's fingers in its warm light. This, however, felt much different; within moments Claire felt as if she had been kicked in the stomach. She could barely breathe, let alone think; the room started to dissolve into darkness, and stopped only when Ms. Stone lifted her hand off of her. Claire shuddered as the energy flow stopped between them, but Ms. Stone only gave her a satisfied smile in return.

"You see what I can do to you? Don't be difficult and answer the question, or you won't live to see the morning."

I doubt you'd let me live anyway, Claire thought bitterly. She decided to answer.

"What about him?" she asked sweetly, inching her hand towards her pocket, where the pin West had given her was currently digging into her thigh. She checked to make sure the nurse was turned the other way as she gave her pocket a tug. The pin fell neatly into her hands, hidden from the nurse's view.

"What do you know about West Anastos?" Ms. Stone asked testily, whirling around to face Claire. She prayed her captor wouldn't notice the beautiful pin in her hands. Oblivious, Ms. Stone breezed past her, leaning over a pile of chairs get something from a desk drawer. Claire shifted the pin in her hands, careful not to drop it.

"West is a friend," Claire said evasively,

"Cut the crap. I know you know about his job. But how much do you know?" she spoke to the window, and Claire closed her eyes and gritted her teeth, bracing herself for the pain as she scraped the sharp edge of one of the petals along her wrist. *Once...Twice...Three Times....*

"Well? I'm waiting." Ms. Stone's reflection smiled mockingly at Claire from the cool glass. *Four times...*Finally, a flow of sticky, warm, wet liquid onto her fingers told her the pin had done its job. She watched as her captor's fingers froze onto the glass.

"I'm bleeding," Claire pointed out. "Unless you want me to bleed to death or something, you should help me."

Claire's heart pounded erratically in her chest as Ms. Stone walked towards her, bending to examine her wound. *Please let this work...*she pleaded silently. Ms. Stone's eyes were trained on Claire's wrist, which was bleeding freely onto the cream colored carpet. Claire clutched her pin gingerly, and caught Ms. Stone's fingers with her own. As the energy flow between them resumed, Ms. Stone couldn't seem to move away. She paused for a moment, as if struggling with herself; then something within her snapped. With an almighty snarl she leapt at Claire, her claws ripping and tearing at the chair in an effort to get to her. She growled, ripping Claire's flesh with claws that were long and charcoal black, making furious swiping motions at her neck. A thought seemed to occur to Ms. Stone, and suddenly, her lips were inches from Claire's throat. *This is not going according to plan.*

Claire ducked as Ms. Stone's teeth clamped onto the headboard of the chair behind her, and the splintering wood gave way to her jaws. Claire had barely registered she had full use of her limbs again; she bolted, her arms free from her chains thanks to the desperate nurse. In her haste she tripped and fell, noting in dismay that the ropes around her feet were still tied halfway. She tugged, desperate, and the ropes slipped loose. The nurse reached for Claire, crazed for energy, but Claire jammed the pin in her face, its facets glistening with ruby blood. Claire shoved it with as much might as she could into her captor's mouth, and the nurse swallowed it whole. She shrieked as it went down her throat, which immediately started to blister. Her neck began to glow with a fierce white light, but Claire didn't bother watching. As Ms. Stone's shriek rang in her ears, she took a broken fragment of the chair and crashed it through the window, the glass raining down on her mercilessly. She caught a brief glimpse of the dark grounds two floors below, and as she heard the fatal snarl behind her, she took a deep breath and jumped.

Chapter 17
A Lost Survivor

Her world had ended, so why was Saphirra still living? Alex was gone, so why was her heart still stubbornly beating? He was.... he was *dead*. She slumped onto her bed, her hands curled into fists.

Why? She'd never lost it like this before. She hated this feeling, the feeling of weight on her heart that was impossible to lift. It felt like she was suffocating. She just couldn't believe it. Saphirra had held onto the vain hope that he would still call tonight, just like he was supposed to. That maybe the ring was a fluke of some sort, that he had somehow managed to win the struggle. She'd checked her phone and found an unavailable number, but when she'd redialed it the phone had rang over and over again. No one had ever picked up, and she assumed it was just the junk phone calls she normally got. It couldn't have been Alex calling from another number. She didn't know whether it was brave or stupid that she had accepted the worst, especially from Ms. Stone, of all people. Still, reality rang through; he was really, truly gone. The ring proved it.

She had even refrained from telling West, on the slight chance that Alex was still alive. She didn't know how she could explain to him what had happened without telling him about the events that had plagued them since the beginning of the summer. Saphirra couldn't even think of where to start. It was as if her mind was fogged over, the haze blocking any rational thought. She didn't want to have to tell West that his best friend was a Viceprus, not now. Not with Claire missing, too.

If both Alex and Claire were gone, she didn't know how she would be able to cope. Saphirra had debated calling Claire's mother, but immediately thought against it. It was the same reasoning she'd thought of when West had asked to call the police. Everything was unraveling before her eyes, and she couldn't take it. Her heart was falling apart, piece by piece. She should have made him stay, she should have told him not to go. She should have talked to him in the beginning of the year; she should have told him everything.

When the very ground you stand on is pulled away, where do you stand? She couldn't move. Her vision was blurred by tears, falling hot and fast onto her lap. The thought of losing Alex was so much more painful than when her mother had died, because Alex had never hurt her. They had been through everything together, back then and even now. She wished she could hear his voice again, and to see him smile again. Saphirra sat in the dark room she normally shared with Claire, curled up on her bed, watching the stars twinkle down at her. To-night was the full moon. The thought brought an upsurge of memories that pierced her heart, and she doubled up.

Death. The thought of sent pain through her.

Would she have to mourn Claire, too? She held on to the vain hope that Claire was alive, constantly fighting the hopeless feeling that threatened to overwhelm her. She just couldn't give up hope. Even now, a tiny part of her was still trying to believe that Alex was alive, too. Memories of him flooded through her: meeting him for the first time, all those hours they'd spend together in his small, cha-otic house, and the days they'd spend in her spacious lonely one; see-ing him again this summer, the feeling of everything finally going on track; him, saving her from Lockson; their first night during the full moon; the amusement park...everything formed a vivid collage in her mind, killing all other thoughts. She examined Alex's ring, twisting the thick leather cord over and over in her fingers. She tied it around her own neck, and the pain lessened a little. The dark was peaceful and calm. In the darkness it was as if time stood still.

She got up and began to walk, hoping some fresh air would clear her head. She hadn't been on the roof since the last moon, and it seemed fitting that she walked there now. As she climbed up the attic stairs, she focused on the memories of this summer, smiling a little as she remembered their first conversation. Had he known, back then, what had happened to her? She had always tried her hardest to act like nothing was wrong, and most of the time it had worked; still,

Alex had always been the one who saw through her lies. *He must have known something was wrong,* Saphirra reasoned. She just never gave him the chance to ask.

She forced the roof door open with more force than necessary. A burst of cool night air filled her lungs as she walked out onto the roof steadily. As she settled back into the corner she tilted her head up to the sky, trying to clear her mind. She didn't want to think anymore. Not of Alex, not of Claire, and certainly not of the memories that constantly threatened to overwhelm her. The full moon shone brightly above her, drenching the rooftop with its silvery light. Saphirra shifted, trying to gaze at the grounds below, but to her alarm she couldn't move. She was frozen to the ground, and she felt the breath leave her body as her surroundings began to dissolve into piercing darkness.

"Wait. What's going on?"

Alex's voice seemed to reverberate through her, but it was faint, like a whisper in the wind. Mute shock swept through her, but it was too late; Saphirra was pulled into the darkness, swiftly succumbing to unconsciousness.

Alex looked around, bewildered. He was watching the same starry sky, but Validus wasn't beside him. In fact, he was completely alone. Alex blinked and got up slowly, trying to find his bearings on the familiar rooftop. Every movement felt forced and cumbersome, as if he were pulling up twice his weight. Something black swung into his vision, and he swatted it away, alarmed, but it just swung back again.

It was his hair.

He examined his hands, surprised at the soft, nimble fingers he now had. He looked down at himself, and was shocked to see he wasn't wearing the same clothes he had been moments ago. Confused, he ran as best as he could to the attic stairs, taking them two at a time in his strange form. As he passed by a darkened window, he saw a familiar reflection in the glass.

Saphirra stared back at him, looking utterly bewildered as to how he had gotten there. He raised a hand in greeting, and Saphirra raised the same hand. He blinked, and she blinked, too.

"Saphirra?" Alex asked, except for it wasn't his voice at all that issued from his mouth. It was higher pitched and slightly musical, almost like...

Saphirra's voice.

Alex *was* Saphirra. Or at least, he seemed to be.

What the hell is going on? Alex thought. It was entirely too weird to be back in Rose University, and even weirder when he was like this. *Is this a dream?* He pinched himself, and felt no pain. Confused, he tugged on a strand of hair, surprised that he didn't feel a tingle in his scalp. Or was it hers? He walked down the familiar hallways, brushing his hands across the walls. He couldn't feel a thing.

He was either in a very vivid dream or something else entirely. He turned down an unfamiliar hallway, and recognized it to be the girl's dorms. Curious, he headed towards the only room whose door was open, and stepped inside.

He figured that it was Saphirra and Claire's dorm room, since it was still fully furnished and the bed looked half-made. He sat down on the bed, bewildered. What was happening? He decided that it was an extremely accurate dream, and looked down. Next to him was Saphirra's cell phone, as well as his.

What is my cell phone doing here? He thought, confused. Hadn't he lost it back at Validus's hideout a few days ago? He ran his thumb over the smooth metal, nonplussed. If he'd lost it back in Canada.... What was it doing here?

He looked around the dorm room as he tucked the phone back into his pocket. A mirror on the far side of the room caught his eye and he walked up to it, staring down at the reflection within. Saphirra's neck and arm were covered in bandages, and a small bruise had begun to appear above her left eye. *What happened to her?* He thought, reaching out to touch the mirror. Her slim fingers danced across the glass, and he unconsciously reached towards his neck before realizing he would never be able to grasp his mother's ring again. It had been lost too, along with his cell phone, at the hideout.

And yet, his fingers had connected with something round and smooth. Surprised, he glanced back in the mirror. There, nestled in the hollow of Saphirra's throat, was his mother's ring, looped around a thick leather cord that Saphirra had tied around her neck.

Why is my ring here? Everything he had lost was somehow with Saphirra. He frowned, tracing the edge of a bandage that had come undone. He tugged a little and it unraveled, revealing the small bite mark he had given her a month ago.

It was glowing.

He let go of the bandage, startled. A faint golden light emitted from her skin, barely noticeable in the bright moonlight. It was then that he noticed her eyes.

A bright violet that glowed like hot coals had replaced her electric green ones. He staggered back in shock. *What have I done to her?* Were the wounds from him, too? He glanced down and saw long, thin scars crisscrossing her arms. He fell against the mattress, his head spinning.

What did I do?

Before he could move again, however, he felt as if someone had pulled him to the ground. In frozen wonderment he watched the mirror as the glowing violet in Saphirra's eyes began to fade back to bright green. He heard a shuddering, choking gasp, and then he fell into impermeable darkness.

Saphirra awoke on her bedroom floor, although she had no idea how she had gotten there. Hadn't she been on the roof moments ago? She looked around her in bewilderment. Had she been on the roof, or had she simply fallen out of her bed? She felt incredibly exhausted, almost as if she had spent the night helping Alex.

Did I heard his voice, or was that a dream? She thought, rubbing her aching head. She was too tired to even think, and as she shifted on the carpet, she felt something hard push against her thigh. Curious, she reached into her pocket, pulling out Alex's red cell phone. *What is this doing in my pocket?* She thought, confused. Saphirra threw it onto her bed, not really caring where it landed. *I must have sleep-*

walked or something, she decided. As she crawled her way back onto her bed, she sank into the covers contentedly. She'd never been this tired before. She glanced out her window, rubbing her tired, sleep deprived eyes. She must have been out for a while, because the dawn seemed to be creeping up on the horizon, painting the skyline a soft pink. The long, unkempt grasses swayed in the morning breeze, dotted with dew, and birds sang. Everything was too cheery. She squinted, watching something move across the quad. She could just make out a figure, swaying unsteadily on her feet, walking towards the girl's dorms. Claire.

Claire was back!

Saphirra jumped to her feet with renewed energy, pushing the door open and running as fast as she could to the other side of the dorms, to West. She passed the common room and stopped there, noticing West examining something in the dawn's soft glow.

"West. *West!*" She shouted, running over to him. He glanced up at her, startled, and shoved whatever he was holding behind his back. She recognized her own grief in his eyes.

"What was that?" she asked suspiciously, eyeing his hidden hands. He shrugged.

"Nothing you need to know about. What did you want?" he asked indifferently, the pain in his eyes replaced nearly instantly by a turbulent grey.

"I–I think I've found Claire."

Chapter 18
Forbidden

Claire's blonde hair was matted in blood. She was limping, her other ankle dragging behind her pathetically. Her clothes were ripped and torn, and dark patches showed where they were soaked in blood. And yet, she could barely feel it. The pain of last night barely registered in her mind—she'd made it, she was back where she wanted to be.

"Claire! Oh my god, Claire, what happened to you?" She heard Saphirra's voice, so distant in the dawn, and Claire swayed. She saw what looked like three Saphirra's run over to her, and felt two warm hands catch her before she hit the concrete steps. She saw West out of the corner of her eyes, and felt stronger hands knock her knees out from under her. She was cradled in West's arms now, and the strange way the quad was spinning unsettled her. She was dragged into blackness, and then pulled out of it just as quickly.

Claire felt herself moving and saw classrooms rush by her in a blur, but knew she couldn't possibly be walking. Her legs weren't moving, and the stabbing pain in her ankle had reduced to a dull minimum. She felt lightheaded and dizzy, and jolted a little as she was launched onto something soft. She closed her eyes warily, and when she opened them, Saphirra's face swam in and out of focus. Slowly, the two Saphirra's merged into one anxious face as her best friend peered down at her. Someone was wiping her face with a wet cloth, and a second later, she heard a low voice that sounded like West's mutter,

"How did she get like this?"

"What happened, Claire? I am so, so sorry!" Saphirra cried, her voice sounding oddly broken, and she threw her arms around Claire. She winced, and Saphirra pulled away apologetically. Slowly, between random dabs of a wet cloth, she was able to tell them a story. Not the right one; West was in the room, and Claire wasn't sure he knew about Alex. West interrupted several times, and by the time her story was over, both their mouths were wide open.

"...and so I ran, but I think I twisted my ankle, because it hurts a lot. The person didn't follow me as far as I know." She stopped abruptly. Trying to edit the story with both of them staring at her was hard enough, but with them looking at her as if she was a hero...Well, that just made it worse. "I got a cab, and the driver really wanted me to go to the hospital, but I came here instead. Apparently, I was in the outskirts of Chicago," she said, talking determinedly to Saphirra.

Saphirra took over wiping down her arms, telling West to go find more gauze. West walked out of the room reluctantly, looking like he wanted to say something but had thought against it. Dread filled her heart as she struggled to talk. It was now or never.

"West...West's a Viceprus hunter, Saph. He had a dagger and everything."

Saphirra simply stared at her.

"No he isn't," Saphirra said firmly. Claire shook her head, and stopped immediately--- it hurt too much.

"No, I'm serious, Saph--"

"Claire, you're just delusional. They don't exist. He can't be a--"

"*Saph!* Listen to me. I'm serious," Claire gave her a meaningful look, and Saphirra slumped down on the bed. After a moment of silence, she spoke. "Why didn't you tell me before?" she asked hollowly, her face disbelieving.

"It's not something I can exactly blurt out!"

"*Alex* is a Viceprus, Claire! This is dangerous to him, too! What do you even mean by Viceprus hunter?" Saphirra asked, her voice an octave higher than usual. Claire winced at her reproachful look.

"He wounds them or kills them or something, depending on what his boss asks him to do," she said quietly. Saphirra's eyes widened in alarm.

"Is there a cult or something that I don't know about, too? Is there a whole league of Viceprus hunters?" Saphirra nearly shouted, practically hysterical. She took a deep, shuddering breath, and then continued. "Sorry. It's just...how did you even know about this? *When* did you know about this?"

Claire told her about the night she'd followed West, skipping over the Siren encounter he'd had at the end of it all. Saphirra seemed to have been stunned into silence; her mouth hung slightly open, as if she couldn't believe it had happened. The whole effect was slightly comical.

"Is that why you two seemed to be avoiding each other so much lately?" Saphirra asked her after a moment. Claire nodded, suddenly unable to meet her eyes.

"I wasn't supposed to find out. We'd agreed we'd act as if it had never happened."

Saphirra nodded musingly. "I guess I understand now." She didn't seem inclined to say anything else, so Claire switched the subject.

"Where's Alex?" Whatever drug West had given her was making her tongue too thick to speak properly. Saphirra cringed at the sound of his name, and her eyes welled up with tears

"He hasn't returned yet," she said hollowly. Claire stared at her, dumbstruck.

"Well that's okay, isn't it? Maybe he just stayed longer or something," Claire suggested, startled by Saphirra's tears. She studied the bandages on Saphirra's neck and arms, surprised, and tried to calm her friend down as best as she could. "What happened to you?"

As Saphirra explained to her what happened after Ms. Stone had taken her, Claire's eyes blurred, and she couldn't find the strength to blink them. Hot tears trickled down her face and onto her neck.

"He's not," she whispered hoarsely. "He can't be dead. Ms. Stone could have been tricking you. There's no other explanation for it. Don't believe her, Saph."

Saphirra shook her head furiously, reaching behind her neck to untie something. She tossed it onto the bed and looked away, unable to meet Claire's eyes. Claire cautiously picked it up, running a hand over the rough leather cord.

"Alex always wore that. He would never take it off unless he was forced. Something happened to him," Saphirra said, her voice ringing with certainty. "This proves it."

Claire shook her head, seeing the flaw in Saphirra's logic, but her friend had already started speaking again. "It's easier this way than keeping up some tiny sliver of hope, you know? If I was wrong...I *hope* I'm wrong," she said forlornly. Claire sank into the pillows tiredly, trying to ignore the ache that had spread throughout her body. How could she explain to West what had happened to Alex if he was gone?

"I'm going to let you sleep," Saphirra said quietly, backing out of the room. Claire watched West pat her on the shoulder comfortingly as the door closed behind them, her frame shaking uncontrollably. Claire felt hollow, and the ringing in her ears told her that Saphirra had actually said those words. *He never came back.*

Claire opened her eyes to find West staring down at her worriedly. She struggled to get up, deterred by the throbbing pain in her head. She looked up at West, waiting for him to speak. West had been unusually nice to her since she'd showed up again, and she wasn't used to it. He looked at her as if he wanted to say something, but turned to her bandages instead. They couldn't send her off to a hospital, because of the questions that would arise from her injuries. Besides, they weren't that bad. West had taken to tending to her wounds instead, and was wrapping her arms in bandages as best as he could, his eyes widening as he saw the extents of her injuries.

West worked on her bandages silently, unconsciously tying her bandages with more force than necessary. West was smart; if she didn't know better, she'd have said West had figured out what Alex really was.

"Claire..." West began. She was shocked to hear how much regret was in his voice. "I...Would you mind if I tried something?"

Claire tilted her head to one side and winced. That hurt too.

"What do you mean?"

"Just hold still."

West pointed to her arm, where a particularly large gash had opened up again. The blood had just begun to stain the bandage as West untied it.

"What are you *doi*—"

"Just watch."

West pressed his palm over her wound, and it began to glow with a soft, golden light, not unlike what usually happened to her if she took Alex's hand. She felt a warm, tingling sensation, and slowly the pain ebbed away, instantly replaced with the same warm feeling. West moved away, and the sensation stopped, but the sting from the injury didn't return. She looked from West's jubilant face to her arm. The gash had vanished.

"H-how–?"

"I've been able to do that since I was little. I always knew I was different, Claire. That was why I took the Viceprus hunting job without questioning it too much. My mother always believed that mythical creatures were alive in this world, and so I believed in them, too. I guess I now have proof that she was right."

Claire watched him, unsure of how to respond. He'd never told her this much about himself before. In fact, he'd never strung this many sentences together in a conversation with her either.

"Why are you telling me all this?" she asked finally. West shifted uncomfortably.

"I want to trust you, Claire. I'd assumed you were dead when that Viceprus took you, but you somehow survived. I hate to admit it, but you really surprised me. How'd you get away?"

Claire frowned. "I shoved the pin down her throat, West. It wasn't some sort of fluke. I can't believe your confidence in me was that low," she said reproachfully. West's eyes were hard.

"If you had died it would have been my fault. Never mind the fact that you had followed me in the first place, or that you somehow found out about me being a Siren. Your death still would have been on my head, and I couldn't live with that." He ran a hand through his hair, taking a deep breath. When he spoke again, his voice was gentler. "I just...If you disappeared again, or if something happens to you, I want you to know the truth. About me, about everything. Will you hear me out?"

Claire weighed the options. If West told her everything, it would help her find a cure ultimately for Alex, but what use would that be if he was gone? She didn't think she could handle any more secrets. West took her silence as a refusal, and she watched West's fingers work on fixing a bandage underneath her neck. It had been so scary, to stumble through Chicago in the middle of the night looking for a friendly face. She'd never wandered into the part of the city she was in, and if it wasn't for the taxi turning the corner, she might have been dead. West seemed to realize the same thing, because their eyes locked, and his deep blue eyes held a fire she'd never seen in them before.

"Please let me help you, Claire."

Claire stayed silent, wondering whether she could trust him. "Okay."

A memory came to her—after waking up to find herself lying face down on a soft bush, wincing in pain as she clutched her ankle and looked up at the building in front of her, a single wall shattered to pieces. What was the name she'd called? The person she'd cried for so desperately, before fainting onto a bench? Who's face was it that drove her to move on, to try and get away before Ms. Stone found her? *West.* She'd known to keep moving, to keep seeking help, because of him. She'd wanted to live, no matter how much her injuries hurt, because she wanted to see his face again. She'd wanted to *be* with him again. That was enough for her to consent to his hands pulling her close, enveloping her in a strangling hug.

"Can't...breathe..." she muttered half-jokingly, and she felt the rumble in his ribcage as West laughed. She hadn't heard the sound in ages, and it calmed her a bit.

"Sorry," he said as he pulled away from her a moment later, his voice now tinged with a softness she'd never heard before. "Those gashes were deep in some places."

"Were?"

Claire looked down at her body. There wasn't a single scratch on her, and the only thing that hurt was her ankle. She glanced at it, and noticed the sickening purple bruise was almost completely gone. The room spun, and she sank further into her pillows.

"How did you–"

"I wouldn't walk on your ankle, though. I don't think it's completely cured," West said, grinning from ear to ear. She pushed herself up onto her elbows, testing her wrist. It didn't even hurt.

"You are a miracle worker," she told him, and he laughed. The sound seemed ridden with relief. She wrapped her arms around him and gave him a giant hug with her newly repaired arms.

"Thank you."

"No problem," he laughed, breaking away to pull open the curtains in the infirmary. The room flooded with light. This new, light-hearted West was strange to her, but she liked it. It was almost normal.

"West?"

"Mmm?" he asked peacefully, turning to her. Icy grey met warm hazel, and she blushed a little.

"I want you to trust me with whatever you have to say. When you want to talk, I'll listen," she assured him. He only nodded in response, turning again to look out the window. She lay next to West for a while, the silence surrounding them like a comforting blanket. She didn't know how long she'd sat there—all she knew was that neither would break the spell, for fear of losing each other.

Saphirra walked out of grocery store, her arms laden with bags. With the budget she had been given by her father she had barely managed to get enough food for the four of them. She'd debated buying Alex's share of the food but bought it anyway, just in case. She wasn't ready to give up on Alex, even if all signs pointed to it.

As she walked down the city streets back towards the campus, she thought about West, about his hunting job. What if he had gone after Alex, and Ms. Stone had only found the pieces? The thought sent a chill through her. West wouldn't attack his best friend...

Reedhima Mandlik

Would he?

Saphirra turned down a side street, passing by an alleyway as quickly as she could. She wanted to go back to Claire, to ask her more about what she knew. Before she could take another step, however, a familiar voice stopped her in her tracks.

"Saphirra?"

The voice was broken and hoarse, and she whipped around, looking for it. People bustled past her irritably, their voices mingling into a dull buzz. She turned to the alley and saw something move within the damp darkness. She walked slowly into the shadowy crevice between the buildings, watching curiously as the person shifted further into the darkness. It looked like some dark potato sack, or some sort of large garbage bag. When she was close enough to the black, feathery lump, she reached out a tentative hand.

"Be careful, Saph."

Each word pierced through her, and she sank to her knees in pain and shock. She'd hoped she would hear his voice again, but not like this.

"Alex?"

The name made her shake. She clenched her fists and touched the lump. It quivered, and with a snap, both of his wings retracted into his back. Saphirra gasped.

"*Please* listen to me this time when I tell you I'm not feeling like myself," he warned, and Saphirra felt shock radiate through her body. She walked to the other side of Alex, and gaped at him.

He was the Alex she knew and remembered, but he looked so... vicious. Purple rings underlined his eyes, which were glowing bright violet. He was whiter than ever before, and his body tremored under her touch. His eyes widened as he looked her over, whether of fear or surprise, she didn't know.

Alex was *alive*.

Chapter 19
Reliance

Alex couldn't move. He couldn't think. All he knew was that Saphirra had enveloped him in a strangling hug, stifling his common sense.

"Thank goodness you're okay," she said, relief flooding into her voice. They sat there for a long time, Alex stunned into immobility by Saphirra's hug. He didn't know what had come over her.

"I was only gone for a while," he said as confidently as he could, but his voice was hoarse; it scratched at his lungs like bristled wire. He began to cough uncontrollably, and he doubled over at the sudden pain in his stomach. Saphirra backed away from him almost immediately.

"What are you doing in a place like this?" Saphirra gestured wildly at the grim alleyway they were in, trying to keep her voice low enough so the passerby wouldn't stop and stare. Most people weren't stupid enough to duck into a dark alleyway in Chicago anyway, but it didn't hurt to be careful. Alex blinked at her, rubbing his sleep-deprived eyes.

"I fell," he croaked as she touched his forehead lightly with her fingertips, as if checking for a fever. The tenderness in her eyes was alarming. Didn't she know what he'd done to her? Or had she passed it off as a dream, like Alex had nearly done?

"What? Why are you looking at me like that?" Alex asked her, his voice so weak it was barely over a whisper. Saphirra bent closer to him, her expression concerned.

"Well...I thought you were dead, didn't I?" she said quietly. Alex simply stared at her, unsure if he'd heard her correctly.

"What? What would make you think that?"

Saphirra looked up at him, her hand still resting unconsciously on his shoulder. "So she *was* lying..." Saphirra mused, more to herself than to Alex. He shook his head, more confused than ever.

"How could you have thought that I had died?"

As Saphirra explained to him how Ms. Stone had taken Claire and then returned a day later, giving her his cell phone and his mother's ring. It took Alex a moment to realize she had his ring entwined around her neck. Alex's mouth fell open. *That* was how his ring had found its way to Saphirra's neck, and his cell phone had wound up on her bed.

But how had Ms. Stone gotten his things?

He thought back to the last week, trying his hardest to remember. Validus *had* told him visitors were coming, and had told him to hide...

He'd rolled out of his makeshift bed, eyes blurry with sleep. Validus had given him something that had resembled incredibly strong tea a few hours before in the hopes that Alex could maybe find some sleep. It had almost worked...Until Validus decided to interrupt him. Alex glared at his new friend, but Validus wasn't even looking at him. He stood over Alex, looking cautiously over his shoulder. "You've got to hide. You aren't supposed to be here. Hurry up, kid. There's only so long that I can protect you."

Alex had scrambled to his feet and followed Validus into a corner of the small, dimly-lit room. The Viceprus had pushed on the wall, opening a small indent just big enough for a person or two to hide in. Alex peered into it uncertainly.

"Well, what are you waiting for? Go!" Validus ordered, pointing to the tiny space. "I can't have a half-Viceprus running around when members of the Council arrive! Now go!" he shooed Alex in and closed the tiny alcove, suddenly plunging him into total darkness. Alex could barely make out noise in the other room as Validus frantically shuffled about, hiding Alex's things from view. Soon, he heard voices, and knew that people had entered their hideout.

Validus lived with four other Vicepruses in a small house tucked away in the crevices of the hillside, hidden from view by the spray from the roaring Niagara Falls below. The other four hadn't been alerted to his presence, and so Validus had chosen the right time to call Alex to his home; the less people that knew about him, the better. Validus was the only one not at what he called the "Council meeting", for what he had declared as more reasons than one. He'd helped Alex as he'd craved energy the first few days, asking him what had caused him to need so much of it. When Alex had explained about the pills, Validus was not amused.

"Taking pills like that is dangerous. Don't you know *Navitas* is Latin for energy, boy? You walked straight into a death trap. You're lucky you came to me when you did," he said, knowingly tapping his nose. Validus was one of those people that seemed stoic and tough, but would care for anyone that needed it. Despite Alex's obvious stupidity he'd helped him, teaching him how the bitterroot herb would help him stay subdued for long periods of time. He'd promised to answer the rest of Alex's questions after he tried resting, but now Alex wondered if he would ever get the chance to ask anything at all.

Validus's deep booming voice echoed through the small space.

"Welcome Ryan, Evelyn, Aenor. I'm afraid I'll have to entertain you by myself; my companions are still in London, of course." The edge to his voice was unmistakable.

"Of course," a voice replied icily. Alex was shocked at how recognizable the voice sounded, but couldn't quite place a finger on where he'd heard it before. It was achingly familiar, and the thought nagged him, even now. He listened as hard as he could, but couldn't make out any more of the conversation save for a few mentions of the Council. Finally, a voice drew closer to where Alex stood, and he held his breath.

"...be right back. Yeah I know where it is," came a bored, sarcastic voice from the other room. He heard footsteps and waited for them to pass, but they continued to draw closer, finally stopping in the room he was in.

"Interesting." The soft, musing voice was closer to Alex than he would have liked. It was a woman's voice, soft and musical, tinged with a hint of sarcasm. He heard something move in his room and then the footsteps started again, fading off into the hallway.

"I couldn't find the..." The voice faded away again, and Alex sighed and sank back into the tiny space, his heart pounding. When he'd finally been let out of his hiding spot, his ring and phone had disappeared. He'd assumed he'd left it in a drawer somewhere in his haste, but he'd never found it afterward. He hadn't been able to search for it due to Validus's haste to get Alex home before another unwanted Council member appeared. As he told Saphirra what happened she frowned, though out of concern for his still-weak voice or what happened, she didn't know. She curled up next to Alex.

"Saph, I *called* you. Why didn't you check your cell phone?"

"With both you and Claire gone, there wasn't really anyone I cared enough about that I would expect a call or text from," Saphirra told him. "Besides, I got a call but when I traced it back the phone just kept ringing." Saphirra fell silent, her voice shaking. Saphirra had been clutching his ring all this while, and she finally seemed to have noticed it; she released it hastily, a faint blush staining her cheeks. The ring had embedded itself onto her palm, leaving a red circular mark. Saphirra reached behind her neck to untie his necklace and he watched as she fumbled with the knot. Finally he reached behind her and gently pried her hands away, taking the ring off its leather cord and putting it on her finger.

"Keep it. It's my way of saying I'm sorry." He gritted his teeth as another shudder ran through his body, freezing him to the ground. She wrapped her arm around his shoulders and the shivers ceased, just as they had before. He finally felt as if he could move again, something he hadn't been so sure of. As he pulled himself off the ground, Saphirra kept a firm, steady grip on his arm.

"I'm okay," he laughed, reading the worry in Saphirra's eyes. Truthfully he wasn't feeling too well; his vision swam in front of him, and each step was precarious, as if he would fall at any moment.

Still, he would act as if he was fine if it kept that look from Saphirra's face.

As they turned out of the alleyway into the sunlight his headache grew worse. After a few blocks, he could barely walk.

"This sucks," he said through gritted teeth, glaring up at the unrelenting sun. His headache was unbearable in this heat. He staggered a little, leaning unconsciously onto Saphirra. She gave him a worried look.

"Alex, we don't have to move if you don't want to," she said, pointing to a coffee shop down the street. "We can always rest for a while." Her voice was light and cautious, as if she was trying her hardest not to ruin the comfortable feeling that had settled around them like a warm blanket. He nodded wearily and was greeted by blast of cold air as the door chimed open and Saphirra pulled him inside, sitting him in a small booth. He sank into the cushions gratefully as his headache began to ebb away and he could finally look at Saphirra properly.

Dark circles underlined her tired eyes, which were glassy from lack of sleep. Her hair was tied back sloppily in a bun with strands falling out at random. He was tempted to tuck a strand back in.

"Saph, when did Ms. Stone tell you about me being...*gone?*" he whispered the last word, watching her face. She was devoid of emotion as she answered back.

"Two days ago," she said quietly, putting her hand, palm up, casually onto the table. He took it gratefully, smiling as the pleasant heat flooded into his chest. He'd missed her, and the thought left a pang in his heart.

"Are you okay?" he asked finally. She scoffed, looking away towards the coffee counter, where a blender was whirring loudly. She squinted her eyes as if she was trying to read the menu. He gripped her hand tighter, ignoring the tingling feeling that had nothing to do with her energy, and she looked back at him, eyes fathomless.

"I thought you were dead," she said, her voice tight. "Give me a minute."

He sat there watching her, never letting go of her hand. Something was different about the way she looked. As soon as he thought about it, he realized it.

Saphirra's golden aura had disappeared.

He couldn't believe it. He blinked at her, and she gave him a funny look.

"What?"

He simply shook his head, unable to speak. He could still feel her energy coursing through him, so why couldn't he see her aura? He looked around at various customers in the tiny coffee shop, surprised to see a faint glow emitting from every one of them. It was just Saphirra.

"What's wrong?"

"I...I can't see your aura," he said quietly. She looked puzzled.

"What do you mean?"

"Your golden aura! It's gone. I can't understand why." Saphirra looked as confused as he felt, and for a brief moment he wondered if he might have turned her into a Viceprus, after all.

"Alex?" her voice broke into his thoughts. He looked at her, startled by her change in tone. It was almost vulnerable. "I think...I think that maybe...since you'd bitten me, my aura disappeared. Like a mark. You can see everyone else's auras, right?"

Alex nodded solemnly, and Saphirra let go of his hand, twisting the corner of the tablecloth nervously in her fingers. "Maybe it's like you'd claimed me. Like I'd already been bitten, so I'm not new."

"Like...I'd *claimed* you?" he scoffed at the notion. Saphirra blushed.

"I don't know how to explain it...It's like you marked me, I guess. I'm not a valid source of energy anymore, I guess." She laughed to herself. "I don't know what I'm trying to say. Never mind. What did you do? In Ontario, I mean."

He smiled, settling back into the cushion behind him. "It's a long story. Would you like to hear it?" she nodded, and he took a deep breath. "When I arrived, Validus looked a little confused. I don't think he expected me to be back that early." He retold the story, pausing at points to catch his breath.

"He was a tall, burly Viceprus with an impatient smile.

"Who are you?" he asked me curiously, cautiously blocking off the cave entrance. I had had tried and failed to jump over a broken pathway bridge on my way there, so of course I was dripping from head to toe.

'I'm...I just have some questions, okay? I'm new to this stuff,' I said unconvincingly. After another questioning glance from Validus, I grabbed a jagged piece of coal black rock and pulled. It snapped off almost too easily into my hands. With understanding eyes, Validus nodded and gave me wide berth as I made my way in.

'So who are you, really?' I asked him as he sat down next to an old-fashioned fireplace. I sat down next to him and put my hands close to the flames, comforted by the dancing orange glow.

'I am Validus.'

He reached out and touched my shoulder, as if it was the most natural thing in the world. When his hand made contact with my shoulder it felt like I'd been blasted away from his body. I couldn't see anything but darkness; I couldn't move, I couldn't feel, I couldn't think. I had no idea how long he'd sat in the shadows of his mind before Validus lifted his hand from my shoulder, and I was brought back jarringly to reality.

'You may be blinded and your heart may be scarred, but nothing can hold you further from the comfort you seek than yourself,' Validus mumbled in a faraway voice, his violet eyes glazed over and unfocused. I started to speak, but Validus cut me off.

'The girl helped you, didn't she?' he asked me suddenly. I jumped a little, startled.

'What? What do you mean?' I asked him, a little guiltily. 'What did you do to me?'

'Nothing you need to know,' Validus said impatiently. 'You bit her and didn't kill her afterwards? This is bad.'

He turned away from me, apparently thinking he'd given a sufficient explanation. He followed him to the next room.

'*Kill* her? She's my best friend! She's...' I shook my head, realizing how stupid I sounded. Validus didn't hesitate to emphasize that.

'You bit your best friend?' he asked, a stern note to his voice. I didn't know what to say—"

"*Kill* me?" Saphirra screeched, snatching her hand back. People turned around in their chairs, staring at the two of them in the small coffee shop. Alex shushed her.

"Careful! Remember where we are!" he hinted, nodding his head towards the customers. She sank lower in her seat.

"Sorry. Why did he want you to...do *that*?" she asked him nervously. He held out his hand and she took it. He gave her hand a reassuring squeeze.

"He told me why you weren't affected by the bite. Actually, you were, but you don't exactly remember it, do you Saph?"

She stared at him. "What? What are you talking about?" he swallowed nervously.

"If I don't bite someone for long enough to take all the energy from them, they survive. If they survive and they don't know how to block their mind..."

"Block their minds from what?" Saphirra asked nervously. Alex looked away.

"From me."

Saphirra stared at her friend, unable to process his words. Alex's ring burned against her skin, and she was visited by the violent urge to yank it off.

"Finish your sentence," she told him through gritted teeth. "Why should I block my mind from you? What happened to me?"

It was Alex's turn to glance around the small coffee shop, his piercing blue eyes finally fixating on a set of posters on one end of the wall. When he spoke, his voice was barely more than a whisper. "Saphirra, do you remember the last full moon? The one that just passed a day or two ago." She nodded, wary. "No, Saph, I want you to really think. Do you remember *all* of it? Or were there parts you didn't remember or understand? Did you have a very vivid dream?"

"Yeah, but it was just a dream," Saphirra said unconvincingly. Alex sighed irritably.

"Saph, I don't know what I did, and I barely understand how I did it, but I took over you. I was the one who made you walk back down the attic stairs and go into your room. I was the one who put my cell phone in your pocket."

'I took over you'. The words sent shockwaves through her. Alex had controlled her body, without her knowing. All it had taken was a few moments, but it had been enough. And she hadn't even realized it.

"I can't believe this!" she exclaimed, moving to stand up. "Can you take over me by will now? When I'm not thinking of anything, you can just waltz in and make me do things I won't even remember? What did you make me do last night?" she was unable keep the accusatory edge out of her voice. Alex shifted uneasily in his seat.

"Nothing else, I swear. I didn't even know what was going on until I saw my—err, I mean *your* face in your mirror. Your eyes were glowing violet, Saph. It was strange to say the least," he said quietly. Saphirra felt extremely self-conscious and weak at the same time. If she couldn't even have her own body anymore, then what was she? A thought sent a chill down her spine.

"Could you hear my thoughts or see my memories?" Saphirra asked sharply, instinctively shifting her hands under the table. This did not go unnoticed by Alex, who was watching her with a newfound curiosity.

"No, of course not. I took over your senses, not your brain. I couldn't feel pain either. I was overriding *part* of your mind, not taking over your whole body. Until the venom from my bite gets out of your system, I can essentially do what I did on the full moon. At least, that's what Validus told me."

Saphirra shook her head, bewildered. "Venom?"

"From the bite. Didn't you wonder how it healed like that? It's supposed to help extract energy from you or something. The venom affected your brain, and until your body builds up enough cells to repair or fight whatever damage it did, I can take over that part of you. I can see and hear and touch everything you touch, Saph. All you have to do is keep an open mind."

Her horror must have been apparent in her eyes, because he looked away from her, focusing on the wall once again. She wasn't fooled by his stoic tone; the panic in his eyes was clear, and she knew this wasn't a quick lie on Validus's part. The Viceprus had told a lot more to Alex, she could tell. She was just afraid of how much he knew.

Chapter 20
The Fatal Call

West sprinted towards the entrance to yet another building in Chicago, the afternoon sun so piercing that it made his eyes water. *Do all Vicepruses stay in penthouses or something?* West wondered irritably as he stood in front of the "out of order elevator" sign scribbled across the doors. Aggravated, he climbed the stairs one after another, listening to the echoing clang of his footsteps on the rusted metal. The calls were more frequent now, more urgent. It bothered him. West climbed one stairwell after another, anxious to get back to the college, where he could be with Claire. The sound of his ringtone had shattered the silence between them, jolting him to his feet. He'd promised he'd be right back after he took care of this last job, but the look she'd given him was reproachful. It haunted him. He panted his way to the door of the penthouse and paused to calm his breath. His boss had never asked him to kill two Vicepruses in such quick succession before. There would be days at a time where he wouldn't get a single call, and then days when his boss decided to make up for it by asking him to hunt four Vicepruses at a time. What had caused his boss to be so sporadic? It made West constantly question what he was doing. Who was he really working for? He felt his phone vibrate in his pocket and pulled it out, noting the blocked number. There was only one person it could be. He flipped it open wearily, leaning against the wall as she spoke.

"Yeah?"

"West?"

"Who else?" he answered coldly.

"Don't do the job I just assigned. I have something else for you to do."

West swore under his breath. Couldn't his boss have called twenty flights ago? "Well, what is it?" West asked exasperatedly as the pause on the line grew longer. He started going down the steps he'd just climbed as he waited for an answer.

"I told you about that Viceprus. The one that I said you should keep an eye out for—do you remember?"

It took a few moments for West to think back—afternoons were not the best time for him. "Yeah, and?" he prompted, dreading the answer. His boss was no doubt talking about Alex, and he didn't want to deal with that now. When his boss spoke again his voice was cautious, almost suspicious.

"I want you to kill him." He paused at West's sharp intake of breath. "But not right away. Give it a few days, maybe a week. You should be able to find him easily, West. You are my best Hunter for a reason."

"Where?" West hid the resentment in his voice with difficulty. His heart sank.

"He's around Rose University of Chicago a lot. No specific location, but what I know he has unusual hair."

"How *unusual?*" West asked dryly. His boss had never been this cryptic before. It was almost as if he was waiting for something.

"Red hair." Pause. "Bright blue eyes, kind of tall. He shouldn't be so hard to spot if he's on campus. Good luck, and report back in a week. I'll know if he's been taken care of."

West swallowed nervously as the phone clicked shut. He didn't want to tell his boss that Alex was gone, and probably never coming back until the beginning of the school year. *Unless he's decided to disappear completely,* West thought with a shudder. What if he couldn't find Alex this week? What would his boss do? West stopped for a moment, shaking his head at himself. Did he really just consider killing his best friend? Was he so inhumane that he would worry about himself without even thinking of what his boss's order had meant? West jumped the last couple of stairs, landing easily on the floor. He couldn't hurt Alex. He'd find some other way. He just had to.

He sprinted back towards the university, dodging honking cars in his efforts to get there faster. He had a week. He thought about where he was headed, and immediately thought of Claire. He'd promised he'd tell her everything. The thought almost made him smile, but he didn't know why. Talking to Claire lifted a weight on his heart that he wasn't even aware of, but he just didn't know how much he should allow himself to tell her. She was the only one to discover his secret in years; she'd survived a Viceprus kidnapping with only a small pin for aid.

Claire, in short, was his personal miracle.

He passed the entrance to the college, slowing to a walk as he reached the infirmary. He'd promised himself no one could know, because if they did they'd almost definitely get hurt. West thought back, trying to remember the face of her attacker. All he remembered was the burning of her gaze, boring into his heart with such a ferocity that he could only stand there, frozen. Something about her seemed familiar, even though the vicious rain that had surrounded her. *How did she find me here?* He'd been unsettled enough by risking having his prey escape by not killing them; hunters don't leave their prey out in the open. There was a reason his boss usually had him kill and never capture.

Still, someone had found him.

It was unnerving to West. He'd always considered himself infallible, untraceable. He knew the maze of alleyways and back streets in Chicago by heart. He'd been working this job for so long that he knew which streets were easiest for someone to lose themselves in. After five years of wrong turns and run-ins with people he'd rather never have met, he'd learned laying low was the key to avoiding another scar. And after all this time, he'd been found. Was it even safe to stay around the college anymore? If Alex came back, he didn't know what he would do. As he walked the cobblestone path towards the infirmary, a cool breeze played across his face, brushing his arms and twining around his shoulders. He didn't want to leave the one place he knew he could call home. Not after having been displaced so many times in his life. His childhood had been a chaotic mess filled with the constant packing and unpacking of boxes. His mother had always been free-spirited, going wherever her whim took her. He'd assumed she was simply dragging him along for the ride. The thought had never even crossed West's mind that she might have moved from place to place for their protection. He'd learned to lose himself in books rather than try to exchange stories with his mother, who wasn't inclined to start conversations very often. When she did, it was usually about school, or work, or both. He'd stopped asking for his father when he reached his tenth birthday, when he realized the question simply shut his mother down. She refused to talk for hours, which then stretched to days. West remembered fearing she'd lost her voice completely. Silence had always unnerved him, but back then it had been downright unbearable.

It was this same silence that fell between Claire and him that made him want to tell her about things he'd shoved to the back of his mind to gather dust. He'd held on to the foolish hope that the memories would have no reason to resurface, that they'd never have an ounce of importance to him.

As he turned the corner, his gaze fell upon the windows of the sun-lit infirmary, where Claire sat peacefully. As he neared the doors she turned and caught his eye and something in him broke, shattering into a thousand tiny shards that pierced him all over, nearly paralyzing him. It was as if her presence knocked something out of him, leaving him raw and defenseless. She destroyed him from within, and yet encased him with vibrant warmth. It took all he had to walk into the infirmary, to keep from running away. The power she had over him made him both nervous and ridiculously happy all at once and somehow always resulted in an unwanted blush that crept up onto his cheeks.

Claire grinned at him as he walked into the long ward and the shards in his heart splintered into a thousand more, coursing through his veins, numbing him. He didn't trust himself to speak, for fear of stumbling over his words. Instead he sat down next to her, watching her hazel eyes. It was nearly impossible to describe the true effect she had on him. All he knew now was that the pain from the shards had melted away, to be replaced with a new kind of euphoria he couldn't quite place. She didn't speak, and neither did he; it could have been seconds or maybe even minutes before he noticed the silence. It pressed down upon them, subduing any peace they'd had. He fidgeted, then took a deep breath, startled to hear the shakiness in his voice as he spoke. It felt weary.

"I believe I owe you a story."

Claire laughed, sending a tremor through him. "You don't owe me anything."

He touched the scar above her ankle, concentrating until her skin became flawless once more. "I owe you more than you ever know."

She sat up on her elbows, her blonde waves falling over her bare shoulders. If he tilted his head closer, one soft curl would brush his cheek. The thought made him lean away instead, the flush returning to his face. He ran a hand through his hair, avoiding her dancing eyes, avoiding the bright spark of her soul that lay within.

"I think you should begin, then," she said teasingly. He couldn't help but agree.

Ry marched into his destroyed office, outraged.

"What happened?" he spat at Evelyn, who sank lower into her seat. The office was a train wreck. His entire glass wall was smashed to pieces, with bright, glittering shards scattered all over the carpet. A chair, cracked in half, littered the middle of the room, covering a deep red stain. After a moment Evelyn stood, her voice shaking as she spoke.

"I thought I could get it out of her. I didn't think she could hurt me."

"With a *pin,* Evelyn? She nearly killed you! Do you realize how long it will take for your throat to fully heal, even with the salve I gave you? How could you have not known?" he couldn't place where the increased anxiety that had settled in his stomach had stemmed from, but he didn't like it. Evelyn hadn't come that close to death in years. If one slip could cause this much of a drawback...he was right not to trust her.

"It was your Hunter that armed her, Ry. You of all people should know that your Hunter is handing out gifts made with Sunstones." Her voice cut through him like ice. He looked at her, unsure if he'd heard right.

"She got it from who?"

"He gave her the Sunstone pin," Evelyn repeated irritably, coughing a little as she spoke. Her voice was raspy, as if she was just getting over a bad bout of the flu. He felt a twinge of sympathy, but ignored it.

"Why would he do that? He couldn't have gotten any extra Sunstones. Unless..." He paused, thinking back. *West only had the dagger,* Ry thought. *But he wouldn't have gone through all the trouble of picking out the stones and putting it in a different setting...would he?* West was his best and only Hunter for a reason, after all. Ry wouldn't put it past him to want to protect someone who had something to hide. And if he'd suspected that girl was in danger, he'd do anything to keep her from getting hurt, to keep her death from weighing on his conscience.

"He made it," Ry said in a hollow whisper. "He used my own stones against me."

Evelyn seemed to find this amusing; she let out a snort of laughter, which quickly turned into a painful cough. She clutched at her throat, rubbing a thick green paste into her skin.

"Where did you find this, anyway?" she asked curiously, eyeing the salve. "It would have been useful to have this in the winter." She gave him a significant look, and the pang of guilt tugged at him once more. He knew better than anyone how hard it was to get energy in the winter, especially around the holidays. They always waited for New Year's Eve, but they could only siphon energy a few hours at a time, since it was an official Council Day. A mass murder every year would have looked suspicious, after all.

"Bitterroot. I found it growing near Validus's place years ago, and I've been testing it ever since. Only Validus knows all its properties." He shrugged, ignoring the sting he felt whenever he thought of the more accomplished Viceprus. Another member of the High Council he had to be wary of. "More importantly, what did you find out?"

She bowed her head and muttered, "Absolutely nothing. She got to me before then. What happened wasn't my fault. She's too smart for me, always has been. She covered that," she pointed to the flower hairpin, sparkling happily on the floor, "with her hands, which she'd somehow cut open. I moved before I had time to think! Her energy was too strong for me to resist. You know I hadn't had any pure energy in a while. It was a reflex reaction, and I'm sorry."

Ry shook his head at her angrily, his hair falling into his eyes. "Can't you do anything right?" he pressed his fingers to his forehead and took a deep breath. "Did you at least get any information on Saphirra?"

She looked as if she wanted to mention something, but thought against it. He recognized the faint glimmer in her eye—it was the same look that crossed his face when he withheld information.

"What are you not telling me?" he growled at her, shaking with rage. At her continued silence, he bent down and picked up a shard of glass, twisting it around in his fingers. With a sharp flick of his wrist, he pelted it across the room at Evelyn, who dodged it easily. The look she gave him was murderous.

"Honestly, I don't even know why I keep you around," he murmured. He turned to face her exasperatedly, and found her massaging her neck, looking hurt.

"At least I *tried* to kill her. I tried, okay? So don't blame me for instinct, and shut the hell up," she said coldly, getting up from her chair. Ry watched her, taken aback. Had this fury been building within her for years, and he'd simply failed to notice it? Ry watched her with a new found interest, and she glared back at him.

"What? Are you going to blame me for the hole in the ozone, too? Or maybe global warming, while you're at it? Why don't you just blame me for other things like that that aren't under my control?" She stopped talking as he moved closer involuntarily. She stared up at him in surprise, eyeing him suspiciously.

"Tell me?" he murmured, giving her his best penetrating gaze. She seemed entranced for a moment, on the verge of speech. Then something seemed to snap within her, breaking his concentration. This wasn't enough. He pressed closer, his eyes searching her face for some sort of weakness, some sort of break. She'd never fought this hard to keep something hidden. He couldn't stand it. He touched her arm and she jerked away. He was surprised; she'd never done that, either. He took advantage of her temporarily taken aback stance to let his hand brush across her cheek, shocked to feel the warmth that just bordered on pain at the touch of her skin. Her hand floated to catch his, this time less guarded than before. Ry leaned in and let his lips meet hers, his mouth moving persuasively against her own. Evelyn's lips opened at his touch and her sweet breath washed over him, leaving him temporarily dazed. This feeling was new, too. She pulled away from him, eyes hard.

"What was that for?" her voice had a sharp edge to it, and Ry was surprised to find that he liked that too.

"I want to know." He shrugged and smiled, but Evelyn's expression didn't waver.

"You of all people know not to disclose information that's best left alone. Not if it's essential, anyway," she said teasingly, her stoic expression faltering, giving way to a playful grin. Ry was taken aback. For the past twenty years, she had never rejected him so completely. Until now.

"Is that supposed to be a good thing?" he asked incredulously. Evelyn gave him a wicked smile.

"A very good thing."

"The first thing I have to do is teach you to guard your mind," Alex told Saphirra matter-of-factly, waving a blade of grass in her face. They had left the coffee shop and were now stretched out on the grass behind one of the buildings on campus, tired of attempting to talk over the whirr of the blender. Saphirra frowned and reached out for his hand, encasing it within her own. The tingling warmth that rushed through her had nothing to do with the sun, so high and hot above them. Alex grinned and let his hand drop to his side. "You've got to be able to stop me from breaking in."

"Why can't you stop yourself?" Saphirra asked dryly. The last thing she wanted was for Alex to break into her thoughts. Alex laughed again, which sparked a prickle of irritation in her. He seemed to be finding all this a lot funnier than she thought it was.

"I can't. That's the whole point. I was just pulled in. One second I was next to Validus, asking him about bitterroot, and the next I was you." He seemed unsure of how she would take it, so he plunged on before she could respond. "When I came to, Validus said I had been sitting still for hours, just watching the sky. I hadn't moved at all; it was as if I was a statue. It was then that he explained my mistake." He shrugged. "I bit you for a few seconds, at least. That was enough for me to get your energy and leave my venom in your system, but not enough to kill you. As long as you block your mind, I won't be able to do what I did that night again. Validus said it gets easier for me as the nights go on. He even said if I kept breaking into your mind I'd eventually take over you completely." His voice was devoid of emotion, and she resisted the urge to laugh. She wouldn't have believed he could break into her mind if he hadn't already done it once. Resigned, she twisted to face him.

"But you bit me a month ago," she said cautiously. "It didn't happen then, right? Or did it?" she added as an afterthought, shuddering. He laughed and shook his head, smiling.

"I only became aware of it when I needed the energy, when I was starved of it. Now that I'm aware of it, though, I don't know if I'll be able to stop myself."

"I don't understand," said Saphirra. Alex frowned, thinking hard.

"Let's say you walk to the store down the block every day, and didn't think twice about it. If you suddenly found out there was a shortcut, but it was dangerous, you'd contemplate taking it anyway, right?"

"What if you chose to not take it?"

"Doesn't matter. The fact that it exists is still in your mind, and you'll keep thinking about it, whether you want to or not. And that's enough for something like this. If I think about it and I'm weak enough, pure adrenaline would get me in, even if I didn't want to."

She nodded, smiling at his terrible analogy. Still, she understood a little.

"Okay. How do I do it?" she asked cautiously. Alex squinted at her through the strong sunlight.

"Well, Validus said there's a few ways, but they were never truly tested. Only one of the Vicepruses he lived with in Ontario could explain them to me." He shifted to his elbow, considering her. "You won't like it."

Saphirra sighed. "Let me hear it, at least."

"You have to tell me whatever it is you're so scared of. When you hide something you watch yourself at every moment, checking to make sure you don't give away any clues." Almost as if on cue, Saphirra unconsciously shifted her arms from view. Alex nodded to them, and she blushed. "See what I mean? The problem is, your mind is just as open, if not more so, when you sleep. Tense by day, relaxed by night. The less you have to worry about the easier it will be for you to protect yourself unconsciously."

"Who told you this?" Saphirra asked suspiciously. Alex laughed again, and the sound mingled with the light breeze, sweeping through the quad, through her hair, through the grass around them. She suddenly felt very light.

"Fama. One of the Vicepruses." He didn't seem inclined to say more, so she swallowed her newest barrage of questions, unsure of what to say next. She couldn't tell him everything. Not yet, anyway. He seemed to understand this and sat up, yawning slightly.

"Think about it, okay? You don't have to trust me. Still, it might be better than me coming around as you every night."

Her heart felt leaden as she watched him get up and walk off towards the kitchens. Half of her wanted to call him back, to apologize, but what could she say? She wasn't ready to tell him about her past. She couldn't even try to think about it herself. She rolled back in the grass, watching cotton fluffs float through the sky. It reminded her of his eyes, wintry blue and piercing. She closed her eyes and grimaced, torn. No matter what she decided, she knew she would have to tell him. And soon.

Chapter 21
Losing Control

"Claire, it might be a long story. Are you sure you don't want to rest first?" West asked her cautiously. He sat perched on the edge of her bed, his eyes stormier than ever. Claire settled back into her pillows, smiling up at him.

"I don't think I could get you to tell me again if I asked. Trust me, I'm okay," she assured him. He looked out the window, almost as if he was preparing himself. When he turned to her again, his eyes were carefully blank.

"I was born without a father. My mother worked two jobs just to keep us alive, and it would have been enough if we hadn't moved all the time. We moved, a lot." He stopped for a moment, shaking his head, frustrated. "No, that's not right...Can I start over? I..." his eyes became clouded again as he struggled with his words, "I can't think of where to begin..." The tone of his voice was so desolate that Claire almost told him to stop, to keep it inside. Almost.

"Take your time," she said instead. West nodded and fell silent, fidgeting with the edge of her blanket. They sat together like that for a while until West spoke up abruptly.

"Like I said, we moved a lot. It was always just my mother and I. At first, I would ask where my father was. My mother came up with tireless excuses, ranging from business trips to long vacations, until she finally had to tell me the biggest lie of all—the lie that would stick with me for ten years.

"I don't blame her for it. After all, she couldn't exactly explain it herself. She'd always read mythology books to me, and I'd always paid more attention to the hero than anyone else. She read me the works of Homer, and I began to envision my father as someone like Odysseus, who'd abandoned his family to go on the next greatest adventure and rid the world of evil." He got a faraway look in his eyes then, and for a moment Claire thought he wouldn't continue, that he would return to his snappish behavior and act as if none of this had even happened. She half expected him to walk out the door and never look back. He didn't move. After a few minutes he spoke again, his eyes trained on the windows.

"It was then that my mother told me Dad was gone, that he wouldn't come back. She never told me he'd died, because she didn't know. Hell, she still doesn't know. I don't know what to tell her..." he trailed off, swallowing nervously, and then continued. "I didn't know what to think. I was only nine, maybe ten, after all. I threw myself into books, knowing that a different world would be easier to live in than the reality I was currently stuck in. When one book ended I simply grabbed another, fearful of the reality that had set upon me like a weighing stone. This was made easier by my lack of friends, since my mom and I continually moved from place to place. I had no one to distract me, and so I stayed in my world of books.

"When I grew tired of them, I found a new preoccupation—studying. Textbooks were almost an adventure for me, and I learned to hunt for things teachers usually didn't even bother to cover. I could live knowing my father was gone if I tricked myself into thinking I had his mind, his command over every subject. I built up an image of my father in my head, something even the bravest man couldn't reach. It was a ridiculously large expectation for anyone to live up to, but as a bookish boy of twelve I had nothing else to believe in. I knew I could look up to my mother, but back then all I saw her as was a hindrance, someone restricting how much money I could spend, and where I could go. As I grew older I began to abandon my books, searching for destroyed souls like myself. I didn't have to look far." He stopped then, rubbing his eyes almost sleepily. Claire noted the darkening sky, surprised at how fast night had fallen. When was the last time she'd looked out the windows? She looked at West's tired face, and realized he'd been talking for almost ten minutes straight. The silence permeated the room, prickling at them uncomfortably. West ran a hand through his hair, eyes darting from window to floor and back again.

"Please say something," he pleaded, his voice quivering slightly. She took his hand but, unsure of he wanted her to or not, dropped it again. He looked at her imploringly.

"I don't know what to say," she said, surprised to hear her voice was shaking. She drew her legs to her underneath the blanket, hugging them protectively. "Please don't stop now," she added hastily, afraid that he would shut down, that she would never be able to understand him. He looked into her eyes, and she was startled to see that they were fathomless and dark, filled with something much deeper than sorrow. She shifted uneasily under his gaze, unsettled by the way he seemed to look through her, into her very soul. It pierced her like an arrow. West sighed, resigned.

"You don't have to hear this," he said quietly. Claire shook her head, saying adamantly, "I want to, West. Please, just trust me."

West nodded, almost to himself, and before she could take a breath his voice had filled the room once more.

"I began to neglect schoolwork. My grades dropped, but of course my mother never noticed. She was too busy working. Instead of helping her, I was idiotic and complained, always complained." His voice was tinged with bitter regret. "It wasn't until I turned fifteen that I was truly scared back to my senses. And this time, from my mother.

"I heard the first sign that something unusual was going on when I went home early from school one day. There my mother was, bustling about the kitchen as if she spent every day like this. It was almost eerie, seeing her at home so early. When I walked in she smiled this bright cheery smile, as if something had gone right for once. But the situation was just the opposite. Her smile seemed forced. Something had gone wrong, terribly wrong. It wasn't until I stepped into the kitchen that I saw we had a visitor. I never knew his name, or what he had been there for. Still, I could take a few guesses. He might have been sent there to scare my mother into what she had been putting off for quite a while. It was a job offer—no, an *order*. I had to take the job, or my mother would be killed. It was some sort of debt I owed because of my father." His voice faltered as he gazed at the same spot on the glass, his eyes glassy and his expression impassive. He was like some great still statue, sitting at the foot of her bed. Claire waited patiently until he spoke again, suspecting he didn't like the silence any more than she did.

"The first thing my boss had me do was train. I went to a weapon's master on the north side of town. He was anything but normal..." West trailed off, his eyes glazed. After a moment of silence, he cleared his throat and continued. "I learned to fight with my dagger, to handle it with great care. I learned which parts could be used to blind the Viceprus, and where to thrust my dagger to kill." He began to count off his fingers. "The heart. The neck. A twist in their back. A jab to their leg. A slice down their abdomen. None of these would be effective if I didn't have the right kind of dagger. My master made it very clear. I got used to not knowing the names of my superiors, just as I had gotten used to the ominous absence of both my mother and my father. I fell into an easy routine, knowing if I didn't my family would be killed. My mother was all I had left, and my superiors knew it. They reminded me of it daily."

"Didn't you wonder what you would have to do, why you were being trained?" Claire interrupted finally, unable to keep her barrage of questions under control anymore. "Didn't it seem suspicious to you, that you were being trained to kill?"

West seemed relieved that she had interrupted and swept a hand through his hair with ease. "When you have nothing to lose, even the most ridiculous request seems reasonable. Especially if it was the only thing keeping my life from being torn apart. I didn't care if I was being recruited into a gang, or if I was being trained for some other malicious intent; all I knew was that I finally had a way to keep my mother safe."

Claire nodded, sinking back into her pillows. She hadn't realized that she had been leaning towards him until she'd broken the spellbinding power of his voice by her inquiry. She felt herself blush, but she wasn't sure why. When it was clear that she had no more questions, West continued, sounding more tired than ever.

"I was ready for my first assignment. By the time I had gotten it, the word *kill* didn't bother me anymore. It was almost normal. I was sixteen, and I had committed my first murder. The Viceprus was the one I had seen in my apartment the day everything began. The second one I murdered was a man...my weapon's master. Somehow, I expected it. I was ready for it. I was unfazed." He began to rip tiny flyaway threads from Claire's blanket unconsciously, each thread bigger than the last. She watched his hands as they methodically unraveled the corner of the sheet. "When I was seventeen, I began to wonder if I should kill so blindly." Rip. "It was the first crack I had experienced through my numb shell, and I hurried to patch it up with excuses. My mother needed me, my livelihood depended on it, and the job was bringing in money to the family. All of these were valid excuses, but not moral ones. I killed out of my own selfishness and greed." Rip. "I wanted a better life for my mom. She had finally been able to quit her second job because of me. I hoped if I got into a good enough university and did something worthwhile, we would have enough to move away again and hide for good." The edge of the sheet finally tore. The sound echoed through the silent room like a gunshot, and West looked down at the corner of the sheet in his hands, as if startled to see it there. "When I got to the university, I thought I might be able to ditch the job and start over. I assumed my boss didn't want me anymore. Then all this happened." He gestured around him, then to her. "I didn't mean for you to get hurt, Claire. That was the last thing I wanted you to do. I even kept you from thinking too much about Vicepruses." With a furtive guilty look, he pulled something out of his pocket and pressed it into her palm. She unfolded the slightly crinkly piece of paper, running a fingertip along its familiar torn edge.

"When did you take this?" she asked sharply, eyeing the drawing. It was the one ripped out of her sketchbook, the one she had been working on when she and West had first met.

"About a day or two after I saw it," West said regretfully. "I couldn't think of another way for you to not think about it." Claire's pulse sped up.

"Were you the one who had ripped out everything on Vicepruses in the library? Did you crash the computers with that virus on purpose?" she asked, her voice rising angrily. West looked taken aback at her abrupt change in tone.

"No?" he said, confused. "I didn't touch any of the books in the library, and I couldn't hack computers if I tried. I swear I opened that virus on accident. It was sent to me through this random email." He stopped for a moment, eying her suspiciously. "Why were you looking up information on Vicepruses, anyway?"

Claire was spared having to answer by a flash of red hair out of the corner of her eye. West saw it, too, and sat up rather suddenly.

"Alex?" he whispered softly, sounding horrified. Claire tried to get a glimpse of his expression but he had gotten up already, hurrying towards the door. She watched him practically sprint outside, embracing Alex in a bear hug. Alex looked startled, then confused, then finally settled on patting West awkwardly on the back until his friend let him go. Claire sighed in relief. She had been so close to telling West Alex's secret. She watched the scene in the courtyard from her bed, wishing she was out there with West. *Alex is back.* She would have put it off as a sleep-deprived hallucination, but there was no need; moments later her living, breathing proof walked straight into the infirmary.

Clandestine listened to Evelyn's screams echo off the walls of the cellar, her fury drowning out all other emotion. She was counting on Ryan punishing Evelyn, maybe even killing her off for good. Somewhere along the way, he'd gone soft. The thought sparked another prick of irritation within her. Well, she would do it, and do it properly. With another flash of gold from her eyes, Evelyn dragged Clandestine's Sunstone dagger across the smooth skin of her wrist, screaming helplessly as a seam of pure sunlight poured out of her.

"Stop! Please, please stop..." She sobbed, her honey–brown hair falling into her face in disarray. Clandestine coldly looked on.

"What did you find at Validus's hideout?" she hissed, her expression livid. Evelyn didn't answer, and Clandestine made her pierce her other wrist. Her scream of pain seemed to rattle the stone walls around her, but Clandestine smiled frostily, concentrating hard on the struggling woman in front of her. A snake of gold flitted through her purple eyes as she spoke.

"Tell me, you ignorant girl."

"Nothing," Evelyn gasped, her violet eyes wide with fear. "Nothing, I swear."

"You lie," Clandestine hissed, narrowing her eyes on the writhing form. "And for god's sake, *stop moving*." Her voice was sweet and dangerous as she spoke, and Evelyn fell silent and limp, her body still shaking slightly as she watched Clandestine with fearful eyes.

"Good. Now, give me that dagger." It was a command Evelyn couldn't refuse. She staggered towards Clandestine, holding out the small silver knife. It's pointed golden tip was as beautiful as it was deadly. Clandestine took it lithely and then commanded,

"Kneel. Then don't move."

Evelyn kneeled like a frozen statue, and Clandestine took the tip of her dagger and traced it along Evelyn's white skin. She gasped in pain, and Clandestine smiled. With the golden tip of her dagger, Clandestine slowly carved an elaborate C into her neck. She watched the C glow for a moment, shining as if the sun was captive in her skin, and as it started to fade, Evelyn's screams pierced her ears.

"Fascinating. It actually shines like sunbeams," Clandestine murmured, watching the C sink into Evelyn's white skin. "This will not fade until you tell the truth," she said haughtily, throwing the dagger across the room, which made a metallic clang as it hit the opposite wall. "And believe me, I *will* know the truth one way or another." *She is such a waste.* Clandestine thought sourly, pacing around Evelyn. She only whimpered in response. Clandestine had concentrated with all her might, and still Evelyn had managed to tell her nothing. Either Evelyn's mind had learned to match her own, or...Clandestine shook her head, dismissing the thought. Her power worked fine over Ryan, didn't it? It should work the same for Evelyn. Still, Clandestine waited for a long moment before giving up completely. "You will not remember me, or the conversation we have just had. You will, however, think Ryan Lockson did this to you." With a flash of gold, Evelyn crumpled to the ground. Evelyn's eyes closed, and as Clandestine's powers took their course, she walked away. As long as Ryan didn't recognize her, her efforts would not be fruitless.

She climbed the stairs up to Ryan's office, glancing around amusedly at the wreckage no one had bothered to clean up. She had expected him to be there, waiting for her. More than likely he was out somewhere in the crowd. Sighing exasperatedly, she set off down the stairs again, out of the building and into the busy street.

Unlike Ryan, her appearance was much more obvious; people immediately began to stare at her as she wove her way through the crowd, searching for the telltale tuft of black hair. Although the real Sirens never had the bird–like, fish–like appearance that Odysseus and many others had come to believe was their true form, they still kept some powers. The ability to lure humans by looks, for one. For another, they had the ability to sing alluring notes that addled the brain, doing different things depending on the pitch. They depended on souls for sustenance. Sirens couldn't life forever, after all. None of them could. They needed human souls to keep on living, once every six months or so. Some of the original Sirens, such as herself and her brother, were able to turn nearly anyone into a worthless lapdog, willing to bend to their will at the snap of a finger. Finally she spotted him, waiting idly at a deserted bus stop. She neared him and he looked up eagerly, then suspiciously as he had no doubt noticed her aura.

"What do you want, Siren?" Ryan demanded, not even bothering to look at her. Clandestine spun him around, and as his golden eyes met her violet ones, he froze. Her eyes flashed, and a vacant expression replaced his suspicious one.

"Call him. Make him do it this week, preferably as soon as possible. You only have *one* week. If he isn't dead by that time, you will be," her voice was normal, so as not to trigger his memory with a high, girly falsetto. She wondered idly if threats would really work against him. It seemed improbable that Waterford would be dead by this week, but if Ryan's Hunter managed it...

"I already told him he had a week, and now you want me to tell my Hunter to kill him off immediately? Why?" Ryan asked blankly. This was strange; usually those under her controlling gaze didn't make suggestions...or think for themselves, for that matter. She concentrated harder as she repeated,

"I have my reasons, but if it cannot be done, then a week is your deadline. You won't remember me, or me telling you any of this. You will think it is your own idea. Just do it," she ordered. Ryan sank to the gravel below. Smiling slightly, she took off, leaving her most useful tool behind her. Everything was falling into place.

Chapter 22
Falling

"West!"

Relief, wonderful relief swept through Alex as his friend ran toward him, nearly tackling him into the grass in his haste. As West looked him over with his tired grey eyes, Alex hesitated. West's aura was dark and threatening, despite his friendly grin. The concern West showed over Alex's reappearance was unusual as well. He shouldn't be so relieved that Alex had come back when he did. He gave a sidelong glance to Saphirra, who shrugged almost imperceptibly, as if she too couldn't explain West's strange behavior. *So he doesn't know.* Alex didn't know whether to feel reassured or anxious at this thought; after everything, he still had pretenses to keep. The thought was almost unbearable after all that had happened.

"Hi!" West said brightly, clapping Alex on the back. He stumbled a little, wary of this new side to West. He hadn't been this cheery in a while. Alex grinned up at him.

"To what do I owe this enthusiastic welcome?" he joked. West smiled sheepishly, running a hand through his hair.

"It was weird not seeing you every day, I guess," he said finally, not meeting Alex's eyes. He glanced at Saphirra again, giving her a look. *Are you sure?*

She shrugged and shook her head again, mouthing *I didn't say a word.* Alex moved to sit down on a bench and West followed suit, his gaze constantly traveling back to the infirmary.

"So how is Claire now? Is her ankle still healing? I heard she took a nasty fall," Alex asked nonchalantly, gauging West's reaction. He kept his expression smooth, but not before Alex noticed a flicker of discomfort. So it was true. West knew Claire had been attacked, and probably by something he'd considered as not natural. For all he knew, West could be rejecting the idea that Vicepruses exist that that very moment. Alex could practically see the gears whirring in West's brain, trying to deflect anything that could lead to the supernatural. West was too practical to believe in that sort of thing.

"We should go in and see her," came West's abrupt answer. Before Alex could say anything he'd stood up and walked towards the large oaken doors, not hesitating for Saphirra or Alex to catch up. As Alex made to go after him, Saphirra caught his arm.

"There's something you need to know," she whispered urgently. He shrugged away and began walking towards West again, who was now waiting impatiently at the doorway.

"Not now, Saph. Tell me later, okay?"

"It's about West."

Alex slowed down, searching her face. Saphirra's blazing green eyes bore through him pleadingly, silently begging him to stop before it was too late. He opened his mouth to question her, but West interrupted him.

"What are you guys doing? Come on, she won't be awake for much longer."

As West rushed them into the infirmary, Alex saw Claire's bed, pushed to the back of the ward. A nest of pillows surrounded her slight frame, making her look incredibly fragile. At the sight of them her face lit up.

"Alex! You're here!" she said delightedly, shifting until she was upright. Other than her disheveled appearance, Alex couldn't see any lasting damage from whatever her attacker had done to her. Saphirra hadn't been able to explain anything about how she had been taken or how she got back in one piece. Alex looked at her, confused, as West and Claire started up a conversation. She should have looked more wrecked than this. Saphirra hadn't mentioned any fuss over Claire's disappearance from West's end, which seemed odd. Surely she would have a complaint or two over how hard it would have been to keep West from calling the police, wouldn't she? He watched Saphirra join into the conversation, but couldn't catch her eye again. He would just have to wait until Claire could tell him himself.

"...don't you think? Alex? Alex!" West said, obviously irritated by Alex's lack of response. He shrugged apologetically.

"Sorry, what was that?"

"Don't you think Claire should switch her major? I mean, anthropology is fine, but—damn." He cut himself off as his shrill ring tone cut through their conversation and pulled away, practically sprinting towards the door. Claire rolled her eyes as the door slammed shut behind him.

"So what really happened?" Alex asked, moving to sit on the edge of Claire's bed. Claire checked to make sure West was out walking in the quad again before answering.

"Ms. Stone is a Viceprus, Alex. She took me from here a day or two after you left. She thought I'd have information on you or—" She stopped suddenly and froze, as if she didn't want to say any more. Alex sighed impatiently.

"And then Ms. Stone told you..." Saphirra prompted. Claire hurriedly continued, explaining to Alex how she'd managed to escape. Something was missing from her story; she kept looking away from him as she spoke, as if she couldn't bring herself to meet Alex's eyes.

"How did you manage to get away by only using a pin?" Alex asked suddenly. Saphirra and Claire exchanged a quick glance.

"I don't know. Come to think of it, that *is* weird," Claire said thoughtfully, leaning back against the bed frame. Once again, she refused to meet his eyes.

"Where did you get the pin from?"

When it was clear that Claire wouldn't answer, Saphirra piped up. "Alex, that's what I was trying to tell you. She got it from West. He's—"

"Great!" Claire blurted. "He made it for me." Alex watched them exchange another glance, even more puzzled than before. Why would West be able to make a pin so sharp that it would puncture Ms. Stone's throat? Unless...Validus had told Alex about the rare stones around the same time that he had explained the properties of the bitterroot herb. Validus had warned that using it was the quickest way for a Viceprus to die.

"What was the color of the stone on the pin?" Alex asked abruptly, interrupting their silent exchange. Claire bit her lip.

"Yellow. Actually...Gold." She seemed inclined to say more, but Alex had heard enough.

"I'll be right back."

"Wait!" Saphirra cried, but it was too late; Alex had already slammed the infirmary doors open and was taking the long, loping steps down two at a time, scanning the quad in front of him. He had to catch up to West, to ask him how he'd made the pin. More importantly, he had to know why his best friend was suddenly in possession of something that could kill him, and why he'd given Claire a pin embedded with them.

What was West doing with Sunstones?

"You should have told him," Saphirra told Claire sternly. It had been hours since Alex had left to no doubt go looking for West. Saphirra had gone out to do her daily errands with the vain hope that she would find either of them and warn one about the other before it was too late. She had returned to the infirmary just as the sun had set, dumping her groceries on a counter, and hoping for some good news. It had proved to be disappointing, however; Claire hadn't seen them, either.

"I know I should have," Claire sighed, defeated. "I couldn't bring myself to do it. I don't know why. When I told you I was still a little scared. I couldn't help telling you something like this. But you saw how Alex reacted just now. What if he knew for sure? What would he do?" Claire's voice wobbled, but Saphirra couldn't think of any way to comfort her. For all they knew, Alex could have figured it out already. Did he know, or was he simply going on his vague suspicions?

"Why didn't you?" Saphirra asked quietly, turning to face Claire. Her friend kept her eyes trained on the rapidly darkening sky as she spoke.

"Saphirra, if they knew about each other, it would be chaos. Alex might already have figured it out. It's a matter of time before the hunter is hunted." She shuddered. "I don't know what to do."

Saphirra put a comforting arm around Claire's shoulder. "We'll figure this out, Claire. They're best friends. They won't hurt each other." Saphirra tried to keep the edge of uncertainty out of her voice, forcing a jovial smile instead. Claire returned her smile shakily, her eyes drifting once again to the darkening quad. Saphirra gathered up the groceries that she had brought with her and began walking to the door, balancing her bags with her knee.

"I'm going to make a snack or something. Do you want anything?"

"No, I'm fine," Claire replied indifferently. Saphirra shrugged and walked towards the Union, still scanning the quad for her missing friends. *Where could he be?* She wondered, pulling the doors open. It wasn't like Alex to simply run off without offering an explanation. As she peered around the quiet study area swathed in darkness, she found it to be empty as well. As she entered the desolate kitchens in the basement of the Union and put away her groceries, she couldn't help wondering if he was with West right now. Would Alex confront his best friend, or leave him be? What would West do if he found out about him?

He could already know, Saphirra reasoned, piling bread and cheese onto a plate. After all, West was smart. He would notice Alex disappearing every night only to return the next day looking worse than the last. Saphirra looked down at her half-made sandwiches, her appetite vanishing. *How could we have been so stupid?* Saphirra's heart sank. Of course West would have figured something was wrong by now. What they had been doing was much too obvious, even with the precautions they had taken. What if West was trained?

Come to think of it, she didn't know anything about West at all. Did Claire know more than she let on? What else was West Anastos hiding? Saphirra slumped down onto the table. The situation was so muddled that she felt like she was walking blindly into a storm. Ms. Stone could waltz back in at any moment and finish any of them off, and no one could do anything about it. What sickened Saphirra the most was that there was an apparent method to Professor Lockson's madness; bit by bit, he would consume their lives, destroying them from within. No doubt the nurse worked for him, or with him. How many other Vicepruses worked around their university? What else did they not know?

Saphirra felt sluggish and exhausted. The events within the past few hours had drained her of all the energy she had, and Alex definitely hadn't helped that. The relief she had felt at his return had been too much, too soon. The emotions had crashed into her all at once; fatigue, restlessness, curiosity, and most of all, a strange warmth that had swept through her like a blanket, erasing all traces of anxiety from her. That feeling was long gone now, replaced once more by a seemingly permanent worry that threatened to overwhelm her. She rested her head down on her arms, ignoring the forgotten sandwiches. She didn't want to move or think. She wanted Lockson and Stone to vanish and never return. Saphirra didn't know what she would do if the professor *did* come back. She was ashamed to say she hadn't thought that far ahead. He could go after Alex this time or maybe even West. Anyone she was close to was a danger.

She pulled the sleeves of her sweatshirt down over her scarred arms, hugging the soft material to herself. She had always had a knack of hurting the people she cared about the most, and they had always shied away from her. *Everyone but Alex.* He'd been the one to give her space when she needed it, to talk to her even when she wouldn't respond. He had the strange way of knowing something was wrong even when she didn't know what it was herself. His eyes had a way of shattering her from within, breaking a barrier she didn't even know she had. She couldn't explain how it felt to be around him; it was almost like being surrounded by a warm blanket. A blanket in a cozy fort made of pillows, with a cup of hot chocolate in your hand. It was that security, that childlike feeling of contentment that she missed now. She wished he was sitting beside her, joking about her poorly made sandwiches, gazing at her with those piercing eyes of his. She knew he'd see something was wrong now, that her tiredness had less to do with him and more to do with her nightmares. It was the same one every night. She shook her head, as if it would help to clear the memory away, and shut her eyes instead, resting her head on the smooth, cold surface of the table. If she fell asleep now, Claire wouldn't mind. Claire could wait for her sandwich for another half hour, couldn't she? Something told Saphirra that she would wait longer, if possible, to prolong eating another one of her sandwiches. Smiling, she allowed herself to drift off.

Alex peered over the edge of the slippery stone, waiting. *He's been in there for hours,* Alex thought irritably. *What could he possibly be doing?* It was an accountant's office building, after all. There wasn't much for him to do as it is. Alex sat back dejectedly onto the rooftop, careful not to slip for fear of falling. The stars already shone brightly in the darkening sky, the crescent moon barely lighting the musty alley West had disappeared into. Alex told himself he would wait for a little longer, just in case. After all, West couldn't stay in there forever.

He'd followed his friend to the building as covertly as possible, dodging in slim shadows and taking flight whenever he could. Still, West had managed to nearly lose him almost twice. Alex had to hand it to him; his friend knew how to deter trackers—novice ones, at least. West had finally stepped into the doorway of a building after looking carefully over his shoulder around four hours ago, and hadn't emerged since. Alex had taken his post along the rooftop of its neighboring building, inching his way along the slippery glass until he had a good view of both the front and side entrances. After hours of waiting, however, Alex could feel his eyes drooping. The slim, energy-efficient glass was pleasantly warm in the cool night air, making it harder than ever to concentrate.

Alex listened hard, waiting to hear some sort of screeching, grating nuisance that would confirm his suspicions. Why else would West have copious amounts of sunstones, enough to arm an unwitting Claire with? *He can't be a Hunter, though,* Alex thought uncertainly. If he was, then wouldn't he have noticed a change in Alex right away, and done something about it? He had plenty of opportunities to kill Alex over the course of the past few months. West couldn't have known.

But it would explain where he keeps running off to, Alex reasoned. West's continued unexplained absences were only further proof that he could have been called out on a job. Still, Validus had told Alex that the League of Hunters were ruthless and scarce. What would cause them to choose a nineteen year old? None of it made sense. West wasn't ruthless, just logical. He wasn't cruel, simply blunt. West had a good heart, and Alex knew he wouldn't hurt people. Why, then, did all signs point to West being a Hunter? None of it was making sense.

Alex lay his head down, closing his eyes wearily. He hadn't felt this exhausted in weeks. His body itched for sleep, and yet he couldn't even if he tried. The feeling was unnerving. He got up once more to stretch, but slumped quickly back down against the glass, enjoying the warmth. He tried to clear his head, wary of jumping to conclusions. What had Saphirra been about to tell him? Something about West?

Saphirra.

It was so sudden that Alex barely had time to react. He began to hear a faint noise, almost as if someone was whispering to him.

"*No, please.* Please!"

It was Saphirra's voice, but from where? Alex whirled around, looking for her familiar face, but by the time he had realized what was truly happening it was too late; he was sucked in once more.

He opened his eyes to find himself in a white room, the voices in the other room so fast and low that all he could hear was a faint buzz. Something shattered through the silence, and he felt himself walking towards the noise, but he couldn't control himself this time. The same black hair hung around his face, only this time it was shorter. He passed by a mirror, and tried to move his head to catch his reflection, but only got a peripheral view—he was Saphirra, but somehow shorter. *That doesn't seem right.* Last time this happened, he had been able to move by himself. Where was Saphirra?

"Jade, don't do this again!"

A gruff, low voice was issuing from the other side of the door. Saphirra lifted her hand to rest it on the door, opening it only a crack. She looked down, and Alex noticed her forearm, unblemished. As Saphirra peered in, a woman with straight black hair stood behind the counter, her knuckles gripping the counter so hard they were white. *Saphirra's mother.* But...her mother was dead. *Am I somehow in Saphirra's past? A memory, maybe?* Alex reasoned with himself. He didn't want to continue watching, but it was no use; Saphirra put her eye to the crack in the door and waited. Alex saw, through her eyes, a glimpse of a leather jacket, worn at the elbows, resting peacefully on the countertop.

Glass was everywhere, framing a sticky liquid that had spilled onto the floor. Voices pierced his ears, each slightly more hysterical than the last.

"Don't do what? Ruin your life? Ruin what you have for us? Ruin *this*?" Smash. Another shard of glass flew onto the floor. "Do you honestly care anymore?"

"I never stopped caring, Jade! Just, at some point, it stopped being about you!"

"Oh, so you don't mind me doing this?" *Crash*. Something rolled onto the floor, spilling red powder onto the blinding tiles. "You can just fix it up again, can't you? Just like you want to fix and patch our family back together until it's flawless?"

"All I said was that maybe you need some help. This is ridiculous!" Saphirra's father was shouting now, his voice booming off the walls in the spacious kitchen, piercing Saphirra's ears. Saphirra squeezed her eyes shut, and for a moment all Alex could see was darkness. When she opened her eyes again the door had been pried wider, and from his vantage point he could see everything.

Saphirra's mother stood just a little to the left of the pile of powder now, her hair disheveled, her eyes darting from her husband to the broken spice rack on the floor nervously. Saphirra's father was leaning against the refrigerator and had lit a cigar, almost as if this argument was trivial. Saphirra's mother took notice, and her eyes flashed angrily; within a moment, another object had been thrown, this time aimed at him. Saphirra's father dodged it in the nick of time, and Saphirra cringed as the object crashed into the refrigerator and onto the floor, scattering what he recognized as salt. Saphirra let out a small whimper, and Alex wished he hadn't seen this scene, that he wasn't in her head now, that he hadn't invaded this moment; he knew he wouldn't be able to look at her the same way anymore. Not after knowing that she'd gone through this, probably more than once. *This is probably why Saphirra never told me what was going on,* he reasoned. She would have known he'd want to comfort her so badly that it ached. She would have seen the sympathy in his eyes, and resented it.

Saphirra's father still held his cigar carefully between his fingers, as if it was the only thing that mattered now. Saphirra's mother glared at it.

"Put it out, Robert. *Now.*"

"I don't think I will," he said calmly, putting it to his lips. Saphirra's mother stood still for a moment, as if she couldn't believe what she'd heard.

Then she snapped.

Saphirra's mother charged across the kitchen, clawing at her husband's outstretched hands, trying to knock down the cigar.

"I...told you...not to do this...here!" she growled, but seconds later she let out a yelp; Saphirra's father had jabbed at her with the lit cigar, burning her forearm. Saphirra's mother leapt back in surprise, nursing her wound, watching her husband with reproachful eyes. Saphirra's father remained stoic.

"You see? You aren't in the right mind, dear. You knew it was lit. Now look, you've gone and burned yourself."

"You burned *me,*" she spat at him, but the strength had vanished from her voice. She rested like a wounded animal against the wall behind her, her eyes trained on his face, which showed no flicker of emotion.

"That's not my fault," he said flippantly. "I called the clinic a few hours ago, they expect to see you tomorrow morning."

"No!" Saphirra's mother sounded panicked now, her voice inching back into hysterics with every word. "I won't go! I don't need this, I know I'm not sick! How could you hurt your wife? I want a divorce."

Saphirra's father smiled cajolingly. "Dear, they warned you this would happen. They warned you that, even at the most unstable of times, you'd think you were fine. Remember, Jade? Remember what the psychologist said?"

Saphirra bowed her head down, her grip on the door so tight that the paint had begun to chip away beneath her small fingers. Alex heard Saphirra's mother murmur, "No...No, I'm not sick."

"Yes you are, dear." The voice was commanding, as if his word was final. Her mother's voice rose another octave as she fumbled with something on the counter.

"You're wrong, Robert. Nothing's wrong with me. Nothing ever has! I want out, and you can't tell me anything different this time!"

A cruel laugh echoed off the bare walls. "Oh go ahead, Jade. And go back to what, your family? Don't be stupid. Maybe you need your medication agai-"

Slap. The sound seemed to reverberate through Saphirra, and her small hand nearly let go of the wood as she raised her head to meet the scene before her. Her parents stared each other down silently, blazing green boring into bright blue. Saphirra pushed the door a little farther, then all the way, stepping quietly into the room. Neither parent noticed—they were too busy shouting at each other, each trying to outdo the last. She padded across the gleaming tile, stepping carefully over the spilled spices, when a scream caused Saphirra to snap her head up. Her father had slammed her mother against the wall, growling, "You're insane. You need help."

"Let go of me!" she shrieked, writhing against her husband. Saphirra ran towards them, stumbling over something sharp and falling onto the floor. Pain, white hot pain, screamed through Saphirra's mind, tearing at her insides. She sat there, stunned for a moment, but the moment had passed as quickly as it had come. Her palms stung as she scrambled up back onto her feet and continued to run towards her father, trying to wedge herself between them.

"Let her go!" Saphirra screamed. Her father looked down at her for a moment, as if he didn't know what to do with her. Saphirra's mother smiled down at her child, tears streaking down her face.

"Mommy and Daddy are having a discussion, dear. Go upstairs."

"*This* is a discussion?" Saphirra screeched, still fruitfully trying to pull her father's hand off her mother. Her father reacted almost instinctively, his hand sweeping down to push his daughter away. It was

245

then that the glowing embers caught Saphirra's eye, and she began to back away, lifting her arm to protect her face, but it was too late.

"Robert!"

Saphirra's mother's shocked tone faded into the background as pain pierced through her, and Saphirra screamed. The sound reverberated off the walls and stabbed her ears, but Saphirra didn't care; something red, something worse, had caught her attention.

Her arm had been cut open, in four, five, six different places, and blood was streaming onto the spotless floor. She turned around, looking for the source, and there it was; the broken glass, the sticky wine that had spilled onto the floor. Saphirra's parents were shouting again, but Saphirra couldn't hear it; all her attention was focused on her bleeding arm, on the droplets of blood that seemed to pool on her damaged skin before falling softly to the floor. Saphirra turned her forearm and there was the burn, the shining pink skin, the stinging pain. She sat there, frozen, until another crash caught her attention; Saphirra's mother had thrown something down the stairs from the other room. Saphirra hadn't even realized she'd left. She looked around numbly, just barely registering the phone on the counter, and ambled over to it, dialing the numbers almost automatically.

"911 response, what is the nature of your emergency?"

Someone pushed her to the floor of broken glass and the pain redoubled, causing Saphirra's eyes to water again. She looked up to see her mother standing over her, holding the phone in her hand.

"What have I told you, Saphirra? Never call the police when Mommy and Daddy are having a fight." Her eyes were wide and empty, her hair wild. She looked slightly insane standing above her, turning off the phone then dropping it to the floor.

"I'm hurt," Saphirra said, her voice weak. Her mother's expression flickered for a moment, and she crouched down beside Saphirra.

"I know honey, and I'm so sorry. We'll fix you soon, I promi—"

Her father stepped into the room, and her mother whipped her head up, grabbing the jagged edge of broken glass beside her.

"Stay away from me," she warned. He turned around but suddenly he wasn't the same person anymore; his eyes were red as if from lack of sleep, his arms outstretched. The image wavered before Saphirra's tear streaked eyes, and panic that wasn't his overwhelmed Alex as Saphirra's mother shot up, grabbed her bag, and shouted something over her shoulder. Within moments, she was gone. All that was left was Saphirra's father, who had somehow grown older, his eyes no longer red, his cigar still lit in his hands. As Saphirra focused on it, the cigar seemed to grow larger and larger, until it eclipsed Saphirra's vision completely, and all she could see was the brightly glowing embers...

Alex jolted up with a start, banging his head on something that had been left on the table next to him. Saphirra's long hair still swung into his vision, but how was that possible? He stared around, surprised to see he was in the basement kitchens of the university. Four half-made sandwiches littered the countertop in front of him, the mustard bottle still half open. He rubbed his head as he stood up, wondering. How was he still in Saphirra's body? It didn't make sense, unless what he'd seen was a dream. As he pulled a pot out of a drawer, he caught sight of his reflection. Saphirra's shaking hands barely managed to keep the pot still, and as he glanced down at the shining chrome, he caught sight of himself.

Saphirra's face was streaked with tears, her eyes puffy and red. Her green eyes had been replaced with iridescent violet. As he gazed down at himself, stricken by the tortured look on Saphirra's face, a thought that was not his own echoed through his mind.

Why?

Alex dropped the pot, but it didn't matter; seconds later he was sitting up on the rooftop, gulping in the cold night air. Saphirra's grief-stricken expression had burned itself into his eyes, and he sat immobilized for a moment, unsure of what he had just seen. Before he could process it any further, however, a noise from below caught his attention, and he heaved himself back onto the ledge of the roof. There below him was West, quietly emerging from the entrance to the building. He tucked something silvery into the pocket of his jeans and disappeared into the darkness, his footsteps padded by the slow traffic in the street ahead. Alex watched as West passed underneath a streetlight before turning left, heading into the dark alleyway from which he'd come. That brief second of light was all Alex needed to confirm his suspicion. It wasn't his ruffled hair or his slightly torn clothing that stood out—it was the slash of blood on his shoulder that, to Alex, glowed even as he disappeared into the darkness of an alley that proved it.

West was a Viceprus Hunter.

Chapter 23
A Midsummer's Nightmare

West walked down a familiar dark pathway, his nerves jangling. It had taken him ages to find the link he needed, the clue that had brought him here. His phone had rung, but it wasn't a normal Viceprus he had been told to kill this time; at least, not one with the signs he usually recognized. This one was strong and well hidden, which probably meant he had been around for quite a while, and hunted for at least twice as long. What had possessed his boss to believe he could be killed? West sighed, watching the starry sky overhead. The small pinpricks of light blurred and faded in and out of his vision, and he rubbed his eyes sleepily. Why tonight, of all nights, had his boss chosen to talk to him? West squared his shoulders, anticipating something to leap out at him around the next corner. Of course, nothing did. West relaxed slightly, but still kept a hand on his pocket, where his new gun now lay, protected. He ran a finger along the edge of the cool metal, shivering slightly. A gun. His boss had now made killing Vicepruses convenient. West shook his head sadly. How many more hunters were there in the world, doing something along the lines of what he was doing right now? How many of them would fail this task? He lifted his hand from his pocket suddenly, as if the metal had burned him. He didn't want to kill whoever was inside. He didn't want to hurt anyone else, whether they be a Viceprus or some other creature. How could he, when his best friend was one himself?

West frowned and began to walk slower, dreading the long night ahead of him. He wouldn't kill this one unless it was necessary, he resolved. The only reason he came in the first place was the intrigue of what his boss had told him; he'd never given him a reason before. His boss had refused to explain West's assignments for years,

Reedhima Mandlik

and West had grown used to it. So why tonight, of all nights, had his boss decided to explain that the person inside would know about his family, about his father? He had told West to meet the man, get the information he needed, then kill him. West grimaced as a gust of cool air blew through the small alley, rustling the fallen newspapers around him. The extra noise was almost too much for West; his paranoia escalated and he whipped his head around, his icy grey eyes searching the darkness around him. Not a soul was to be seen.

West had felt eyes on him ever since he'd left the college, and it unnerved him. The many detours he'd taken to shake the feeling hadn't helped much, either. Was it paranoia, or was his tracker really that good? He peered up at the night sky again, scanning the skies for a sign of life. What he heard, however, was a small thud, followed by a grunt of pain.

West froze. The sound seemed to have come from the rooftop in the building next to his. West began to walk again, slowly this time, keeping his eyes trained on a spot a little to the left of the glass building. Something bobbed in the corner of his eye, and West whipped his head around just in time to see a flash of bright red. *Alex.* He couldn't believe it. Only the heavy presence of the gun in his pocket reminded him to move and not stand there, mouth agape, waiting for another telltale flash of his best friend's vibrant red hair. Alex had followed him. West felt numb. *Does he know?* What other explanation was there, unless Alex had decided to hide on rooftops every night? West couldn't fathom it. *Alex followed me, and I hadn't even noticed it.* The thought sent a chill down his spine. Would he have to confront Alex now, right here? Before West could even dismiss the thought, however, his feet had found the step to the building the person was supposed to be in tonight. West looked up at the tall skyscraper, looking for some sign of life. The whole building was dark. Shrugging, West pushed in the key code his boss had given him and entered the building, wincing a little as the door shut with a resounding thud behind him.

The interior of the office building was bleak, lit only by a few safety lights in the back. The reception area's glossy wood surface looked as spotless as the rest of the room. West walked across the dully patterned carpet to the elevator, debating if its noise would startle whomever lie in wait for him. At the prospect of climbing all those stairs, however, he entered the elevator instead, standing idly until it had reached the thirty-fourth floor. Thankfully, its doors whispered open without so much as a chime. He stepped out cautiously, his hand flying back to the weight in his pocket, but there was no need; the floor looked deserted. Desks spaced at even intervals littered the main section of the floor, leaving room for only two rooms on either side, most likely for accountant offices.

One of them had the door open, bathing the floor around it in a glowing halo of light. He inched towards it, nearly jumping a foot in the air when someone inside slammed a drawer shut. He heard the ruffling of papers, then silence. It pressed down upon him, expediting his thoughts. *It was stupid of me to come here,* he realized. After all, what was he supposed to say? *Sorry I broke in, but I heard that you could tell me about my dad?* It was ridiculous for him to even assume that the man beyond the door would try to help him without question. *What if I have to kill another one tonight?* He didn't know if he could. He sighed, resigned, and turned away, only to be stopped by the sound of a single step behind him. West whipped around, startled, but his eyes only met darkness. The rustling continued in the brightened office, occasionally punctured by the slamming of drawers. West shrugged and turned around again, heading towards the elevators. It was a few more steps before he heard it. A short, cynical laugh punctured the silence.

"Just who do you think you are? This building is under tight security."

West's hand flew to his pocket protectively as man loomed out of the shadows before him. He was tall and reedy, and appeared to have just stepped out of his office; his tie was loose and flung over his shoulder, and the first few buttons on his shirt had come undone. His face was shrouded in darkness, but there was no mistaking it; this was the person his boss had wanted him to meet. The faint glow around him proved it.

"You know why I'm here," West said coldly. The man cocked his head to the side, flashing a grin at him. His bright teeth glowed eerily in the shadows.

"No, I'm afraid I don't," he said after a while. He sounded tired. "However, I *do* know that you are trespassing. Would you like to make this a problem, or would you like to leave now and escape with your dignity?" He smiled, almost as if he was joking, but his voice had a hard edge to it that West hadn't noticed before.

"You knew Faron Anastos, right?" West asked quietly. The man glanced up at him, a hint of panic flashing in his tired violet eyes.

"Yes. I did."

"Then you can tell me what happened to him?"

"That I am certain I cannot do. Please leave."

West ignored him, walking back towards the room, where a lamp had left a small pool of light in the corner. "You knew who Faron was. You knew he wasn't just the office manager at some company. You must have known *what* he was. What he did."

"Why are you here?" he asked suspiciously, following West further into the lighted room. As the shadows around him receded, his features became garishly prominent. The man looked tired and worn, with deep circles under his brilliant violet eyes, and his fine blonde hair appeared to be thinning. He did not seem to be the sinister villain his boss had portrayed him to be.

"More importantly, what is your name?" West countered, turning to face him. Ice grey pierced shocking violet for a moment, their gazes unwavering. Finally, the man looked down.

"I am Akakios. Akakios Alexiou." He looked up, as if hoping for a sign of recognition. When West showed no sign of identifying him, he continued. "Faron was one of my good friends."

"Even if he was a Siren?"

Akakios stood very still, looking at West as if for the first time. Then he let out a laugh, one so terribly agonized that it shot through West's heart like lightning.

"It's you," Akakios said tremulously, his eyes shining. West was taken aback at his abrupt change in mood, but before he could say anything the Viceprus had moved on. "Faron has come back from the grave to haunt me," he whispered, watching West fearfully. "He's come back, hasn't he? He's you."

"Don't be idiotic," West said impatiently, watching as Akakios slowly backed away from him. "I'm his son."

"No!" Akakios shrieked, his back now firmly against the wall behind him. "No, you don't know! You don't know! She'll kill you all and replace you with Faron! She swore it, she swore it..." He sank to the ground, shaking uncontrollably. West crouched down next to him concerned.

"Akakios, you don't know what you're saying. I understand it might be a shock for me to be here—"

"No!" Akakios shouted, his palms clamped to either side of his head, his fingers digging into his scalp. "You're here because of *her,* aren't you? She told you to kill me, didn't she? It's a trap, it's a trap!"

West looked down at the sorry mess before him and frowned.

"What do you mean, *her?*"

"My sister," Akakios whispered. "Clandestine."

His stomach dropped. His *sister?* It didn't make any sense. *Akakios is a Viceprus, and Clandestine is a siren. How is this possible?* Akakios glanced at West's confused expression and let out a snort of derisive laughter.

"She's gotten to you, hasn't she? You have no idea how many Hunters she's possessed before you. Oh, but wait," he said slowly, scrutinizing West, "she hasn't possessed you, has she? No, you still have your wit about you. Who do you report to, then?"

"No one," West said carefully. Akakios laughed again.

"Still, its obvious Clandestine is familiar to you. Just look! Look at that spark of recognition in your eyes! She's already talked to you, hasn't she?" The haunting sound of song still echoed in his ears, vivacious and bold. West nodded. "And yet you don't believe me?" Akakios continued disbelievingly.

"You don't seem to be anything—"

"Anything like her? Of course not, you fool, Vicepruses age. Sirens do not, or if they do its excruciatingly slow, to the point that it is rarely noticeable or relevant. Sirens do not die of age. Of course she seems younger."

"B-but your surname—"

"Don't be thick. You think she hasn't changed her name before? Always trying to shed the family name. What is she under this time? Mandeliv? Baron?"

"Margaux, actually," West amended feebly. "But why would you think your sister would try to kill you?" he asked cautiously, a hand still resting on his pocket. The gun felt heavy and warm against his thigh. Akakios didn't seem to be listening to him; he pulled himself up and straightened his collar, finally eye level with West. His expression was smooth, determined. West stood his ground as the Viceprus came closer.

"She would do this to me, after all she put me through," he whispered, almost as if to himself. "It is in her nature. Keep around only the most useful until they too become worthless." He smiled at West, his expression smooth. "You won't have the chance to kill me," he said to West after a moment. West slid a hand into his pocket.

"And why is that?"

"Because you'll be dead before you can even lift a finger from your gun."

Before West could stop him, Akakios struck his leg, ripping his jeans. Searing pain caused West to crumple to the ground, and Akakios struck again, his long claws raking West's cheek. West stumbled back, caught off guard at the sudden flow of sticky liquid down his neck. Akakios stood over him, dangling West's gun lazily from his finger.

"Do not underestimate me, West. I know I may look weak, but looks can be deceiving. When you are ready to talk without the influence of my sister or a weapon, we shall. Until then," he flicked the gun casually onto the carpet beside him, "I bid you good day."

Akakios walked off into the open elevator, his violet eyes fierce in the darkness. West scrambled to his feet, but by then the Viceprus was gone, leaving him with long claw marks tracking down his leg and cheek. West gathered up his gun, wincing as his leg sent another burst of pain up his spine. Since when was Clandestine the enemy? West knew not to trust her, but not to this extent. Clandestine couldn't be using him; on the contrary, she hadn't contacted him in weeks. How could someone use him and then simply leave him there? It didn't make any sense. West stumbled into a bathroom and began trying to wipe the stinging blood off his neck, wincing again as the cold water hit his burning skin. His thoughts flashed back to Alex, who was no doubt still waiting on the roof. How long had it been since he'd walked into the building? One, maybe two hours? West ran a hand over his leg, deciding the cuts weren't deep enough to worry about. He had to hand it to Alex, though; the guy sure had patience. A flash of anger flared up inside him at the thought. How could Alex simply watch him like that? All this while, West had been trying to avoid harming Alex as much as possible, and now Alex was one step closer to hurting him instead. *Alex could be waiting for me right outside the building,* West thought grimly. After all, survival colors even the strongest friendships in the most dismal hues. West sank to the floor, trying his hardest to ignore the throb of his leg. Here West was, trying his hardest to keep Alex from harm, when he could have known about his job the whole time. *What else does Alex know?* The thought sent a chill down his spine. Did Alex know he was a Siren? Did he know about Clandestine? About everything? West held his head in his hands, and groaned when that hurt, too. *What do I do?*

West didn't know how long he sat there, staring at the tiled floor, before he willed himself to get back up again. The pain had ebbed away slightly now, and as he gave himself a last glance in the mirror, he made a split second decision. He ran a hand over the length of his wounded leg and smeared the blood on his shoulder until he got the desired effect. As he walked out of the elevator doors moments later into the darkened lobby, he tensed, as if expecting Akakios to jump around the corner. He paused by the glass doors as well to peer out the window, searching the night sky for the telltale flash of red hair. All he could see was the vast expanse of stars in the unusually clear night. Cautiously, he stepped out onto the quiet street, digging into his pocket to retrieve his phone. It was nearly nine. *I'd been in there for hours,* West thought. *He's probably gone by now.* At least, that's what he hoped. He dialed his boss, his heart sinking a little further with each ring. *It's the first and only time I have ever failed. What will he say?* The thought hadn't occurred to him until now. Before he could come up with a legitimate excuse, his boss's voice flooded into his ear.

"Yes?"

"I...I c-couldn't." West swallowed hard, his mouth suddenly dry. His boss let out a short derisive laugh.

"You couldn't find him? Catch him? Kill him?"

West let out a shaky sigh. "Yes."

"Of course you couldn't. That Viceprus is one of the hardest to catch. Let this be a reminder to you, West. Do not get too contemptuous about your skills."

"I never would, sir."

The silence on the other end was unnerving. Finally, his boss spoke, his voice sounding more distant than usual. "Just remember you have less than a week now. You are not the best. You will never be the best. So do not even begin to think of how you can defy me, because you will never be able to." And with that, the phone clicked shut. West stared down at his cell phone, amazed. What was with the controlling speech? *There's no way boss knows,* West assured himself. He couldn't know that he'd been thinking of how to avoid hurting Alex ever since he'd gone missing...could he?

Something caught the corner of West's eye and he turned, certain he'd seen Alex's flaming hair. As West walked underneath a streetlight, his wounds were thrown into even greater relief. He could almost see the thoughts running through Alex's head if he was watching him now. *I bet he'll think twice about messing with this,* West thought savagely, relishing in the thought. *He's got to. Or he'll never survive.*

Saphirra woke up face down on the floor next to a fallen pot, a strange ache pulsing through her body. She sat up and rubbed her eyes sleepily, wondering how she'd gotten so far away from the table, where she was sure she'd fallen asleep. Saphirra pulled herself off the floor and bent down to pick up the pot, lifting the lid to check if anything had been inside. As she replaced it she saw her distorted reflection, and nearly dropped it again; her eyes were puffy and red, her cheeks stained with tears.

All too late, she realized what had happened; *Alex saw.* She didn't know how, or why, but it was clear Alex had seen. Saphirra sank to the floor, noticing for the first time how much the pot shook in her hands. *He knows.* She didn't know how what to do. Hot, fresh tears spilled onto her cheeks, but she did nothing to stop them. How would he react? What would he say? She hugged her knees to her chest, watching her tears *plip* softly onto the tiled floor. This was not happening. Why'd she have to dream of that night? *Why?* Something shifted beside her, and she screamed. Then someone's arms had encompassed her, holding her tight, and she caught a glimpse of fire red. Alex. She was sobbing now, and she willed herself to stop shaking. She couldn't. Why was Alex here? How long had she been dreaming? She willed herself to stop crying, but she couldn't do that, either. After a while, she had calmed enough to say one thing.

"You saw." It wasn't a question. Alex turned her around so that they were face to face, his expression somber.

"I didn't mean to."

"But you saw what happened. All of it?"

"No, not all of it." Alex's voice was understanding, his eyes pouring into hers. She wanted to look away, but the ice blue of his eyes trapped her. The tears began to spill over once again. She wanted to scream at him, to warn him, to make him understand that she didn't need his sympathy, that she didn't want it. At her silence, Alex gently pulled her wrists to him. She allowed him to turn them over, to pull up the sleeves, to expose the jagged scars that littered her forearm. He stared down at them, speechless. Saphirra resisted the urge to pull them back.

"She never came back."

"What?" Alex looked slightly dazed as he glanced over at her again, his eyes unfocused. She cleared her throat.

"She died that night. She never came back. She got into that car and drove straight off a bridge into the ravine and killed herself, probably because I called the police. She didn't want to go." She began to shake again, and Alex pulled her towards him. She buried her face in his chest, uncaring of how it looked. It was oddly comforting, having someone know. For once in her life, she felt as if she wasn't alone in the dark.

"Saph, I'm sorry." The place where their hands touched had begun to glow, but she felt no different. She was exhausted and confused. Saphirra had convinced herself that no one would want to know, that no one needed to. It wasn't until she looked up into Alex's face that the full extent of what he had done hit her. She recoiled from him, scrambling backwards until she hit a chair. Alex made no move to go after her; instead, he watched her with fathomless eyes. He seemed unsure of what to say.

"Don't look at me like that," she said sharply, pulling herself upright. Her hands were still shaking uncontrollably, but she tried to mask it as best as she could. Alex said nothing, but continued to watch her fruitless progress around the kitchen as she picked up the fallen pot and set it back onto the table, fighting back tears. *He shouldn't know. He can't. It'll ruin everything.*

"I told you not to look at me like that!" she shouted at him after a second, unable to keep the tears from spilling over once again. He simply stood there. "Stop!" she cried again. Her voice echoed off the walls, and her knees suddenly felt weak. "Stop watching me like I was wrong! Like I caused her death! Like it was all my fault—" her voice caught as a new sob escaped her. Her heart hurt. Her lungs ached. Everything around her blurred, and suddenly Alex was there, encompassing her once again.

"It's okay," he murmured, his voice soothing. "It's okay." He stood there for a while, patiently holding her until her shivers had somewhat subsided, before he spoke.

"Everything fits now. I remember wondering why your house was so quiet, why it felt so empty. I remember your parents never being home. And yet," he said, turning Saphirra's face up to his, "you needed someone to hear you so badly. I was just too dense to listen." The intensity of his gaze made her blush, and she hastily wiped her tears on her sleeve. *Finally, someone else knows.* It wasn't until she realized this that she felt a great surge of relief, a tidal wave of years and years of holding on to something she never wanted uncovered. He needed to see both sides, to see *her* side. She was suddenly overcome by an urge to explain everything, *anything* to get him to stop looking at her like that.

"After my mom left, I ran. My dad found me the next day at the park. He told me my mother was dead, and I caused it. It was because of me," she said softly, turning her head away from him. She didn't want to see his reaction to this.

"My dad went on a straight streak after that, giving money and charity to people, as if it would erase the past, and I went along with it. Alex, I could have stopped what happened to my mom. My *dad* could have stopped it. I let her kill herself."

Chapter 24
The Legendary Dagger

Clandestine stood in the center of the room, a phone in her hand and an unresponsive Ryan Lockson at her feet. Her fingers gripped it so hard she was sure it would snap in two. Frustrated, she kicked Ryan's side and he flopped over, his eyes glazed and unfocused.

If West couldn't kill her brother, who could?

Clandestine sank down into one of the many chairs in Ryan's office, dropping the phone to the plush carpet below. What use was it having a wealth of people at her disposal if none of them could finish the job she wanted? Akakios was still alive, and West was too, which could only mean one thing; he had convinced West to give up. West, the stoic, hardened assassin had been convinced to not harm his assignment. *What did Akakios say?* Her brother wasn't one to mince words. He had, no doubt, talked about her. How long would it be until West asked her why she hadn't explained about her twin? Why she hadn't bothered to mention that he was a Viceprus, or that he was one of the most powerful on the Viceprus Council? She hadn't decided yet whether answering him would benefit her plans; he could easily become emotional and disrupt everything. *Visiting him now would be detrimental,* Clandestine decided. After all, one meeting could ruin everything. Clandestine stared out of the window, her eyes searching past the thick-pained glass into the starry sky above. The blue moon was nearly upon them, and so much more had yet to be done.

She had been counting on West to harm Akakios, just enough so that she could finish him herself. Akakios was faceless in her mind's eye, and extremely distorted from how he would appear to be now; it occurred to Clandestine that she hadn't seen his face in over a hundred years. Although Vicepruses aged more quickly than Sirens did, she imagined he looked much older than the young boy of seventeen she remembered. Hell, even *she* looked different now. Clandestine thought back to when they hadn't gone their separate ways, back when they stuck together for fear of being alone. *No,* Clandestine realized, *he'd always feared being alone.* Wasn't it Clandestine who had chosen to venture out into the world, to find the council in Europe, to find people like her? Wasn't it she who had told her brother over and over again that they could not be the only ones like this in the world, that being truly unique was nearly impossible? *But Akakios refused to believe me,* she recalled spitefully. Had he still kept his original name, or was he called something else now? Clandestine rubbed her forehead in frustration. She didn't care about him. She shouldn't.

So why did she still believe that he didn't deserve the fate she had lain out for him?

Blame. Thousands of years of scorn and regret. She wanted to eradicate these feelings from her mind once and for all. If Akakios was alive, she'd never be able to carry out her plans. He wouldn't allow it. He'd taken the "good" path in life, doing all the right things for all the wrong reasons. No matter how much she tried to show him her ways, he continued to condemn them. How could he not see that Sirens, and all ancient creatures, were superior to humans? It frustrated her. *How could he not realize that hiding our world is unreasonable? That we should be out in the open?* She'd convinced the Siren Council of this, after all. They were not freaks of nature; they were ancient beings, gifted with intelligence and wisdom far beyond the human mind. Humans were their *prey.* Who in their right mind would let them rule the world? When asked this, Akakios had no concrete answer. Sure, he would prattle on about minute things such as being "humane" and learning to "coexist", but is that what they were doing, really? Clandestine didn't believe it. If the Viceprus Council and Society wanted to believe it, fine. They were no brighter than humans.

It was this that had brought a clear solution to Clandestine's mind; overpower the Viceprus Council, overpower the world. If she could just get the world back to the way it had been. What about the Elymphs, the nymph-like creatures full of mischief? Their kind thrived on the freedom of nature, the blending of the wind in the trees, the sun on leaves, and the rustle of water in the brooks. What about them? What about all the other creatures that were legendary, broken into submission? Wasn't it their *right,* their *duty,* to protect their own race from similar damage?

It was a stroke of luck that she had even gotten this far. The Council had sent her on an assignment, to find the culprit of a series of mass murders of the Siren Society. Clandestine had jumped at the chance. *Hunters.* She stared down at Ryan's motionless body now, marveling at the genius of his idea. It had only just occurred to her that he had been well beyond his years with his careful planning. It had taken her weeks simply to find out the general base of his operations, and another few months to find out the correct address. When she realized he wasn't part of the Hunters League, however, she began to get suspicious. The Viceprus Society had set up a system of skilled Hunters in defense of the Siren attack they constantly braced against. Clandestine scoffed, nudging Ryan's back with her foot. Granted, their League was illegal, but it was too large to do anything about it. None of the Societies followed the laws set in place, knowing that doing so would be their downfall. Each section of the Triumvirate had their own backup, in case of another War like the terrible First War. Sirens, Vicepruses, and Elymphs all had their clear boundaries, but all were too afraid to cross the line. Their populations had suffered enough during the First War.

So why had Ryan started a black market Hunters League?

Clandestine had quickly found out Ryan had had his own plans. Like her, he believed the dominant species should not be humans. Unlike her, however, he'd decided his target would be the Siren Society. Under his Hunters, more and more influential Sirens had been disappearing day by day. After weeks of studying him, she had realized a peculiar trait of his; Ryan would kill off the Hunters once they had filled a certain quota. He never killed them because of incompetence, nor for an egotistical kick; no, his Hunters were simply getting *too good* at their jobs.

Still, there had been one Hunter that stayed in his employment years later; West Anastos, then a surly teenager of fifteen, had managed to kill and not be killed. Clandestine had allowed her curiosity to get the best of her the day she'd seen West, wondering if he would take ridiculous orders, whether he would do as his boss bid, no matter the expense.

"And here we are," she muttered softly to Ryan, bending down to pluck his dagger from his pocket. The tip was emblazoned with olive branches and a tiny stone well was etched into the handle. A boy with wings had been carved carefully onto the hilt, and a demonic looking girl rested on its tip. Each part of the small dagger seemed to tell the tale of the Old Healer. She laughed bitterly and slipped the dagger into her pocket, her fingers gripping the handle so hard her knuckles turned white. She would return it later. The horror of seeing it again proved it; Ryan knew. Why else would a dagger designed to kill even the most skilled Siren lie in his pocket? *I suppose I'm not erasing his mind as much as I used to,* she thought, unsettled. *But what if...*What if his mind had learned to combat her own? What if he'd somehow built up resistance to her? The thought sent a chill down her spine, and she kicked at his head, smiling slightly at the sickening thud that resulted.

"That was for the betrayal," she told his unresponsive frame smugly, turning to the window once more. The light from the street poured into the dimly lit office, scattering soft beams of light across the faded carpet. Clandestine watched Ryan for a while, waiting for the twitch, the slight stir that would tell her he'd woken from his stupor. To her relief, he didn't move. Smiling softly to herself, she slipped through the door and began to head down the poorly lit stairwell. Akakios was not dead, but that was fine; she'd expected it.

She'd just have to do it herself.

Ry blinked, startled to see a long expanse of white stretched out before him. *Where am I?* It took him moments before he realized the strange, light fuzziness around him wasn't an obstruction of his vision but the carpet of his office. As he attempted to lift his head he winced as his head gave a particularly nasty throb. How had he gotten here? He'd waited to find if Akakios would spare West...and he had. Akakios wasn't one to show mercy, especially to someone who had come to assassinate him. But if West had mentioned Faron...if Akakios had seen something in West's tired eyes...

Ry knew that Siren powers were hereditary, but he'd held onto a vain hope that they would be nullified if the head of the family died before his son. *Apparently not.* Ry had no concrete proof, however, that West was indeed a Siren. How could he prove it? It had taken him ages, after all, to discern the two. Faron was so lithe and daring, so valiant and mysterious. His story was the stuff of legends to Sirens, so many of whom still looked up to Faron Anastos, even in his disappearance. Not many knew he was dead, save for the ones who'd come to find him in the first place. Faron's miraculous recovery in the First War only added to rumors that he'd had healing powers, something so rare of other Sirens. There was no doubt that Faron had been unique. Still, his missions during the First War had been a mystery to him, and no matter how much he pried, none of the Vicepruses knew. It was a secret only the Siren High Council knew of. *And the Triumvirate,* he thought to himself bitterly. He resented their power. *No matter,* he thought savagely, *I'll be one of them soon enough.*

When he had hired West, he'd searched for signs of recognition of the mythical realm, and had found none. *Perhaps I did not look hard enough,* Ry chided himself. West had been in his adolescence, moody and uncontrollable. Of course it had been foolish to search for signs then. The boy was handsome, sure, but that wasn't an indication of anything.

"What are you doing on the floor?"

Evelyn had appeared at the doorframe, hair disheveled, looking bemused. Ry sat up suddenly, groaning as something in his back ached.

"The question is," he said gruffly, pulling himself up onto a chair, "what are you doing back so early?"

Evelyn's cheeks tinged bright pink as Ry brushed past her into the hall, and it took her a moment to catch up to his quickening stride.

"He's already healed."

"What?"

Ry turned to look at her, panic gripping his heart. She shrugged indifferently. "I followed him back to the university. He'd had a large cut in his shoulder and his leg looked to be nearly ripped in half. By the time he'd gotten to the gates his shoulder had nearly healed and his leg's wound was about half the size it had been." Her long fingers wrapped around his, and he wrenched himself away, mind whirring. *He has Faron's powers. What else can he do?* He had a sinking feeling that it wasn't the only part of Faron he'd inherited. He turned to Evelyn, whose shrewd eyes were watching his face warily. *Can I trust her?* Evelyn didn't know why she had been called to watch over his Hunter, and he preferred to keep it that way. Still...

Someone had been watching him lately. He could feel his memory lapsing randomly, and he knew he'd done things he couldn't recall now. How else would he have ended up on the floor with no recollection of having left his desk in the first place? *Someone has been controlling me.* And from the looks of it, for quite a while, too. His mind had only just learned to combat it, and only barely at that. How long had it been going on? And who had been erasing his memories?

"Ry? Ryan? Are you okay?"

Evelyn's voice broke through his thoughts, and he blinked in surprise. He'd forgotten she was even there. Frowning slightly, he ran a hand through his hair.

"Fine," he mumbled. "You did well. Wait," he said sharply as a movement caught his eye. He brushed her long hair off her neck, startled to see a long, glowing, ornate C carved into her ivory skin.

"Who did that?" he asked slowly, his voice shaking in anger. She raised her fingers to meet his, her eyes lost and confused.

"Who did what?" she asked curiously, a playful smile beginning to form on her lips. He shook his head urgently, tracing the C lightly with a fingertip. Didn't she see he wasn't playing around? Someone had branded her with *Sunstones*. Why couldn't she see that? A flash of hot anger raced through him, and he grabbed her wrist roughly. Enough was enough.

"Come here, I need to get you a salve," he instructed, pulling her back into the office. As he rummaged through his drawers, her hand reached over to cover his. When he looked up again, her face was dangerously close to his. She gently closed the drawer, drawing his mouth to hers, and giving him a soft kiss. As she pulled away, Ry had completely forgotten about her salve, because another problem had just become evident. As she'd pressed him back into the desktop, he'd expected the sharp edge of his dagger to prick his thigh, but his pocket felt oddly light. He rummaged through it, but his hand came out empty. He looked up at Evelyn, who was smiling smugly to herself, and glared.

"How dare you."

"W-what?" she asked, caught off guard. Ry stalked around his desk and put a hand to her throat, his eyes flashing dangerously.

"How dare you take my dagger?"

"I-I didn't! Ry, what are you *talking* about?" her voice trembled, and she squeezed her eyes shut under his scathing gaze. It was the only logical explanation. After all, she'd been the first one to find him on the floor, hadn't she? Unless...He let her go and she stumbled back, massaging her neck.

"Go," He growled. Evelyn's frightened face swam before his, and he gripped onto his desk for support. He would not panic. He would not panic. He would not—

"But why?"

"*Go!*" he shouted, pointing a shaking finger at the door. Evelyn nearly tripped in her haste to leave the room, not looking back as she ran down the stairs, her long hair flying out behind her. Ry collapsed onto his desk, holding his head in his hands. Of course, how could he have been so stupid? It was a Siren that had done this to him. It had always been a Siren. And now they had his only weapon against them.

Chapter 25
Revelation

"She did *what?*"

Alex's hands were frozen, still half outstretched towards her. He was staring at her with the same look she'd imagined, only something else was mixed in it. Was it sympathy? She took a deep breath, and even though tears were streaming silently down her face, she managed to speak. She had to explain, to make him understand.

"After what you saw...she walked back in. She was drunk, and she...she tried to force me into the car. My dad just watched. I had called the police again. Once she found out, she just left. Drove away before I could call her back."

Her voice cracked, but before Alex could say anything, she plunged on.

"My dad didn't come back downstairs for hours. When he did, it was to tell me that whatever happened, I had caused it. If I had kept my mouth shut, none of this would have happened. The police came, and my father told them I'd slipped on some broken glass. He couldn't tell them what had really happened. I couldn't think straight enough to tell them myself. She never wanted to go like that." Her voice shook as she tried to stem the flow of tears that threatened to engulf her. She didn't dare to look at Alex's face now. She watched his hands instead, half outstretched toward her, perfectly still. She was afraid of the rejection she'd brought upon herself. The strange feeling knowing she wasn't alone had dissipated now, leaving her only with the sinking feeling that he'd do exactly what she expected him to; leave, and never come back. She expected him to leave, to say he never wanted to come back, but she never expected him to simply *stand* there. His silence was unnerving. She refused to meet his eyes, staring instead at the patterns on the tiled floor. Finally, he spoke.

"I know you're not going to like it, but you've got to hear it from someone. I'm sorr—"

"No!" Saphirra said sharply, turning to him. "Don't. I don't want your sympathy. I don't need it." *I don't deserve it.* She turned to the kitchen counter and picked up a pot aimlessly, turning it over in her hands. More silence. And then—

"So that's why. No wonder you don't like your dad, Saphirra." His voice, so close to her ear, sounded disgusted. Not angry at her, but at her parent's behavior. It just made Saphirra clutch the pot harder. Didn't he see? She'd basically let her mother die. She couldn't even contradict her father when he had said, with certainty, that her mother's antidepressants had taken her too far, that she'd needed help and refused it, and that Saphirra had pushed her over the edge. Did her father really think she was that blind? He'd never needed help coming up with stories. *He was so good at it himself,* she thought bitterly. Still, she had repeated part of that story to every burly, hairy policeman that asked her, never telling what really happened, never mentioning that it *was* partially her fault. Wasn't she at fault too, if she kept it quiet? Wasn't that just as bad? It took her a moment to realize that she hadn't said a word. The silence around them was suffocating.

"I'm sorry," she said finally. "I didn't mean to—"

"I know," he said quietly. She was afraid to turn around, for fear of being trapped by his ice blue eyes once more. She swallowed hard, willing herself to loosen her grip on the handle.

"But your parents were so *nice* when I used to come over...Saphirra, why didn't you ever tell me?" he asked her gently. She tried to stem the flow of tears before answering.

"B-because I didn't think you should worry about me. You kept asking about those scars, and I just...I didn't want you to look at me differently, I guess," she said quietly. "I couldn't tell because....because I was afraid. God, I'm so stupid! I could have told the police, I could have put my father in jail for abuse and who knows what else, and I didn't. I'm a horrible person. I was just as bad as he was. Only I knew the real reason why we moved. It wasn't to start over; it was so no one could start an investigation. It was my fault, too."

"Saph, it's horrible, what they did to you...but they're far, far away now. You're with me, okay? You're safe. So please...please don't cry..." he pleaded, his voice aching with effort. Saphirra shook her head. Why couldn't he understand?

"Don't you see? I could have tried to save my mom; I could have sold out my dad. He would be in prison, where he belongs."

"But how could you?" Alex interrupted hotly, turning her gently towards him. Electric blue locked on emerald green, and she couldn't tear her gaze away. "How could you, with the way he twisted things around? Your mom wasn't sick. Your dad just made her think that way, just like he's done to you."

The words sent a shockwave through her. "W-what do you mean?"

"None of it is your fault," he said firmly, his grip on her shoulders reassuring. "None of it. You couldn't stop whatever twisted games your dad had played. You couldn't stop him, and you couldn't have stopped your mom. *None* of it is your fault. Saphirra, you've got to believe me." His voice was earnest, and each word he spoke felt like a blow to the wall she'd set up for years, the wall she'd thought was impenetrable.

"You don't understand!" she cried. "You go through pain every single day because you saved my life. That doesn't seem fair, does it? All I do is cause trouble for everyone," Saphirra said miserably. To her surprise, Alex smiled.

"You have to listen to me, Saph. You aren't a horrible person. If you had told who knows what your dad would have done? And what evidence was there? If he could convince his own wife..."

"He could convince the police, too," Saphirra finished softly. Alex nodded, relief flooding into his eyes.

"You see? It's only logical to someone that young. And how many times do I have to tell you that you would be *dead* if I hadn't showed up? Any human being would have saved you in that kind of situation." He took a deep, steadying breath. "I don't regret saving your life. Do you?"

He tucked a loose strand of her midnight hair behind her ear and looked at her, waiting for a reaction. Her throat felt tight, her eyes sore, but a sudden wave of relief flooded through her. Someone finally knew. Someone understood. It was as if he had crumbled her wall down just by his gaze. Everything within her had crashed with every word of explanation she'd spoke. She hugged him then, thankful beyond measure. He had stayed. The nightmare was over. He was here, and currently giving her such an intense look that she wanted to look away, but somehow couldn't bring herself to.

"Saph...Do you remember that day, in the empty classroom, when we heard that noise? Do you remember how I was going to say something?" he sounded nervous, almost cautious, as he spoke. She tilted her head to one side, feigning confusion. Of course she remembered. She shook her head instead, unsure of what brought on her lie. Alex laughed softly, his eyes twinkling.

"I was going to thank you. To thank you for being my friend, for being *alive*. You're more than I could ever have asked for."

And then he kissed her.

Her hands tangled in his vivid red hair, and he pulled her closer. Emotions she never knew she had flooded into her. Joy beyond anything she'd felt before. Pain tinged her heart, but it was a good kind of pain. Something inside her shattered into a million small tingling pieces, sending a shockwave through her body. She kissed him again, taking in the smell of his skin, the feel of his lips against hers. It was all too good to be true. He was so kind to her, and she'd done nothing to deserve it. The thought that he might lose control flitted through her mind, but only briefly. She knew it wouldn't happen again. He wouldn't let himself, she was sure of it. As if agreeing with her, the small scar on her neck tingled. She felt her limbs slowly getting heavy, her breathing more ragged. She pulled away, barely able to breathe.

"I-I'm sorry," Alex stuttered, a crimson blush tingeing his cheeks. He shook his head. "No, I'm not sorry. I mean—"

"It's okay," she giggled. The sound made her feel as light as air. She pulled him closer, kissing him again. His hands found her jaw line, his thumb stroking her cheek lightly. She pulled away, unable to erase the wild happiness that had taken over her. Alex smiled as she walked unsteadily towards the table, sitting down. He joined her, taking her hand in his.

"I think those are staring us down," he said jokingly, gesturing towards the half-made sandwiches on the countertop. Saphirra got up suddenly and sat down again just as quickly, dizziness overcoming her. It wasn't because of the kiss; rather, it was more likely because of the energy Alex had unknowingly taken from her. Alex seemed to understand this and smiled apologetically as he helped her up, walking her towards the food. She leaned on him, feeing more peaceful than she had in years. It was as if everything they had been worrying about had melted away. For the first time in her life, Saphirra felt truly safe.

West had no idea how long he'd been pacing the quad, but the night was slowly disappearing, and with it all his fruitless ideas. He walked the brick bike paths briskly. Another night gone. Would he actually have to kill his best friend? He knew his boss would be watching every move he made, and unless he killed Alex, *he* would be dead. He knew Alex was the Viceprus he was supposed to kill. Maybe a part of his brain didn't want to believe it, but now it was as real as anything. Alex seemed normal, and yet he'd followed West to his job. What else did Alex know? *And if his suspicions were confirmed,* West thought grimly, *would he try to kill me, too?* Another thought struck him. Did Saphirra know too? He saw the way she looked at Alex. She might even love him. What would happen if she found out? *Unless she already knows.* The thought sent a shiver down his spine. Falling for a Viceprus. *How disgusting.*

He hardly realized he was walking anymore. The long grass was in desperate need of cutting and tickled his legs as he walked, while a breeze played lightly across his face. It was warm for the first day of August, and he ran a hand though his chocolate brown hair nervously. *What should I do? What can I do?* he wondered anxiously. He loved Alex like a brother; he couldn't imagine goofy, unaware Alex as a Viceprus, much less with big, bat–like wings on either side of him. He tried to picture Alex with pale, white skin, his reddish–brown hair falling into his purple, vicious eyes, his mouth twisted into a ferocious snarl, and shuddered. He couldn't deny that Alex was a Viceprus, no matter how badly he wanted to. The only question was who was going to confront the other, and when.

West was so used to the forestry silence of the meadow–like quad, surrounded on one side by towering oak trees, the other by university buildings, that it startled him to hear voices. Alex and Saphirra were heading into the quad, and they were far enough away that they wouldn't see him. He made a split second decision, diving into a hedge. He stifled a cry as he untangled himself from the vines.

Damn rosebushes. He cursed. *What are they doing up so early?* He crouched behind a different set of foliage, peeking over its thick leaves at the two halfway across the quad from him. Alex had his back to him as they walked, and he paused, looked around, and muttered something to Saphirra. Her face lit up, and she giggled. Giggling was so uncharacteristic of Saphirra that West watched on in amazement.

"No, don't!" she said suddenly. Their voices floated to West clearly. He saw Alex pause for a moment, his hand still grasping Saphirra's. In the blink of an eye, two long, black, feathery wings had materialized onto his back. *She* does *know.* The thought made his blood boil. West stifled his noise of irritation as Alex picked Saphirra up none too gently, pulling her laughing frame into the air.

"Alex, someone's going to see! Stop!" Saphirra cried, and her annoyed tone floating effortlessly to him. Alex grinned and set her back down sloppily on the ground. West's knees were growing numb and prickly from crouching uncomfortably in the same spot for so long.

"Ow," Saphirra mumbled, and after trying to push herself away from him fruitlessly, she crossed her arms over her chest huffily. "I don't know how I survived the past few days. They felt like hell," Saphirra told Alex, and West silently agreed. Thinking his best friend was dead wasn't the best feeling.

"Well, I'm not dead. I only avoided impending doom, that's all."

"You make coming back from the dead sound easy."

"You make living sound easy."

"It is," she said, still sounding huffy and irritated, but with a hint of confusion in her voice.

"Not without you."

She laughed uproariously at this, and he pushed her a little, a faint blush creeping onto his cheeks. Saphirra took his hand and smiled at him, murmuring something inaudible. West watched them talk, strangely moved by their words. For some reason, the urge to visit Claire overwhelmed him.

"You know what's strange?"

"What?"

"I can hear your heartbeat. I can hear West's and Claire's better now, too," he told her. Saphirra smiled playfully.

"What does it sound like to you?"

West could hear the curiosity in her voice, and Alex said something too quiet for him to hear. West could have sworn she rolled her eyes. He kissed her and West sat back a little, stunned. *When did that happen?* Alex paused for a moment, and West could have sworn he saw his back stiffen. Alex whispered something to Saphirra again, making her jump a little. She gasped slightly, and West thought she glanced directly at his hiding spot.

"What? Wait, no, Alex–" He'd taken off again, leaving Saphirra to sprint after him. Cold dread clawed at his heart. Before West knew what was happening, Alex was right next to him, making him jump. Alex frowned down at him as Saphirra glared up at Alex, struggling to pull him back from West. Alex's face was livid.

"Spying?"

Chapter 26
Face to Face

West had left Claire so she could 'get some rest'—as if she actually needed it. The only thing that hurt now was her ankle, and it had gone back to its natural size when West had healed it. She stared out of the window, watching the quad bathed in the morning sun's light. The brick buildings surrounding the east end of the quad sparkled, and the forest–like trees swayed in a sudden breeze. Claire sank lower into her pillow nest, wondering. Now West knew about Alex, but did Alex know about West? It was all so confusing, and she could barely keep her stories straight anymore. She had hated to lie to West and Alex, but she wanted to keep them both alive. An assassin and his target, living together in the same dorm room. The situation was just asking for trouble.

She turned on the TV just for something to do, waiting for the image flitting across the screen to meet the sound. Bored, she stared out the window again, watching a robin try to peck its way through the glass. She thought again about the prophecy, and about the strange look that had crossed West's face at the mention of his best friend. She had a sinking feeling that West knew a lot more than he was letting on. She wished the animosity between her two friends could be over, that they could somehow accept each other and move on. Claire cringed at this childish thought. How could a Viceprus and a Viceprus Hunter be anything more than enemies? She pitied West. At least Alex didn't have to feign happiness when he saw his friend, but West had to cover his tired expression every day. And if West knew about Alex...Claire closed her eyes. She didn't want to think about what would happen. After a minute's worth of irritating static, she turned the TV off. Her head hurt, and she couldn't think straight. What was the point in trying to figure out anything when her brain refused to work?

She settled down into her pillows again, and was on the verge of falling asleep when loud voices floated through the window, jarring her awake. She glanced out the window, and was startled to see Alex and West, pointing at each other and yelling, and Saphirra between them, trying to force them apart. Claire leapt off her bed, throwing her pillows aside in an effort to get up, and wincing a little when she stepped on her ankle. Although it was healed, it still throbbed a little. She ran out of the infirmary, leaning on the oaken doors to catch her breath. *What are they fighting about?* Claire wondered, even though she thought she knew the answer already. She half-ran, half-limped across the long grasses of the quad, wincing as the slight pain in her ankle morphed into a throb. She reached the group faster than expected, out of breath.

"...and since when have you been a *Viceprus?*" West was yelling hotly. She'd never seen him so serious and angry before in her life.

"Since when have you been a *Hunter?* Two *years,* and you couldn't be bothered to mention that you were the best Hunter the Council had ever seen? Two years, West?" Alex countered, scoffing at the word 'Hunter'. Claire ran in between them to help Saphirra force them apart, yelling,

"Stop, stop!"

Together, she and Saphirra pried them apart, keeping them at arms distance from each other. West glared daggers at Alex, and Alex glared back. For a second, Alex's eyes broke the silent staring contest between himself and West to glance at Claire, and then he determinedly looked away.

"You're bleeding, Claire," he said indifferently, not looking at her. West's arms came out of nowhere, pulling Claire protectively to him. She struggled, wincing as another stabbing pain from her ankle shook her. *Why are they acting like this?*

"You'd like that, wouldn't you? To touch her, to absorb her energy? Look what's happening to Saphirra!" West accused, and Claire noticed a hard edge to his voice she'd never heard before. Indeed, the place where Saphirra and Alex touched had begun to glow a soft golden. Alex growled at him, and Saphirra stood in front of him in a herculean effort to restrain him. He looked down in surprise at Saphirra, who had dug her heels into the soft grass to keep him from launching onto West, and he stopped abruptly.

"I never thought about ever hurting Saph–"

"Oh yeah? Then why does she look so tired? She can barely hold herself up, look–"

"Because you're *pushing* her so hard!"

West stopped resisting and simply stood there, watching Alex with burning eyes. Alex stopped, too, but both girls still kept their hands on them, in case they decided to go at it again. Alex looked down at Saphirra coldly.

"You're no better, Saph. You knew about West. Don't lie," he said quickly as Saphirra made to speak, "I can see it on your face. You didn't bother telling me that West could kill me in an instant? That I was in danger? What else have you hidden from me?"

Those words seemed to jolt them apart; Saphirra pushed him away from her, a look of hurt shock crossing her face. Before they could argue any more, however, West spoke.

"I hadn't told her. If she figured it out, it was on her own. Claire didn't even know up until a few days ago. That doesn't excuse what you've done. You still sucked the life out of her, didn't you? You've done it for months now!" West countered, and Alex fell silent. Saphirra glanced between them, and broke the silence warily.

"West, I asked him to. Both of us did. It's not his fault–"

"But he could have refused!" West shouted angrily.

"He was about to *die,* West! So don't blame him, blame me!"

West looked down at her as if seeing her for the first time. When his eyes slid to Claire's heaving frame, Saphirra seemed to have realized her mistake.

"What did you mean by 'us'?" West asked slowly, his voice shaking with anger.

"We both decided to help him," Claire squeaked. "He needed it–"

"You *knew*!" West shouted at her. "You bloody *knew,* and you didn't tell me? Do you know what I had to do to keep *him,*" he pointed a shaking finger at Alex, "alive? I nearly got killed saving his neck!"

"If you knew what I was, why didn't you warn me?" Alex shouted hotly. "Why didn't you tell me what you were?"

"Oh don't make me laugh!" West spat bitterly, turning his blazing eyes on Alex. "I know you followed me last night! You've obviously known for a while. I know you saw what I do."

Alex looked stunned. He couldn't seem to make his mouth form words; after a long moment of silence, he spoke.

"You knew I followed you?" he sounded confused. West's expression softened a little.

"Of course I knew. I've been a Hunter for years."

The sentence sent a chill down Claire's spine, even if she already knew. Alex stared at him.

"Years..." He said, sounding lost. Saphirra whipped around and looked at Claire, somehow conveying that she hadn't expected this, either. West frowned at them.

"Oh don't be stupid. You know what a Hunter can do. And you followed me, which means you know my newest job."

"And what would that be?" Alex asked sarcastically, a hard edge returning to his voice. West gave him a significant look, and the next few words he said made Claire's stomach drop.

"I have to kill you."

❧

What else have you been hiding from me?
The words had reverberated through her heart, slowly but surely returning it to the stone it once was. She wanted to cry, to shout, to scream. It hadn't been a choice. Hiding her past had been the only way she could live her life without remorse, Alex knew that. She didn't mean any harm by it, but she'd needed it. Of all the things to shout at her...She looked up into Alex's face, but found she was, once again, unable to meet his piercing eyes. She had to say something. Anything.

"You can't! He's not going to harm anyone! He's not dangerous, are you, Alex?"

Saphirra's cry shattered the silence, causing every eye to turn on her. She pushed Alex further away, ignoring her shaking knees.

"Saphirra, let him think what he thinks. I'm not a savage, and I know that," Alex told her quietly, putting a hand on her shoulder. West glared at them both.

"Then what do you call what you do? You *kill* innocent people, just to absorb their energy. And you think you aren't dangerous," he spat coldly. Saphirra looked up at his face, and the twisted fury it held scared her. Alex looked down solemnly.

"I...I didn't chose to be this way. Professor Lockson bit me. He turned me into what I am, and I wish I could go back to being normal, being *human,* but I might not be able to anymore," he looked downcast, and tightened his grip on Saphirra's shoulder as she made to speak. Saphirra looked up at him instead, puzzled. Something was off here.

"West...What are you *doing?* Don't get mad at him, he's—" Saphirra began in a whisper, but West cut her off.

"Don't worry," he said loudly, then bent down to whisper in Claire's ear. He looked up again and said venomously, "He'll only suffer for a bit. I have to kill him, no matter what you say. Why would I if he wasn't bad? I didn't choose to be asked to kill him either! I have to be this way." His eyes never left Alex's face. Saphirra's expression was frozen in horror.

"What are you *talking* about? You know what? Never mind. You want to kill me? Fine. Let's see if you can," Alex said, gently pushing Saphirra aside. She stumbled towards Claire as West pushed her aside too. Alex took a step forward, his eyes glinting in the morning dregs of sunlight. His face held contorted fury. West smiled grimly.

"Fine."

"No, please, you guys are best friends! Don't listen to your boss, West! Please!" Saphirra pleaded, but Claire held her back silently.

"Saphirra, it's a trick."

Saphirra glanced at Claire for a moment, bewildered.

"What?"

"He's not actually going to hurt Alex. It just has to look like it. He's under a contract, so he has to kill whomsoever his boss tells him to. He has to make it look like he's going to kill Alex, because he thinks someone's watching. It'll be fine," she assured Saphirra.

West pulling a revolver out of his pocket, pointing the barrel steadily between Alex's eyes, which had turned the deepest shade of violet. Saphirra tried to run between them, but Claire held her back. All too late, she saw a flaw in West's plan.

Alex didn't know West was only putting on a show. Alex thought this was *real*. And if she told him now, whoever was apparently watching them would hear her.

"Saphirra, move aside!" It was an order, and Saphirra hated that.

"Don't, you idiot!" Claire hissed at West, glaring up at him. *"Alex thinks it's real."* West shook his head.

"I'll tell him somehow. Now, let *go*," he yanked his arm away from Claire, and she let her hand fall to her side. Saphirra suddenly felt the ground leave her feet, and she looked around. Alex had half-carried, half-pushed Saphirra and Claire into the corner of one of the buildings. Saphirra glanced at Claire's panic stricken face, and knew she had to say something—and fast.

"Alex, you have to listen to me, West is–"

"What? A traitor? Bent on killing his best friend? I know!" he shouted at Saphirra, and she saw something break within him, as if he knew it was the end. Saphirra held on to him, trying desperately to pull him back. Her fruitless efforts caught Claire's attention, and together they pulled Alex aside.

"For god's sake, listen to me! West is trying to–"

"Watch out!" Alex shoved them aside just as something exploded onto the rooftop, shining bright golden light like a firework before reducing to smoke. Saphirra cringed in pain as she landed on her side, tumbling into Claire.

"What was that?" Saphirra asked, disoriented. Alex picked up a shining silver capsule, with the remains of golden dust inside.

"I think West has a gun now," Claire muttered to Saphirra as Alex swore loudly. He took off into the air, flapping his feathery wings carefully. He flew as far away from their spot as possible, and as he flew, Saphirra noticed huge, black claws protruding from his fingers. Claire moved over to Saphirra, staring at the place where the sun bullet had landed. This would be worse than she thought.

"You are going to regret this!" she heard West call angrily. He wouldn't forget that he was only acting; would he? She peered around the corner of the building apprehensively. Claire looked extremely distraught; she was wringing her hands nervously, watching with both awe and disgust as Alex swooped down over West, obscuring their view.

"He's a Siren."

If Saphirra hadn't seen Claire's mouth move, she wouldn't have believed she'd said anything at all. Claire's voice sounded hollow, as if she'd given up.

"What?"

"West is a Siren. A soul-sucking, Viceprus-hating Siren!" Claire cried, looking slightly insane as she sank to the ground. Saphirra stared blankly at her. She'd heard the words, but was unable to process them.

"I-I don't understand."

"Of course you don't!" Claire wailed, looking positively tortured. "Sirens *hate* Vicepruses, they always have! It was in my mythology textbook, but I hadn't put it together until I realized how West's job and this fit. If his boss knows what he is, wouldn't it make all the more sense to hire him? His hatred of the creatures wouldn't simply be because of how he's lived, it would be ingrained. Primal."

Saphirra gasped, and watched with new found fear as West pulled the trigger of his revolver.

"What happens if his Siren instincts take over?"

"I was thinking the exact same thing," Claire said grimly. It was as if Saphirra was frozen to the ground; she couldn't move even if she wanted to. What looked like a tiny sun shot out of the silver barrel, blasting towards Alex so fast that all she could see was a glowing blur. Alex dodged, and the tiny sun hit one of the university buildings, showering that side of the quad in broken glass. Sunlight scattered like beams from the explosion, and Alex narrowly dodged them, too. The noise was oddly muted, as if she was hearing it from far away instead of being right next to the noise. Alex flew from building to building, dodging the bullets West shot at him with reckless abandon. West seemed to have lost all sense of what he was doing; he stood with feet planted wide, one steady hand holding the silver gun as he shot coolly at Alex, barely missing the mark each time. Something in him seemed to transform before her eyes; the once calm, caring West had turned into someone dark, someone cold. The ground shook slightly as West shot bullets at Alex, his expression calculating, his eyes narrowed. A tiny explosion occurred each time he missed his mark, and the ground beneath her feet tremored from the impact. The corners of buildings exploded one by one as each bullet struck, and bricks fell down to the quad about thirty feet below.

Saphirra backed away from the corner to turn to Claire, whose eyes seemed glassy and unfocused. After a moment, Claire spoke.

"I can't take this anymore! I'm going out there."

Saphirra watched her get up, unable to do anything herself. She couldn't will her legs to move, no matter how much she tried. Instead, she watched out of the corner of her eye as Claire searched for a fire escape to climb onto the roof.

"Why would you go up there? It's dangerous!" Saphirra shouted as Claire's hands wound around the first rusty rung. Claire looked down at her, eyes fathomless and dark.

"I need to let Alex know before it's too late. That West's a Siren, that he'd initially meant to pretend but..." she cut herself off, watching as West coldly shot another bullet, hissing angrily when it missed. "I'm not so sure anymore. He needs to hear all of it. I don't care what it takes." She grit her teeth and watched West, pausing at the end of the stairs. As West bent down to reload his gun, she began to climb. As she reached the top and disappeared onto the roof, Alex swooped down to the ground, his eyes lit with fury. He seemed almost demon-like as he barreled towards West, who dodged in the nick of time. One of Alex's wings clipped West's mouth, and he screamed as a long line of red marred his cheek. Saphirra heard Claire's gasp from above, all to evident in the eerie silence caused by Alex's attack.

*That didn't look like acting to me...*Saphirra thought anxiously. Panic started ebbing through her determined calm, and she clutched the edge of the roof in anticipation. Alex turned over in the air, opening his mouth, and to Saphirra, it seemed like he was about to apologize. His wings beat automatically to keep him aloft, and his wing accidentally smacked into West. West went sprawling through the air, landing on his side. This time, the groan was evident; Alex's wingtip had cut through West's shirt, slashing his forearm. Saphirra's squeak of horror mingled with West's shout of agony.

"West!" Claire screamed from above, looking back down at the fire escape as if contemplating coming back down again. Saphirra willed herself not to run out, not to scream at Alex for what he had done. She had to stop them, before they ended up killing each other. West's murderous scream cut through the quad.

"Fine. You want to play that way, then we will!"

Saphirra's heart turned to ice as she looked just in time to see West twist around on the ground, pointing his silver barrel towards Alex. This time the tiny sun hit its target; Alex screamed in agony as it exploded into his leg, making his jeans shine as if the residue sunbeams were struggling to get out. He crashed to the ground, clutching at his leg in pure agony.

"Alex!" Saphirra's panic stricken squeak was echoed in Claire's voice. She sank down to the gravelly floor, shaking.

"Alex, stop! West's acting! It's not real; he's not trying to do anything!" Claire had somehow made it back to the ground, and passed Saphirra as she ran further out into the quad, calling to Alex. None of them seemed to have heard her, which was just as well; Saphirra dragged Claire back behind the shelter of the bricks, clamping a hand firmly on either shoulder.

"Claire. Don't shout that, it could ruin everything."

"I know," Claire said, tears brimming in her hazel eyes, "but I couldn't help it. Look at them out there! They're killing each other!"

Claire's statement seemed to be true; West stood over Alex's cringing frame, his gun pressed to Alex's temple. Alex had curled into a ball, and Saphirra could tell he was shaking. She started running towards him, calling out. In the second that West looked up to the sudden noise, Alex had kicked out, his feet connecting with West's knees. As West crumpled to the ground, Alex took to the air again, dodging a sun bullet as he went. West shot again and missed, hitting the edge of the building they were hiding behind as if in slow motion. It exploded, the deafening bang piercing through her skull, the force of the blast throwing Claire and Saphirra into the wall of the next building.

The whole world seemed to be muffled. Nothing made any sound at all.

Saphirra fell to the floor, bits and flecks of gravel biting into her cheeks. She was dimly aware of the rush of blood to her head, and the shiver of something wet trickling steadily down her neck. Her head throbbed and her ears rang. For a moment she wondered if the blast had made her go deaf, but then she heard Claire cry out in pain next to her.

"West, stop! You've hurt them!" Alex roared, and Saphirra urged herself to speak, but it was impossible. She silently thanked him with her eyes, and her vision of the quad was wavering, as if she was looking at it through a glass of water. She fought to keep awake, and as her vision focused, she saw sunbeams pouring like blood from Alex's leg. He was careful not to put pressure on it as he took to the skies again.

"No, Alex! This will end, *now*!" West's furious call echoed oddly in her ears. She watched them fight, trying to call at to them, to make them stop, but her voice stuck in her throat. She glanced at Claire, who was curled up, clutching her wrist in a futile effort to stop the bleeding. She looked as bad as Saphirra felt—a small gash on the side of her head was letting blood pour down the side of her face, and her knee was soaked in blood. The scars on her arms stood out in the haze in her brain, as if to remind her she'd been hurt worse before. She turned her attention back to West as Alex came to him. Alex's shape blurred and disappeared, and Saphirra heard another sun bullet miss its mark, crashing into a building a few yards away. She saw Alex's shape reform behind West, and as he gripped West in a stranglehold, West cocked his pistol at Alex' head. As Alex's wings disappeared into vapor and his eyes turned back into bright blue, she could have sworn West whispered something quickly into his ear. Alex nodded, and West flicked a switch on his gun. They stayed like that for a split second, and then a shot rang through the quad. The tiny sun made contact with Alex's head, and he was blasted off his feet, landing sprawled onto the grass.

"No! Alex!" Saphirra shouted, struggling to get up. Claire did the same, collapsing onto the ground a second later. Saphirra saw West's swimming figure flick open his blue metallic cell phone, waiting as it rang on the other end. Saphirra fought back the arms of sleep that threatened to pull her under, straining to stay conscious. As the world around her faded away, West spoke into the phone, his words echoing oddly into her ears.

"Hey, boss? It's done. The Viceprus is dead."

Chapter 27
Safe Haven

Claire didn't understand. How *could* she understand? West had just shot his best friend to death. She saw Saphirra pass out beside her, and she continued her fruitless efforts to get off the gravel and onto her feet. What had just happened was playing on a constant loop in her mind: Alex, his wings disintegrating, West, his chocolate brown hair flopping into his eyes as he aimed the gun at Alex's head; and then the fatal gunshot. She'd watched Alex, only a few yards away from her, be blasted backwards from the force of the blow, sprawling onto the warm, uncut grass. The sunbeams from the last shot on his leg had faded, leaving a golden glow around the bullet hole.

She knew she should feel the same despair she'd felt when she'd thought Alex was dead only days ago, but she couldn't. She felt numb, and she knew something wasn't right. West was walking all too casually towards Alex, peering around the quad as if he should be looking for somebody. As he glanced at the building above her, she did the same, wincing as her head throbbed painfully. She thought she saw a whirl of black and white, a blur that looked suspiciously like Professor Lockson, but maybe she was imagining things. Maybe she imagined everything, and she would wake up soon, cold sweat running down her back, sighing as she would realize it was all a dream.

Claire winced again as her head throbbed. No, it couldn't be a dream; it was impossible to feel pain in dreams. She turned her gaze back to West, who was kneeling over Alex and murmuring something, as if he expected Alex to talk back. She stared at West with disbelief. Pure hatred coursed through her veins as something inside her broke. How could he let his anger get the better of him? How could he—

She blinked, hoping she hadn't imagined what she just saw: Alex had *moved*. She rubbed her eyes, trying to get a better look. West was standing over him, his eyes glued to the corner of one of the buildings. A flicker of confusion crossed his face, and then it was gone, replaced by stoic indifference. He hesitated another moment, his gun frozen over Alex's motionless body, and then bent back down towards him. Within moments, he had pulled Alex to his feet. Alex was moving, talking, even *laughing* a little, clutching onto West for support as they walked over to the girls. Alex glanced towards the unconscious Saphirra, and his smile slid off his face as he raced over to her.

"...How?" Claire asked weakly, sliding further down the wall she was leaning on. West ran to her and cradled her in his arms, and she dimly noticed how comforting his heat felt.

"Sun bullets don't work on humans, remember? West shot me at just the right moment, when I'd turned back into a human," Alex explained quietly. He clasped a hand to his head and sank to the ground, squeezing his eyes shut, a grimace taking over his expression. "Damn it West, you nearly gave me a concussion." She could have sworn she saw the tiniest smile flit across his face.

"But...But I saw him shoot you. It hit your head–"

"And it glanced right off," he interrupted, smiling grimly. "He didn't mean to kill me, in the end. Although I wish I had known sooner," he said angrily, turning to West. West shrugged and sat back on his heels, running a hand through his hair.

"I assumed you'd have your doubts and figure it out," West said. Alex smiled and nodded.

"I knew something was off when you kept aiming to the left of me," he admitted. "Still, some of those were really close. You could have nearly blown my head off!"

"It's hard to ruin a perfect shot," West grinned and shrugged again. "Especially if I never miss. At least my boss thinks Alex is dead, and that's all that matters. I was right—he was watching us."

West had stretched his hands over Saphirra's wounds as he spoke, and Claire watched in wonder as the cuts and bruises slowly began to disappear. It never ceased to baffle her how the same glow that Alex used to draw energy could be pushed out to heal. West turned to her next, and within a minute, the pain had eased enough for Claire to see that the blood vanish from her arms. Claire got up suddenly, wincing as her stomach rolled.

"I don't think you're fully cured, Claire. Saphirra looked like she sprained something, and I don't think I cured that. Do you feel okay?"

"Not really," Claire mumbled, holding her head as the world around her spun.

"What happened to the cuts? What happened to the bruises?" Alex asked in a panicked voice. Something seemed to be processing behind Alex's tired eyes, and he glanced from West and back to Claire with new found interest.

"You mean they have powers? Hunters have powers?"

"No, actually. I'm the only one." He turned to Alex, healing his scrapes and bruises as fast as he could. Claire noticed his voice seemed taught, but she couldn't muster up the strength to comment on it. He paused at the place his bullet had hit Alex's leg, frowning as he concentrated with all his might. Claire watched the two of them hopefully, but Alex simply sank lower onto the ground. "It's not working, West."

"I'm really sorry about your leg," West said apologetically, glancing down at the glaringly open wound as if in disbelief. *He can't heal damage caused by sunstones?* The panicked thought seemed to cross West's mind, too; he paused for a moment, then pulled out his cell phone, dialing for an ambulance. "Change of plan. We're going to get you to the hospital, see what they can do. Chances are that stuff will poison your system. I wouldn't know; I've never missed a Viceprus's heart before. They always died before—"Claire gave him a scathing look, and he swallowed and continued. "Right. Anyway, you'll be fine. Don't worry, Alex." He said the last sentiment without conviction, as if he didn't believe it in the slightest.

"What are we going to tell the hospital about my wound? We learned how to bottle sunshine and accidentally injected it into my leg?" Alex asked sarcastically, a hint of a smile playing across his face.

So they're joking around. Good. She struggled to speak, to reach out to West, but she couldn't bother. She was suddenly very sleepy. It wasn't long until Claire heard police sirens wail in the distance, and something brushed her lips lightly, almost so that she thought she could have imagined it. She opened her eyes one last time to see West turning away from her, and wondered if he'd just kissed her. She thought she heard West mutter,

"Claire's not fully cured, either. Something's wrong. My healing abilities aren't working as much as they used to." The panic in his voice almost dragged Claire out of the stupor she was in. "I think they might need to stay in the hospital too."

Before she could contemplate this further, she had been dragged down into unconsciousness. Her own salty metallic taste of blood was the last thing she remembered.

Evelyn stared into her mirror, her worried expression reflected back at her. She lightly touched the glowing C on her neck, feeling the intense heat it gave off. She whisked her fingers away, as if burned. It didn't hurt anymore, but it still felt strange. She had no idea how it had gotten there, but she had the strangest feeling Ry had something to do with it. She could only remember pain, all concentrated on her wrists, her arms, and her neck. It had been a while before she'd remembered hearing a cold, merciless voice, but it wasn't Ry's voice. This one was as not careful and thoughtful as Ry's was; it was bored, calculating, and above all, a woman's voice. She remembered kneeling on the soft, plush carpet of his office, gazing up at someone who remained faceless in her mind. It was as if her figure was enveloped in black, and she couldn't see her features at all. Ry's face swam to the surface of her mind once again, and she shook her head angrily. It couldn't have been him!

Ry couldn't tamper with memories...could he? He had intelligence beyond anything anyone has ever seen before, but...*He couldn't do this to me,* she told herself firmly, gazing again at the faint mark on her neck. *He wouldn't.* Somehow, she couldn't help doubting it, if only just a little. Then again, there were times when she felt like she wasn't herself, like she was under someone else's control. Evelyn sometimes found herself on the floor with no idea of having gotten there, and even in places that she'd never even visited before. Panic gripped her heart as she let her fingertip touch the ornate mark on her skin once more. It glowed brightly, and she withdrew her hand again. *What's happening to me?* She'd constantly denied the possibility that someone had been wiping her memory, but now she wasn't so sure. What else had this mysterious person done to her? *Rather, what did they make me do?* Evelyn walked away from the mirror in disgust, pulling up the lapel of her shirt to hide the mark. She needed energy more than ever, if only simply to distract herself. She walked through her tiny apartment and out the door, turning onto a familiar street. She began to run past alleys and streets, the building's features blurring as she ran faster. The shops and neon signs of Chicago blurred as she ran, turning into a swirling haze of pinks and oranges. Only a trained eye would see her now, but only as a brown and white blur. It was time to hunt.

She headed towards Lake Michigan, darting behind anything that could give her cover as she went. The sun was especially strong, and she didn't want to risk another energy overload. She needed someone, *something,* to remind her she was in control.

That she will *always* be in control.

As she turned down a side street, the blazing sun above seemed to direct all its rays down at her, making it excruciating to move. She decided on ducking into a shady alleyway the next chance she got, but she never made it that far.

She felt like she'd burst into flames.

Evelyn glanced at her hands in horror, freezing where she stood. Her skin had begun to glow a bright golden, and a blinding heat had begun to creep up her spine. She looked around frantically, ignoring the stares from walking pedestrians as she searched desperately for shade.

Too much sun exposure, she chided herself, trying frantically to get her limbs to move faster. As powerful as they were, they weren't any match for the sun. Suddenly, powerful arms were pulling her down the street and into a grimy bar. The faded paint chips of the tavern sign flecked onto the ground as her savior yanked open the door and let it slam behind them. The scent of stale beer and smoke immediately wafted to her, and she tried her hardest not to gag. Images blurred as the person holding dug into her shoulder and forced her upright, muttering into her ear in a low, gruff voice,

"Follow me."

She turned around to try and see who had saved her, but her eyes only met hazy shadow. Another tug on her sleeve and she followed into the dim bar, weaving past a large crowd watching the television screen, and into a back room. She looked around for a moment, allowing her eyes to adjust to the dim light through the dirty window, then sank to the damp cement floor, chest heaving. She couldn't move. She looked up as the person entered in behind her, his violet eyes glittering.

"Thank you." She couldn't keep the relief out of her voice as she spoke. "I'm Evelyn."

"The name's Akakios. Pleased to meet you," he said, sitting down next to her. "Where am I?"

"A bar," he said sarcastically. She didn't push him for more information, and after a moment of silence he sighed. "These drunken idiots supply me with more than enough energy when I need it." She stared blankly at him, irritated when all her eyes met were shadows once more. She felt around the room for a light switch, but he stopped her.

"I'd rather you not know what I look like," he laughed. "We got to be careful in these times, after all." He shrugged.

"Interesting," she said quietly, studying her surroundings. "Why'd you save me?"

It was his turn to study her. He watched her for a moment, as if he was choosing his words carefully.

"Vicepruses like you don't like mixing with my type. We stay our separate ways, but you don't seem like the type to wander willingly here. And I've been in the same situation myself once or twice," he said grimly. "I know I wished someone had been there for me." She nodded and let her hands rest on the damp floor. Its coldness felt lovely on her feverish skin. Akakios watched her for another moment, and then spoke up hesitantly.

"...Ah, I see my sister has branded you. You must be very important," he said, more to himself than to her.

"Your...*sister?" she* managed. Panic pulsed through her. *Is he the same one that's been controlling me?* She wondered. But...it didn't make sense. Vicepruses couldn't control people...At least, not that way. She was sure it was a Siren. Still...She waited for him to elaborate.

He didn't.

It took a moment before the burning heat faded from her skin, and she could fully get a look around the room. As her eyes adjusted to the darkness, she noticed piles of beer boxes in their corner, nearly walling her into the room. She suddenly realized that Akakios was blocking her only exit. Her head began to spin. She sat up suddenly, remembering where she was, *what* she was. She needed to get out of there, and fast.

"Thanks for helping me, but I really do have to leave," she said carefully, pulling herself upright. The sudden movement made her dizzy, and she clasped onto Akakios's shoulder for support. Evelyn was startled to feel like she was being sucked into a vortex. Colors swirled, and suddenly, she wasn't in the same room anymore. She was in an alleyway, and Akakios had mysteriously disappeared from her side. She stared into the grungy side street, and was shocked to see the same person, his eyes a brilliant violet beneath his drawn hood. Someone with very similar features as him stood by his side, her violet eyes turned to the mud splattered ground beneath her. Her long blonde hair whipped around in the wind, and she spoke quietly, murmuring into his ear. Evelyn stepped closer, and caught the word "brother". He nodded at her as she spoke. She watched the scene un-fold, uncertain whether anybody could see her. Akakios continued to talk to his sister.

"You want me to catch Evelyn when she runs?" he asked incred-ulously. "How do you even know what she'll do?" she started at the mention of her name, and drew even closer to them. Neither figure paid any attention to her. The wind began to whip up as rain fell in straight sheets around them, and the girl drew her coat closer to her, bowing down against the gale.

"Yes. I think she will try to run away. She will figure it out soon enough...Something's wrong. I'm detached from myself." She frowned, sounding bitter. Akakios drew closer to her comfortingly, but never touched her. He held dark suspicion in his eyes.

"And what exactly is it that she will have figured out?"

The young woman looked up at him, as if startled that she'd said anything at all. "What? Nothing. No one. Forget what I said. Just get rid of her."

"Fine. Have your way, Clandestine, just as you always have."

Something clicked as the word Clandestine flew out of Akakios's mouth. Before she could hear more, however, the scene began to dissolve, and the feeling of being sucked though a vacuum overpowered her. Suddenly, she stood back in the dark room, her fingers still lightly pressed into Akakios's shoulder. He looked up at her with saddened eyes.

"I couldn't kill you. It wasn't right. Clandestine couldn't understand what it was like to destroy a life. She doesn't understand much of anything." Heavy misery weighed his words. Evelyn looked down at him, a mixture of despair and sympathy clawing at her heart. This poor man listened to his sister, but something told her that he was forced to. Akakios got up, resting a hand on Evelyn's shoulder. "I know what you saw. I let you see it for a reason, Evelyn. You should go. I have to run, too. I need to get away from her, before…" he shook his head and looked away. "Before something else happens. She carved that into your neck, and she knew you'd find out."

Cold fury began to overwhelm her senses. "She would do this to her own kind? Why me? Has she been the one controlling me?" She was so confused. Within a span of a few moments, she'd finally found out the person controlling her. If only she knew *why*.

"I'm sorry, I don't quite know. I don't understand my sister anymore. She's…she's gone down a different path." He spat the words bitterly at her. Evelyn stared at him.

"What did you just do to me? How could I see this? Why—"

"You shouldn't ask so many questions," he said abruptly, cutting her off. With a sweep of his hands, he opened the door. "You can leave, if you'd like. I know you want to." Something about him seemed desolate, as if he'd already given up. It saddened Evelyn, and beyond reason she wanted to help him. She stood where she was, unsure of what to do. This man held answers for her. And yet...there was her escape route, waiting for her.

"You can leave. Or," he said suddenly, sounding eager, "we can escape together. Run somewhere, far away, and figure out what to do from there. Goodness knows I'd like a companion."

Evelyn bit her lip. She knew she should go back to Ry, but for what? He didn't explain anything to her, and treated her like dirt. She hesitated, one foot towards the door, her eyes trained on his face. His violet eyes slowly faded into a dark brown, swallowing up his face in darkness once more.

"Go," he sighed. "I understand. However, if you change your mind, travel to New York City and look for one of us. Ask for me, they'll point you in the right direction. I don't stay in one place for too long, but for you I'll make an exception. I see what she's done to you," he whispered. "She'll never quit, Evelyn. She'll hunt you down and torture you without you knowing and create chaos in your mind. She won't rest until she gets what she wants. I'll give you a few weeks, maybe two or three, to decide. After the third week I'll be gone. Don't do this to yourself," he told her, gesturing around the room. "We can start over, start better off. I can give you a better life. Think about it." With that, Akakios whipped out the door and into the dark tavern, nodding at someone behind the bar. Evelyn stood frozen for a moment, unsure of what had just happened, and then made her way back through the smoky bar and out the door into the intense sunlight, feeling unsure of herself. What scared her was that she would have taken his offer in a heartbeat, if he hadn't interrupted. She took off down the street, taking a different route back towards Ry's office and her apartment. She suddenly didn't want energy anymore. She felt paranoid, as if Clandestine was looking over her shoulder, watching her. *Why is a member of the Siren Council after me?* She couldn't possibly be aware of what Ry was doing. No one was, not even her. Evelyn slowed her pace and ducked into a small ice cream shop, relishing the cool air. She needed to think. Ry would have noticed her absence, and would most likely be furious when she returned. The thought made her shudder. Why did she put up with him and his miserable mood swings? Why did she care? It was as if some primal instinct took over whenever she saw him. She realized now that she didn't care for him at all, and yet...*I still act so stupid around him,* she thought bitterly. Evelyn contemplated Akakios's offer. Move to New York, start a new life. It would be nice having an ally for a change. She bought an ice cream cone and headed back to their building, still deep in thought. As she rounded the corner and saw Ry standing expectantly on the steps of their apartment building, fury lighting up his cold dark eyes, she repressed another shudder. *Maybe New York wouldn't be so bad after all.*

Chapter 28
Poisonous Alliances

West gazed through the glass at Claire and Saphirra's beds, side by side in the stark white hospital room. Neither was stirring.

What have I done? He thought, holding his head in his hands. He was trying to act like he hated Alex, but when Alex had hit him like that, something had snapped. He could barely control the Siren in him anymore; he had had to bite his lip to keep the upsurge of swelling song from escaping his lips. It had taken all his strength to regain control of himself, to not blast Alex off his feet. He had ended up hurting more than Alex in the process—he'd hurt Claire and Saphirra, too. He fingered the bandage across his cheek, remembering the nurse saying their injuries were a lot less than she had imagined. After she had patched him up, she's said none of them were in bad shape, and that they'd be fine soon. She must have said that to console him, but it just made him desolate. *What happened to my healing abilities?* West wondered. The thought that they weren't as effective as he had thought worried him. He thought back to the destruction he had caused, knowing they wouldn't have injuries in the first place if he hadn't lost control. Couldn't he have made it realistic without blowing up half the quad? The construction crew Saphirra's dad had assigned to the university would be moving from the south building to the quad in a few days, and they probably had much more to repair than her dad had paid for. West sighed, shifting uncomfortably in the hard white chair across from Alex's room. Apparently, the nurse knew Alex—she'd explained in detail to him that there were no more squirrels around the hospital. West had no idea what that was supposed to mean, but he'd watched the nurse ramble on long after Alex had fallen asleep.

They hadn't had much to fix with West, but for some reason his wounds from Alex's wing wouldn't heal on their own. He'd had to have his arm stitched up, and he had winced as the bustling nurse knocked into his shoulder. She'd been talking the whole time, glancing out the window every few minutes, obviously wishing she were anywhere else but there.

"You four were pretty lucky. That was a pretty bad gang attack, wasn't it? I bet the media are eating up that college you four stay at right now," she'd shaken her head as she put some sort of liquid on the thin line on his cheek. "Those news crews are always looking for something bad in Chicago—it's not like everyone that lives here are criminals!" she sighed and continued when West didn't interject. "Oh, it's going to leave a thin scar, but it won't be very visible. It's too bad, with your looks and all." she continued, running a cotton swab down his cheekbone, spreading a thick liquid down it.

"Thanks."

The nurse mmhmmed at him, taking the cotton swab and dipping it into some sort of oozing clear liquid. He sighed as the nurse continued.

"Your blonde friend here told me about it in detail. You're lucky you didn't get killed! There," She said, patting a bandage into place, "You're all fixed up. Your friend is going to be a while, though." She jabbed a thumb in Alex's direction. "That one won't wake up. They found hundreds of fragments of a golden half–glass half liquid thing in his body. It started poisoning his system before his antibodies stopped it. Good thing you guys came in when you did. The doctor reckons we've saved his life. Sucked the poison right out of him. Strange, isn't it? Using weapons like that. I swear, gangs, shooting in a university, especially such a prestigious one..." she shook her head disapprovingly. "I expect the news crews already showed up and left. Things like this aren't that uncommon, but blowing up the place..." The nurse had trailed off, and lead had enveloped West's heart.

"Oh that's just from the construction," he said hurriedly. "The university is—"

"Getting a new wing, yes, I know," the nurse said tiredly. "Your friend explained that to me, too. Still, it's unsettling, isn't it? Are you sure you wouldn't like to talk some of the counselors here?"

"I'm sure of it," he'd said grimly.

Now he got up gingerly, wincing as the stitches pulled at his arm. He'd...He'd poisoned his best friend. He felt horrible. As West pushed open Alex's door and approached his bed, he stared at the various monitors hooked up around him. They beeped irritatingly, and the IV drip echoed oddly in his ears. Alex's eyes were closed, and he looked extremely pale. His leg was wrapped in a thick layer of gauze. West reached out a tentative hand, but couldn't bring himself to touch him.

"You're pretty good at feigning sleep. How long has it been since you couldn't? Sleep, I mean," he asked coyly. Alex's eyes snapped open, startled. He smiled slightly.

"At least a month or two. You have to know I wasn't born this way, West. It happened near the beginning of the summer. For weeks I didn't know how much damage I could cause. I didn't know anything, really." He swallowed, and continued in a quieter voice, "Hey, at least we're all safe from your boss, for now." He winced as he tried to sit up, clutching his leg. "You hurt them though. Saphirra and Claire, I mean."

"I *poisoned* you, Alex. I–I don't know what came over me, I didn't mean to hit you, I'm sorry, I–" Alex cut him off with a shake of his head.

"It's fine. Seriously," He added, seeing West's doubtful look, "I'm perfectly fine. I gave you that scar, and those stitches on your shoulder, so we're even," he smiled at his own lame joke. "Have you actually hit a Viceprus with one of those stupid bullets before?" Alex asked. He must have guessed the truth from West's eyes, because he sighed and sank into the stiff pillows surrounding him, his eyes filled with pity.

"At least that explains your aura."

West froze.

"What?"

Alex nodded, avoiding West's eyes. "You look different. I can't really explain it. It's like you've got this dark aura about you...almost like anti-energy. I know that sounds weird, but..." Alex wrinkled his nose, and West laughed nervously. *It's the Siren blood in my veins,* he thought sadly. *Will I ever be able to tell him?*

Reedhima Mandlik

"When I fought you, it looked like you'd done it thousands of times before. How many have you killed?" Alex asked bluntly.

"Too many to count."

Alex sighed again. "West, I've been thinking about what you said...about how your boss said you needed to kill me, so I must be bad. I know it was an act then, but...do you really think that way?"

West shrugged, hating himself for his answer. "Sometimes. I can't really go against him anyway. It's just easier believing I'm doing something good." The truth of it bit at him like ice. Alex frowned.

"Maybe some of the Vicepruses you've killed were good, West. Did you ever think of that?" he asked gently. West nodded solemnly, grief filling the pit of his stomach. He followed his boss's advice so frantically, and hadn't thought of *what* it was he was really doing until these last few months. West buried his face in his hands. How could he trust someone he'd never met so blindly? And yet...He was being blackmailed. He had no choice...right?

"I didn't really think about it until Claire mentioned it a few weeks ago. I know that sounds bad," West said hurriedly. "I wish I could quit my job, but I'll be killed. My *mom* will be killed." His voice was hollow as he remembered his countless victims' screams. He was cruel, he understood that. He'd accepted it as his fate. It wasn't until he'd met Claire that he'd seen he could have another path in life. He hadn't really considered it as something worth trying for before her. She had changed his whole world. *And now, thanks to me, she's lying in a hospital bed.* The thought made him cringe, and he hurriedly pushed Claire out of his mind.

"West, why did your boss tell you to kill me? Who *is* your boss, anyway?" Alex broke through his thoughts, his reddish hair falling into his eyes. West shrugged, wincing as his shoulder screamed in protest.

"That's the problem—I have no idea who he is, or why he wanted to kill you."

"So you just—"Alex groaned, cutting himself off, and West looked at him in alarm. He was clutching onto his leg, trying to tighten his gauze on what West assumed was the bullet wound.

His wound.

"Until I find a way...until *we* find a way for me to become fully human again, I'm stuck like this," Alex told him, groaning and laying his head down on a pillow. "You'll help me, right? I'll explain everything, in time." West watched him guiltily as Alex winced in pain again.

"Alex, I'm–" He began, but Alex held up his hand.

"I think Claire was trying to tell me what you were doing, but I didn't listen to her. I was too furious to care. I'm the one who should be sorry," he admitted weakly. West stretched his hand over Alex's wound, surprised when the familiar warm feeling rushed to his hands. His fingers began to glow, and West concentrated until the leg wound was nothing more than a shining circle of new skin. West grinned at him.

"I guess without the shards it's a regular wound, and if you're not a Viceprus when I heal you, it works." West felt elated, glad he was good for something. Where a dark wound should have been, thin, slightly golden skin had appeared. As West looked closer, he realized it would leave a mark that would no doubt remain there forever. Alex stared at it, and then looked back at West incredulously.

"I was bleeding a few hours ago..." he said thoughtfully, touching it with one cautious finger.

"You sure heal fast," West hinted, sighing with relief. He wasn't sure if he'd put enough force into closing the wound properly. Alex laughed appreciatively.

"No harm, no foul. After all, you're a good fighter...for a Hunter."

"So are you, for a newbie. How'd you.... Well...You know?" West shrugged towards Alex, and winced again as his shoulder cried out in protest. As Alex told the story, West began to feel worse and worse. He'd never known *how* Alex became a Viceprus, and now that he knew, he felt a burning hatred towards Professor Lockson. How could they do something like that? *Why?*

"We have no idea what to do, or what Professor Lockson is up to. Plus, your boss is on our backs too..." Alex finished, swinging his leg gingerly out of his starched white covers and onto the iron bed stand next to him. He cautiously rewrapped the heap of gauze until his leg was completely covered again. Alex grinned again and swung his leg onto the ground, attempting to stand up. Wobbling slightly, he gripped the bed rail as he took another step. With a screeching crunch, he'd pushed the bed a few inches as he'd nearly lost his balance again.

"Whoops."

West jumped to his feet as Alex tottered into the next room. He raced after his surprisingly quick friend, catching up to him moments later. Both walked steadily towards the girl's room, and West paused for a moment. There was something he wanted to do first. Alex watched him with confused eyes as West reached down, pulling out the only part of his old dagger he hadn't used to make Claire's pin, the edge that had always driven into his victim's hearts. He'd had it molded it into a type of smaller dagger, just in case. Alex glanced at it apprehensively.

"This was part of my original weapon," West explained, pointing to the dagger unnecessarily.

"You killed Vicepruses with a tiny dagger?" Alex asked, incredulous.

"No, this is only part of it," West said seriously, examining the tip.

"You carry a dagger around?"

As they passed a nearby window, West opened it as wide as it could go, then stepped back and aimed. With a flick of his wrist, he tossed the dagger out of the window, watching it sail across the grounds, landing in a nearby bush. Alex stared at him wordlessly.

"Not anymore."

West held out his arm. Alex leaned on him gratefully, and the two friends walked into Claire and Saphirra's room, their friendship closer than ever.

Clandestine stormed into Ryan's office, ignoring all reason. Mad fury swelled within her as she gripped his desk her nails splintering the wood.

"Is he dead?" she demanded, making him jump. He whipped around, his shock of black hair falling into his pureblood golden eyes, and cursed silently as he saw who was approaching him. He leapt at her, and within a split second she was in a stranglehold on the plush white carpet.

"Not again," he hissed at her through gritted teeth. "You will never take over again." His glare turned into a mild look of confusion as he looked over her. "It's you," he whispered. "Clandestine." His grip on her loosened enough for her to wrestle his wrists away from her, forcing him to look into her eyes.

"Let *go* of me," she said calmly, a snake of gold flitting through her irises. He released her abruptly and she pushed him aside, getting to her feet lithely. He stayed crouched on the floor, glaring at her with venomous hatred.

"Why would you target me? What do you *want* from me?" he asked for what felt like the thousandth time. She rolled her eyes and ignored him.

"Sit upright," she ordered. Ryan sat up, still glaring daggers at her. Clandestine smirked at him.

"Is he dead?" she asked again. Ryan tried his hardest not to answer; she tipped his chin up until his eyes met hers.

"I *said,* is. He. Dead?"

"Yes," He gasped finally. "He's dead. I saw it with my own eyes."

Clandestine's mood lightened. Finally, something was going *right*. Still...she tilted her head to the side, contemplating Ryan's resilient stature. He continued resisting, even when under her control. It had taken all her concentration to even get this far. She was at a loss. How could she keep him from remembering? She mulled over her options, staring out at the stormy sky. Rain whistled through the trees and onto the window, as if it intended to blast the windows apart.

"What do you want with me?" Ryan shook as he struggled to get the words out of his mouth. Spiteful hatred lined every word.

"I want you to continue with your plan," she told him coldly. "Attack Validus last. He has too many allies, and the Council will no doubt be guarding him the most. In fact," she said suddenly, "take a break for a while. Lay low. We have a week or two, after all. We don't need more suspicions drawn to the prophecy."

"How do you know about the prophecy?" he asked numbly. He was beginning to look lost and confused, and Clandestine noted the force behind his words had grown weaker, more lethargic. She smiled to herself and concentrated harder. Her process couldn't be explained, even to herself; it was as if explaining to someone how to breathe. The natural flow of thoughts and processes were subconscious to her; she'd never had to think about it before. But now, as she drew her attention to the missing links between Ryan's memories, she found her concentration lapsing; she began to doubt herself, to wonder if she'd really cleared her mind this way, or another. The puzzle pieces of Ryan's mind dissected themselves before her, and his mouth went slack. She scrambled to reattach them best as she could, her mind's eye concentrating on her one goal. Confusion was not an option. Not now, anyway.

"I know all," she said finally, satisfied as her haze of panic cleared and she could understand once more. She concentrated harder until an image formed in his mind, one strong enough to wipe out all others. She grinned as it enveloped him, and he collapsed to the floor, completely unresponsive.

"This time, you will *not* remember me," she said quickly, whirling around towards the door. She heard the thud of Ryan falling over, and felt satisfied that her mind tricks had done their job, even if it was a little later than usual. Sprinting down the stairs and out the door, she practically knocked into a young man, his blonde hair soaked with rain. She looked up into his violet eyes, and smiled. Her twin simply frowned at her.

"Are you done torturing others, Clandestine? Are you finally through? I see the smug look on your face. Don't pretend it's over. Don't lie to me." He sounded tired, as if he knew what she would say. Clandestine pulled him into the shelter of a nearby building, ignoring the pedestrians bustling past them.

"You *dare*—"

"Yes, I very well *dare*. I know what you tried to do. You really are pathetic, Clandestine."

So he does know. The thought didn't surprise her; after all, how could she expect him to let it go, to ignore a Siren in his midst? Surely he'd caught that much. He confirmed her thoughts moments later.

"Sending Faron's child after me, Clandestine? What other dirty tricks are you going to pull?"

"It was necessary," she said indifferently, biting back her harsh reply. How could he understand what she wanted, if he had already closed his mind to it? It was no use trying to convince him anymore. And since he was in the way...

Either save a few lives or save many. That was her choice. She'd chosen many, and he'd decided to try and stop her. What did he expect, that she would let him roam free? That she would let him ruin everything?

"Similarity in the mind and body is crucial, brother. We must think alike," she said, twisting around to check no one was listening. "I gave you the option years ago. My offer still stands. You don't seem to be doing too well right now, maybe you'd like to reconsider?" she couldn't help but sound hopeful. She'd loved him, once. Before his morals got in the way of reason. Her brother did indeed look worse for wear; his blonde hair had begun to thin out, his features becoming gaunt and reedy. He looked pale, withdrawn. A frown seemed to be set onto his face, with no signs of changing. He shook his head, and when he looked at her his eyes had changed back to a deep brown.

"Never again, Clandestine. I'm done with your crazy plans. Don't try to follow me, unless you or my attacker wants to die a painful death."

"Then why did you come here?" Clandestine shouted at him, frustrated, as he began to walk away from her. He stopped, his back still to her, and called over his shoulder,

"I wanted you to know where I stand. I gave you the option years ago. My offer still stands. You don't seem to be doing too well right now, maybe you'd like to reconsider?" His mocking tone stabbed through her, and it took all she had to repress the blind fury that had threatened to engulf her.

"Akakios, do not go against me," she warned, "Or you will regret it."

"Why? Because you're the strongest, the most elusive? Because you believe you are superior to everyone and everything, just as you always have?" His spite bit into her, and she lost it.

"Because I will rip you to shreds if you hesitate," she growled. He turned on his heel and brushed past her, ignoring her last words. His arrogance made her blood boil. She ran after him, but he had already disappeared into the growing crowd, the rain washing him away into the darkness.

Chapter 29
Forgiven

Saphirra climbed out of a cab, loving the feeling of being able to stretch her limbs again. She was just glad she didn't have to breathe in the strange hospital air. As Claire climbed out behind her, she knew Claire was just as glad as she was that they were finally home. The hospital had healed Claire's swollen ankle in an instant, chiding her for not coming to them sooner. Apparently, they had slept for a while; the nurses had commented on their lack of cuts, but never made the connection to West. Their remarkably short stay at the hospital had been slightly deterred by their long, restless sleep; the nurses had explained that so many events had happened so quickly that it was all her body could do to cope with it all. Saphirra smiled to herself as she approached the open gates of the university, ignoring the fact that she had another mile or so to walk before she reached her dorm room again. She felt better than she had ever felt in her life, something she attributed to the aftereffect of the drugs the hospital had given her.

"Saph, wait!" Claire called, waving her phone in the air as she ran to catch up to her friend. Claire was listening intently to whoever was on the other end, nodding unconsciously at times. Saphirra had tried to push away her disappointment, but she still couldn't help but feel detached—this was the second time the hospital had called her father, and he hadn't bothered to respond. *Deal with it,* Saphirra told herself firmly. She'd come to expect nothing more from her father, anyway. Why should this be any different? He never called her for anything, unless he wanted a favor.

Claire hung up, smiling brightly at her friend. Saphirra raised her eyebrows; Claire's cheery smile didn't quite reach her eyes. Claire stuffed her phone back into her pocket and matched her stride with Saphirra's, scuffing the heels of her shoes on the dry grass.

"My mom left a voicemail," she said dryly as they turned into a gap between the two art history buildings. "All she did was lecture. She said it was bad publicity for the university, and that I acted irresponsibly." She sighed heavily, her hazel eyes turning to meet Saphirra's. Misery lay underneath her cheerful gaze. "I don't think I'll ever get through to her."

"At least..."

"At least she knows, yeah. I'm sorry, Saph. I know he would have called you if he'd known."

Saphirra shook her head, looking up to avoid Claire's heated gaze. She fixated her emerald eyes on a particularly fat cloud, taking a deep breath before answering.

"He knew. He's always known. He just chooses to forget."

She remembered Alex then, and West, both of whom had declined letting anyone know what had happened to them. Alex insisted his father didn't need another burden to bear, and West had simply sat there, stoically refusing all logic. Saphirra had seen a hint of sadness in his eyes, the same look all four of them now had. It had been nearly a week since the last moon, and Saphirra couldn't help wondering why they hadn't done a thing.

"Well, Professor Lockson sure got his wish, didn't he?" Saphirra said bitterly, keeping her voice low so the construction workers wouldn't hear. They sat busily repairing the crumbling bricks and minor damage West's bullets had caused, unaware of the fact that the extent of it wasn't what they had been paid for. She waved to a couple of them and turned back to Claire, mind whirring.

"What do you mean?" Claire asked quietly.

"He just distracted us for two whole weeks, and used Ms. Stone to do so! If she hadn't taken you, maybe none of this would have happened."

"*Life* got in the way, Saph. West's boss, Alex coming back, all of it. It's just getting worse. We haven't even begun to look at the prophecy yet!" she said quietly. "Our deadline is getting closer and closer by the second! If we don't know what to do when the time comes..." She trailed off, giving Saphirra a meaningful look. Of course she knew what that meant. Alex would be stuck this way forever.

She made a beeline for her favorite tree, plopping down beneath it. As Claire sat down beside her, Saphirra ran her hands over the warm, familiar grass. There were so many aspects of her life she never wanted to change; her friendships, her way of life. This summer had affected that so much that she didn't know what was normal anymore. It amazed her how easily people could lose their sense of reason. West and Alex had both shown that in the course of a few minutes, after all. How could they count on preparing for something so monumental if none of them could keep a clear head?

"Found it."

Claire had been rummaging through her bag, tipping it into the sunlit grass until a piece of folded paper flew out. She smoothed it out against her thigh, holding it up to the sunlight to read out loud:

One controls the mind,

Another the heart.

Their bodies fierce,

Their hearts sound.

Both take life,

And yet fear death.

When blood hangs in the sky

And the moon appears twice,

Fates shall be revealed.

One will find peace,

The other betrayal.

Their key to survival

Is hidden within the jewel.

Saphirra frowned at it. "Where did you find it? I thought we'd lost the translated prophecy after you'd been kidnapped. Isn't that what Ms. Stone wanted?"

Claire shook her head. "She might have asked me a ton of questions, but I only remember a part of it. I'd been really heavily drugged,

Reedhima Mandlik

after all. But that makes sense, too. Actually...she took me because of West."

Saphirra tried to meet her eyes, but Claire was firmly staring at the paper in her hands, her fingers shaking slightly. "You mean, about his job? Because he was a Viceprus hunter?"

"*Is* a hunter," Claire corrected spitefully, "and if I knew he didn't have a valid reason for it I'd hate him. Saph..." she trailed off.

"What? What is it, Claire?" Saphirra asked hurriedly, catching Claire's uncertain tone. Claire shrugged.

"Nothing."

She was spared another barrage of questions from Saphirra by the entrance of Alex and West. It seemed that they hadn't noticed the girls beneath the tree; the two crossed through the quad and plopped down on the soft grass a ways away from them. Neither were smiling, but it didn't seem as if they held any animosity towards one another, either.

"We should talk to West about this," Claire said quietly, indicating the fluttering paper in her hands. "He has a right to know." Saphirra nodded and got to her feet.

"Might as well do it now. Do you want to explain it, or should I?"

Claire bit her lip, watching the two boys. Alex was holding his head in his hands, and West was now leaning himself back to gaze into the sky, murmuring something. Alex nodded and looked up at him. His dejected expression sent a pang of sympathy through Saphirra's heart.

"I think I'll tell him," said Claire, breaking through Saphirra's thoughts. "He might take it better from me." She paled a little as they began to walk towards their friends. Although West looked up expectantly at the sound of their footsteps, Alex didn't even bother looking up as they approached him.

"Hey," West said comfortably, smiling up at them. His lazy happiness vanished at the look on Claire's face, and out of some unspoken agreement, he stood up and followed Claire further into the quad.

Saphirra sat down cautiously next to Alex, hugging her knees to her chest.

"Why are you doing this?"

She was taken aback at the abrupt question, the blunt tone. She frowned at him.

"What do you mean?"

"Hiding things from me. I said you could trust me with anything, and then all this happened." He waved his arms, pointing out the building in front of them, where a pile of broken bricks lay, slowly crumbling into a dusty heap. "I ended up wrecking the whole place." Saphirra thought for a moment before replying, her dark hair dancing in the light breeze.

"I'm sorry, Alex. I wanted to protect you. *We* wanted to protect you."

"Did West tell you himself?"

"No, Claire did."

"And how did she know?"

"Alex, I don't know. I tried to tell you when you came back that day, but you didn't listen. She would only told me when she thought you were dead, gone for good." She choked on her words, and swallowed hard. It took her a moment before she could speak again. "I had to hide it from you, especially now that you had just gotten back. One day isn't enough to process all this rationally," she told him quietly. Alex scoffed.

"Well *you* seemed to manage it pretty well," he pointed out dryly. Saphirra blushed.

"I'm not the one who can kill with a swipe of my hand," she countered heatedly. "I'm not the one who is a danger to himself and everything around them."

Alex turned to look at her, and his eyes held a faraway look, almost as if he wasn't sitting next to her at all. She took a deep breath. "We decided to trust each other, and I was the one who betrayed that. None of it is your fault," she said firmly. "Still, I *did* try to warn you."

"But why not before? Why now?" he sounded so hurt and confused that it took all Saphirra had to restrain herself from hugging him.

"I never realized just how important trust was until yesterday, until you showed me. Until then, I thought what I had done was right, that hiding it from you was the only option. I see now that maybe I had assumed wrong." She tried to catch his eye and failed. He prodded the ground instead, rolling the grass around in his fingers.

"No," he said finally. "You were right to keep it from me. I mean, look what happened to us because I got angry. We were stuck in the hospital for two days, West has scars he can't heal, and I got shot." He tried to make it sound humorous, but his voice came out strained.

Saphirra didn't hesitate to answer. "You had no way to know what West was doing. But if you had just *listened* to Claire..." She trailed off, and Alex mumbled,

"Sorry."

Saphirra laughed. "It doesn't matter anymore. We only had a few bruises to show for it, and West healed those too."

Alex laughed shakily, and she tightened her grip on his shoulder. *Everything's so messed up...and it just seemed to get worse since last week...* she thought, gazing down at the dehydrated grass. She scratched her neck and let her hand rest there, above the suddenly warm scar that lay there. It glowed like a hot coal under her touch, and then faded back to a shimmering gold. As the days progressed, the bite scar on her neck had gone from cold to burning warm, and it worried her. Still, she had constantly checked to make sure she hadn't changed, and for the most part she hadn't. Only Alex had noted the difference when he said he couldn't see her aura anymore.

Alex's hand caught hers, and she looked up absentmindedly. She was startled to see how serious his expression was. Her scar prickled uncomfortably as his grip tightened on hers, and as it became vice-like, a shot of pain stabbed through her, nearly causing her to cry out. Her pain was echoed in his eyes.

"It's getting worse," she stated. Alex nodded hollowly, turning to gaze up at the sky. *This has to stop.* She had to figure out a way to keep Alex from feeling like this every few minutes. She couldn't believe it had taken almost two months to even get this far. Even with a translated prophecy, they were nowhere near finding a solution. Alex leaned back, his fiery hair catching the sunlight, and propped his elbows up on the grass.

"Doesn't the sun hurt you? Isn't it too much energy?" Saphirra asked cautiously. Alex squinted into the midday sun and shook his head.

"It's not so bad now," he said quietly. "The sun isn't as strong, so I'm not absorbing as much energy, I guess. Not after what we went through in the hospital." He closed his eyes, letting the sunlight play across his eyelids.

"Why don't Vicepruses just lay out in the sun then? If they need the energy that badly?" Saphirra asked curiously. Alex shrugged.

"I don't know. Validus said it felt...*empty,* somehow, like being promised sweets and getting vegetables instead. I...I guess I can see what he means, now." He made a disgusted face, and let go of her hand. Saphirra settled down next to him, watching West and Claire bicker with each other in the distance. They seemed to be calming down, and their voices didn't carry over to them as much anymore.

"Are you going to forgive West?"

Alex seemed to think about that for a moment. Saphirra couldn't blame him; he had blasted buildings apart, nearly poisoning Alex and wounding everyone around him. Still, he had done it for a good cause, after all. He had tried to protect everyone.

"Yeah, I guess so. But I'm not sure Claire will," he said, nodding over to the squabbling couple.

"We have to fix this, Alex. For everyone." Saphirra hated the finality in his voice.

"What are we going to do?"

His light blue eyes searched her face as he sighed.

"I don't know, Alex. I just don't know."

"You hurt your best friend, almost killing him in the process; you hurt Saphirra, and you've hurt me! You didn't listen to me, and you expect me to *forgive* you?" Claire shouted at West, her voice so loud that it upset a flock of birds that had crowded near them .

How could he do that to us? He's blasted half the college apart! She stormed away from him, turning into a part of the college she'd never been in before. She heard Saphirra call questioningly to her and the

Reedhima Mandlik

sounds of West sprinting to catch up with her, but she ignored both of them.

"How many more times should I apologize for you to forgive me?" West pleaded. She didn't slow down as he caught her shoulder. She shrugged him off and continued walking. If she didn't, she knew she'd lose her head of steam. She couldn't stay mad at anybody for long, especially West.

He came out of nowhere in front of her, blocking her path. She walked around him, startled to see she was facing the mouth of a dead-end passageway. She turned around, and West was blocking her again. She glared at him.

"A few thousand more times should be a nice start," she replied coldly. She could feel her resistance crumbling when she looked at his piercing grey eyes.

"Please?" he asked sweetly, catching her wrists gently. She tried to twist away, but a note of beautiful song escaped his lips, filling her entire body with a sweet kind of tingly warmth. Suddenly, she couldn't remember why she was struggling.

West. Poisoning Alex. Blasting the college apart.

Right.

She pushed him away from her as quickly as she could.

"Did you just try to use a *Siren* song on me?" her shock reverberated through the room, and West held up his hands.

"No! I mean, I didn't mean to...It just slipped out," he insisted wearily. "Please, just stop for a moment and *listen* to me, Claire!"

"It was stupid for you to do that, and you know it. You should have listened to me," she said sternly. West shrugged.

"Okay, I guess I deserved that," he admitted. She glared at him.

"Please forgive me?" he pleaded. She felt her anger ebbing away, and she tried to hold on to it fruitlessly.

"I've already forgiven you for whatever happened these past few days. What happens in the future, however..." She shook her head at him disapprovingly. "We'll have to see about that."

West shrugged and moved aside, letting Claire through. Claire strode back into the quad and through a pair of double doors into the Union, making a beeline for the computers.

"West, do you know what's been going on?" she called over her shoulder.

"Not really."

As the computer began its slow, weary revival, she began to explain about the attack in the beginning of summer, and then the finding of the prophecy. She thrust the piece of paper that held its translation onto him, ignoring his bewildered look. "Try and make sense of it, West," she said as the computer groaned to life. "Even if it's been translated into English, it still doesn't make a bit of sense to me. Maybe you'll understand it better than I do. I know you must have suspected at least a little of this before. I just can't make sense of it," she said exasperatedly. He stared at it for a moment silently, as if unsure of what to do with it. Claire was surprised at how he had taken it so well, so *quietly*; then again, she hadn't explained what had happened with Ms. Stone. She decided she wouldn't mention that just yet. Just as she was about to repeat the question, West said sharply,

"Look up when the next blue moon is."

"We already know, the blue moon is sometime this month, but that doesn't mean—"

"Just look it up," he said sternly. "Nothing ever turns red during a blue moon. It just looks like any regular moon. But...during an eclipse..." He trailed off thoughtfully, resting his chin on his hands. Claire searched for it, smiling triumphantly as the links came up.

"See? Less than a week away," she told him. West shook his head urgently.

"No. Blue moons are special, but not special enough to be in a prophecy for hundreds of years. Search 'lunar eclipse'."

She did, surprised when another link came up. "It says...It says it's a huge phenomenon. 'The blue moon will be accompanied by a lunar eclipse, something that hasn't happened in hundreds of years,'" she read out loud. West nodded next to her, and pointed out the picture in the article. The moon was a blood red.

"It's the lunar eclipse," he said excitedly. "The moon turns red during a lunar eclipse. It all makes sense now!" he waited a moment for that to sink in, and then plunged on. "This is a whole lot bigger than just us and Professor Lockson. This must deal with the whole mythical world," said West. "It says 'their key to survival is hidden within the jewel'. Something tells me that it isn't just about the two people in the prophecy," he mused. "It sounds too general." Claire studied his worried expression, wondering just how much West knew about, as he termed it, the 'mythical world'. She hadn't even been aware that more creatures like Vicepruses and Sirens existed.

"What do you mean?" she asked curiously, turning away from the computer. West bit his lip, as if unsure of whether to continue or not. Finally, he consented.

"There are so many more creatures than just Vicepruses and Sirens, Claire. There used to be thousands of different kinds of creatures years ago. It's why you can read about them in the ancient Greek and Roman texts; humans and mythical creatures were equals once. Then pride and judgment got in the way," he said bitterly. "The creatures were forced into hiding, and have been ever since. Since then, three groups proved their dominance over the rest; the Sirens, the Vicepruses, and the Elymphs. Sirens deceived their way to power, Vicepruses fought their way in, and Elymphs captivated everyone around them until they got in, too. The leaders of each came together to form the Triumvirate, a powerful tri-dictator alliance that has kept the rest of the mythical realm in control for years."

"How do you know any of this?" Claire asked suspiciously. West looked down, as if fighting back words. Finally, after a deep breath, he spoke.

"My weapon's master explained some things to me. You didn't think I walked into this Viceprus hunting thing blindly, did you?" His tone was short and clipped, and Claire knew he wasn't about to say anything else.

"Sure seemed like it..." she muttered, turning back to the computer. It bothered her when West got secretive like this, as if he had a wealth of information and she wasn't important enough to explain it to. It made her feel like they hadn't made any progress at all in their friendship over the summer, despite all they'd been through.

The silence stretched between them, until she finally said, "Okay, well what do you think it means, then?"

"Well, look at how the prophecy is worded. They constantly single one side out against the other, except for three lines, where they're suddenly combined. What if...what if they were talking about the different mythical creatures, not the person anymore? I mean, look at how generalized it is. 'Their bodies fierce, their hearts sound'. It doesn't sound like they're talking about one person," West said. Claire bit her lip.

"That would have made sense," she said, still not taking her eyes off the computer screen, "if they had mentioned anything about Sirens—"

"Or Elymphs," West interrupted. Claire rolled her eyes.

"Or Elymphs," she conceded. "But they didn't, so it doesn't work. The prophecy is about Professor Lockson and Alex, not a whole population. Plus, Saphirra must 'the key'. Why else would Lockson attack her?"

"But that makes no sense!" West said, sounding frustrated. He seemed to be getting more agitated by the minute. "Just because Saphirra's name has the word 'sapphire' in it doesn't mean she's suddenly the jewel the prophecy was talking about! I bet you anything there are about ten girls you know named Ruby or something. And even if it *is* true that this can only be Saphirra, why wouldn't Lockson attack everyone else first? Why specifically her?"

"You're right," Claire sighed. "He must know something we don't." The thought had never occurred to her before, and she was glad West could finally help.

"He could have been there when the oracle showed him the prophecy," West said after a long moment of silence. "He must have lived a long time, after all. And in Greek mythology, oracles are everywhere. I'm sure this one is more recent than that, though."

"But if it was found in so many books, it's got to be old, right?" Claire asked. "I doubt Lockson could live that long, even if he isn't human."

West nodded to himself. "What if.... Couldn't someone else have told him what the person looks like, or where he'd meet her and when? Passed it on, maybe? Or written it down somewhere else? We might only have half of the real prophecy. Can I see the original Latin one? Otherwise none of this makes any sense."

"It never made sense in the beginning."

He laughed at her dry tone and flashed her a brilliant white smile. "True. Still, I don't think it means Saphirra. Maybe it means a jewel of some sort? Do we know of any important jewels?" he asked mockingly. Claire laughed.

"Besides the Sunstone pin, no. And that didn't seem altogether that powerful, anyway. I mean," she said, correcting herself hurriedly at the hurt look on West's face, "It saved my life, but I doubt it can save four. Or five, or a whole population of creatures or people."

"So that's a dead end, then?" West asked. "What else do we have?"

"We know the date is on the lunar eclipse, around six or less days from now. We know it might involve a lot more than we planned for." She sighed, running her hand through her hair anxiously. This was a lot more serious than she thought, and they were running out of time. "The first two lines—something about the mind and heart—sound strange to me. Different, somehow."

"But you still think it's only about Professor Lockson and Saphirra and Alex?" West asked quietly. "You sure it's not like what I said?"

"West, it can't just not be about Saphirra at all!" Claire said exasperatedly, dismissing him with a wave of her hand. "Maybe it is bigger than just us, but it's got to come down to them. Why else would Lockson attack Saph in the first place?"

"Because he's stupid?"

"Because he knows something we don't, like you said. And we need to find out what that is," said Claire. She took the piece of paper back from West and attempted to smooth it back out again, staring at it hard. "Whatever it is, we have to be ready. We've got less than a week. We should get moving and try to find Saphirra and Alex. They need to know your theory," she said. "You're right about it sounding funny, but I don't know if it might just be a translation thing."

"Do you have the original Latin?" West asked suddenly. Claire nodded and rifled through her bag, eventually handing him the original page. West examined it and then pushed it towards her, shaking his head.

"Nothing's wrong with the translation, which is a miracle. Whatever you did you did it right, Claire." This compliment, for whatever reason, brought a blush to Claire's cheeks.

"I used a lot of different websites and resources," Claire admitted. West grinned at her.

"Well it's perfect. The wording *is* purposely strange, for whatever reason," West said, getting up from his chair as Claire shut down the computer and got up too. West held his hand up, stopping her. She turned to him and was startled by his intense gaze.

"Do you know Latin?"

She studied him for a minute. *What is he getting at?* "Not as well as you do."

He laughed an almost relieved laugh, and she watched him, puzzled. *"Ego diligo vos pro totus vicis quod usquequaque."* He whispered in her ear, and she puzzled at them. The words had some familiarity to them, but she couldn't remember what they meant.

"What does it mean?" she asked curiously. West laughed again, and this time the relief was apparent in his voice.

"You'll find out later, I suppose."

"Why don't you just tell me what it means?" she asked as they started walking back towards the main quad, talking just a bit louder as the traffic near the college gates increased.

"I'd rather you find out what it means yourself."

She studied him again, barely watching where she was walking. *What was that supposed to mean?*

"What do you—"

"Well anyway, let's go find Alex and Saph," West said abruptly, tugging her arm. As Claire followed him bewilderingly, she noticed West's eyes watching the rooftops warily, as if he expected something. She followed his eyes, and could have sworn she'd seen a flash of something on the corner of the rooftop; seconds later, however, it was gone, swallowed up by the blue sky.

❦

Evelyn was running blindly through a dark tunnel, holding her hands out on either side of her to feel her way forward. She tripped, and suddenly she was falling further and further into this impenetrable darkness, dark shapes passing by her alarmingly fast. She twisted in the air and before she knew it she was on the floor, her face pressed hard against the cold ground. Something wet dripped steadily from the ceiling onto her cheek, which was excruciatingly sore. In fact, everything was sore. She tried to move, but her body felt thick and raw, as if her limbs were so disconnected that she couldn't move at all. She could only look upward at the dim cement walls and the worn staircase leading to the only door above. Something creaked, and her body instinctively braced itself for pain; the door open, letting a sliver of light shoot through the blackness that surrounded her. Something told her it was better to pretend she was unconscious, and so she closed her eyes and lay limp. Someone moved slowly down the stairs, and she cracked one eye open confusedly. He never sounded so cautious before. He'd always charged down the stairs, allowing his voice to boom through the excruciatingly silent room.

She opened both eyes, and had to stop herself from crying out; someone else was here, his face bending down to examine hers.

"Who are you?" he asked faintly. His black hair flopped into his molten golden eyes as he looked down concernedly at her. "What are you doing here? This isn't the place for someone like you. Did you owe him money? Were you a—"

He just found me; she wanted to tell the man in front of her. He came for my brother, and now he came for me. Let me be, or he'll come for you too. She wanted to say this with all her heart, but all that came out was a whimper. He looked torn; he glanced up at the room above him, then back down at her.

"We need to get you out of here. Can you walk? Can you move?"

She tried to shake her head, but all that came out was a whimper. The man took her in his arms then, so gently that she barely felt herself move. He looked deep into her eyes, and seemed to like what he found there.

"You need energy," he said, more to himself than to her. He looked at her again, and regret tinged the edges of his words as he spoke. "You needed this, please remember that. I- I can't leave you here with Max. He'd do horrible things to you. Worse, really, than this." He paused, listening for footsteps above once more. "I came to collect. I'm sure he wouldn't mind another fee. I'm leav-

ing here, anyway. Thinking of heading to Chicago soon." He kept babbling, his eyes never leaving hers, and for that she was grateful. She needed to hear a kind voice, a caring voice.

Within seconds he was kissing her unresponsive mouth, almost as if waiting for a response. Despite everything, her body decided she needed to kiss back, and so she tried bewilderingly. The man kissed her neck and stopped between the base of her throat and her shoulder.

Then he bit down.

If Evelyn wanted to scream, she didn't; if she had the ability, she couldn't. The shock of what he had done radiated through her...or was it something else? Her body suddenly felt revitalized, the soreness vanishing as a tingling warmth spread through her. The man had pulled back the second he'd bitten her skin, watching her progress warily. As she began to move again, he smiled a relieved smile.

"What do you say? Want to come with me?"

Evelyn didn't even have to hesitate. As soon as her jaw was working again, the word flew through her lips.

"Yes."

"Evelyn? What are you doing here?" Ry's surprised voice called, breaking through her dream. Or was it a nightmare? Cold sweat dotted her neck, and she realized her breath was shallow, her fists balled up against the pillows beneath her twisted frame. She flipped over, surprised to find Ry in her apartment. But her surroundings didn't look like her apartment at all; she turned around, startled to see the couch she had laid on was not her own, but actually Ry's. In fact, everything here was his. *How'd I get in his office?* She wondered, gazing around bemusedly at the room. She'd been thinking hard, but not enough to be completely unaware of where she was going. Evelyn rubbed her head, looking up to find Ry standing with his back to her, gazing out at the skyline of Chicago.

"I have no idea, actually," Evelyn admitted. *What was with that dream?* Evelyn wondered. She didn't think her past had been like that at all. Sure, her brother had gotten into trouble, that much she recalled; she remembered being beaten for his mistakes, but never this badly. Ry turned to her, and she saw something she'd never seen in his eyes when he looked at her—dead callousness. *What happened to the man who saved me?* Evelyn wondered sadly as she gazed at him. It was one of the reasons that had her contemplating joining Akakios. Safety, warmth, food, and someone to be with. A friend. She needed a friend.

"So are you saying you don't remember how you ended up here?" Ry asked sharply. He didn't wait for a reply. "Don't bother, I know what you meant. It makes sense, actually. I'm forgetting a lot of things, too. I don't know what's wrong." He pinched the bridge of his nose agitatedly. "I overreacted," he said suddenly, causing her to look up at him in surprise. "You couldn't possibly have my dagger. You didn't know it existed in the first place," he mumbled, more to himself than to her. She didn't know what to say. She contemplated telling Ry about Akakios, but settled on mentioning one name, instead.

"Clandestine branded me, Ry. That's who did it. The soon-to-be-Chief of the Siren Council did this to me." She pulled down the lapel of her shirt, where the ornate C still glowed faintly at her touch. Ry seemed to be beyond asking obvious questions, like where she'd gotten the information from in the first place; instead, he asked her to repeat the name.

"Clandestine," she spat. Ry's eyes tightened with sudden understanding.

"We have to move. We're in danger."

We're in danger. Isn't that what Akakios had warned her about? Being in danger? She glared at Ry, who had begun to pace. *What did they know that they weren't telling her?*

"What? Why, what about the prophecy? Ry, there's nothing to fear–" She started, but Ry cut her off with a shake of his head.

"No, we have to *move,*" he started tugging her towards the door, but she dug her heels in. She was surprised to find she was almost as strong as he was.

"I am not moving until you tell me where we're going, and why!" she said, yanking her arm away from him. "I need to make some plans before we decide to abandon everything we've worked for and just waltz out."

"There's no time–" He started, but she cut him off furiously.

"Then explain what's going on!"

She bit her lip, wondering if she'd gone too far. Ry was studying her with the most peculiar expression on his face, almost calculating.

"Do you remember what I had said to you the day we met?"

"I promise to protect you," she echoed quietly. She thought of Akakios, who had promised her the same protection. *Who do I follow?*

"Exactly. And right now, the reason I haven't explained anything is because I'm trying to protect you. You have to trust me. Please Evelyn, don't let me lose you again." His voice was so sincere that she did a double take to make sure he was talking to her. He hadn't spoken to her like this in years.

"And if I don't care?" she asked, her eyes blazing. To her surprise, he laughed.

"I'll save you anyway. Evelyn, I'll never stop caring about you. Trust me." He held out a hand, beckoning for her to take it. She was so stunned that she consented.

Chapter 30
Racing the Clock

Ry had pushed Evelyn towards the direction of the university, telling her to distract West somehow, but he barely remembered doing it. Even now, as he sat in his office, staring aimlessly at the Chicago skyline, he didn't think he could function. At the word "Clandestine", it was as if something had clicked in his brain. Evelyn's branded skin, the Siren Council's sudden interest in the Viceprus Council's affairs, all of it made sense now. Except...He patted his pocket absentmindedly, missing the heavy weight of the dagger against his thigh. How had Clandestine known that he even had a weapon against her?

He had been stupid to assume that Evelyn had his dagger. After all, she wasn't the brightest. Ry's fists clenched as a new kind of nervousness settled in the pit of his stomach. Evelyn had never been so commanding, and definitely had never questioned his motives before. Ever since the day he had found her she had complied willingly with his demands. Why had she suddenly changed her mind? He frowned at his reflection in the darkening glass. *At least the Waterford boy is gone.* That was the least of his problems, it seemed. He had seen it with his own eyes; West had shot Alex to death. That much was certain. He hadn't hung around to wait for the paramedics to appear, nor to watch the remaining drama unfold below him, but he knew the end result would be the same—Saphirra was still alive. Ry had contemplated asking West to kill her off, too, but quickly thought against it. If the boy was heartless enough to kill what Ry assumed was one of his closest friends, he could definitely do worse, including hunting Ry down. For years, West had complied simply because of the threat Ry posed to his mother; now, however, he seemed more resilient, more *angry*. West had apparently had enough. Ry had expected this to happen, but not so late in the game. Either way it was beneficial to him; there were only three more key placeholders in the

Council Ry needed to eliminate, and then he was in. If West couldn't handle them, Ry would kill the council members himself, and then get rid of West. The boy was his most skilled Hunter, but once he made it to the High Council Ry assumed he wouldn't need him.

And yet...

Validus had visited him a few days ago, only to pass on one message; the High Council had reviewed the prophecy, and requested to see him immediately. This only meant one thing; someone had given them outside information, something beyond the prophecy itself. Something he had thought only he knew. Validus had neglected to provide any more information, and it had taken him a great deal of persuasion to leave Ry, if only for the moment. Still, he knew he had to disappear. He had to draw out his time until the blue moon, until the full eclipse. If he could last until then, he could save himself.

The oracle had left an imprint of his prophecy in an Elymph-made ball, something so in-tune with the earth that it could project an image of whatever had been preserved if the orb was in the same place as it had been made. Ry had happened upon it entirely by accident, and upon seeing its contents, had attempted to get rid of it. He'd thrown it into the Mediterranean Sea long ago, hoping it would sink to the bottom and never resurface.

But someone found it, thought Ry. *They found it, and they saw what I saw.* The thought sent a jolt of horror through his heart. They saw the girl reach for his neck, saw the boy dive at him with all his strength, saw what would ultimately mean the destruction of the Viceprus race. Ry knew prophecies could be proven to mean something else entirely, and he hoped it was true in this case as well. *I won't die,* he told himself firmly. After all, all his work couldn't possibly go to waste this easily.... Could it? *I need to speed it up,* he thought suddenly. He needed to time his acceptance into the High Council with the blue moon perfectly, especially with the aftermath being so unclear. He pulled out his cell phone, contemplating. He needed the Council out of the way, but what about Evelyn? The thought hadn't occurred to him until now that she could be a hindrance. But with her new aversion to his hidden agendas, he had no choice. If Evelyn failed to carry out his instructions one more time, it would kill them all.

Her death was eminent.

West sat in the library of the university, his wealth of weapons scattered out on the table, many of which he'd just unearthed from his room this morning. Saphirra and Claire stood next to a gleaming bullet, examining it closely, while Alex stood a wary distance away from it all.

"I don't know," West said carefully, picking up his gun. "I might need this. My boss isn't going to quit just because he thinks I killed Alex. He was just another one of my jobs," West argued. "I can't just give you my weapons."

"Then why did your boss stop calling, West? What if Alex was the one he was after, and now he's done?" Saphirra's voice sounded so hopeful that West couldn't help but laugh.

"Why would Alex be the one my boss is after? He hasn't caused trouble. In fact," West said thoughtfully, "I wonder how my boss knew Alex existed at all." *He* hadn't even realized it for a while, and Alex had been right under his nose. He couldn't believe Claire and Saphirra were able to keep Alex from him for so long through what Claire had explained to him were monthly transformations. If they could keep it a secret for so long, how could his boss have known? He was even more surprised that Alex had no idea that West was a Siren. Weren't Vicepruses supposed to be intuitive about these things? His stomach dropped as a new possibility popped into his mind; if his boss knew about Alex, what else did he knew about? What if he knew West was a Siren, too? West glanced at Alex, who was staring obliviously at the scenery outside. Just how much did his boss know?

"I've been wondering about that." Claire's voice broke through his thoughts as she carefully placed a bullet back down onto the table. "It seems really peculiar that he knew about Alex."

"Validus could have mentioned it," Alex piped up. West recalled Alex telling him about his visit to Validus, and wondered how Alex had managed to even get out of there alive in the first place. High

Council members weren't supposed to help new Vicepruses roam free, let alone ones who were half-developed like Alex was. Something didn't add up.

"That doesn't make sense. High Council members aren't supposed to help people like you," West said matter-of-factly. "I highly doubt he'd go around parading the fact that he helped you, let alone announce it to someone like my boss." Claire gave him a strange look, which he ignored. She didn't seem to want to let it go, though.

"How exactly do you know that?"

Alex and Saphirra turned to look at him, as if this hadn't occurred to them before either. West glared spitefully at Claire, who only gave him a smug smile in return. *I can't explain it!* He wanted to shout. When Clandestine had sung to him, it was as if she'd awakened a treasure trove of information in his brain he'd hidden long ago. He *couldn't* explain how he knew what the Council did, and how it existed; he just knew. But he couldn't say any of this without sounding incredibly stupid, let alone revealing the fact that he was a Siren.

"I told you, my weapons master told me bits and pieces about it when I was younger," West said dismissively. "Anyway, I can't let you guys use these." He gestured towards the massive pile of bullets on the table before him.

"Then can't you ask for more and say you need them for another job?" Saphirra asked.

"It'll look suspicious to ask for them when I haven't used any in a while. Besides, my boss always sends them to me when I need them. I've never needed to ask for more. He's always just *known*."

"And it didn't occur to you that that was weird?" Claire asked sharply. "You didn't consider that maybe he was following you?"

"So what if he was following me, Claire?" West asked exasperatedly, throwing up his hands. "What do I have to hide? He's already taken everything I love away from me, what else could he do? Kill me?"

"Exactly that!" Claire cried, her gaze burning into him. "He could kill you, like he had you 'kill' Alex. Why are you so blind?"

"Calm down," Alex said hastily, quickly walking between them. The mood in the room was suddenly supercharged with tension.

West hadn't even noticed he'd gotten up from his chair; he was now glaring daggers at Claire, who stared defiantly back.

"I was forced into this, Claire! I had no choice!" West shouted at her, ignoring Saphirra and Alex's protests. "But that doesn't mean I was *blind*! I knew what I was getting into! I knew I might die!"

"And how would your death keep your mother safe, West?" Claire asked him. "How would you know if your boss would keep his word? The guy didn't even trust you with a name! How could you trust him with two lives?"

Her words were like a heavy blow to his chest. He stood there, his mind reeling, as Alex tried to get him to sit back down again. Of course he'd considered it. Of course he knew he was being stupid by trusting this person, but what else could he have done? West supposed she was bringing this up because she was stressed to the limit, but they all were. *You don't see Alex and Saphirra jumping at each other's throats,* West thought bitterly. Why did she need to bring this up *now*? He took a few deep, settling breaths, trying to calm down as best as he could. She only meant well, after all.

"What other choice did I have? Claire, what do you think I can do?" he asked her quietly. She looked startled at his calm tone.

"Well...For starters, you could tell your mom to run somewhere, to hide," Claire said reasonably, bending down to pluck another book from the mountainous pile beside her. West bit his lip. He'd been brought to the brink of doing exactly that numerous times, but always something had stopped him. Worry that his boss would somehow know and go after his mother, worry that he would be killed if he tried. Claire hurriedly continued before he could interrupt her once again. "If you don't want to do that, then you could maybe...maybe next time you get a call, have Alex go in your stead? He could warn the Viceprus, maybe even save their life."

"And if my boss finds out? What if he's always watching, like you said?"

"Your boss thinks Alex is dead, and you can't kill a dead man. Besides, Alex could tell them to go into hiding somewhere, make it seem as if they're dead, or they disappeared. No one will know."

West liked that prospect. All these years, he'd been wondering if he'd been killing for good or for evil. Now, he'd never have to worry about that again.

"Alright. For the next few days, we'll try that. After the blue moon eclipse…" he trailed off. *Would we even survive it?* The prophecy said something about survival, after all. And whether it meant the race in general or simply Alex or Professor Lockson, he didn't know. Either way, someone's life was in peril. He shook the depressing thought, turning to look at Saphirra instead, whose relief at his composure was clear in her expression.

"Maybe I should call. If something happens—"

"It won't," Saphirra and Alex said together.

"But if something does," West continued, "I want her safe. I'll make the call."

He stood up and walked out of the library, pulling out his phone as he went. Claire had confirmed the doubts he'd been having for months now. *Was* his boss trustworthy? He hadn't sent West into a situation he couldn't handle yet…*Except for that day with Akakios,* West corrected. That Viceprus had been ready for him, and had wounded him in the process, leaving scars that would never heal down his leg and shoulder. He looked back down at his phone, and his heart leapt to his throat. He stared at it as if it were a time bomb. Calling his mother…It was something he hadn't done in years. He missed her terribly. West was visited by an urge to drop everything and leave, to go back to where his mom was. Sighing, he flipped open the phone and dialed the number. After the regular questions and casual greetings, he warned her to hide.

"It's not safe anymore, Mom. You've got to leave. I can't let my boss hold you over my head anymore!" he'd said exasperatedly, cutting through his mother's protests. The other end of the line fell silent. West asked the question he'd been wondering about ever since that Siren had talked to him. It felt as if he was going to burst.

"Mom, how long have you known? About me, about my past? Who am I, really?"

A pause on the other line. "Sweetie, what do you mean?"

"Mom, I know. I'm a Siren. Clandestine found me."

He heard his mother's gasp and shuddered a little. "West, you have to avoid that woman. She's been looking for me for a long time. She loved your father, West. Clandestine would do anything to get him back, even though it's not possible. She'd even try and kill you."

He'd stumbled a little in shock. He'd expected her to ask who Clandestine was, not warn against her. "What?"

"West, I'll go somewhere safe if you listen to me. That woman... She can control anything and anyone. She could have you kill yourself if she wanted to. You have to avoid her at all costs. She told you the truth earlier than I would have liked, but it's all true, sweetie. All of it."

"You mean–"

"There's no going back. You're a Siren, but you would have stayed a human if you hadn't come in contact with another Siren. I don't know how much your father had to do to keep me alive, but it must have been more than I will ever understand. You have to protect the ones you love, sweetie. Keep Clandestine away from you and your friends. Keep her far away. She's more trouble than its worth."

At that, his mother had hung up. West had stared at his cell phone for the longest time, his mother's words echoing in his ears. *So it was all true,* he'd thought. Even now, he'd refused to believe it. He started heading towards the student Union, his mind reeling. *Stay away from Clandestine? But why?* Wasn't she the one who had provided the answers he sought? She couldn't be that bad, could she? West watched the cloudless sky, unsure of what would happen next. He knew he really should return to the library, but he didn't think he could face his friends just yet. He'd almost forgotten the sound of his mother's voice. He felt a pang in his heart at the thought of her, having to uproot her whole life once again to save herself. Hadn't his mother already suffered enough? White hot anger flared through him then; anger at his boss for doing this to him, and anger at his father and Clandestine for screwing up his life. He hadn't asked to be caught in the middle of a love triangle. He hadn't asked to be any part of this.

He walked through the doors of the student Union blindly, not really caring where he ended up. His only goal was to put as much distance from the library and him as was possible. He didn't want Claire to see him like this. He turned the corner and jumped a little when

Reedhima Mandlik

he saw Saphirra there. She was mixing something in the blender of the smoothie counter, and she smiled at him when she saw him enter.

"Here. Take these," she said warmly, thrusting two large cups at him. He drank out of one of them carefully, trying to hide his somber expression. Saphirra didn't appear to have noticed anything.

"This is good! What's in it?" he asked, draining the cup in one gulp. Saphirra shrugged, turning on the blender again.

"I don't know. I just threw stuff together."

She poured herself a glass and stepped away from the smoothie counter, and West cringed as he saw a glowing purple sphere beyond her emerald eyes—her soul. It expanded until it surrounded her in a kind of glowing violet cloak, shimmering slightly along the edges. West gritted his teeth, frantically trying to squelch whatever it was that threatened to burst out of him. Did he actually want her soul? Was he already that far gone? Saphirra glanced quizzically at him.

"Why are you looking at me like that?"

He quelled another upsurge of some kind of song, leaning against the counter as he felt the energy slowly drain out of him with the effort.

"Nothing. What are you doing down here, anyway?"

"I felt we needed a break," she told him. She didn't question how the phone call went, and for that West was grateful. Together, they headed back towards the library, West trailing unwillingly behind a cheerful Saphirra. As he walked through the huge double doors Saphirra walked right past him, setting the drinks down next to Claire. She reached for one unconsciously.

"Where's Alex?" West asked, glancing around. Claire looked up at them.

"I thought he was with you, Saph."

Saphirra was examining West's gun again, turning it over and over in her hands. She shrugged as a response.

"He probably needed a break too. Anyway, West, why did you only give us these today," she asked, gesturing unnecessarily to the pile of bullets and weapons on the table. "How could you have possibly lost this? Is your room a black hole or something?" she waved the gun carelessly in the air, and West took a step back as her finger came close to touching the trigger.

"It probably is. Right after the battle, it had disappeared. I just found it today," he shrugged, taking the gun from her and flicking on the safety switch. It felt familiar in his hands, and he turned it over, examining the golden tip. He ran a hand over the warm metal. He didn't want to admit to them that he'd hidden the gun from himself, in case he was tempted to hurt another Viceprus again. It occurred to West just how little his friends really knew about him. He'd thought he was finally opening himself up with Claire, something he'd vowed he would never do. *I guess I can still keep my promise,* West thought as he observed Saphirra crack a book open. *They don't know anything about my Siren abilities at all.* None of them knew he'd taken a week off work to prepare for this, either. Somehow, the only person he wanted to know this was Claire, and currently she was ignoring him, her nose pressed in a thick volume.

"Do you know how to use it?" he asked Saphirra, gesturing to his gun. She shook her head. "I can train you, if you'd like," West said suddenly, perking up a little.

"*Train* her?" Claire interjected from across the room. "Why would you want to teach her to kill?" her words held so much poison in them that West took a step back from her. *What's her problem?* He thought she'd accepted the fact that he killed Vicepruses on a daily basis by now, that she'd understood. *Apparently not.* When he turned around, Saphirra was in front of him.

"I don't think that it's worth it, West," Saphirra said quietly. "I don't want to have to kill anyone." Claire gave an appreciative huff at Saphirra's words, which West ignored.

"Even if they're trying to kill you, Saph?" West asked darkly. Saphirra shrugged.

"If Lockson wants to come after me, let him. Whatever happens in the prophecy will happen, there's no going around it. We'll see if I'm meant to kill anyone after all." She held no emotion in her tone as she walked away from West towards Claire, who had begun shifting books out of a large bag at her feet. The library's navy blue walls were covered with shelves of books—hundreds of them, outlining ev-

Reedhima Mandlik

erything. Where they couldn't fit on the shelves, they were dumped onto the floor in semi–organized piles. Claire had been searching through one such pile now, pushing piles of books into what West could only assume was the discard pile. West glanced up at the large windows, noting how the sky had gathered a cloudy canopy in record time. *Please let this work. Please let us survive this.* He begged to the skies. The massive grey clouds just rolled on by.

Chapter 31
Anticipation

Saphirra walked past the building crew on the second floor of the East wing of the college. The builders were going to have to renovate way more than her father had asked for. She hurried past the gaping hole in the wall, ignoring the mutterings of the workers as she went. She glanced at the brick walls bathed in the glow of a fading summer, wondering if she'd ever get to see the college like this again. *Survival.* That one word stirred up a mess of emotions in Saphirra; she felt her nervousness gnawing at her as she thought of how close the deadline was. *Three days,* she thought hollowly. Three days, and they weren't ready for anything. But how *could* they prepare? The prophecy was too ambiguous, and Professor Lockson had successfully consumed the last few weeks of their lives by piling on one disaster after another. If he was that cunning, who was to say he wouldn't succeed on the blue moon? According to the newspaper Claire had rescued from the pouring rain yesterday, the eclipse would be at its full around three in the morning. Everything about that day seemed ominous to her, and she couldn't help but wonder if they'd make it through alive. As she turned down the corridor and down another flight of stairs, Alex popped into view, refolding his wings surreptitiously. She jumped a little at the sight of him.

"I thought you were in the library with West and Claire," Saphirra said curiously.

"I couldn't take it in there. It was worse than finals week. Besides, West's boss called and gave him a job. West told me to warn them instead," he explained. "I just came back from my first rescue mission." His smile was strained.

"How'd it go?"

Reedhima Mandlik

"Terribly," he admitted. "The Viceprus didn't want to listen. I had to bring up Validus before she'd stop asking questions and listen to me. I think I got a few death threats, too."

"What kinds of questions?" Saphirra could feel the dead weight of the conversation, but she knew she had to keep talking. It was the only way she could keep herself from going insane from fright and worry.

"She kept asking who sent me. She was so skeptical that a Hunter would even try to go after her...Something about being on the High Council and how that commanded authority." He shrugged as they began to walk into the building, heading for a study room. "Either way, she's in hiding now. She actually seemed *angry* with me, though. I don't think she understood that I'd saved her life."

"Did you find out her name?" Saphirra asked curiously as she made a beeline for a plump couch.

"No. I was a little too busy trying to figure out why she needed to know who I worked for," Alex admitted. "She kept asking if he was a member of the Viceprus council."

Saphirra buried her face in her hands in frustration. "Things could *not* get any more confusing," she sighed heavily.

"Sounds like we all need a break," Alex said, pushing the pile of papers surrounding her to the side to sit down next to her. "What if West's boss *is* part of the Viceprus council? That would make sense, since he knows so much about them."

"What if he knows about the prophecy, too?" Saphirra asked suddenly. The thought hadn't occurred to her before. If Lockson knew, and Validus knew, wouldn't West's boss know, too? Even if they didn't know it was three days from now, the Viceprus council could be expecting it. *Now what?* They exchanged a hopeless look, and Saphirra knew Alex was thinking the same thing—*What did it matter if he knew? If the whole world knew?* Their situation seemed to keep getting worse by the second, and Saphirra was done trying to find a way out.

"Then we better hope West doesn't pick up his phone," Alex joked. Saphirra tried to smile, but she was so tense that she couldn't

338

think of anything else. Their *lives* were on the line. As the dull panic began to set in, Saphirra spoke.

"Alex, you know you might have to kill Lockson, right?"

Alex didn't answer.

"I know it won't be easy, but—"

"Not *easy?* Saph, you're telling me to kill a *person*—"

"You mean Viceprus?"

Alex glared at her. "Whatever. He used to be my *professor!* He's way more powerful than us, and he's been trying to kill us all summer long! Just because his ego is the size of Greenland doesn't mean he's stupid enough to think that he doesn't need help defeating us. He could have us killed in an instant, but he didn't. He knows we're a threat. Saph, this prophecy is telling me to go against the odds, and logic tells me that just isn't possible. What would you do, Saph? What can *I* do?" he finished dejectedly, sinking lower in the plush couch. Saphirra put her hand over his. She could feel his pulse under her shaking fingers.

"It scares me too, Alex. I—I honestly don't know how we've gotten this far. It took us so long just to get the prophecy translated, and now we don't even have a week left. But...We've got to try. We *have* to. We can't give up. It's taken so much out of all four of us, and we can't just give all that up. We'd be letting Lockson win."

Alex shifted beside her, and she glanced up at his face. His expression was unreadable. "We need to go find Claire and West," he said abruptly. Saphirra was taken aback.

"What? Why?" she asked. Alex didn't answer, but grabbed her hand instead, walking quickly out the door and into the deserted courtyard outside. He took off towards the library with her in his arms, letting Saphirra skim the top of the trees with her Finally, the library came into view; Claire and West were bending down over what Alex thought were sheets of diagrams. Before he could slow down enough to make a smooth landing, he'd touched down on the ledge.

Bam.

Something bright and golden narrowly missed them, hitting the edge of the brick they were perched on. As it exploded, Alex was forced to fly up into the air again, dropping Saphirra suddenly onto the roof.

"Do you have a death wish?" West called irritably from where he was crouched on the ground. Alex didn't move from where he was up in the air. As Saphirra looked around for the source of the light, she finally realized what had so narrowly missed them—one of West's Sun bullets.

"What was that?" Alex shouted. West turned to Claire.

"You didn't tell him?" he asked accusingly. She shook her head.

"Alex, it's one of our traps, remember? We were going to rig the roof today," West told him. Claire glanced concernedly at Saphirra, whose worried expression must have been apparent.

"Where were you?"

Just figuring some things out," Alex answered for her, flying down cautiously next to Claire. Nothing launched itself at him, and Alex sighed with relief.

"Don't move," Claire said, running over with a roll of red tape. She boxed it around where the mini sun had hit the brick, cautiously stepping around what Saphirra now saw were fishing lines. Then she switched to blue tape, boxing them in with it.

"Thanks, by the way," she said to Alex. "Now I know they can't only land there, they could land anywhere," Alex gazed around, startled to see more fishing lines crisscrossed throughout the rooftop. "But hey, my trajectories were right!" Claire said cheerily, sticking her tongue out at West, who replied coolly,

"It didn't even hit Alex."

Claire's face fell.

"Well that's just great. Tell me when you need target practice, okay?" Alex said sarcastically. He turned to Saphirra, who was thoroughly confused now.

"Saph, I talked to them about it, but I haven't told you. I *could* get help...But it would cost a few days. One or two, if I fly fast. I know the way now, I won't get lost—" Alex was talking to himself more than to Saphirra, and she studied him, puzzled.

"What are you talking about?"

"I'm talking about going back to Validus to get them to help." As Saphirra opened her mouth to protest, he cut her off with a shake of his head. "Saph, we need all the help we can get, and Validus has three others with him, I think. I'm sure he'll help me if I ask. Saph, I've got to go get help before time runs out and it's too late. West and Claire say it's worth it for me to go, too."

Saphirra remembered how Validus was a member of the High Council, and decided he might have more information than he'd told Alex. She nodded. It was for the best.

"Just be careful," Saphirra said, sitting down Indian style on the floor. "Make sure you hurry, because we don't have much time left. Where should we wait for you?" Saphirra asked, her voice sounding much calmer than she felt. The prospect of Alex leaving again wasn't exactly comforting, but she knew they would need all the help they could get. Claire and West seemed a little shocked that she was so calm.

"Saph, I promise nothing's going to happen to me, or you, or any of us. We'll get out of this just like we always have. We're four college students-- what could possibly go wrong?"

"Every time someone says that, something bad happens," Saphirra said quietly. Alex took her face in his hands, gently raising her eyes to meet his. His azure eyes flashed deep violet for a moment, and then it was gone.

"We will be fine," he assured her. "Be careful." She shivered as he kissed her once last time, and she watched him get up and walk to the edge of the roof.

"You too," she whispered as he took off in a flurry of black wings. As she turned back to West and Claire, she realized her entire body was shaking.

"So, when did all this happen?" Claire smirked. Saphirra blushed. She hadn't realized that Claire and West didn't know they had kissed.

"It just happened," Saphirra shrugged. They stared at each other and then West suddenly burst out into laughter, finally breaking the tension Saphirra had been bearing for days. Their laughter was cut short by a startled cry from Alex; within seconds, he'd crashed back down onto the roof, miraculously avoiding landing on a fishing line.

"What are you playing at?" Alex shouted at them. West looked taken aback.

"What are you talking about?"

"I know you just set off more traps!" Alex said angrily. "They missed me by inches! Couldn't you check to see if they work *after* I'd left the area?"

"We didn't shoot anything!" Claire insisted, looking around pleadingly for support. West backed her up.

"None of our traps were shot off, Alex," he persisted.

"Well, *something* shot at me," Alex grumbled, stretching out his wings once more. West watched him oddly, and Saphirra realized he still wasn't used to Alex's wings yet. "Next time, make sure you didn't leave any stray traps out, okay?" And with that, he took to the skies once more. Claire looked as bewildered as Saphirra felt.

"Did you guys leave any extra traps out?"

Both of them shook their heads. "We only set up traps on this roof," West repeated. Saphirra frowned, searching the sky until her eyes found Alex's frame, growing smaller into the distance. She looked down at the grounds, and a flash of something caught her eye. Something honey-brown. Something that suspiciously looked like Ms. Stone.

Evelyn stormed through Ry's office, searching frantically for him. She had been looking for him for hours, all because of one monumental flaw she'd found in his plan; *Alex was alive.* When she saw him take to the skies at the university, she'd tried to shoot him down as best as she could. Evelyn didn't care about being hidden or stealthy anymore; the college students would never be able to find her, anyway. What did it matter if they knew she was out to get them? It would only strike a higher level of fear into their hearts. The fact that Alex was alive was a flaw she couldn't let Ry forget. After years of her having screwed up, it was *his* turn to regret it. For the first few hours Evelyn had been ready to gloat, but now her air of superiority had dissipated, replaced by a gnawing anxiousness. It was almost midnight. *Where is he?* They were supposed to stick together, for fear of losing each other. It was essential that they knew where the other was; what if one of them got hurt? She searched the olive green walls, turning slowly in a circle until she saw something glitter out of the corner of her eye.

Evelyn furrowed her brow as she walked closer to it. It looked to be a long dagger, its hilt glittering eerily in the half-darkness. *Is this the dagger Ry accused me of stealing? Idiot.* She picked it up lithely, turning the beautiful metal over in her hands. It had been emblazoned with a kind of metal that seemed to flow at her touch, like a river. *Elymph-wrought metal,* Evelyn thought appreciatively. It was extremely hard to come by, especially for a Viceprus. *What is Ry doing with this?* She thought curiously, inspecting the metal. If she looked hard enough, she could make out figures etched onto it. A girl with a pail, an olive tree, an old, haggard woman beneath...tiny scenes had been depicted all around the edges of the dagger, resulting in the tip, where a beautiful girl and a demonic looking boy lay, their hands intertwined. Something about the scene seemed familiar to Evelyn, and as she passed a hand over the etchings, it occurred to her just what this dagger was.

The dagger from Siren Rock.

She stared at it in horror. It was the legendary dagger that could kill any Siren simply by piercing their throat. The Elymphs had insisted it was stolen from their kingdom centuries ago, adding to the high animosity between the creatures and the rest of the world. *How in the world did he get it?* She wondered, letting it clatter noisily onto the table. He wasn't supposed to have it, let alone use it. What would he need it for? He wanted to take over the High Council, not kill off all Sirens. Unless...She stared at the dagger once more, disgusted by how its gleaming metal seemed to call out to her, how she wanted to reach out and take it. What if Clandestine was controlling him, too, and he found out? She had been wondering what a member of the Triumvirate would want with her or Ry, and now it all made sense. Ry's plans weren't simply about the Viceprus Council; he planned on killing off everyone who stood in his way, including the Sirens. *Clandestine must have figured it out,* Evelyn realized. What other explanation was there? Ry had brought Clandestine's fury upon himself and Evelyn. Dismay clawed at her heart as she realized how stupid she had been. Evelyn had been ensuring the destruction of the carefully balanced mythical world, and she didn't even see it. Clandestine knew, and now Ry was planning on killing her, too.

Evelyn glanced up at the clouds, seeing the hint of the moon halfway up in the sky. It was only a day or two until the blue moon, something she had looked forward to with eager anticipation. Now, she wasn't quite sure what Ry had planned. If he held this dagger, then what else could he have in store? *He could have planned my death,* Evelyn realized. He could have decided to kill her once she was useless once more. It didn't seem uncharacteristic of him, after all. *I could have helped him plan my own destruction,* she realized. Fury boiled through her veins. She wanted to kill him, to make him pay for using her like this. *Revenge,* she decided. He needed to realize not everyone would comply with his plans. But how? She began to pace, and paused at the dagger once more. Fine. If Ry wanted to manipulate her, she would do the job herself. Evelyn would kill him in the worst way possible. She let her fingers curl around the dagger, letting the welcoming feel of the smooth metal envelop her palm. Smiling to herself, she slipped it into her pocket. Ry would be no match for any Siren without it. She would get rid of Clandestine, and then get rid of him. She would kill them all.

Chapter 32
Once in a Blue Moon

Saphirra proceeded up the narrow stairs leading to the roof with West and Claire. She felt like she was in a funeral procession, all silent and filled with dread for the hours to come. Their preparations over the last two days came down to tonight. They had spent the days looking up last minute information on Vicepruses, living on coffee and anxiousness. Claire trudged behind the rest, her eyes bleary with exhaustion. She was the most sleep deprived out of all of them, because she finally had to admit that there wasn't a single book in the library that could tell them how to defeat Professor Lockson. Of course, she'd tried—the entire library was now sorted into two piles: almost-useful and worthless nonsense. Her anger towards West seemed to have dissipated as well, more than likely replaced by the terror they all felt.

Saphirra now held West's gun in her pocket, because West insisted she needed it more than he did. She narrowly avoided walking into him as he paused by the door, fumbling with the latch. They walked onto the roof nervously, expecting an ambush. Nothing happened. West settled down cross legged, while Claire dumped the remnants of West's sun bullets onto the ground. West had shown them how to break the bullets open to reveal the dangerous powder inside, and how to make them into something more useable. They had rigged the bullets to explode on contact if they threw them, something Claire had been especially proud of. As they settled down onto the rooftop, Saphirra glanced up at the sky. If the lunar eclipse had already begun to swallow up the full moon, she wouldn't have known it; dark storm clouds had obscured the sky, making things darker than they should have been. Saphirra felt her pulse speed up as her phone vibrated in her pocket, and she pulled it out.

"Is it Alex?" West's voice broke through her thoughts, but she was spared having to answer as her phone rang. Saphirra glanced at it fearfully. To her relief, Alex's name lit up the display.

"Hello?"

"Saph! It's me. We're coming." Alex's voice flooded through the receiver, washing her anxiety away. Saphirra smiled; *this* was the call she had been waiting for.

"You want me to meet you?" Saphirra asked curiously, shifting to get a better look at the dark sky. She couldn't see anything for miles.

"Yeah. Meet us near the gates," he conceded. "Try to hurry, please." He hung up, and Saphirra looked up at her two friends, who were waiting patiently for her to explain.

"He says he's almost here," Saphirra announced. "I'm going to go to the gates to meet him."

"What? Don't go alone!" Claire cried, alarmed. West laid a comforting hand on her shoulder.

"It's fine. We can hold the fort up here. Go," he insisted. "We'll see if anything happens from here, and we'll be able to help you. Don't worry."

Saphirra nodded to the two of them and maneuvered quickly down the stairs and out the door. If she could save Alex, it would all be worth it. She ran out into the quad, sprinting close to the buildings so no one could see her. She ran past the shrubbery spelling out their university's name which now decorated in rubble, and sighed as she reached the old fashioned golden gates. She stood next to them, still as a statue.

Was it stupid, going out on her own like this? She could see bright flashes of light from one of the roofs, which told her Claire and West were still fixing last minute rigs. She clutched her cold cell phone in her pocket fearfully, tracing the cool metal with her thumb. She had traveled Chicago at midnight before, taking long walks by herself when things got too hectic. The streets were nowhere near empty tonight, even at two in the morning; drunken men tittered as they walked past her, swaying to a rhythm no one could hear. Saphirra rolled her eyes as lightning streaked across the inky black sky. As the first fat wet raindrops hit her face, she moved towards the street corner instead, moving to stand under an awning that would protect her from the rain.

Saphirra stared around, the rain making sharp edges fuzzy, the neon sign of the scrap booking store staring her in the face. The phone booth there was empty, along with the rest of the street. She felt chills trickle down her spine as she looked around. She had the uneasy feeling that she was being watched, even now. The gates were only a short distance away, but she still felt nervous. Her wet hair was clinging to her face as her phone beeped, signaling it was three o' clock.

Then the pain hit.

She crumpled to the ground, clutching her neck as the pain seared through her. *What's happening to me?* She wondered as her eyes filled with tears. She was on fire, her neck was on fire, and she screamed as the pain shot through her again. A group of people walked past her, muttering about lunatics. Staggering, she pushed herself up, slipping on the wet sidewalk. She could barely stand, the pain was so intense. The fire was spreading, and she clutched at her neck, even though he knew her hand would get burned, too. Why wasn't the rain, falling fast and hard against her face, putting out the terrible fire? She groaned as she touched her hand to the burning bite mark Alex had left on her neck, frantically trying to stop the wild burning that had consumed her.

She was running now, blinded by the pain. She collapsed again near the college gates, in the brink of an alley, her legs unable to carry her anymore. She pulled herself up, trying to reach the gates. A scream ripped from her throat as the pain stabbed through her. She didn't know what was happening, she didn't understand, she just felt her hand start to burn up, too. Removing it at once, she examined her fingers through shots of pain that reverberated through her body, stabbing at her insides. Her hand was burning, she could feel it—but no flames were dancing on her skin, licking her fingers with the ferocity she felt. She wasn't on fire. If so, then what was happening? She clutched her neck as tears spilled over.

"Saphirra!"

She heard Alex's voice as if it was inside her own head, booming and panic-stricken. Suddenly, she felt something new, something else; a swooping sensation enveloped her, and then she was enveloped in darkness, Alex's shout reverberating through her body.

When she awoke again, she had made it into the college somehow, and had collapsed on the muddy ground. The pain returned, ferociously tearing at her insides. This must be what Alex felt every moon; this must be what he was feeling, even now. Had they somehow combined? She struggled to her feet, but the swooping darkness veiled her once more, causing her to fall to the ground.

She came to behind the bushes that spelled out the university's name, her head throbbing, pain searing through her heart. Every cell in her body was crying out silently to end the pain that Saphirra knew she and Alex somehow shared, for Alex to stop the burning she could now feel. What was happening? She wasn't like him; she shouldn't feel like this, should she? She wished for anything to take the pain away. Was this what the full moon did to him? Was this the blue moon's effect, the *eclipse's* effect? Either way, Professor Lockson would get what they wanted, wouldn't they? Because Alex had no idea where she was, Alex wouldn't hear her cry out to him, begging him to save her, and she was dying. She was dying, sinking slowly into the muddy, rain-streaked ground and no one would know.

Alex heard thunder reverberate through the sky, and knew he had to move, and fast. Below him, Validus was urging his companions to move closer, urging them to move quickly. Alex beat his wings faster as the Vicepruses below him ran through the streets, dodging bleary eyed humans as they went. Alex watched Comis run, watching her lithe footsteps as if in slow motion. Kind, friendly, beautiful Comis—if he didn't know better, he would have thought she was a Siren. Her long brown hair danced as she ran, whipping Validus in the face. Validus, who had shown the most affection towards her, the most he'd ever shown since Alex had first met him, ran to keep up with Comis. The Viceprus called Fama followed behind, shouting out orders as she took to the sky.

Callidus was flying with them now as their little procession entered the heart of Chicago. Callidus was the smart one of the group, as Alex had quickly realized. The new additions to Validus's hideout hadn't been very surprised to see Alex standing there. Validus had touched his shoulder upon his arrival, and Alex was propelled into black oblivion After he could finally see again, Alex watched Validus tell the others what he needed. Validus had explained that the High Council knew about the prophecy, knew Lockson was in for them. He'd never suspected it to be this serious until now, until the Viceprus Alex had rescued came to him for help, explaining what Alex had told her. They followed Alex grimly as he flew deeper into the city, guiding them to the college as fat raindrops started to fall, lashing him with water. He heard Validus curse beside him, and heard Fama comment at the eeriness of the blue moon, now peeking through a storm cloud, far away from where they were. It was almost three in the morning, and the eclipse would be at its peak in a few minutes. They didn't have time to waste.

Suddenly he heard a piercing scream, shocking him out of his stupor. That scream...it was Saphirra's, and it was loud, louder than anything else. The note pierced him, and he bent over in agony. *What's happening to me?* Strong pain cascaded though him, and he crumpled to the ground. He pulled himself up at the last minute, staggering with the pain. He felt claws growing from his fingers, longer than before.

"Saphirra's in trouble," he said through gritted teeth. As if to confirm this the piercing note rang though him again, sending a shiver down his spine.

"Can't you hear that?" he called to them as they swooped down to the ground, staggering a little as they landed next to him.

"I can't hear anything," Callidus told him. Comis was watching him, concern etched in her face, and Alex got up, staggering though the pain. Fire seemed to be burning through him, blocking out everything else; he curled into a ball, his wings dissipating onto his back. The rain pelted him mercilessly, as if the heavens were trying to put out the fire within him. He heard her scream one more time, and he shouted,

Reedhima Mandlik

"Saphirra!"

Before he knew what was happening, he'd been sucked into her, enveloped by something else entirely. He blinked, and saw he was on the pavement, inches from the college gates; he pulled himself upright, running staggeringly towards the grounds, pushing the gates aside as quickly as he could. As he reached the muddy grass he fell to his knees, his body incapable to going on. Saphirra's hair was plastered to his face, and her entire body shook; he looked down at his hand, and was surprised to see his mother's ring glowing slightly on her finger, as if begging to be taken off. Seconds later he was back on the street, surrounded by the four new Vicepruses he'd met only hours ago. He shook himself, ignoring the burning that had renewed in his veins as he bounded off the pavement, flexing his wings until they caught in the air.

"I'm going to look for her. Wherever she is, she isn't on that roof." he cringed as another round of pain pierced his heart, throbbing through his skull. "I'll fly to the roof when I find her; I'll bring her back, I swear. Please take care of West and Claire. Validus, you've seen where we're going to meet, so please go there and protect my friends. Thank you all so much for what you're doing for us," he told them, speaking mainly to Validus as he took off, making a beeline towards the college.

The pounding in his ears didn't match the rhythm of his heart anymore; it was something else entirely. It was a second until he could understand what he was listening to—Saphirra's heartbeat. *No wonder they couldn't hear it. I'm the only one attuned to it like this,* Alex thought grimly, flying past neon signs and street cars, the rain whipping him in the face, making it harder to see. He didn't care if any people saw him anymore; they'd just think they were delusional.

Lightning ripped through the sky again, and he finally heard Saphirra's voice groaning, "Help..." faintly. He fell to the ground once more, this time hitting the pavement hard; he was Saphirra again, lying motionless on the ground where he had left her. He struggled to get up, pulling himself until he was next to a row of bushes, before her body collapsed; as he was dragged back into his own body, he saw her ring glowing more brightly than ever, nearly pulsing with light.

He struggled to his feet and began to run, ignoring the pain burning though him until he finally saw her. Alex landed next to her, cradling her in his arms, and her face twisted from terror to relief as she saw who was holding her. He walked with her into the shadows, frantically searching for a way onto the roof. He didn't think he could handle flying just yet; the pain had begun to mount, suffocating all reason.

"I'm...I'm dying..."

"No, you aren't...you can't," his voice broke at the last word as despair clutched at his heart, clawing at it. She couldn't die, and yet, her heart was slowing down. The throbbing pulse he could hear had begun to slow down, its power diminishing with every beat. *What's happening to us?* Alex wanted to shout. His hands began to glow from where he touched Saphirra, and he had to control the urge to drop her. He didn't want to suck energy from her, not now...

" Alex...I'm on fire...cold fire..." She groaned as his hands touched hers; she was gripping her neck oddly, her fingers digging into the skin. He pulled her clutching hand away gently, gasping at what he saw. The bite mark he'd left on her neck was glowing with the eerie, soft golden glow, beckoning to him. Saphirra cringed in pain, and the same pain swept through his body.

"You can't die; you won't, I won't let you!" he said desperately as Saphirra closed her eyes, wincing in pain. He looked at her, fear coursing through him, and she coughed, trying to open her eyes. Her heart was stuttering, it was failing, and she was dying–

No!

Saphirra coughed again, her body shivering uncontrollably. Alex gritted his teeth and unfolded his wings, putting every conscious effort into flying towards the roof. As he lifted off into the air, Alex frantically called out into the night for Validus, for anyone that could help. They didn't respond. He was nearing the roof with more force than necessary, but he couldn't stop himself. His body seemed to have taken control, propelling himself forward with a new kind of ferocity. He felt pain spread once again from his arms to his neck, down his chest and into his heart. He looked down at the feeble girl in his arms, voraciously vowing he would keep her safe. Saphirra opened her mouth, coughing as she spoke.

Reedhima Mandlik

"Alex...What have you done to me?" Saphirra gasped.

And as the pounding in his head seemed to cease, she fell limp in his arms.

Chapter 33
Splatters on a Rooftop

West stepped to the side of the rooftop, trying his hardest to avoid Claire. He couldn't stand being near her right now, not when he felt like he was going to explode. He was shaking all over, and he doubled over as something in his brain stirred. For a second, he saw Claire glance at him worriedly, and felt like lunging at her. He could see her soul, and it shone brightly at him, almost as if it was beckoning to him. *What's wrong with me?* He hadn't felt this way in a long while. He shuddered as Claire put a hand on his shoulder.

"West? Hey, what's wrong?" she asked softly. West glanced up again, and it was as if something took over his body for a second, pulling at him, trying to make him attack Claire. He'd seen the white sphere beyond her hazel eyes, and a part of him yearned for it. That part was bigger than West would have liked it to be. The urge to attack Claire, to have the soul within her, had been building slowly for the last week, and he didn't think he could control himself anymore. Lightning ripped through the sky, and the first small raindrops started falling onto the rooftop. Claire bent down so she was at eye level with West.

"West?"

He gritted his teeth before answering as he watched the moon disappear behind a cloud.

"Seriously, Claire. If you want to survive this night, *get away from me.*"

Claire stepped back as if he'd slapped her. The rain started to fall in earnest, and she backed away from him silently. He couldn't tell whether she was crying or whether it was raindrops rolling down her face. He reached out to her, to apologize, but he couldn't get the words out without some sort of note escaping him, overpowering his senses. He'd never even been able to tell Claire what the Latin words really meant—*I love you, forever and always*. And now he might not even be able to. He couldn't even open his mouth to say sorry. *I hate this. I hate this so much!* West thought irritably. He couldn't understand why all his Siren powers seemed to be ganging up on him at once, especially at a time like this. Lightning ripped through the sky again, and he couldn't control himself anymore. He ran at Claire, who didn't make a single sound. Her eyes weren't focused on him, but he could still see her soul, brighter than ever. Just as his fingers grasped her wrist, something jerked him back. Someone had their hands around his neck, choking him, and Claire simply watched silently.

Saphirra felt like she'd been thrust into six feet of snow. She struggled to open her eyes. She could hear something distantly, and it sounded like Alex. Something wet was hitting her face with astonishing speed, making it nearly impossible for her to open her eyes. She felt her body sway, and memories of a few moments ago flooded back to her. It was raining, and then...throbbing pain. As if to remind her, a flash of stinging heat burned through her veins. She felt like she was on fire. She couldn't move. She couldn't talk. As the rocking motion stopped, she heard Alex groan. Was he carrying her?

What happened to me?

She heard Alex shouting in her ear, and struggled to open her eyes, to no avail.

"Validus! No, let go of him!"

She heard a thump as something, or someone, fell to the ground. Someone's gruff voice answered.

"The boy is a Siren, and you want me to calm down? You never informed me that we're working with the enemy!"

Alex stopped moving.

"He's a what?"

Saphirra was lowered to the ground, and after a moment she opened her eyes.

Alex was staring at someone behind her, his violet eyes glowing in the darkness. Somehow, he seemed illuminated. Claire's worried face looked down at something on the tiled floor of the rooftop, and she twisted around to see what Claire was looking at. West had been knocked to the ground.

"Saphirra?"

She looked at Alex again, noting the sound of pain in his voice. Why did he sound so apprehensive?

"What?" she asked him quietly. He looked at her, confusion and horror flickering in his violet eyes, which were slowly changing back to blue.

"Did you know about this?" Alex asked her, astonished. Claire swept her strawberry hair behind her shoulder, staring at the both of them as if for the first time.

"I...I can't..."

She couldn't talk anymore, she couldn't move. Alex crouched down beside her, leaning against the wall for support.

"West...You're a *Siren*? How–"

"Not now, Alex."

West was glaring at the four Vicepruses Alex must have brought with him, and was shaking so hard he could barely get up again.

"You mean to say you've been working with a *Siren*?" Someone spat.

"I didn't know," Alex said, sounding as lost and confused as Saphirra felt. *He's a Siren?* The thought made her head spin. He leaned against the wall as he stood, and helped Alex up. Claire put a hand to Saphirra's forehead, blocking her view.

"How touching. The last thing you will see is each other."

Professor Lockson's harsh voice rang through the silence, and something blurred out of Saphirra's vision. As Claire dived to the side, pulling Saphirra with her, a blinding flash sent Alex sprawling backwards into the brick wall.

It had begun.

Claire jumped to her feet as West's traps did their job, blasting bullets towards Lockson. With lightning speed, he dodged each bullet, leaping around like he was walking on hot coals as trap after trap went off with a bang. West grabbed his gun from Saphirra's pocket as

Reedhima Mandlik

Alex took to the skies, pulling Saphirra with him. Claire scrambled along the edge, hurling as many sun bullet sacks as she could. This was what they'd been preparing for.

Lockson howled in pain as one sack hit its mark, blasting onto his arm. Shrieking with rage, Lockson knocked into the wall, blinded by what Claire assumed was immense pain. West raised his gun and took aim as Alex dived, his wings knocking the professor forward. Instead of halting and hovering near the ground, however, Alex crashed into the tiled floor of the roof, setting off more bombs. She had no time to process or even try to understand why West had attacked her, or who the new Vicepruses were; chaos had broken loose around them, and Claire could barely see straight. The entire rooftop exploded all at once in an eerie golden light, and Saphirra and Alex's screams mingled with Claire's as she fought to see.

"What? You're my best Hunter, and now you're trying to kill me? How ironic. You didn't even kill *him*," Professor Lockson spat, pointing at Alex, "and yet I let you live. How *dare* you go against your own employer?" Professor Lockson shrieked in rage. Claire dropped the sack she was holding. *Did he just say–*

"You are my *what*?" West growled.

"Can't you hear, boy? Are you deaf?" he sneered. "I was your boss. You were working for your enemy. Now, how does that make you feel?" he mocked. West seemed too stunned to answer. Professor Lockson took advantage of their momentary pause and leapt towards Claire. She saw Alex shout at a beautiful brown haired Viceprus, but the burly one who had put West in a stranglehold only moments ago shoved Claire aside.

"Move!" he hissed roughly, pushing Claire to the floor. She felt her hands scrape against something warm, and pain blossomed on the back of her head as she hit the wall hard.

"Comis! Get him!"

The brown haired Viceprus, Comis, whirled towards Lockson, her arm outstretched. The professor neatly dodged, only to find his way blocked by a tall Viceprus.

"Get out of my way, Validus," Professor Lockson hissed.

356

"You *dare* go against the High Council?" Validus boomed, stepping menacingly towards him. "You will *never* be one of us."

"I knew from the beginning what the prophecy meant!" Lockson's wild yell shattered the stillness Validus had imposed. He looked slightly deranged as he faced Validus head on, his claws clutching the brick behind him for support. "I *warned* you, and none of you listened! None!" he let out a shriek of laughter, which was promptly cut short as Validus clawed at his throat. The two grappled for a moment, before Validus was blasted off his feet. Lockson had pulled out his gun, and was now shooting at anything that moved, laughing maniacally as he went.

"You didn't listen!" he taunted. "You didn't listen, and now you'll die!"

As the remaining three Vicepruses dived at him, West appeared beside Claire and put a hand on her shoulder.

"Are you alright?" he asked. She nodded.

"Lockson was your boss?" she grimaced as she spoke.

"All the more reason to kill him," he growled. He shielded Claire with his body as he pulled out his gun and aimed, taking a deep breath as his finger pulled the trigger. A burst of golden light illuminated the whole rooftop, and then West cried out in pain. As the flash ebbed away, total silence echoed throughout the rooftop. Claire saw West kneeling on the ground, a gash across his chest spurting blood everywhere. The bullet had missed its target, hitting the wall behind Lockson as he'd dodged. Lockson had pushed West to the ground, swiping at his chest, which resulted in the blood.

West put a shaking hand over his own chest, squeezing his eyes shut as his hand started glowing. Just as the wound started closing up, Professor Lockson knocked a petite Viceprus aside and crashed into West. He was now crouched over him, getting ready to take the fatal swipe with his unearthly claws. Claire screamed.

Before she could do anything, Validus had charged at the professor, surprisingly faster than Claire thought he could be. He'd barely had time to dodge the burly Viceprus before Alex fell onto him, tackling him into a fishing line. As the wall next to them exploded, Alex got knocked down to the floor. Claire sensed movement out of the corner of her eye and turned just as West had begun to stand. His chest was still bleeding slightly, and he was breathing heavily. Claire started to help him up, but he shook his head. Determinedly, she pulled him out of the wreckage. She knelt down beside him, He groaned weakly as she helped him to the corner.

"Claire, get away from me."

Claire shook her head, one arm on West, the other on the wall, not daring to take her eyes off the deadly dance that had ensued in front of them. Their lithe, precise movements scared Claire.

The two female Vicepruses were working as a team, and they cornered Professor Lockson, practically diving at the same moment towards him.

All at once a flash broke out, and the two were thrown backwards, writhing in agony as the sun bullet's poison took its toll. A scream of pain broke through the night sky like a thunderbolt, and Claire tried to see through the rain that was now falling thick and fast onto the rooftop.

Professor Lockson had apparently clawed Alex on his way down, and Alex's body was now streaked with red. West clutched at Claire's arm, and she felt him shaking. He staggered towards Alex, ignoring the battle that had ensued between the remaining Viceprus and Professor Lockson. The others had either been seriously wounded, or were already dead, a deep scorch marking where they had lain. Claire's heart sank as she helped West walk, one arm on him, one arm dragging Saphirra's limp frame towards Alex. As West gritted his teeth and reached out to touch Alex, Saphirra's frame shuddered, and Claire let go of West in order to fully support Saphirra's weight.

West was bent over Alex now, and as his hands glowed with healing powers over Alex's body, Saphirra's began to faintly glow as well. The rain flew into Claire's face, blurring her vision. She crouched down next to West, and found that Alex and Saphirra's hands had somehow entwined, and were glowing once more. West was positively quaking now, and was looking away as if he couldn't figure out where to go. Claire reached out a shaking hand.

Alex groaned and stirred feebly, never letting go of Saphirra's hands. The light golden glow between them grew brighter, and when

Claire inspected Saphirra's hand more closely, she saw a pinprick of white light shooting out. Within seconds, the glow between their hands turned an iridescent white as Alex fell limp.

Alex's ring was glowing.

Professor Lockson was shouting something at the Vicepruses who had charged at him, but Claire took no notice; West was leaning against the wall, his breathing shallow and heavy. Claire put a hand on his shoulder, blinking the blinding rain from her eyes. Lightning streaked across the sky as she saw West turn to look at her. There was something about him that seemed almost *hungry* in a way. He stared at her for a moment, and then suddenly lunged at her, throwing her onto the floor and into a wall. His breathing sped up as he gazed at her.

"West, what the–? Let *go* of me!"

West shook his head, and for a moment, his grey eyes flashed with recognition.

"I warned you to get away from me."

It was the last human word he'd spoken. He opened his mouth to say something more, and a beautiful song poured from his mouth. Every Viceprus was brought to their knees with the noise, screeching in fury and pain. They struggled to cover their ears, all but Professor Lockson, who took the opportunity to fire a deadly bullet into a Viceprus's back. As West sang in her ear the song changed pitch, and as Professor Lockson was brought down to his knees as well, her world went black.

Alex was burning. No, he was sweating. Now he was burning again. He tried to open his eyes, but everything around him swam. He felt something cold in his hands, and turned to see Saphirra out cold beside him, her hands entwined in his. A faint white glow emitted from their hands, as if there was an invisible force holding them together. Then out of nowhere, Professor Lockson was on top of them, pummeling them further into the ground. Saphirra's screams echoed throughout the deserted college, and Alex realized he was screaming too. He felt the wings on his back evaporating, and his strength diminishing; he looked around frantically for help, but Validus lay unconscious on the ground, and the rest didn't seem in any fit state to help anyone. He pulled Saphirra closer to him protectively, and her body felt lifeless. He shook her and her eyes fluttered, then snapped open, looking Professor Lockson squarely in the eye. Her hand, still entwined with his, reached out and took hold of Lockson's neck, sending him reeling back from them. He screamed loudly, clutching at his neck as if burned. Alex furrowed his brow, watching on as Saphirra fell back into a state of unconsciousness. *What just happened?* Had Saphirra just unconsciously saved their lives?

Claire was screaming now, and Alex squinted through the rain to find West grabbing Claire, singing something loudly. It sounded like nails on a blackboard. One ear burned with the noise, but the other just processed it as noise. Alex struggled to get up, but the world spun. He collapsed, writhing in sudden pain and agony. Saphirra jerked awake suddenly, screaming with the same pain Alex suddenly felt. Were they somehow becoming part of each other? Were they combining through the venom that existed in his body and the venom he'd accidentally injected into Saphirra when he'd bitten her? Maybe the venom held the link. Alex winced as another shock of pain radiated through him, and he looked at West, who was crouched over Claire. Claire's mouth was open, and something was slowly emerging from it–

West's Siren side has taken over. Alex registered as a pure white sphere of light, something Alex dimly understood to be Claire's soul, began to materialize from her mouth.

"West! Stop!" Alex managed to shout out, half reaching towards him. An invisible force pulled him back down, making it so he couldn't move. West shook his head at the sound of Alex's voice. His hands tightened on Claire's shoulder, and he seemed to force his mouth shut. Deep gash marks appeared on Claire's shoulder, and blood began to stream down, staining the tile below. West closed his eyes.

"I...I *can't.*"

With that, a swell of song flooded through the rooftop, and Alex shuddered at the noise. Claire's soul rose faster than before, up and towards West.

Fire was spreading through his body, Alex was sure of it. He should be freezing in his wet clothes in the ceaseless rain, but he was on fire. Something hit him hard, and he was pushed up against the wall. It took him seconds to realize Saphirra was the one pinning him to the wall, a strange look in her eyes. He didn't understand what was happening; only that Saphirra was acting on her own, holding up their entwined fingers to her eyes. His ring shone bright white through the haze of yellow that was transferred energy, somehow instilling a feeling of calm through him. *I love her,* he thought, looking up into her eyes, then back down at the ring. He didn't even know what he was saying anymore; the next words that flew out of his mouth made it seem as if he was talking to his mother's ring, almost *insisting* with it:

"I love her," he repeated out loud. The ring flashed a brighter white, almost in recognition, but her emerald eyes remained blank. As if in answer she kissed him, and the fire vanished, and bone chilling cold replaced the fire. But now Alex felt Saphirra's skin burning up, saw her cheeks flush; he kissed her, and lightning ripped through the sky. The moon was barely visible through the storm cloud, but it's red light still shone through; *as blood hangs in the sky,* Alex thought numbly. For the first time in three months felt relatively *normal.* Saphirra's skin lost its feverish temperature, and she pushed away from him, breaking the link between them. Within seconds, his world had dissolved into darkness, dragging him along with it.

Chapter 34
Zenith

Saphirra came to as the wall above her exploded, showering her with bits of rubble. Saphirra could barely make sense of what was happening. *Why am I standing?* She wondered. She was no longer shivering, and yet a strange eerie calm had taken over her senses, making her thought process slower than usual. She couldn't feel anything but a strange heated sensation in her left hand. For a moment, time stood still.

Then everything crashed into her at once.

Her vision slowly came into focus as she tried to make sense of it all. Professor Lockson was heading towards her, his black hair glinting in the half darkness. He was shouting now, looking about as if expecting someone to appear. No one came.

Who does he expect to show up? Saphirra thought bitterly. *What idiot would help him?*

She glanced up at the sky, where the blue moon was peeking through a cloud, its eerie red light shining on the rooftop like a spotlight. Hadn't it been raining before? The rooftop was drenched, but raindrops no longer fell from the sky. An unmistakable air of unease washed over Saphirra as she looked around, realizing she and Professor Lockson were the only ones standing. The four Vicepruses Alex had brought with him were either injured or already dead, and completely unhelpful at the moment. She searched for West and Claire instead, noting a low note stretching across the rooftop.

Professor Lockson paused in his tracks, brought to his knees by the sound; finally she found them in the furthest corner of the rooftop. West was bent over Claire, struggling as a golden sphere rushed up from Claire's mouth. He opened his mouth, and his cruel, beautiful music washed over the entire rooftop, this time with lyrics sung in an alien language. His voice made her forget everything and everyone around her for a moment, and she stood where she was, mesmerized by his music. The sphere of light above Claire's mouth flickered and swelled a little, and suddenly Saphirra realized exactly what West was doing.

He was going to suck out Claire's soul.

I have to get to West. I have to stop him, she thought, watching warily in case Professor Lockson tried to get up. He didn't move, however, so she sprinted across the rooftop towards West and Claire, dodging debris as she tackled West onto the ground. His song was still pouring from his mouth, and it was as if she couldn't think for a moment. Claire's soul flitted higher into the air, and she shook herself out of West's Siren spell.

"Keep...your...mouth...*shut,*" she growled at him, hitting him hard in the jaw. His mouth snapped closed but he didn't seem hurt, to Saphirra's relief. She reached out to grab Claire and pull her away from West, noticing with shock that deep gashes had appeared on her shoulder. With West's Siren song gone, the Vicepruses were able to move again, and bangs and crashes echoed throughout the college. She pulled Claire nearer to where Alex was, in case she had to make a run for him, too. She watched the golden sphere of light just hovering above Claire's face, and moved to touch it, to push it back into her mouth, but a voice made her stop.

"Don't touch it."

A Viceprus lay next to her, clutching at his leg, where he'd apparently been hit. She glanced at him uncertainly. "If you do, it'll shatter into a million pieces, and she will die. Worse, she will be without a soul," he informed her monotonously, grimacing as wave after wave of pure song crashed into him. She glowered at him.

"How do I make it go back in, then? Just stare at it?" she asked irritably. The Viceprus shook his head, shifting his lanky, bony frame towards her.

"Only the Siren can make it go back. He's the only one with the power to manipulate souls."

"But he tried to *kill* her! You expect me to trust West after this?" Saphirra interrupted, pulling Claire closer to her.

"You trusted Alex when he lost control, but you can't trust his friend? It's hard enough for us to trust a Siren, but you're a human. You should put your prejudices aside," he said carefully. Saphirra ignored the fact that he seemed to know way too much about their situation and hoisted Claire up instead, making sure not to touch the sphere that was her soul. West made to help, but she slapped his hand aside.

"If you want to help, *fix her,*" she growled, thrusting West away from both of them. A commotion from behind her caused her to whip around. Lockson had gotten to his feet and was now charging towards Alex, his gun outstretched in his hands.

I love her.

The voice was Alex's, but that was impossible; he was unconscious. Saphirra looked down as her finger suddenly grew warm, and noticed something odd about Alex's mother's ring. It had begun to glow an iridescent white. Before she knew what she was doing she charged forward, her hand outstretched. It was as if her hand had a mind of its own; it pulled her towards Professor Lockson. As she moved the ring began to expand before her eyes, the metal sprouting from the diamond of the ring and uncoiling itself into a tangle of long, thin threads. *What the—?* She stared at it, alarmed, but before she could tear it off her finger it had pulled her forward again. It continued to unfurl itself, slowly blossoming out of the diamond of the ring. Professor Lockson saw this and screeched, alarmed, at the sight of the glowing white metal.

The key to their survival is hidden within the jewel. Is this what the prophecy meant? Saphirra wondered numbly. Was West's theory about the prophecy really true? Was it the ring, after all?

Suddenly, something white and brown flashed in the corner of her eye, and Saphirra whipped around, trying to see what it was. Her gaze only met night air. She saw the flash again, and this time her eyes caught it; Ms. Stone, sprinting towards them. Saphirra turned back to Professor Lockson, her eyes lit with fury.

"You will never hurt Alex again," Saphirra hissed. A brief spell of warmth shook her, and before she could stop herself the words had flown out of her mouth: "I love him."

Before she even knew what she was doing Saphirra's out-stretched hand had grabbed onto his shoulder. The ring expanded as if it had a mind of its own, its long spindly threads twining themselves around Professor Lockson's shoulder. He shouted out in pure agony as the ring continued to spiral up his shoulder blade and onto his neck, gathering there and squeezing. It appeared the metal was burning his flesh; Lockson howled in pain, his golden eyes conveying pure horror as he struggled to push Saphirra away. Within seconds he appeared to have lost the ability to speak; garbled shouts of anger issued from his blistering throat, and then his hands were on Saphirra, struggling to push her to the ground, struggling to tear her limb from limb.

"Elymph...metal..." He gasped at her, fumbling with the continuously growing ring.

I love her. Alex's voice shook through her, and once again the unconscious words escaped her:

"I love him. You will never hurt us," she spat. As Professor Lockson made to retaliate Ms. Stone appeared, her expression livid. It happened so quickly that Saphirra barely processed it; Ms. Stone gripped his head on either side, her claws digging into his skull. Time stood still as Ms. Stone tugged violently and twisted. A sickening crack echoed throughout the college as Professor Lockson let out one last scream of agony. His neck had been broken, and his head lolled uselessly at his side now, only supported by the eerie spindles of Alex's mother's ring. The ring didn't seem to be done, though; it began to glow brighter, until it was almost blinding. Searing heat burned Saphirra's finger, and she shielded her eyes against the brilliant white light. Impossibly, Lockson screamed once more as his spots along his body began to glow with the same brilliant white light. The holes steadily grew larger, until it enveloped his whole frame; in another brilliant flash he was gone, a scorch mark the only evidence that he had existed in the first place. His gun clattered to the ground, useless and burned.

"I suppose your pitiful assistant wasn't so useless after all," Ms. Stone whispered, spitting at the mark on the ground. She turned to Saphirra, her violet eyes glittering mercilessly.

"Now I can kill you."

Before she could move to protect herself, a voice echoed from behind Ms. Stone.

"Don't be too sure."

A gunshot echoed throughout the rooftop, and Ms. Stone shrieked in pain and shock. She stared at her leg, where sunbeams had already begun to appear, then at West, who stood triumphantly above her, his gun smoking, breathing heavily. Ms. Stone tottered backwards, backing away from West. Saphirra saw it happen almost in slow motion; Ms. Stone took one wrong step and tripped, falling backwards off the roof into the night. Her scream resounded off the walls until it was cut short.

Saphirra stood frozen, unsure of what had just happened. Alex's mother's ring had returned to its original form on her finger, almost as if she had imagined the whole thing. West dragged her away from the spot Professor Lockson used to be, his voice snapping her trance.

"Get to Alex, *now*."

Saphirra obediently ran to Alex's side and crouched down, alarmed to see his eyes still closed. *I thought he couldn't pass out!* The thought, panic settling into her stomach. Saphirra touched Alex's wrist, checking for signs of life. *He can't be dead, please don't let him be dead, please–*

"He's got a pulse," she stammered shakily, breathing a sigh of relief. West moved towards Claire, his footsteps echoing loudly in the sudden silence. West reached out a hand to touch Claire.

"Get away from her. You'll kill her!" Saphirra started, but West held up a finger and opened his mouth. For a moment, Saphirra thought he was going to actually do it, that Claire's soul would be gone forever. Instead, song poured from his mouth, gentle and sorrowful. Saphirra was hit by all the pent up emotions in West's heart, and she sank to her knees, the tears that had spontaneously sprung spilling over. *He loves her,* Saphirra realized. *I can hear it in the song.*

West sang, and the entire college reverberated with the sound. For a second, the cars honking in the street so far away had muted, and nothing mattered except West's song and Alex's gentle breathing. The intensity of the song grew, and Saphirra's heart ached just like it used to before she met Alex.

She was crying in earnest now, silent tears sliding down her face. She noticed West was shaking, and that he was crying, too. She felt Alex's fingers twitch in her hand, and she realized she'd had a death grip on them. She loosened her hold on him as she watched Claire's soul float back into her mouth. For a moment, she couldn't breathe. She could hear the words of the alien song and suddenly they made sense;

Claire, come back to us; Ego diligo vos pro totus vicis quod Usquequaque. Claire, come back to me, please.

The beautiful music lowered in pitch, and Claire's body jolted as if she'd been shocked. West put a hand on Claire's shoulder as the Vicepruses around them started to come to, stirring feebly. Validus was the first one to move, but Saphirra could see how hard it was for him to go against the Siren song. *Entrancing to humans, excruciating pain to Vicepruses,* Saphirra thought. West stopped singing and slumped against the brick, Claire in his arms, his chest heaving heavily. He smiled shakily as Claire started moving.

"Oh thank God," he sighed, Saphirra echoing him in a whisper. Validus got to his feet, standing around Alex and Saphirra. Saphirra looked at him, searching for answers.

"Is he...Is he still..." She gestured towards Alex, and Validus shook his head.

"He's not a Viceprus anymore. Whatever the lunar eclipse did, he's cured now." Saphirra sighed with relief.

"Thank you all for saving us. We'd be dead in minutes if it weren't for your help. We wouldn't have survived this. We owe you our lives," Saphirra said gratefully. Validus shrugged.

"I think they would appreciate that if they were here," Validus said sadly.

"If they were..." She trailed off as the reality of the situation took its hold. *Validus was the only one left.* The others had left similar scorch marks on the ground where they had been hit by Lockson's bullets vanishing forever into the night.

"I'm sorry," she said quietly. Validus nodded, his violet eyes unseeing.

"It was the price they were willing to pay," he said softly. "I just wish so many of them hadn't lost their lives because of him. I wish we had known sooner."

Saphirra nodded, and glanced about the now silent rooftop. Scorch marks marked where Ms. Stone had disappeared, and rubble littered the cracked and singed tiles. There was a gaping hole in the opposite wall, exemplifying the damage they had done. Saphirra glanced to Alex. He was sleeping peacefully, his head on her lap.

"What about West?" she asked with concern. West looked up at the mention of his name, worry flitting across his grey eyes. Validus tapped his chin.

"I *could* get him to talk to other Sirens," she said, glancing over at West. He interrupted her.

"No. No *way*. I'm done trying to understand the unnatural. I'm not talking to any other magical creatures. I'll just figure it out on my own," he said determinedly.

"In that case, you might be able to reverse your condition." He waited for a response from West, who was thoroughly ignoring the two of them. "Well, let him know I might be able to help," he told Saphirra in a low voice. She nodded, swaying a little as exhaustion finally hit. Validus looked uncertainly at her, his eyes falling on her ring.

"Why do you have a ring made with Elymph metal?" he asked sharply, beckoning with his hand. She showed him the ring, which had reverted back to its innocent size. "It's Alex's. Actually, it's his mother's engagement ring," she explained. Validus recoiled from it, then bent down closer to touch it once more. Nothing happened.

"Interesting," he murmured to himself. "The ring is exquisite."

"I kept hearing Alex's voice in my head," Saphirra said thoughtfully. "I couldn't figure out where it came from, but..."

"What exactly did Alex's voice say?" Validus asked gently. Saphirra blushed as she mumbled the answer.

"He said he loved me."

"And did you find yourself saying you loved him back?"

Saphirra nodded, blushing even more. "I didn't even consciously say it. It just...flew out."

"That ring was made with Elymph metal, but was welded with care," Validus informed her. "Whoever Alex's mother was, Alex's father wanted to protect her. Whoever bears this ring can protect the person they truly love. This ring will destroy whoever endangers that person. Genius," he murmured appreciatively.

"How did Alex's dad get a ring like that?" Saphirra asked, staring down at the delicate ring. If she hadn't seen it herself, no amount of convincing would have had her believe that the tiny band of metal and diamond could kill anything on its own. She shook her head, marveling at it. Everything suddenly made sense.

"That's the question, isn't it?" Validus said, bending down to brush rubble and dust off himself.

"So what I saw in the beginning of the summer *wasn't* my imagination?" Saphirra mused. Validus gave her a confused look.

"What did you see?"

"Professor Lockson tried to bite me like he'd bitten Alex, but he couldn't. When I looked over at Alex, his ring was glowing. I thought it was my imagination," she said quietly. Validus smiled warmly at her.

"The ring protected you. Alex must have loved you for a long time," he informed her. Saphirra blushed deeper. "He may not have known it himself, but his ring apparently did. Your heart," he said, tapping his chest, "always knows what is right, even if your brain denies it. Nothing's bigger than love, Saphirra. Always remember that." Validus smiled. "Anyway, I best get going," he said, gesturing to the sky. The moon was half covered again, and no longer the blood red it had been moments ago. Saphirra nodded and waved as he unfolded his wings and took to the night, calling over his shoulder,

"Let your Siren know he can come for help from me any time!"

Saphirra brushed the hair off Alex's forehead as West moved closer to her, cradling Claire in his arms.

"We did it," she said softly. West nodded next to her, closing his eyes peacefully. She did the same, leaning against the wall. She'd never felt so exhausted in her life, but it had been worth it.

It was all over, and for the first time in months, they were safe.

Chapter 35
Perpetual Calm

Claire woke up to the sounds of two people muttering over her head. No, it was way more people than two. Four? Eighteen? Now someone was shrieking with derisive laughter.

Now someone was patting her head.

Where am I? Claire thought, trying to open her eyes. They met blinding sunlight, and she squinted as her eyes adjusted. She was lying on something yellow and soft, and the pattern of the wall looked extremely familiar.

"Saphirra?" she said groggily, struggling to get up. Saphirra's worried face swam into view, and suddenly she was being fiercely hugged.

"Claire! You're awake!" Saphirra said cheerfully, her blazing green eyes twinkling. Claire propped herself on her pillows, squinting through the glare of the sun. The windows in their dorm room had been propped open, and the curtains had been thrown wide. She tried to move her hands and realized they felt like there were no bones in them at all. She swallowed, and winced as her throat burned. People flitted by in the hallway, calling greetings and rolling their luggage through the college. Alex was sitting on the edge of Claire's bed, watching apprehensively.

"Saphirra, she got up twice and said the same thing, and then she collapsed again. And you've hugged her three times now. How many more times is she going to be possessed by her own soul?" he asked, putting a hand over Claire's forehead. Claire shook the fog out of her brain.

"What? I have? When?"

Saphirra and Alex glanced at each other nervously. Claire glared at them.

Wait. What is he doing here?

"What are you not telling me? And why are there people at the university?

It's—"

"Claire, it's been almost a week. The roof has been repaired, everything's fixed, and people are coming back to the college again. Drink something before you ask more questions," Saphirra said authoritatively, pouring water from a giant pitcher into a glass and handing it to Claire. She drained the glass greedily, holding her hand out for more without a word. She'd drunk the contents of half the pitcher before realizing Quinn and Demitri wasn't there. *Where are my other friends?*

"Where's Quinn? Where's everyone else?" she asked through the mouthfuls of breakfast Saphirra had brought her. Alex and Saphirra exchanged another look.

"Do you remember *anything* that happened last week? Over the past three months?"

Claire thought back. Yesterday. Wasn't that the day she'd met that one kid...wasn't his name West? *Yeah, I remember talking to him at the fountain. Then he had to leave, and we went to the classroom together to pick up Saph, and...nothing.* She couldn't remember what happened after that. It was as if there was a huge blank white hole in her memory.

"Wasn't yesterday the first day of vacation? Why are people coming back if it's the first week of vacation?" Something was terribly wrong, Claire knew it. "What do you mean, 'the roof is repaired'? When was it damaged? Weren't they just going to build an east wing? Saphirra?"

Saphirra was giving her a look of pure horror.

"Please tell me you remember who West is."

Claire shook her head. "Well, isn't he that one kid I met yesterday? But how would *you* know him? And what are you doing with Alex? Since when are you two such good friends? Since when—"

Claire felt like she'd been hit with a bowling ball in the stomach. All the wind had been knocked out of her.

"I can't remember. I–I...Something happened to me, didn't it?" she asked in a whisper, tears pooling in her eyes. *What have I forgotten? Who have I forgotten?*

"Oh no," Saphirra whispered. She took Claire's hand. "Claire, you've *got* to remember what happened. Please," her voice broke, and she looked away. Alex pulled her into a hug. Claire watched the two of them, confused. *When had they ever been more than friends? When did they get like this? What's going on?*

"Don't you remember, Claire? The hospital, Professor Lockson? I became a Viceprus, and you got kidnapped, and West–" Alex stopped, waiting for a sign of recognition. Saphirra got up and closed the door. The sounds from the hallway were instantaneously muted.

Claire looked at the two of them, dumbfounded.

"Is this some kind of joke? You two must be insane! There's no way anyone can just *become* a Viceprus. And how could I have gotten kidnapped? I'm right here!" she said, shrinking away from them. "You two need psychological help if you think that stuff is true. Maybe you guys just had a weird dream or something."

Just then, the door burst open. The kid she'd met yesterday walked in with a bowl of cereal. He looked thinner than before, and paler. When he saw Claire he dropped his spoon. It fell to the carpet, and everyone watched it fall as if it was the most interesting thing in the world. West looked at Claire cautiously.

"Claire? Is that really you?"

He remembers my name? Weird, she thought.

"Of course it's me. Who else would it be?" she looked down at herself, realizing her clothes had miniscule rips in them. Her shoulder had three thin white scars that almost looked like claw marks, and she connected them to West, for some strange reason. West walked over to her and tried to touch her, but she slapped him away.

"Claire?"

He sounded hurt and confused. She tilted her head to one side. "Do I know you?"

Alex walked out of his dorm room and slumped against the door, sighing heavily. He'd just unpacked his new school books onto his desk, which was threatening to cave under the weight. He sank to the floor, gazing out of the floor-length window that made up the wall of the hallway. Surprisingly, the corridor was void of students, and Alex sighed in relief. He couldn't really stand talking to anyone else right now. He felt drained, but it was much better than the alternative. It was such a relief not to have to restrain himself from walking outside in the sunshine. He let the sunshine streaming in through the window play across his closed eyelids, and felt like he could just sit there forever.

A week ago he'd been passed out on the rooftop, leaving West to drag him back to the dorm room. He'd woken up then next morning with no idea what had happened, forcing West to explain the details. *Saphirra killed Professor Lockson, and I shot down Ms. Stone, almost killing Claire in the process. I think I'm still a Siren. Validus said he could help me if I needed it. Saphirra's watching over Claire. She still hasn't woken up yet. Everything has been repaired, and students will be coming into the college tomorrow.* Alex suspected West had given him the *Cliff Notes* version, but he really didn't care. As long as West, Saphirra and Claire were all right, he'd figure out a way to deal with it, too. He really didn't understand how Saphirra had managed to kill Lockson, or how Lockson hadn't killed *her* in the process. Alex sighed loudly, turning his head lazily to look at the wall. He enjoyed being able to stay in the sun, letting it soak into his skin and warm his fingers. He stared at the clock on the wall, jolting to his feet when he saw the time. He needed to talk to Saphirra, to sort everything out.

He walked into the common room and took a sharp right, trudging up the stairs and past shrieking clusters of girls babbling about their summers. He pushed the door of Saphirra and Claire's dorm room open, shocked to see that Saphirra was nearly exactly in the same position she had been in when he'd left; hovering around Claire, who was fast asleep again, her face buried in a pillow. Saphirra glanced up at his face, and her expression abruptly flickered from worry to alarm.

"Are you okay?"

He nodded, collapsing down on a couch next to Saphirra. "We survived," he said quietly. The fact was blatantly obvious, but he felt the strange need to say it anyway.

"I know," Saphirra smiled at him. "West was right. It wasn't about me at all. It was about the ring."

Alex stared down at the delicate circle of metal on Saphirra's finger, recalling what Saphirra had told him it had done. Validus had said it was made out of some sort of Elymph metal, and that his dad held a connection to that. *What does it mean?* How could something so fragile kill so savagely for love? He blushed as the reality of the moment set in. He'd said it, and she'd said it, but neither had said it to each other.

"Saph?"

"Mmm?" she said distractedly. She was gazing at the prophecy, frowning a little at the words. "It wasn't about us at all," she said suddenly, interrupting him. Alex looked puzzled.

"What?"

"It says 'One controls the mind, another the heart.' Don't you see? West was right! This isn't just about you and Professor Lockson, it's about Vicepruses and Sirens! You and West!"

"How do you figure?"

"You found peace, because you're not a Viceprus anymore, but West was betrayed by Professor Lockson! Plus, West went berserk on that rooftop that night, too. He nearly killed Claire! That only proves that the lunar eclipse had some effect on him, too."

"But one crucial piece doesn't make sense. I see how the 'jewel' saved my life, but what about West? He's still stuck this way," Alex insisted. "I don't see how it's his key to survival at all."

"Maybe the ring still holds answers," Saphirra suggested. "Maybe you could ask your dad about it later on. I mean, if it's made out of Elymph metal, that's supposedly rare. If your father knew anything about it..." She shrugged. "It could be useful. It could hold answers for West, too."

"I suppose," Alex conceded. Just as he was about to say something else, his phone rang. He looked down at it, surprised to see Demitri's name light up the screen. Alex hadn't spoken to him in weeks. He gestured to his phone and took it outside, greeting his friend. Saphirra watched him walk away with unfathomable eyes.

Chapter 36
Ego Diligo Vos

Saphirra sat in the middle of the student union, watching the sun wane behind the large double glass doors leading towards the main quad. It was the eighteenth now; another day gone. How had time moved so quickly? She held a thin golden envelope between her slim fingers, twisting the edge over and over until it ripped. The return address had been from her father, not the usual stamped Rose College emblem he used whenever he wanted to send something to her. She glanced about, smiling at various familiar figures, but never making an effort to talk to any of them. Even after what happened, their problems hadn't ended.

Saphirra laughed at herself, earning a few bewildered looks from her fellow students. Had she actually expected all their problems to melt away, like winter to spring? *I'd expected life to get a little easier, at least,* Saphirra admitted to herself, studying the envelope again. What could her father, who hated her for the fact that she even *existed,* want to tell her? What could he possibly say to her that was so important that it cost him actual effort to write his name on the envelope? Saphirra was afraid to open it. With Claire's memory gone, Alex having disappeared somewhere, and West moping about because he was *still* a Siren after three months of chaos, Saphirra had known something bad was bound to happen to her as well. It wasn't the fact that she now felt more alone than she ever that bothered her, but rather the fact that she couldn't help the ones she loved. She wanted to help Claire, to help her regain her memory. She'd tried explaining to Claire about everything that had happened over the past three months twice, and each time Claire had seemed skeptical. Claire was impervious to irrational thought.

Saphirra had been staring absentmindedly at the double doors, slowly sinking lower into a plush couch. She hadn't even realized that the mob of students surrounding her had thinned a little. She clutched the envelope in her hands and got up, walking outside onto the terrace. The cool dusk breeze washed over her, and the sound of crickets chirping merrily lifted her spirits a little. The college hadn't been this calm for a long time. She spotted West sitting at a table in the corner, and she walked over to him, plopping down in a seat across from him. He barely noticed.

"She...she doesn't remember me," West stated in a broken voice. Saphirra nodded sympathetically, tracing the contours of the white round table as she spoke.

"She just knows she met you at the fountain three months ago."

He sighed, leaning back into his chair. Some friends passed them, and West waved hello dejectedly. Saphirra watched him carefully. *What did he do to her that night?*

"West, how did she lose her memory? What did you do?"

"I was just wondering the same thing."

West stood and walked down the steps and into the quad. Saphirra followed closely behind, waving hello to a few people as they passed. *So many people, so blissfully unaware of everything. What would they do if they knew seven Vicepruses had been on this campus, and that five of them had died? What would they do if they knew West was a Siren? What if Claire never remembers what happened?*

Saphirra walked into the girl's dorm, following West and ignoring the giggles that ensued when he walked into a room. *Can't they get a life for once?* She thought irritably. Saphirra ignored West and walked past him, heading for the stairs and Claire's room. Saphirra opened the door, and seeing Claire awake, West broke into a smile.

"Claire? Do you remember me?" he asked gently, but Saphirra shook her head.

"She's still unaware of...well...you." she hinted. Claire looked up at him.

"I'm really sorry I don't remember who you are, West. I–I wish I *could* remember, but I can't, and Saph's story doesn't make sense, and–" tears slid down her face, and Saphirra watched as West's entire frame sagged.

I better leave them alone, Saphirra thought, walking out of the room quietly. She walked towards the quad, accidentally tripping halfway down the stairs. An arm reached out and caught her mid–trip.

"Long time, no see, huh?" Alex said into her ear. She jumped, looking up into his face. His eyes sparkled happily.

"You're in a much better mood," she noted as he set her upright. Alex laughed.

"Yeah. I guess I am," he said, grinning from ear to ear. Saphirra smiled happily. Alex glanced at her hand. "What's in the envelope?"

Saphirra glanced down at her hand, realizing she was still crushing the golden envelope in her fist. She sighed, loosening her grip and trying to flatten it as best as she could.

"I don't know. Want to open it with me?" she asked pleadingly. Alex laughed again, and she smiled at him quizzically. He hadn't been this carefree since the beginning of summer.

"Sure."

Saphirra nervously ripped open the side and shook out the contents onto her palm. Four thick slips of paper with the Rose College seal fell into her open hand, as well as a folded up letter. Alex took the letter and began to read out loud as Saphirra examined the regal texture of what she took to be tickets.

Dear Claire and Saphirra,

Your father and I are hosting a ball, which will link together the three biggest and most widely known colleges in the world. This ball could extract a huge business deal, maybe the biggest one so far. Your attendance is required, for it is a prestigious honor to be invited to such an elite standing. The tickets are enclosed in this letter—two plus two for your dates. Formal attire is required. The date of the ball is August twenty first, at eight p.m. We look forward to seeing you there.

Best Regards,

Ms. Hill.".

Saphirra shook her head in disbelief. *Unbelievable.*

"They had to send us a *letter* to tell us something so important? The only reason they want us there is to show that they 'understand the young mind'!" Saphirra said hotly, crumpling the envelope into a tight ball. Alex's smile faded. "I love how it orders us to show up. Oh, even better, the signature on the bottom. Can't you tell how much they know about us?" she continued irritably, stalking off towards the quad. Alex jogged to catch up to her.

"So what are we going to do?" he asked curiously, putting a hand on her shoulder to stop her. Saphirra sighed heavily.

"Looks like we're going to a ball."

"Claire, it's not your fault, it's mine. I don't know what I did, but I'm going to reverse it. I promise," West told her, stroking her golden blonde hair absentmindedly. They were still in the dorm room, watching the sunset through the window. Claire looked up at West blankly.

"I really am sorry."

West nodded, resting against the wall, keeping a safe distance from Claire. He could see her soul flitting through her eyes, and he knew he'd messed up. Big time. How had he managed to erase her memory completely like that? Now Claire felt horrible, and it was all his fault. West glanced around the room, wondering if he should try to sing something. *But what if that makes it worse?* he reasoned with himself. He didn't know what he could do to help her, unless...

"Look, I really *am* sorry." She entwined her fingers with West's, who couldn't break away even if he wanted to. She didn't know he'd said he loved her. She didn't know his feelings at all. *What if she's permanently lost her memory, and it never comes back?* West glanced up at Claire's face. She gazed at him dazedly, as if he wasn't even in the room. Making a split second decision, he grabbed Claire and pulled her towards the door.

Claire stayed silent as they walked past the dorm rooms and down to the first floor, out the door and into the central quad. He pulled her towards the library, not stopping for a breath until he'd reached the front steps.

"Why'd you take me here?"

Claire sounded sad, and her soul disappeared out of sight. She looked up at West.

"I just wanted you to see the place you love the most."

She glanced up blankly at the library.

"Why would I love the library?" she asked, puzzled. "I like this place, but I'm not such a bookworm that I love it..."

West shook his head.

"Not there. *There,*" he said, pointing towards the giant maple tree in the center of the quad. Beyond that, the large fountain poured water over its stone pages, glistening in the sunlight. Claire walked silently towards it, passing college students catching up with each other after a summer apart. She walked through the soft green grass as if in a dream, her fingertips brushing the bushes lightly. She walked to the fountain, sitting down silently on the rim. West took her hand and placed it right on top of a stone page. The water ran over their fingers calmly, and West moved her hand so she could read the words underneath.

"*Ego diligo vos pro totus vicis quod Usquequaque,*" he whispered to her. "I carved it a few days ago. It fits, doesn't it?"

Claire's face was turned away from him, and she nodded. Warm water drops fell onto their entwined hands, and West realized they were tears. Claire looked up at him, tears sliding silently down her face and smiled, her hazel eyes twinkling with recognition.

"I...I *remember.* West...I remember *everything.*"

She allowed him to pull her into a hug. He held her shaking frame close to his heart, vowing she would stay there forever.

Chapter 37
The Triumvirate Ball

Claire woke up with a start as a shriek of laughter cut through the silence. Turning to the window, she pulled apart the daisy yellow curtains to let in some of the bright sunshine, and flopped back down onto the edge of her bed.

That's right, there are people at the college now, Claire remembered suddenly. It felt so strange seeing people roaming the virtually deserted pathways around the college, hearing echoes of laughter that she hadn't heard since the beginning of summer.

She tottered groggily towards the bathroom, grabbing a towel absentmindedly. It seemed incredible to her that she'd been able to forget everything that had happened over the summer; whatever West had done to her must have had a powerful impact. *What if he did something to my brain? Something...different?* She twisted the tap, waiting impatiently for warm water to fall into her cupped hands. *Could he have put my soul somewhere it shouldn't be?* Her hand fluttered automatically to her chest, touching the spot where her heart lay, as if it and her soul lay side by side. Claire stopped, glancing up at her face in the foggy mirror.

Have I changed? She thought hesitatingly, refusing to believe it. No, she was still the same person, she had to be—she still felt the same, she still acted the same, didn't she? Claire stared into the mirror, and her reflection stared back.

I still don't know what West said that day, she realized with a start. She still had no idea what *ego diligo vos* meant, let alone what the rest of the sentence was. It was such a long time ago that she was surprised he remembered he'd said it in the first place. She reminded herself to look it up as she splashed water onto her face, and then buried her face in a towel. Sighing, she glanced at herself in the mirror, cringing when she saw the three long white scars across her shoulder. *How am*

Reedhima Mandlik

I going to explain these to anyone? She wondered, touching one with the tip of her finger. It seemed to glow for a moment, and she knew it would be hard to ignore, especially with the dress she was supposed to wear tonight.

Trust my mother to force us to show our faces once in a millennium, Claire thought miserably, walking out of their dorm room and down the stairs. *She just wants to prove she has a teenage daughter that hasn't screwed up.* Claire resented anything to do with social events hosted by her mother, because she always acted aloof and unconcerned with everything. It was the 'relaxed' side that Claire's mother wanted to flaunt at these parties, and that fake personality was something Claire couldn't stand.

Only people she loved could make her this irritated.

Claire burst into the common room and was instantly showered in scattered laughter, compliments and squeals of delight—the normal sounds of the common room. Ignoring the crowd of students that were now crammed into the small space, Claire flopped down onto a navy blue chaise and sighed. Three months away from other people had left her wishing the whole place was silent again. She'd never felt so cut off from people before, and she hated the prickling unease she felt around people she used to be so comfortable with.

Claire glanced around her as the noise around her suddenly died, a hush falling over considerably half the student body. Claire noticed the girls staring at one of the entrances to the boy's dormitories, mouths agape. Their male counterparts wore frozen flickers of annoyance on their faces, their necks craning towards the noise.

It was a second before Claire realized that there really *was* indeed noise washing though the room, melodious and sweet. She rolled her eyes and shook her head, anticipating the strange fizzy lightheadedness she used to feel every time she heard one of West's songs. *What is he thinking, singing in front of all these people?* She thought exasperatedly, waiting for her mind to go numb.

She was surprised to find her mind stayed clear.

"West?" she called, her voice cutting through the room. No one around her seemed to be able to move. "West, stop being an idiot and come down."

The song ceased as West emerged from the stairwell, one hand in his chocolate brown hair, the other steadying himself by the railing. Claire laughed at the childish pout on his face, and she returned his confused glance with a reproached one.

People around her blinked and gazed around dazedly as the spell holding them still broke, completely unaware of what had just happened. Claire wasn't even sure herself. Tiny gasps flew from one corner of the common room as a group of blondes noticed West.

"West, hey, how was your summer?" A brave one walked straight into his path purposefully, altering his course to Claire. He stopped dead in his tracks, staring at the girl as if he'd never seen one before and wasn't quite sure what to do with one. After a minute of this unresponsive stare, her group of friends started to titter, and the blonde bristled.

"West, we've got a few days before class starts, so how about you and I go out sometime? Catch a movie, maybe?" she raised her voice enough to carry around the room, and the girls around her stopped talking in order to watch this new development. The room fell virtually silent. West blinked at her.

"Sorry. Can't," he said absentmindedly, shoving her aside and gesturing to Claire.

"Claire, we need to talk."

His voice was oddly strained, and so she followed him out the door amid hushed whispers. The blonde was now glaring daggers at her from the corner, arms crossed, but Claire really didn't care. They crossed the pavilion and walked out into the quad silently, passing streams of students chattering diligently about their summers. Claire noticed his fists were clenched as he walked.

Something wasn't right.

West would never sing in front of a room full of people, putting his secret in jeopardy. He would never shove a girl out of his way like that. And he would definitely not walk ten steps ahead of her, almost ignoring her but not quite. *What is going on?* Claire wondered as West stopped next to the library building. Claire looked up into his dark blue eyes, and saw only rebellion.

"Claire, how could you not...how were you unfazed by that?" he sounded frustrated, and Claire shrugged.

"Whatever you did to me that night must have rewired me somehow. Come to think of it, it must have rewired your brain, too. How could you be so irresponsible? How could you–"

"Claire, I needed to check. I needed to see for myself that I was right. That I really am a monster." Claire started to protest, but West cut her off. "Claire, if I've done this to you, what else did I change? This—this isn't right, this isn't working, I'll end up hurting someone else next time–"

"So what are you trying to say?"

Claire heard the wobble in her voice, felt the rejection in her heart, but refused to register it. *What is he talking about? After all we've been through, he's actually going to be this stupid?*

"I'm trying to say that maybe we shouldn't be around each other anymore."

Claire wanted to hurl him from the nearest roof.

"The smartest people are often the stupid ones in disguise," Claire threw at him. "Are you sure you really want to do this?"

His eyes said no, but his mouth said yes.

West woke up with a start as Alex slammed drawers frantically, rushing around their room like a cyclone.

"West, have you seen my tie? I need my tie. Where the *hell* is my tie?" he hissed, slamming a cabinet drawer angrily. West blinked at him blearily.

"What?"

"My *tie*, West, my tie! The ball is in half an hour, remember? I wish I didn't have to go. *Dancing.*" He shuddered, and then continued. "Saph would be left alone if I didn't show up, and she would have to face her dad alone. She's the only reason I'd wear a tuxedo."

West barely processed the rest of his chatter as he glanced out of their window. The stars twinkled mockingly at him, quieted by the fading sunset. The ball was tonight, in less than half an hour. How could he have forgotten?

Crap.

"Where's my tux, Alex? I have two, and suddenly I can't find the one I put on my bed–" West stopped halfway out of the chair he'd been dozing in as he eyed Alex's tux.

Scratch that. *His* tux.

Alex grinned sheepishly at him. "I figured you wouldn't need it, so–" Alex cleared his throat and shrugged. "It fit."

West registered the awkwardness in his voice. "What do you mean, *I* won't need a tuxedo? I can't just show up in jeans and a shirt, you know!" West told him, jumping to his feet and rummaging through a pile of clothes on the floor until he unearthed the other tux from the heap. It was considerably wrinkly, but it would have to do. *I can't be late. Claire will kill me.* Alex eyed his friend suspiciously as West pulled it on, rearranging his hair until it looked halfway decent.

"Well...You aren't going, are you?" Alex asked cautiously, unearthing a tie from an equally messy pile. West paused, his shirt halfway over his head.

"What do you mean?" he asked, slowly shrugging it on. The fabric slid fluidly across his shoulder, and he shifted it into place. Alex furrowed his brow.

"Well, there wouldn't be a point in going, since you told Claire you didn't want to be anywhere near her. Don't you remember? You told me in the common room about three hours ago before disappearing up here. You must have fallen asleep over there." Alex pointed to the bed for emphasis. When West responded with a frozen stare, Alex put his hands on West's shoulders and shook him. "West, what's going on with you?"

West sat down on the edge of his bed hard. *I...told her I didn't want to be around her?* West thought, the shock creeping slowly through his tired mind. *I shoved away the best thing that's ever happened to me?*

"Why the hell would I do that?" he asked Alex angrily, snatching a corsage from the center and pulling a scarlet scroll that contained his invitation from a dresser drawer. Alex held up his hands.

"You're the one who did it, you tell me."

Alex watched his friend confusedly as West stomped out of their dorm room, slamming the door behind him. He tripped down the stairs and blundered through the common room, ignoring the snickers that ensued as he walked into the door in his haste. Throwing the double doors open, he walked into the blast of cool night air, aided by blind fury. *How could I do something like this? What's wrong with me?*

West saw Claire and Saphirra walk down the stone steps into the warm summer night, and fingered the package he held nervously. He saw them pause, and ran to catch up to Claire.

"Claire! Wait!" he pleaded. He saw her tell Saphirra something, nodding a little. Saphirra swept away to the entrance, wearing a shimmering blue dress. Claire wore a similar black one; her blonde hair was piled up on her head in elaborate curls, and West felt a pang in his heart.

"Claire!"

She paused, her back determinedly turned to him, tensed as if for a fight. He saw her fists curl, and silently kicked himself for everything he'd done. He didn't mean to do this to her. He didn't want it to turn out this way.

And yet, it had.

"Claire, I–I'm so sorry. Please–" his voice broke, and she turned around. Fury lit up her face.

"I gave you a second chance, and this is what you do to me. I have scars, West."

There was no fury in her voice; just disappointment. West winced as she turned to one side, and the scars he'd given her were thrown into relief in the moonlight, undeniably harsh. He didn't remember how they had gotten there—all he remembered was that he had made each white stroke on her pale skin. Each tiny white line running the length of her shoulder cut West deeply in his heart.

"Please...please..." he pleaded with her, fighting to ignore the sphere of light in her eyes. It had dimmed because of him, and he briefly wondered how his father had managed staring into the eyes of the one he loved like this.

"West, I have to go. I don't have time for this."

She turned to walk away, and West slipped a corsage on her wrist.

"What–?"

"If I can't be near you, at least let my heart be," he pleaded. She gazed at him with a peculiar expression on his face, and he had to quell the sudden upsurge of music that threatened to pour out of his mouth. He hated himself for doing this to her, for taking the brightness out of her eyes. She watched him for a long moment, and then she turned wordlessly away, walking towards Saphirra. West watched her leave, noticing something glinting in the moonlight in the spot where she had stood just seconds before. He bent down to pick it up. The flower he'd given her lay in the palm of his hand, but the ribbon was nowhere to be found. She was gone, and she'd left his heart on the ground, to be trampled underneath her feet.

West watched them walk away, disappointment clouding his brain. *How could I reject someone without remembering it?* Try as he might, he couldn't remember anything. It was as if he'd gotten amnesia. As the two slipped past the wrought iron gate, he watched Alex run from the doors he'd walked through moments before, and glowered as his friend sprinted to catch up to the girls. As Alex's red hair bobbed out of sight, he heard a strange sound. College students streamed about on the pathway a few yards behind him, but none of them seemed to hear the sudden song that had sprung from the trees, the song that erased all thought from his mind, the leaves that whispered his name. He wanted to call out to the music, to tell it to stop, to tell it that there was something important that he was supposed to be doing. He knew he had to chase after the person that had dropped the flower he now held, but he couldn't bring himself to remember her name.

It was as if she didn't exist anymore.

He walked towards the song that was meant only for him, unaware of everything but the strange ache of his heart.

Saphirra walked as calmly as she could up the long marble stairs with Alex, Claire trailing behind a little, looking grumpy. Saphirra was trying her hardest not to bolt from the stairs, sprint across the street, and take the nearest taxi as far away from her father as pos-

Reedhima Mandlik

sible. Alex touched Saphirra's arm lightly, almost as if to remind her
that he was still there. She tipped her head back for a last glimpse of
the stars, the moon still a little full.

"Thanks for doing this," she whispered to Alex, squinting
through the sudden onslaught of camera flashes that enveloped them.
She saw Alex nod out of the corner of her eye as they walked into the
outer pavilion. The press crowded around the entrance, excited to
catch any movement that was remotely insignificant, and blow it up
to insane proportions. The ball was an annual gathering of the world's
most intellectual minds and donors, and tonight was no exception.

"No dancing?" Alex asked hopefully, squinting at her through
the flashing lights. Saphirra nodded, shouting over the sudden upsurge in noise.

"No dancing," she assured him. They made their way into the
marble foyer, nearly knocking into a crowd of donors. Saphirra sand-
wiched herself between Claire and Alex, determined not to accidentally run into her father. Just because she had to talk to him didn't
mean she had to enjoy it.

"Why didn't you at least listen to West? He sounded desperate,"
she whispered to Claire to distract herself. Claire had that stubborn
frown on her face, and her jaw was set.

"I'm not the kind of girl to fall for a Siren's tricks. I'm beginning to think what we were was just some huge lie," Claire replied.
Saphirra could hear the wobble in her voice, and knew she'd explain
it eventually. Claire was strong, to the point of idiotic stubbornness.

"But he said he had made a mistake—"

"My mistake was in trusting him," Claire said, cutting Saphirra
off curtly. They fell silent as the ballroom opened up before them. Vast
columns of marble held up the intricately carved ceiling. Ice sculp-
tures softly melted into larger beds of ice, surrounding a checkered
dance floor that dominated the center of the room. Dancers whirled
past them to the beat of the thumping music that blasted from every wall. Saphirra filtered into the room, narrowly avoiding bumping
into a woman wearing a long baby blue dress. Her long blonde hair
bounced as she walked, just like Claire's did. It was when Claire accidentally let out a squeak of recognition that Saphirra realized who

it was. Claire pushed past her, trying to catch up to her mother. She called her name, but her mother never turned around. Saphirra realized they'd been standing in the same spot for about a minute, simply watching Claire get swallowed up by the thickening crowd.

"Let's get out of here," she muttered to Alex. He gave her a confused look but complied, allowing himself to be towed away from the dance floor and into the bar area. Saphirra slumped down onto a barstool lined in gold, sighing exasperatedly. Alex sat down next to her, his eyes trained on her face.

"Did you see him?" he asked curiously as her eyes darted from person to person, her nerves jangling restlessly. She couldn't take much more of this, and the night had barely started. She shook her head a little too late.

"N-no. I just don't want it to happen by accident." Her voice was shaking, and she straightened the folds of her midnight dress restlessly. She knew she'd eventually bump into her father—that was inevitable. It was partly *his* ball, after all. But if she had to talk to him, she'd rather not do it in front of a crowd of people.

"Do you want to leave?"

Saphirra shook her head again, grabbing a glass of water from the busy bartender.

"I'm going to have to face him eventually. I just want to avoid it becoming a disaster, and—"

At that moment the lights dimmed and a spotlight trained on the doorway. Saphirra watched Claire's mother glide through the crowd to stand next to her father. His tall, strong stature made his proud chest puff out even more as his menacing eyes scanned the crowd. He stepped up to the microphone and gripped the handle as if it was life support; now he was speaking, waving his hands enigmatically as the crowd around him nodded. It was as if his voice was everywhere, crashing into her in waves.

Her arm began to feel the pinpricks of burns long gone, tingling the smooth surface of her skin. She had to bite her lip to keep from shouting. She should have known she couldn't handle being here, being near someone she'd had to trust so completely, only to get hurt to

Reedhima Mandlik

the point of destruction. She was shaking so much she had to set her glass down.

Seconds later, she was running towards the door, unnoticed by the larger part of the crowd, Alex sprinting to catch up with her. She didn't bother to look over her shoulder as she flew into the deserted entranceway, trying her hardest not to let the sudden tears spill over. All she had to do now is walk past the gilded doors and into the outer pavilion, and she'd be free. She was unconsciously clutching her arm, her fingernails biting deep into her skin. She heard the clatter of the door opening behind her, and heard footsteps. They couldn't be Alex's—these were too sure, too brisk, and too arrogant. She guessed who had walked in behind her before he spoke. The same voice she'd been running away from resounded behind her; only this time, it was louder and clearer than before.

"There aren't any reporters here to watch you run out the door and make a scene, although it was wise of you to try and destroy my reputation."

Her father's harsh voice resounded with a boom, making her flinch. Hands balled into fists, she turned to face the one person she wished never existed.

Chapter 38
Uncertain Endings

Claire wandered through the crowded ballroom, her mother long gone. She wanted to talk to her, but knew the feeling wasn't mutual. Her mother had actually liked her at some point in time, she was sure of it; she remembered the times her mother would take her on walks, telling her that one day, daddy would come back, and they would be one big family again. It was one of the many promises her mother failed to keep. She was setting herself up for rejection by looking for her, just like she had done with West.

That idiot, she seethed, momentarily forgetting where she was. She blundered through the room blindly, not caring who she bumped into. She briefly scanned the room, unsure of who she was searching for. Saphirra caught her eye, and they both shared a helpless look. Seconds later the moment was gone, and Saphirra whirled through a gilded door, closely followed by a tall blonde man. Claire watched Alex pause by the door, peer in cautiously, then slip inside. Claire attempted to follow them when a rotund man stepped into her path, shouting to no one in particular over the thumping music, and precariously swishing his drink in one hand. As Claire watched the drink spill onto the sleek marble floor, a hand encircled Claire's waist and yanked her away with a violent tug. Distracted, she attempted to break free, jabbing her elbow blindly behind her. She opened her mouth to scream when a voice stopped her cold.

"Just listen, Claire. Please."

His voice, so close to her ear, sent shivers down her spine.

"Why should I?" she replied angrily, turning to face West. The dim lighting cast his face into shadow, and she wrenched herself from his grip. He was wearing the same tuxedo as before, and was holding her broken corsage in his palm carefully, as if he didn't want to crush it. She glanced at her wrist, surprised to see that the ribbon was still tied to her wrist.

"What are you even *doing* here? How did you get in?" she continued, stepping away from him. He shrugged, and something flickered in his unreadable grey eyes.

"I have my ways," he replied evasively, turning to walk towards a pair of glass double doors decorated with golden ivy. Claire stood where she was near the wall stubbornly, glaring at his retreating back. The thumping music faded to a waltz, and West was swallowed by the twirling dancers. She sighed and turned towards the bar area, sidestepping dancers as she went.

What was that about? It's like he just showed up to make me mad, she thought crossly, plopping herself down on a gilded chair. She turned to order a drink, and saw West's face instead. He sat down next to her, smiling infuriatingly. She glared at him.

"You're not going to leave me alone, are you?" she said, pushing herself up. She stomped towards the ballroom again, and West reappeared by her side.

"Are you coming with me, or not?" he asked playfully, a hint of a smile on his lips. Claire frowned, hating how much he aggravated her. She wanted to trust him, but how?

"I thought you wanted nothing to do with me," she growled at him. West's face fell, but within moments he was grinning again.

"I changed my mind," he said carelessly. "Will you come with me?"

"Where?" she said finally, stopping mid–step. West turned her around to face him, his hands on her shoulders.

"Claire, just trust me, okay? Come with me to the garden. I have something I need to show you," he said, his oceanic eyes trained on hers. She forced herself to look into them, and nearly staggered back in shock. His eyes were blank, emotionless and completely uncomprehending of his surroundings.

He isn't himself, Claire realized. *He can't be. This is West, but...something's off.* Instinct told her not to listen, to ignore this strange version of West and walk away. Just as she started to turn, he let go of her shoulders and stepped back.

"It's fine if you don't come with me. Please. Don't listen to me."

Claire looked up at his face, startled. His voice was shaking, the complete opposite of his coy attitude three seconds before.

Does he have split personality disorder or something? Claire wondered, her feet firmly planted in place. *Now he's warning me against himself? What the hell is going on?* She watched his eyes turn blank, and knew she couldn't leave.

"West, something's up. I–I won't leave until I know you're back to yourself."

West looked taken aback. He glanced at her, his eyes flashing. He seemed to struggle with what to say.

"If I go, will you follow?"

Claire found herself nodding, her soft curls brushing her cheeks. Smiling, he steadily led her out into the courtyard, and despite her sinking heart, she followed.

Alex flinched as the full impact of Saphirra's father's frame hit him. He was tall, he was daunting—and at this moment, he was glaring down at Saphirra. Alex peered through a crack in the doorway, debating whether to intervene. He quietly inched through the door, watching Saphirra and her father warily. They were far enough down the deserted hall that they wouldn't notice him, but close enough that he could hear every word.

"What were you planning on doing, once you had run out of here? Surely you didn't expect me to chase after you? I'm only here tonight to remind you of where you stand. You are the reason we had to move from Boston, where I was independent, and didn't have to rely on anyone. Because of you, my work contract is intertwined with the Hill's colleges. Because of you, *I* didn't win an award tonight, *we* won. Do you know that the college is now in more disrepair than when I left it? And because of you, it's suddenly my responsibility to restore it. What have you been doing at that college to possibly put me under this much stress? What," he said through his teeth, "could you possibly have done to result in the disappearance of a nurse and one of our best professors? Saphirra, how could you do this to me?"

Alex saw Saphirra flinch and open her mouth to retaliate, but no sound escaped her lips.

"Can't you even speak? Honestly, you haven't grown up at all," he said irritably, pulling a lighter out of his pocket. He casually lit up a cigar, and Alex saw Saphirra start to tremble as Mr. Rose puffed smoke in her face, eyes gleaming.

I've had it.

"Hello, Mr. Rose. I believe you've got some of your facts wrong, don't you?" Alex said, smiling tightly as he walked in between the two.

"What are you *doing?*" Saphirra hissed at him. Alex smiled cheerily at Mr. Rose.

"Standing up for you, like I should have done years ago."

As Saphirra's eyes widened, Mr. Rose's eyes flickered with recognition.

"*You,*" he jeered glaring at Alex with newfound hatred. Alex smiled blandly at him.

"Hello, Mr. Rose. Nice to see you again."

Now it was Mr. Rose's turn to shudder, his face growing ruddier by the second.

"Well, Saphirra, it seems you can't keep annoying bits from the past back, after all. Just remember that—"

"Mr. Rose, that's enough. I know you can't see the damage you've done to your daughter, but I'm reminded by the scars I see every day. And I believe smoking isn't permitted in the building, is it?" Alex asked, jabbing a thumb towards the no smoking sign on the wall. Mr. Rose glared at him as if he was a disgusting insect he couldn't wait to squash.

"What does it matter? Those scars are her fault, after all. Why should I be blamed for my past actions? I was drunk—"

"And you still don't see the error in that? I'm sorry, but I don't think Saphirra wants anything to do with you, and neither do I. I love her, and I'll protect her in a way you never seemed to manage. I'm sorry, but we have to leave now. It was nice seeing you again, Mr. Rose." Alex smiled at him politely, fighting the urge to shout. *I said it.* Relief flooded through him, mingling with his mounting anger at the man before him. Mr. Rose was the reason Saphirra was shaking beside him–the reason scars littered the length of Saphirra's arm—and Alex was just supposed to let that go? Mr. Rose glared down at Saphirra one last time.

"I have another award to receive, Saphirra. When you leave, please don't let your rude friend make a scene." He bent down and whispered something in Saphirra's ear, then strode away as if their conversation hasn't occurred at all. Saphirra's nails were digging into his palm, and as they walked into the cool night air, she loosened her grip.

"Alex, thank you. I...I couldn't...It was horrible. I never want to talk to him...to *be* with him...again."

Alex squeezed her hand, smiling warmly at her. Her worried eyes stared back.

"He...He just told me...That I should know where I stand, that I'm not worth anything to him anymore."

Her voice was shaking, and as the tears started to tumble down her cheeks, Alex held her close.

"Saphirra...Your father is cruel person. He should never have been worth anything to you in the first place. I meant what I said back there. He never gave you the love you deserved. No one should have had to go through what you had to do. It wasn't right of him, but I can change that. I can *help* you, if you let me. Saphirra...You may not matter much to your dad, but you are the world to me. Please remember that," he told her. She smiled a shaky smile up at him.

"Thank you, Alex." Her voice was choked with emotion, and Alex smiled warmly down at her.

"Do you want to leave? I think we got whatever we needed to do done."

"I need to find Claire first," Saphirra said as they began to walk back down the hallway together. "She went off to find her mother and I haven't seen her since." As they passed by the large bay windows, a movement in the darkened maze caught her eye. Someone that looked an awful lot like Claire was kissing someone. As the moonlight threw their faces into relief, Saphirra realized it was West.

They were talking quietly now, their heads close together. Saphirra gestured to the window, and Alex let out a short laugh.

"Took them long enough," Alex said. "I don't think we should interrupt them, do you?"

"No, I guess not," Saphirra said, smiling widely. "It looks like she'll be just fine with West."

Alex laughed and pulled her to the entrance, hailing a cab.

"I love you," Saphirra whispered as they climbed in. The driver smiled at them through the rearview mirror. Alex felt his stomach swoop at her words, but was cut off by the tired taxi driver up front.

"Tough night, eh? Needed to leave early? That seems to happen a lot nowadays."

Saphirra chuckled, her eyes slowly regaining the happy sparkle that seemed to have fizzled out before. She lightly squeezed Alex's hand, and he squeezed back. Right there, right then, he felt like the happiest man in the world.

"You don't know the half of it."

West led Claire into the courtyard, picking his way carefully past the couples outside. Claire watched him worriedly, unsure of whether to run or to hide. *I don't want to be here, but I can't leave him alone when he's like this,* she told herself. West walked past the thick rose hedges, into the center of a moonlit maze. It occurred to Claire that this was the very last night of summer, the very last night before everything returned to normal. She wondered how she'd be able to go back to being just Claire, and how she'd be able to cover up the fact that if things had gone wrong a week ago, Alex would have been dead.

Shuddering, she unconsciously pulled herself closer to West, who seemed quite unaware of her presence. He led her towards a beautiful fountain, the water cascading down the stone petals and down into a pool below. He slowly turned to face her, his eyes trying to convey something she couldn't understand.

"Claire, I know I hurt you, and I made a mistake. But I want you to know something before I ask you this next question. Do you remember the Latin I engraved onto the fountain of knowledge?"

Claire nodded slowly, whispering, *"Ego diligo vos pro totus vicis quod Usquequaque."* She'd memorized those words, hoping to figure out what they'd meant somehow. West smiled, as if it further proved his point, then pulled her to him. She stood stiffly by his side, unsure of what he could possibly do to make her forgive him.

"Claire, that means 'I love you, forever and always'. I–I loved you, Claire, and I still love you. So please think carefully when I ask you this next question. If I go, will you follow, no matter what?"

Claire felt like she'd been kicked in the stomach. Unable to stand, she teetered towards a marble bench. *He loves me. He actually... he actually loves me.* She felt like slapping him for springing that up on her at a time like this, but what was she supposed to say? West followed her, concern etched in his face.

"West...How is the fact that you love me supposed to change my answer? I–I can't trust you anymore, I thought we established that. It's not going to suddenly make me want to change my mind. I won't go anywhere unless you tell me where I'm being taken."

West's hands froze on the edge of a rosebush, disturbing the carefully arranged leaves. He tilted her face upward towards him almost forcefully, and she had to find the courage to look into his eyes. They glared back stonily at her, all traces of affection gone.

"Claire...please don't make me do this..."

It was moody West again, his voice raw and troubled. He seemed to be warning her about something, but what? She backed away from him, turning to walk back through the maze.

"I'm done with this, I'm going back–"

"Stop."

The harsh commanding voice came from West's mouth, but in the split second it took for her to register it, it was too late. Song, rich and powerful, poured from West, the notes entwining around her, encircling her heart and soul. Suddenly, she couldn't think, she couldn't move—she was paralyzed, betrayed, and broken. *Why is he doing this to me? After all this?* She couldn't work enough anger or dismay into her thoughts when the music was drowning every rebellious thought in her mind. She turned to face West mechanically, walking quickly to get to him. His song rose in pitch, and she stopped in front of him, staring into his eyes. He flinched and squeezed them closed, as if he was trying to stop himself. He made her touch his cheek with one uncaring hand, one that desired to slap him instead of resting on his shoulder. She felt herself kiss him and whisper in words that were not her own, "I'll follow, I promise."

Shock radiated through her body as the full impact of what she had just said hit her. It was her voice, but the strange wistfulness behind it was West's imagination alone. She wanted to scream, but she couldn't work her mouth. West watched her silent rebellion with dismay, reaching out as if he wanted to help her. The song had faded, but it was as if it was still swirling in her brain, obscuring all thoughts. The hand froze in midair as a second commanding voice broke through the still night air.

"Well done, West. *Let her go.*"

His hands fell limp at his sides as Clandestine, the woman from the forest a month or two before, emerged from the maze. Her long silvery blonde hair swayed in a nonexistent breeze, her ball gown looking like she'd stripped it from the night sky itself. Clandestine smirked down at Claire, who glared up at her in silent horror.

"West, I am so glad you decided to work with me. Going against me would have been quite painful. He insisted on you, Claire...Apparently, you will be useful. And since you're quite keen on following him, *no matter what,* I see no problem in leaving tonight, do you? We have plans to make."

Claire's mind was trained on West, on the fact that he could work with the same woman who caused him grief—the same woman who caused all of them grief. *Without her, West wouldn't even be a Siren. Without her, everyone could have been normal. She screwed up our lives, and I'm supposed to come quietly?*

Clandestine seemed to sense what she was thinking, and smiled coldly.

"My dear, you seem to think you have a choice. West, take her. Now."

And before Claire could scream, West had taken her into his arms, a new song pouring from his lips, cementing her lips together.

They followed her into the depths of the rose maze, West forcing a smirk identical to Clandestine's.

Evelyn ran through the streets of the unfamiliar city, dodging pedestrians desperately as she moved. She needed to find the one person she had been told would save her, the one she knew would give her peace.

Akakios. Am I too late? She wondered frantically, turning into a familiar looking bar, not unlike the one Akakios had pulled her into before. She sat down on a stool, exhausted, and looked around. The place was nearly deserted, save for a very tired looking barista. She bustled about cleaning tables that looked like they hadn't had customers in ages, ignoring Evelyn as best as she could. Finally, she cleared her throat loudly, and the woman stopped picking up plates and walked over to her.

"Do you have anything cold?" Evelyn asked dryly, eyeing the strange woman. She looked snidely down at Evelyn, then gasped a little in recognition.

"You're the woman, aren't you? The one he's waiting for?" The woman's whole demeanor changed in an instant.

"The one who's waiting for?" Evelyn asked suspiciously. The barista grinned.

"Akakios, of course. You came to the right place. He's back here," she said, and as she spoke her eyes flashed a glowing violet. The woman disappeared in a back room eagerly, telling Evelyn to wait for a moment. Evelyn frowned at the suddenness of it all. She had expected it to take a lot longer to find him than this. There was some commotion from the dusky back room, and within moments Akakios appeared, looking healthier than he had before.

"Akakios Alexiou," she called out in greeting. He smiled warm-ly at her.

"Evelyn. I see you decided to take my offer after all."

"I see you aren't very good at hiding yourself," she countered. Akakios laughed at that. It was a light, carefree sound that tugged at the corners of Evelyn's mouth.

"Maybe you're just exceptionally good at finding me," he retaliated. She smiled then, walking over to hug him.

"Thank you for this," she told him earnestly. "For helping me, I mean."

"I would enjoy nothing more," he said pleasantly. Evelyn grinned slyly at him.

"You wanted to run from your sister, right?"

He nodded at her. "Why?"

"I was just thinking...Why run when you can attack?"

Evelyn pulled a long dagger out from her jacket pocket, letting the Elymph metal sparkle in the dim glow of the shop. Akakios's eyes widened perceptibly as he took it in.

"Is this...?"

"The legendary dagger from Siren Rock, yes," she said smugly, handing it over to him. He turned it over wonderingly in his hands, finally looking up at her.

"How did you get this?"

"Ryan must have had it for years. He left it on his desk, and had accused me of taking it before. Something tells me Clandestine left it there on purpose, for him to take it and use it. She had bigger plans for him, I think," Evelyn explained. "Either way, I have it now. *We* have it now."

"But we couldn't possibly use this against anyone," Akakios insisted. Evelyn smiled. *His innocence is sweet.*

"Your sister tried to kill you. What else is she capable of? Shouldn't we take care of her before she messes up the rest of the Siren realm, or the entire mythical realm?"

"Yes, but—"

"Trust me," Evelyn said soothingly, carefully plucking the dagger from him and putting it back in her pocket. Akakios stared at it hungrily. He struggled with himself for a moment, but when he looked up at Evelyn his eyes were clear.

"Let's do it."

Saphirra leaned against the bark of the thick oak tree she loved, basking in the sunshine. Alex was sitting across from her, smiling a small relieved smile every time their eyes met. Quinn sat beside her, frantically flipping through notes that Saphirra could barely read. There were a thousand or two more students at the university than there had been last year, and Saphirra wasn't used to it. People were everywhere, and yet the two people she needed to see the most hadn't materialized from the growing crowd.

Saphirra had left multiple messages on both West and Claire's phones, but neither had picked up. Her worry had been assuaged by Alex, who had shown her a text message from West saying he and Claire had left the ball early. The message also explained they were with Claire's family for the moment, and they'd be back when classes started. Somehow the message had sounded strange to Saphirra; couldn't Claire had said something as well? When Alex had texted back asking this, he hadn't gotten a reply. The continued silence worried her.

"That's it. We can't wait for West and Claire anymore. I don't know where they could be, but we really do have to get to class. There's a new mythology professor in for Professor Lockson, and we can't afford to be on *her* bad side, too," Quinn said pointedly, shooting Saphirra a look. Saphirra laughed.

"It wasn't my fault, and you know it, Quinn," Saphirra told her, standing up. Alex picked up his books from the grass and strolled lazily to catch up to the girls, his lengthy stride easily matching theirs. Quinn rolled her eyes pointedly when Alex draped an arm around Saphirra's shoulder.

"I should have known you two would get together the second I leave," Quinn teased, shoving Saphirra playfully. Alex tightened his grip on her shoulder, and together, they walked from the cheery central quad into Professor Lockson's old classroom. It was where everything had begun over three months ago, and it felt strange to walk into the room so calmly again. They sat at the desks in the back, and watched the classroom slowly fill up, waiting for the new professor to arrive, and to get the day over with. It was already the first day and Saphirra wanted for the year to be over. She exchanged an impatient look with Quinn as the volume of the class grew to a dull roar. Finally, a young woman arrived, her straight silvery blonde hair barely brushing the middle of her back, carrying a suitcase. She turned to the class, her light violet eyes resting on Quinn for a moment before scanning the rest of the room. An eruption of mutterings around the room made Saphirra's eyes roll. The new teacher wrote on the blackboard lightly, practically dancing as she turned around to smile at the class. A snake of gold seemed to flit through her eyes as she spoke.

"Hello class. I am your new mythology professor. Please call me Professor Alexiou."

Author Bio

Reedhima Mandlik is currently a Junior in Crystal Lake South High School. She has loved to read and write ever since she was a child, but she never actually got to writing Heartbeat- A Novel until she was around fourteen years old. The beautiful islands of Greece inspired the theme of this novel, as she had written the last words while on the islands. She wishes, more than anything, that one day she could get her wings and fly as well. Until then, she will continue to write. Heartbeat is her first novel.

www.ingramcontent.com/pod-product-compliance
Lightning Source LLC
Chambersburg PA
CBHW070752280626
47162CB00016B/168